For Your glory, Lord

# IN SHEEP'S CLOTHING

## SUSAN MAY WARREN

Although we attempt to carefully select all of the books contained in our library, it is not possible to be familiar with every book and the contents before those books are placed on the shelves.

There may also be values presented within some books that are questionable. We would encourage parents to be aware of the books their children are reading and to discuss those books with them.

It is not our intention to remove all controversial resources from our library. All materials will not necessarily present Biblical values. Our aim for students is to develop perception and an ability to be discriminating

Steeple
Hill®

Published by Steeple Hill Books™

STEEPLE HILL BOOKS

Steeple
Hill®

ISBN 0-373-78544-5

IN SHEEP'S CLOTHING

Copyright © 2005 by Susan May Warren

**Printed in U.S.A.**

# *Prologue*

If the train trudged any slower into the station, American missionary Gracie Benson would be dead by sunset. Five minutes. Twenty steps. Then she'd be safely aboard.

God obviously wasn't on her side. Not today, at least.

Then again, He certainly didn't owe her any favors. Not after her fruitless two years serving as a missionary in Russia.

Gracie purposely kept her gaze off heaven as she hunched her shoulders and pulled the woolly brown scarf over her forehead. Please, *please* let this Russian peasant guise work. The train huffed its last, then belched, and Gracie jumped. *Hold it together, Grace.* Long enough to fool the conductor, and find her berth on the train for Vladivostok. Then she could finally slam the compartment door on this horrific day—no, on this entire abysmal chapter of her life. So much for finding redemption as a missionary in Russia. She'd settle for getting out of the country alive.

She tensed, watching an elderly man dressed in the typical Russian garb of worn, fake leather jacket, wool pants and a fraying beret gather his two canvas duffels and shuffle across the cement platform. Would he recognize her and scream, "Foreigner!" in the tongue that now drove fear into her bones?

Without a glance at her, he joined the throng of other passengers moving toward the forest-green passenger cars. A younger man, dressed mafia-style in a crisp black leather jacket and suit pants, fell in behind the old man. Gracie stiffened. Had he looked her way? *Help me, Lord!*

Just because God wasn't listening didn't mean she couldn't ask. The irony pricked her eyes with tears. This morning's events had whittled down her list of trustworthy souls in Russia to a fine point. She'd give all the rubles in her pocket for someone like her cousin, Chet, FBI agent extraordinaire, to yank her out of this nightmare into safety.

Not that she should give any man a chance to introduce himself before decking him. She'd been down that road once. Never was too soon to trust another man within arm's distance.

Gracie shuffled forward, in keeping with her disguise of tired village maiden. She clutched a worn nylon bag in one hand— her black satchel safely tucked inside—and fisted the folds of her headscarf with the other. As the smell of diesel fuel and dust soured the breathable air and cries of goodbye from well-wishing relatives, grief pooled in Gracie's chest. *Poor Evelyn.*

Biting it back, Gracie cast a furtive glance beyond the crowd and caught sight of a militia officer. The soldier, dressed in muddy green fatigues, an AK-47 hung over his shoulder like a fishing basket, leaned lazily against a cement column, paying her no mind.

Hope lit inside her. Freedom beckoned from the open train door.

Stepping up to the conductor, she handed the woman her wadded ticket. The conductor glared at her as she unfolded the slip of paper. Gracie dropped her gaze and acted servile, her heart in her throat. *Please, please.* The conductor paused only a moment before punching the ticket and moving aside.

The train resonated with age in the smell of hot vinyl and polished wood. The body odor of previous passengers clung to the walls, and grime crusted the edges of a brown linoleum floor. Gracie bumped along the narrow corridor until she found her compartment. She'd purchased a private berth with the intent of slamming the door, locking it from inside and not cracking it open until she reached Vladivostok. The U.S. Consulate, only ten minutes from the train station, meant safety and escape from the nightmare.

Escape from the memories. Surely Evelyn's killer wouldn't follow Gracie to America.

Tossing her satchel onto the lower bunk, Gracie untied the headscarf and shook out her shoulder-length damp hair. Blowing out a deep, shuddering breath she willed her pulse to its regular rhythm.

So maybe she'd been too hard on God. He *had* gotten her this far. Perhaps He hadn't turned his back, completely, on Gracie Benson, a.k.a. foreign-missionary-flop-turned-fugitive.

Gracie grabbed the handle and began to roll the door shut.

A man's black shoe jammed into the crack.

"No!" Grace stomped on it with her hiking boot. The assailant grunted and yanked his foot back. She threw all her weight into the door. "Get away!"

An arm snaked through the opening and slammed the door back, nearly ripping off Gracie's hands. She stumbled back onto the bunk, fumbled for her bag.

How had he found her? "Get out!"

Gracie's heart lodged in her throat. The man was huge. Dark eyes, knotted brow, muscles and menace in a tweed jacket, he stomped into her compartment.

She screamed and flung her bag at him with all her five-foot-two-inch, one-hundred-and-twenty-pound strength.

He sidestepped and caught it.

*God, help me please, now.* Gracie scuttled to the farthest end of the berth. "Get out!"

He reached inside his jacket—for a knife? She kicked at him, panic blurring her vision, and pain stabbed her foot as she connected with his shin.

He winced. "Calm down!"

English? The accent still sounded Russian.

She jerked. Sucked in a breath. "Get away from me." She hated the shakiness in her voice. What had happened to six months' worth of self-defense classes?

"Are you Grace Benson?"

*He knew her name.* Every muscle turned to liquid. She pushed against the far wall, vowing that this time it would be different. If he touched her, she'd go down bruised and kicking and clawing his eyes out.

"I'll take your silence as a 'yes.'"

Was that a smile on his face? She calculated the distance to the door. *Trample over him. Run!*

"I've been searching all over for you," he said, with a sigh of exasperation.

*I'll bet you have.* Had he taunted Evelyn before he slit her neck, too? Her breath left her.

His blue eyes glinted, as if in victory.

Where was the scream that filled her throat? Why, oh why, in times of terror, did she go into lockdown? She shot a glance into the hall.

Where was the conductor?

Her assailant turned and slammed the door closed, cutting off her escape.

Gracie went cold. *Oh God, this is it! Please help me!*

She watched the man drag a hand through his hair as if contemplating her demise. Would he slit her throat? Or did he have different plans? *Not again.*

She erupted like a woman possessed and dove at him. "Get away from me!"

He grabbed her forearms in an iron grip. "Stop it! Please. I'm not going to hurt you, trust me!"

She wrenched away from him. Fell back onto the bench seat. Her breath burned her lungs.

*"Perestan!"* He shook his head as her roaring pulse filled her ears. "My name's Vicktor. I'm with the KGB and I'm trying to help you."

# Chapter One

❧

*Twenty-four hours earlier*
*Khabarovsk, Siberia*

Nickolai Shubnikov knew how to whittle away his son Vicktor's pride with the skill of Michelangelo—one agonizing chip at a time.

"Whoa, Alfred! Slow down." Vicktor Shubnikov wound the leather leash twice around his grip and dug in, hoping to slow his father's Great Dane/Clydesdale. The animal dragged him like a nuisance as he plowed through the row of street vendors, chasing an errant smell.

Two years ago Vicktor might have labeled vet duty sweet revenge. Today he called it atonement.

Vicktor dodged a babushka hawking a bouquet of lilacs, jumped another pedaling sunflower seeds, and skidded to a halt before the metal canister belonging to a wrinkled woman selling peroshke. The fried sandwiches laced the air with the odor of grease and liver. Alfred shoved his wide Dane snout into the sandwich bag.

"Get your beast out of here!" the woman cried. She whacked at Alfred, who didn't even flinch. Vicktor, however, felt her land a hearty blow on his shoulder.

"C'mon, you mutt." Vicktor grabbed Alfred's fraying collar and yanked him away. He thrust the woman a ten-ruble note. She swiped it from his hand.

"Why do you do that to me?" They half trotted down the sidewalk, Vicktor hunched over at the waist and trying to match Alfred's gait. The dog's black jowls flopped and his saggy eyes gave no indication of remorse.

*Penance.* He cursed the impetuousness that had led to this moment. If only he'd been smarter, faster, wiser, he'd be in Lenin Park on this sunny Sunday, slapping shots against Roman, outscoring the former wing. Or maybe he'd be at Yanna's volleyball game. The Khabarovsk Amur volleyball team didn't need help from their fans to bury their opponents—he went for the pure joy of watching Yanna's power spike.

If only David could see her now.

He checked his watch. Noon. Hopefully Evgeny would be in the office. He hadn't called ahead, but the vet kept normal business hours, and Sunday had been a working day since Stalin outlawed the religious day of rest some sixty years earlier.

He muscled the Dane toward the dirt path that led to Evgeny's office. Vicktor had to admire his friend for carving out his dreams into a private practice. He and Vicktor had chewed away long hours in high school, concocting ways to free the laboratory mice from Tatiana Ivanovka's biology classroom. Between the pranks, however, Evgeny had revealed the love of medicine inherent to true physicians. Why he had gone into animal medicine still baffled Vicktor. Then again, Vicktor had sworn he'd never join the militia, and look where he had ended up.

Evgeny's office, a tiny green log house, sat lopsided and forlorn in the shadowy cover of three nine-story concrete high-rises. Vicktor turned up the dirt path and shivered as the sun passed behind a building. He shoved his free hand into his leather jacket pocket, wishing he hadn't taken out the lining. That morning, during his run, the wink of the sun against a cloudless sky and the fresh breeze smelling of lilac had lulled him into believing winter had finally surrendered to spring in Siberia. He'd jogged home, unzipped the wool lining from his jacket, thrown his *shopka* on the top shelf and kissed winter goodbye. Now, as he approached the office, his lips felt parched from the cold, and a faint musty odor curled his nose, like the smell of moldy clothes sitting in old snow.

The Dane jerked out of Vicktor's grip and he tripped, glared at the animal and picked up his pace. Of course Alfred would be anxious to see Evgeny; the vet had treated him for nearly ten years.

Two paces before the door, Alfred skidded to a halt, sat on his haunches and growled.

"It's just a checkup, pal. Cool it." He patted the dog's head. Still, the way the door hung ajar raised the fine hairs on the back of Vicktor's neck. "What do you see?"

Alfred growled again, a threatening rattle in his ancient throat, and curled his lips, showing canines.

"*Tiha.* Quiet, boy," Vicktor commanded. He paused, took a step toward the door and pushed. The door groaned, as if in warning.

Vicktor recoiled as the smell of rotting flesh hit him. He covered his nose.

Alfred whined.

"Stay," Vicktor rasped, and looped the leash around the door handle. Gulping a breath, he stepped across the threshold. It took all his military training not to gag at the odor that poured from the room.

"Evgeny?" Vicktor surveyed the reception area. Broken glass from the smashed display case crunched under his feet, a cash register lay overturned on a ripped vinyl chair. Whipping out a handkerchief, Vicktor cupped it over his nose and tiptoed around broken vials of animal narcotics on his way to the examination room.

"Evgeny? It's Vicktor."

Silence.

In the examination room, the leather bench where Evgeny examined Alfred on occasion had been slashed, the stuffing pushing through the cut like a festering wound. A jumble of medical utensils gleamed like weapons of war where the sun licked the wooden floor.

He backed out, a sick feeling welling in his gut. He crept toward Evgeny's office, rueing the creak of floorboards. When he swung the door open, Vicktor's blood ran cold.

Shards from the ruined glass cabinet littered the carpet. An emptied drawer lay upturned over its contents, a foot-size crater in the middle. Notebooks and ledgers, slashed into pieces, were strewn like stripped leaves. The squash-yellow area rug bled with the black and red dye of crushed pens.

Vicktor ducked back into the hall. "Evgeny?" He heard panic in his voice. He purposely kept few friends, but Chief Veterinarian Evgeny Lakarstin was one of them. With the exception of Roman and Yanna, and two Americans he didn't acknowledge to his coworkers, he depended on Evgeny. He counted him as the type of *paren* with whom he could share a sauna and shed a few secrets while he sweated.

And in Vicktor's world, trust wasn't an easily acquired commodity.

Vicktor headed for the back door leading to the kennels. Even from the hall, the eerie silence gave him chills—no dogs barking, no plaintive mewing.

Two steps before the back entrance, he spied another door to his left. He'd thought it a closet before, had even asked Evgeny about it once. The tall vet had shrugged and said, "Supplies."

Vicktor's eyes narrowed, instincts firing. He grabbed the handle. With a squeak the door opened.

He grabbed the door frame and hung on with a white fist as he tore his gaze away, wincing.

Etched in his mind, however, was the image of Evgeny lying in a pool of his own russet-colored blood.

Three hundred people clapping, cheering, for her, Gracie Benson. It just might have been the worst moment of her life.

How she longed to find a safe place and hide from tomorrow.

Gracie stood on the platform in front of the church, listening to the congregation applaud her for two years of missionary work, and felt like a sham. She was a joke, an embarrassment, a failure, and no amount of applause or kind words from Pastor Yuri Mikhailovich could erase that fact. She swallowed hard. She just hoped God wasn't watching.

She'd had her second chance. And had blown it.

Maybe she could get her job back at Starbucks. She made a mean mocha latte. Her unfinished English degree felt light-years away. She probably couldn't recite a Robert Frost poem even if the KGB—no, the FSB; wasn't that their new name?—put her under the bright lights and stuck needles under her toes.

Pastor Yuri shook her hand, his meaty grip slightly sweaty in hers. "Thank you, Gracie, for your hard work. We won't soon forget it." His brown eyes, deep and holding a lifetime of spiritual wisdom, settled on her.

She chilled. No, they would forget the vacation Bible school, the children's bell choir, the Sunday School classes she taught. Despite her two years serving as a short-term missionary in Far East Russia, as soon as her replacement flew in, they would erase Gracie Benson from their minds.

Whereas she would cling to them forever.

Maybe not all of them, but certainly Evelyn and Dr. Willie Young, her coworkers, and definitely Andrei Tallin, the sweet man with nearly palpable affection staring at her from the front row. She tried to ignore the ache in his chestnut-brown eyes. She'd turned down his proposal for marriage only a week ago, and felt like a jerk. The guy had gone above and beyond his job as her chauffeur these past two years—translator, bodyguard, friend. She'd nearly given her heart to him.

Nearly.

It would be a long time before she trusted a man again. A lifetime, perhaps.

Of all her friends, she would definitely remember Larissa. Larissa Tallin, with honey-sweet brown eyes, tawny hair cut like a man's, a smile so warm it made Gracie reevaluate every friendship she'd had back in America. The woman had even been thrilled with the cross pendant Gracie had given her, despite Larissa's atheism. Larissa may have been ten years her senior, but Gracie knew she'd never forget the woman who'd become as close as a sister.

It was because of Larissa that Gracie wept into her pillow every night. What was wrong with her that she couldn't even lead her best friend to salvation?

Pastor Yuri finished his farewell speech and again reached for her hand, and Gracie thanked the Lord for making her from stoic Scandinavian stock. She managed a convincing smile.

Why, oh why, did Russia have to obey their visa laws? It wasn't like they took any other laws seriously.

The clapping died as she found her seat next to Dr. Willie and Evelyn, career missionaries and the lucky ones who got to stay. The successful missionaries who changed lives and made a furrow in the eternal landscape of the soul.

Gracie's heart felt like it weighed a million pounds and sweat beaded her brow as she stood for Yuri's presermon prayer. The sun poured through the lace curtains of the log church, heating the room like a sauna, despite the lingering chill outside. Still, most babushkas huddled under three layers of wool and headscarves, relying on the masses of clothing as a bulwark against an early death. Gracie shifted in her denim dress, feeling rumpled, hot and empty. She'd leave more than her emotions flopping and bleeding in the former Soviet Union. She'd leave her hopes for a new Gracie. Her dream for a fresh start.

She sat, and Pastor Yuri began his sermon. Yuri's venerable presence on the podium as he gripped the lectern and moved into his impassioned speech reminded her that he had been her champion. He'd stood up for her a year ago when her one-year visa expired, working some behind-the-scenes magic that allowed her to stay. He'd been encouraging, and, although she couldn't understand everything he said, she felt as if he somehow appreciated her. His handshake and solemn eyes had to mean something.

She might have impressed the pastor, but he didn't know the truth. Unless over the next five days before her departure her ministry took a hundred-and-eighty-degree about-face and she turned into Billy Graham or D. L. Moody, she'd be returning to the States the same scarred failure she was when she left it. Only this time, she'd be out of second chances.

As if reading her thoughts, Evelyn reached out and wrapped her soft, wrinkled hand around Gracie's. "You'll be okay, honey," she whispered.

Gracie looked away, blinked tears.

Unless she figured out a way to stay and keep fighting for redemption, not likely.

The fact the militia had sent Chief Arkady Sturnin in response to Vicktor's call meant two things. Either they'd forgiven Vicktor for the past, or the chief was the only one in the office.

Yeah, like Vicktor had to guess at the right answer.

"He was a friend of yours?" Arkady's cigarette bobbed between his lips as he talked. The ash dropped onto the linoleum and sizzled in a muddy puddle.

Scowling, Vicktor waved the smoke away and watched the forensics team prepare Dr. Evgeny Lakarstin's remains for the morgue. Although every door in the clinic had been propped open, the odor from the wreckage of medicines embedded the blue walls, the muddy wooden floor, the cracked plaster ceiling. Nausea dogged him as Vicktor watched the mortal remains of his friend manhandled.

"Yeah."

"Funny no one found him before this." Arkady's bulldog face jiggled when he spoke. "Did you have an appointment?"

Vicktor worked a nagging muscle in the back of his neck. "No, I just stopped by. My father said Alfred's been a bit droopy."

"With a mug like that, doesn't he always look droopy?" Arkady guffawed at his joke.

Vicktor clenched his jaw.

"Have you been to the kennels?" Arkady asked, his laughter dying.

"Yeah. Right after I called you. It's not pretty. Every animal has been gutted."

Arkady toyed with his Bond cigarette, squashing fuzzy eyebrows into one wide brush as he scanned the small clinic.

"What do you suppose this is?" The old man bent over to finger a wad of soggy papers, grunting as he went down, sounding every bit of his nearly sixty years.

Vicktor winced with remorse. Arkady had aged a century since the Wolf incident. Another residual casualty, another cop paying for Vicktor's impulsiveness and reckless pride.

"I don't know," Vicktor answered thinly as he stalked back to the lab.

A fog of saline and alcohol hung low and heavy. Vicktor put a hand to his nose as he stood in the doorway watching technicians gather evidence from the black lab table and smearing it on glass slides. Every vial had been smashed, and a gooey amber liquid covered the table like syrup. What had Evgeny been cooking up in here?

"Vicktor Nickolaiovich." Thankfully, the technicians still gave him respect, using his full name to address him. The technician motioned to him, then crouched behind the lab door.

Vicktor crossed the room and knelt beside him, arms hanging over his knees. The man peered into a thin metal bucket.

"What are we looking at?"

"Ashes." The tech wiggled the can. The orange peels at the bottom shifted and Vicktor made out a thin layer of charred paper, curled as if peeled from a block of chocolate.

"What is it?"

"Looks like the remnants of a *tetrad*, the kind professors use to record lab data."

A notebook. For experiments? Vicktor rubbed his chin and rose. Why would Evgeny burn his lab notes? Turning, he glimpsed another tech slip something into his pocket. "What are you doing?"

The man whirled. Reed thin, with bloodshot eyes and scaly skin, he blanched. Vicktor grabbed him by the collar and shoved the tech against the sticky lab table. Glaring into his eyes an inch from his nose, Vicktor reached into the man's pocket and pulled out an unbroken vial. Novocain.

"*Zdraztvootya?* I believe that's called stealing."

The tech's Adam's apple dipped twice in his neck. "He doesn't need it anymore."

The room went quiet. Vicktor let the kid go and blew out a hot breath. The tech's mottled face, glistening with a scrim of sweaty fear, told Vicktor he wore what Roman would call his "tiger" face. Great. Just when he thought he had a clamp on his emotions.

Good thing Roman wasn't here. Though perhaps, if he were, Vicktor wouldn't feel like the only uninvited guest at a birthday party. The militia stepped up and took notice whenever a COBRA walked into the room—the training the FSB received to become the special agents who fought the mafia guaranteed respect.

Or better yet, the entrance of David Curtiss, Green Beret and Delta Force captain, would get their attention. Only, he couldn't shout that little alliance across the room, could he? Sometimes Vicktor felt like David, better known as Preach, was in his head, his little voice of reason, and he would admit, only to himself, that he needed Preach's words of wisdom way more than he'd thought ten years ago.

Who knew that a pickup game of hockey, a fistfight and an American-style pizza would lead to friendships that felt tethered to Vicktor's very soul?

Sometimes he wondered if Roman and David had planned it that way.

Vicktor set the vial in a tray on the examining table and shot the tech a scalding look. "Get to work."

Stepping into the hall, he fielded a frown from the Bulldog. "*Spequietsye,* Vicktor. This isn't America. Loosen up."

Arkady's voice, although low, tightened Vicktor's gut. He swallowed a retort, closed his eyes and sighed. "Sorry."

Arkady was right. He didn't need a new generation of enemies in the militia, and another stunt like that could route his next urgent phone call straight to the morgue.

Arkady tapped his cigarette. The ash died to gray before it hit the floor. "Your shirt is too tight, Vicktor. You've changed. Ever since you got back from that stint in America, nothing is good enough for you. You see everything through American eyes...American *cop* eyes. Black and white. Don't forget you are Russian. The law has shades of gray here."

A muscle tensed in Vicktor's jaw. Arkady was from the old school, the days of propaganda and the Cold War, the easy days when the bad guys were easily identifiable—they wore red, white and blue.

It hadn't helped his relationship with his former chief when he had accepted the six-month internship in America. The friendship had taken further serious hits when he defected to the FSB, a.k.a. the former KGB, six months ago. The chief just didn't get it—after the Wolf incident, the blunder of Vicktor's militia career, Vicktor had to rescue himself from early retirement. Besides, the FSB had been chasing him like a hound since his training in the States, and after Roman had smoothed over the incident, they'd practically thrown him a welcome bash.

"We're on the same side, you know," Vicktor said.

Arkady drew on his cigarette as if he didn't hear him.

Vicktor suddenly wanted to dump this entire thing in Arkady's lap. A lifetime of chasing the scum of society had left an ugly pit in his stomach. He preferred the intellectual sparring of the international crimes unit where he now worked. But the memory of Evgeny, all smiles and jokes, stripped his anger, leaving only aching.

He needed answers. He wasn't about to disappoint another person he cared about, especially posthumously. He'd find Evgeny's killer even if he had to wrestle his pride into hard little knots.

Vicktor dredged up a respectful tone. "Yes, sir."

## Chapter Two

⊰❦⊱

Vicktor banged out of his apartment building and spied Roman leaning back against his building, arms akimbo, wearing a stocking cap, a running suit and a smile.

"Missed you last night."

"I had to work." The last thing Vicktor wanted to remember was the fact he'd missed out on a group chat. Like he had friends to spare. Vicktor made a face at him and began stretching from side to side. "I found Evgeny Lakarstin dead in his lab yesterday."

Roman went silent at that, his mouth in an O.

"I was up until midnight answering questions and writing reports."

"Fun. Well, then I hate to be the one to tell you Mae's in town. She's pulling transportation duty for some army brass. She told me to say hi to 'Stripes.'"

Okay, that hurt more than he would have expected, even with Roman's warning. "Oh, really?" Just what he needed to make his day—the memory of Mae Lund, her right hook against his chin, the fact that she was over him enough to say hello, and the knowledge that she probably looked better than he had a right to imagine. Only she knew how much he needed her opinion, how he'd relished the nickname she gave him.

"She made captain, by the way. She's flying DC-10s."

Good girl. Mae had earned her stripes through grit and spunk, and in the active, *objective* part of his brain, he couldn't blame her for not falling for the first Russian to flex his muscles. Even if he had done it saving her life.

"I thought she was on Search and Rescue."

"Not when she can speak Russian. They have her translating, too. By the way, David was online, as well."

The rising sun peeked through gaps in the tall buildings. It turned crisp, slightly frozen street puddles bright platinum and hinted at a beautiful spring day.

"Let's run," Vicktor snapped. He didn't know what irritated him more. That he'd been up until all hours describing Evgeny's death scene for his old militia cohorts, that he'd slept with one-hundred and thirty pounds of Great Dane on his face, or that he'd missed a chance to check in with the only people who knew the nightmares that haunted him.

Especially after a day when those nightmares seemed particularly fresh and brutal.

Roman scrambled to keep up as Vicktor shot down the sidewalk toward the wide greening boulevard between Karl Marx Street and Lenin Street. Roman, of course, wouldn't think of asking him to slow down, and that fact kept Vicktor at a speed that pushed his heart rate into overdrive.

He didn't care. Two weeks into his summer running habit, he needed an intense workout to drive Evgeny's corpse from his mind. Internal snapshots of Evgeny had pushed sleep into the folds of eternity.

He hardly noticed Roman behind him the entire kilometer to the river.

The Amur River pushed yellow foam and brown ice in thick currents north to its Pacific mouth. Vicktor let the snappy wind comb his hatless head and chill the sweat on his brow. Next to him, Roman gripped his knees and gulped frosty breaths. Remorse speared Vicktor. He shouldn't wrestle his grief during Roman's workout time.

"Sorry, Roma," he muttered, stopping and leaning against a stone wall that separated the beach from the boardwalk.

Roman straightened, his forgiveness written in his signature lopsided grin. "*Kak Dela,* Vita? I'd say from this morning's sprint we aren't simply stretching our muscles. You trying to exorcise some personal demons?"

Vicktor looked away from Roman's intuitive blue eyes. "You're starting to sound like Preach."

"I'll take that as a compliment. Tell me what's up."

Vicktor turned, braced himself on the fence and leaned in, forcing screams up his calf muscles. "It's nothing. I'm just tired."

Roman crossed his arms and propped a hip on the stone. Wind whistled down the boardwalk, sifting through Vicktor's Seattle PD sweatshirt. He shivered.

"Tired?" Roman echoed after a bit. "Tired of what? Grieving your mother? Trying to make things right with your pop?"

Vicktor tossed him a frown. "You are definitely sounding like Preach, or maybe Mae. Stop psychoanalyzing my life. I'm just…tired." He stared at the dirty Amur. "Sometimes I just wonder if it wouldn't have been better if it had been me who'd been shot instead of my father."

"You gotta go forward, pal."

"Yeah. Well, Evgeny sure isn't going forward. I'm going to find his killer."

Roman nodded. "I know. But when you do, you're still going to be exhausted."

Vicktor shook his head. "I know where you're going with this, and I'm telling you before you start, ditch the God-talk. I'm not interested. You know God and I have issues. The bottom line is God isn't going to solve my problems. Ever."

"Calm down, Stripes." Roman held up his hands in surrender. "As your friend, I get to say that you're wrong, but I'm on your side anyway."

"Let's run." Vicktor jogged back to the boulevard. He heard Roman fall in beside him and set a reasonable pace. They ran in silence, listening to the wind rustle through the trees and traffic fill the streets.

It was just like Roman to foist his religion into Vicktor's problems. He and David had been systematically ambushing him for years.

They just didn't know how it felt to experience God's cold shoulder. He'd tried the God route, once upon a time, and sorry, no thanks. Not that he'd ever mentioned his trial run with God to Roman or David. He'd rather have his tongue skewered slowly.

He was going to find Evgeny's killer without God's help. It just mattered too much to trust to a fickle God who did…or didn't…come through.

They ran in rhythm, vaulting in one accord the craters in the broken sidewalk and murky puddles of mud. Crumpled paper cups and refuse frozen by winter's embrace edged the path. Vicktor wondered if their national disregard for cleanliness irked Roman as much as it did him. Roman, too, had been to America, and Europe and even Japan once, and had seen the swept streets, the manicured lawns and the lush gardens. Nevertheless, Roman was forever flinging an easygoing smile into his assessment of life in Russia. Vicktor wondered if anything ever stymied his optimistic friend. Roman and Yanna were always telling Vicktor to loosen up, as if, somehow, that would help him find a new life for his handicapped father. Or help him wrestle the guilt of knowing he'd condemned the man to his threadbare armchair.

So maybe his run was about more than exorcising Evgeny's ghost from his mind. "Tell me about your latest love, Roma."

"Oh yeah, it's hot. I spent yesterday at the gym, arguing with the dead weights, and the night before having a long and personal chat with a bowl of ramen noodles. I'm the man." He shook his head. "Sorry. My long run as a single guy is in no imminent danger of ending."

"You expect too much, Romeo." Having stood on the sidelines watching Roman trot through numerous short-lived relationships, he knew his friend wouldn't stay single long. The man was a sponge for women, with his tousled brown hair, thick muscles and easy laughter. It was Roman who couldn't seem to figure out what he wanted.

"All I expect is a woman who cares about honesty and living a life for God."

"I'm not sure, but I think there is a rule about nuns getting married."

Roman elbowed him, and Vicktor dodged a puddle, laughing.

"I'm serious. Those types of women don't exist. Sure, you might find a Godly woman—look at Mae. How about Sarai? You had a good thing going with her back in college. But even those women have their hidden agendas. In general, women can't be trusted."

"Ouch. That's a pretty cynical statement, considering two of your best friends are women." Roman veered around a meteor-size crater in the middle of the sidewalk. "Seriously, though, you don't trust women? Mae, Yanna?"

"I'm not dating Mae or Yanna. Nor will I. I learned from Mae that dating warps friendship. Love is a game for a woman—one designed to confuse and decimate men." He gave a mock shudder.

Roman didn't laugh. "Nice. You're a real walking Don Juan. I'll bet the ladies love hanging around you."

Vicktor ignored him and he went on. "Sorry, but that's the truth. Remember what Sarai did to you? She led you on, then blink, walked out of your life without even a goodbye. I'd think you'd be my champion."

Roman's hand clamped on his shoulder, yanking him to a halt. His friend's eyes sparked, and Vicktor recoiled, suddenly aware he'd pushed Roman too far.

"You couldn't be more wrong, Vicktor. About God. About women. About Sarai. I regret losing her more than you can guess. But I don't blame the entire female population for my broken heart."

"Sorry." Vicktor shrugged off Roman's grip, feeling like a jerk for mentioning Roman's first love.

Roman inhaled an unsteady breath, his blue eyes scrutinizing his friend. "I don't know what happened to you yesterday, but you need to get a hold of your fear of trusting people. Trust is a choice, pal. No man is an island, and, unless you choose to believe in people, you're going to live a pretty chilly and barren life."

Roman's words felt like a sucker punch. Vicktor already lived a desolate life, his best friends being attached to a modem. Yes, he had Roman and Yanna, but more often than not he poured out his frustration to a dog he didn't even like. "That's not fair. I trust *you*." He broke their gaze.

"And I trust you, my friend. But you need more than me and Yanna, Mae and David. You need the Savior. And you need the love of a good woman."

"Just like you do?"

Roman smiled. It eased the moment, as well as the band around Vicktor's chest. *"Da."*

Roman released his grip and they fell into step, cooling down from their run with a brisk walk. The winking sun had skimmed the tops of the apartment buildings and the wind was dissected by the wad of budding trees along the boulevard. The smell of freshly baked bread swirled on the crisp air. Vicktor's stomach roared.

"That animal sounds hungry." Roman smirked.

Vicktor ignored him, cut off the path and tramped across the stiff grass toward the Svezhee Bread Factory.

Five minutes later, two loaves of bread tucked under his arm, he rejoined Roman, who waited on the sidewalk, eyebrows high, tapping his foot.

"Gotta feed Alfred," he mumbled.

Roman laughed. "By the way, I found a woman for you. Someone honest and not confusing in the least."

"What?" Vicktor frowned.

Roman jerked his head, indicating a blonde heading in their direction. Her hands were fisted in her coat pockets, her legs, pulling against the hem of her denim skirt as she strode. Her vivid scowl and blazing eyes broadcast her fury as she stalked toward them.

"Just your type, Vicktor," Roman said, voice low, teasing.

Vicktor's eyes roamed over the lady, for some reason empathizing with the frustration written on her face.

Five steps away, she glanced up and met his eyes. Green. Intense. Vulnerable. His heart caught at that last impression and he barely remembered to stumble backward to let her pass.

"*Da.* Just my type," he echoed as he watched her march down the sidewalk.

Gracie felt the man's stare on the back of her neck and picked up her pace. *Way to go, Gracie.* Ex-pat rule number one—don't make eye contact with a man in Russia. Or anywhere, for that matter.

She distanced herself from the gawker on the sidewalk, her heartbeat slowing. Poor guy did look frayed. His pensive blue eyes, a furrowed brow, his black hair in spikes and perspiration running down his unshaven jaw. Her heart twisted in response. She knew all about feeling frayed, worn down, defeated.

A frosty wind gusted through her thin raincoat and she shivered.

The smell of fresh bread wafted after her as she beelined to the bus stop. She would have dearly loved to pick up a fresh loaf for Evelyn, but thanks to Leonid, her absent chauffeur, she was hoofing it all over Khabarovsk. Leonid had better have a wallop of a reason for being late three times in a row. She once again wished for Andrei, but he was already assigned a new post somewhere. Thank the Lord for Larissa, who had come into work at Aeroflot Travel early to meet her. Her travel agent friend even bumped her into first class.

"Your flight is at four p.m. Be there by one p.m. and don't be late," Larissa had said, melancholy in her eyes. "There's only one flight a month out of here now, and it's packed."

Friends like Larissa, and her cousin, Andrei, would be difficult to replace.

Especially since she was leaving, forever.

Gracie's throat closed and she didn't dare look at heaven. She knew she'd blown it. The reality was mortifying—a missionary who had never led someone to the Lord. Why, she couldn't even convince her best friend, let alone the masses. Larissa's heart was as hardened to the gospel as a rock on the Lake Superior shoreline.

With five days left, the time bomb of a ticket in Gracie's pocket ticked away.

She joined a handful of old women waiting for the bus, their wide faces peeking out from fuzzy gray scarves wound twice around their heads. Their desolate eyes matched their headgear. Life took all the guts the elderly could muster, especially on gray spring days.

As a grimy orange bus chugged up to the curb and coughed exhaust, Gracie fished around in her coat pocket and unearthed five rubles for fare. She climbed aboard and squeezed in beside a grizzled old man. The vodka on his breath nearly knocked her to her knees as she snared an overhead bar.

She hoped Evelyn was still home. Her boss wasn't expecting her, but Gracie dearly needed a fresh e-mail from her mother to ward of the feeling of dread that hovered over the morning. She gritted her teeth against the breath of the toothless rummy, and hung on while the bus lurched toward Victory Square. The bust of Lenin towered over the cobblestone parade grounds, a heap of bouquets wilting at the base. Only four days earlier she had shivered on the balcony of the Youngs' sixth-floor apartment and watched Russia revel in the old days of the might and power of the Cold War. They'd pushed out the old arsenal, including tanks and Katusha rocket launchers, and had assembled them in the square, crushing the stones to dirt. She had to admit the sound of a thousand or so male soldiers singing the Russian national anthem had sent pangs of patriotism through her. Indeed, there were times she dearly missed America.

Ten minutes later, she felt nearly soused herself, courtesy of the wino beside her. She gulped fresh air as she stumbled off the bus. Approaching the Youngs' building, she noticed Leonid's blue *Zhiguli* was not parked in front. She'd held out a slim hope he'd actually check in with Evelyn, not relishing the day hiking around town. Still, as much as she needed a lift she had to admit to some relief. The guy gave her the creeps. He ogled her like a starved lion. Her irritation died in the face of the alternative. Hoofing was definitely safer.

Gracie shuffled into the dank corridor and called the Youngs' lift. It wheezed to life and lumbered down six floors. Shivering, she wondered why someone didn't clean the cobwebs, hanging Spanish-moss–fashion from the dark corners. A pile of old cigarette butts, crushed juice boxes and plastic bags added a musty odor to the shadows. She smirked as she read the new chalk graffiti on the already well-decorated walls— "Natasha loves Slava." Some things were the same throughout the world.

The elevator doors wrenched open and a buzzing fluorescent light beckoned her to enter. Gracie hesitated and waged her familiar self-debate. She'd been imprisoned twice in an elevator in Russia and the experience had left scars on her psyche, not to mention her olfactory glands. Still, six flights of stairs waged a compelling case. She pushed the sixth-floor button, charred black from a vandal's lighter, and ascended in the tiny box sticking of dog urine. Perhaps she would walk back down.

The lift stopped on the sixth floor. Gracie stepped out and froze.

The black metal door protecting the Youngs' flat, a standard for foreigners, hung slightly ajar. Talk about creepy—it groaned as Gracie eased it open. "Evelyn?"

The inner wooden door gave easily. Gracie stood there, her stomach coiling into a cold knot. Evelyn was a zealot about locked doors.

"Dr. Willie?"

Silence oozed from the apartment. Gooseflesh rose, pricked her neck.

"Evelyn? Dr. Willie?" Alarm pitched her voice high and it added to the gnawing fear in her gut. *Stop. It.* She took a deep breath. There were simple explanations. Like, they'd gone out shopping and forgotten to lock the door.

She nearly jumped through her skin when she closed the door and found the Youngs' coats neatly hung on the hallway hooks. From the kitchen, the refrigerator clicked on and buzzed.

She startled, turned and braced her hand on the wall. *Stupid girl.* Maybe they were next door. Gracie stepped into the kitchen. A fresh, wet rag dripped into the sink next to the drying rack, which held the clean breakfast dishes. Bacon grease glistened in a cast-iron pan on the stove. On the ledge, an African violet sparkled, freshly sprayed.

"Evelyn?" Maybe she was in the bathroom.

Gracie stalked down the hallway, noticing the French doors to the family room were closed. If Dr. Willie was studying, he wasn't answering. A light streaming from the bathroom urged her down the hall. Gracie stuck her head in, a smile on her face, ready to catch Evelyn hanging laundry. A stepladder and a fresh batch of laundry drying from a line above the bathtub cast gloomy shadows on the white tile.

No Evelyn. Gracie flicked the light off and stood in the hall, listening to her heart beat.

*Stop.* Gracie held up her hands as if to halt the ridiculous fear cascading over her. She would not let the unknown push her beyond the cradle of common sense. Evelyn and Dr. Willie had obviously left and forgotten to lock their door. Odd, but not impossible. Besides, weren't they safely tucked under the protective wing of her Heavenly Father? Gracie bowed her head, shame dissolving her fear. *Forgive me for my lack of faith, Lord.*

Gracie checked her watch. She still had time to download her mail and send her mother a note. She headed for the bedroom office.

Knocking on the bedroom door, she laughed at her silliness. If Evelyn were in the bedroom, she would have heard her long before Gracie's timid rap.

As she pushed open the door, the moment slowed like an old movie on creased film. Horror filled her—starting at her gut and building until it emerged in an all-out howl. Her bones turned to rubber. Gracie collapsed to her knees and fought for breath.

No, *no!*

She whimpered as she pulled herself across the bloody floor toward Evelyn's unmoving body.

# Chapter Three

Toweling off after his frosty two-minute shower, Vicktor caught the phone on the third ring.

*"Slyushaiyu."* He rubbed a hand over his clean-shaven skin and winced at a raw spot. The clock hands inched toward eight-thirty.

"You have some explaining to do, Shubnikov." Comrade Major Mikhail Malenkov's voice grated Vicktor's already throbbing nerves.

"Come again?" Vicktor folded his towel and hung it over a straight-backed chair.

"Maxim. He's supposed to be your partner. Yet you didn't have the courtesy to call either him or me and let us know that one of your best informants is stone cold in the morgue?"

"He was a friend, sir, and unless I missed a memo, my understanding was Maxim just shares my office space."

"Don't get smart. You know he's assigned to you."

Vicktor's eyes narrowed as he surveyed his closet. His voice grew cold. "I was walking my dog. I found Evgeny by accident."

"Right. Next time call your own guys for backup. We don't need the goats in the militia sniffing around our *dela*."

"Since when are local murders our business?"

"Since they are mafia hits."

Vicktor scrambled for balance, his sock halfway on. "Mafia hit?" Hope lit inside him. That meant the case would head to the COBRA force of the FSB. Roman's division. Vicktor schooled his tone. "Sorry about the oversight, sir. Old habits die hard. I'll call our guys next time."

Malenkov's voice softened to a cultured tone. "Aren't you supposed to be here by now, Captain?" The phone hummed in Vicktor's ear.

He slammed it onto the cradle and smirked. With Roman on the inside, maybe Vicktor wouldn't have to kowtow to Arkady. He'd happily shove the raw memories and unending penance behind him.

He tugged on his black suit pants and white oxford. Straightening his tie in the mirror, he caught a glimpse of Alfred, sprawled on an armchair, tearing into the last of his loaves of bread.

Vicktor crossed the room in two strides. "You're a menace, you know?" He tried to wrench the bread from the dog's mouth, then gave up and scratched the dog behind his pointed ear. "Try not to eat me out of house and home, huh? No furniture, no pillows, no shoes and I promise to take you home tomorrow morning, okay?"

He thought he heard the dog sigh with contentment as he slammed the door behind him.

The sun had peeled off the initial chill of the morning. Vicktor flipped up the collar of his tweed sports coat while he coaxed his forest-green *Zhiguli* to life. He felt like flicking on his siren and parting traffic on his way to work. As it was, anticipation sent his accelerator into the floorboard and he soon found himself in the back parking lot. Screeching into his regular space, Vicktor hopped out and shut the door.

"Vicktor!" A feminine voice, high and smooth, sailed over car tops to greet him. Yanna strode over to him, hitching her leather computer bag and gym bag up her right shoulder. The satchels dwarfed her lean body, but she was crisp and pretty in a black leather skirt, hose and matching jacket. Yanna knew how to pull off European fashion.

"Do you have a game tonight?" he asked, melting into her stride.

"Against the Vladivostok Torrents. They're still unbeaten."

"Until tonight." He winked at her. Yanna's volleyball team had taken the championship for the city and was smoking their way toward nationals. Yanna's serve could melt butter and her spike sent him to his knees in terror and admiration. He didn't have a prayer when they played one-on-one down at the beach.

"Come and watch the game tonight. It's at Dynamo Stadium." Yanna flicked back her silky brown hair and looked up at him, those brown eyes so clear and genuine. His heart twisted. Why couldn't he find a girl like Yanna? Roman was right: his life was desolate. Never mind about the Savior garbage, but maybe he could be persuaded to let someone quiet into his life. Someone supportive. Forgiving.

Yeah, *that* was likely. Especially if he let them close enough to get a glimpse of the real Vicktor.

He returned Yanna's smile. "I'll try and make it to your game."

"Great!" She bounced through the door he held open.

They fell silent walking in the back entrance of FSB Headquarters. The mustard-yellow building covered nearly a city block and loomed five stories tall. The rumors ran as deep as the dungeons but few had involuntarily ventured lower than the first floor and lived to tell about it. Vicktor and Yanna walked through the gray corridor in silence, their feet echoing against the cement. They passed abandoned interrogation rooms and doors that led to the secrets below. Vicktor wondered at the wisdom of the FSB occupying the same building its predecessor, the KGB, had occupied for sixty years. Fear was embedded within the walls.

They climbed the stairs and entered the lobby. "I'm ducking into Personnel," Yanna said. "I'll see you tonight."

"Yanna, wait." He caught her arm, a lump rising in his throat. His voice stayed low. "Sorry about missing the chat last night."

She blinked twice at him, as if he'd dashed her with a bucket of ice. She gave a furtive look around the lobby. "No problem." Whirling, she nearly sprinted away from him.

Vicktor stared after her. He was making all sorts of friends this morning.

He took the steps two at a time to his office on the second floor, then threaded his way through a minefield of desks to his office.

Vicktor snorted as he rounded Maxim's desk, buried somewhere under an avalanche of paper. Yesterday's teacup soiled a stack of notes and Snickers wrappers littered the floor, but the desk chair remained empty. Annoyance flooded him as he recalled the major's words. The rookie was slightly difficult to mentor when he never showed up for work. *Partners*. The word made him cringe. Maxim didn't have a clue what it meant and Vicktor didn't have the time or desire to teach him. Vicktor shrugged out of his coat and hung it in his wardrobe.

Grabbing his coffee mug, the one with Mount Hood glinting off the side in gold etching, he scooped in a generous amount of instant coffee, added a spoonful of cream and plugged the samovar in, waiting for it to boil.

He turned on the ancient paperweight they assigned him a month ago, a.k.a. his desktop PC, coaxing it with a few sweet words. While it eased to life, he weeded through his phone messages. Two distraught families from cold cases who would never know what happened to their mafia-connected kids, and a call from Arkady. Filing the other two in the Maxim pile, Vicktor flicked his fingers on Arkady's note while he dialed his father.

Nickolai caught it on the sixth ring. Vicktor didn't know if he should be glad or brace himself for the inevitable.

"*Slyushaiyu!*"

Vicktor forced a cheery tone. He thought he'd make a great undercover cop. "*Privyet,* Pop. How are you?"

Silence.

"Do you need anything?"

"What would I need? A son who stops by and visits once in a while, maybe?"

Right. Okay. Nickolai had his happy face on today. "I'll stop by later. Do you need some bread?"

He supposed he should be grateful his father still spoke to him after the accident. The old man hadn't assigned blame, but he didn't have to. The *Santa Barbara* reruns and the constant tapping with his metal cane turned the knife with precision.

Silence crackled through the line. "Pop?"

"*Da. Da.* Bread is all I need." He hung up and Vicktor stared at the dead phone.

He was off to a great start this morning. Vicktor kneaded his temple. If his mother were here she'd know what to do. But Antonina had abandoned her men on a snowy night two years ago, and the grief and anger had driven the Shubnikov men apart long before Nickolai's accident. The Wolf's bullet had simply pushed them beyond reconciliation.

Steam fogged the room, obscuring the glass windows that separated Vicktor's office from the rookies on the floor. Vicktor filled his cup and stirred the coffee. It wasn't Starbucks, which he'd visited more times than he should have in Oregon, but at least it was coffee. Sorta. Okay, it *smelled* the same.

A cup and a half later, he had read through his e-mail messages and reached for the phone. He hoped Arkady had eaten a full breakfast. He needed the man slightly sluggish when he needled him for information about Evgeny.

"Give us a break! Lakarstin's body isn't even cold!"

Nope. Probably had kasha. Even Vicktor would be on edge after a bowl of cold, lumpy mush. "I know, Chief, but what do you know? Tell me, anything." Please, let him say he was handing the case to the COBRAs. He didn't want to be caught in the middle of a range war.

Vicktor heard Arkady snuffle, and could almost see him lean back in his tattered desk chair and take a pull on his cigarette. "Well, let's see what you can do with this, hotshot. His neck was slit."

"I'm not quite that stupid, thank you. Tell me something new."

"And he had a wad of paper shoved up his nose."

"What?"

"You mean you goats in the 'FezB' don't know a mafia hit when you see one?"

"What mafia? That's not the Russian signature for a hit."

"It's a North Korean superstition. They shove the paper up a victim's nose to keep their spirit from haunting them. Even a rookie would know that."

Vicktor thumbed his coffee cup handle, ignoring the barb. "What would the North Korean mafia want with a veterinarian?"

Arkady's chair creaked as the Bulldog shifted his weight. Probably putting out that cigarette.

"That is a good question. Was your buddy into drug smuggling?"

"Now, how would I know that?"

Arkady laughed. Vicktor tensed.

"You said that dog of yours was a bit sluggish...maybe he needed a fix?"

"At Alfred's age, following a cute poodle just about does him in."

"Your pal was into some sort of *tyomnaya delo*, some nasty business, for the mafia to track him down. They were searching for something, too. We found a charred notebook in the garbage can, like he tried to keep something out of their hands."

Vicktor remembered the orange peels. "Maybe it's some sort of ledger."

Vicktor heard the flick of a lighter.

"Are you doing an autopsy?" he asked.

"Cause of death is pretty obvious."

"Not to the FSB." As soon as the words left his mouth Vicktor wanted to bang his head on his desk.

A chill blew into Arkady's voice. "Something you want to tell me?"

Vicktor's stomach knotted. Why, oh why, couldn't he keep his mouth shut? "I heard the word mafia and…well, it's not personal, Chief."

"Your COBRAs have been banging on my office door all morning. You tell them this is my case and I'll hand it over if and when I want to."

"It's not your jurisdiction anymore."

"I'll say what's my jurisdiction. You just remember, you chose to leave. Nobody forced you out."

"I don't see it that way."

Silence stretched the moment taunt. Then, in a voice so thin Vicktor hardly recognized it, Arkady whispered, "You watch your back over there, Vita."

Vicktor opened his mouth. Nothing emerged.

"I gotta go round up the boys," Arkady said, his voice fully recovered. "They're probably out stealing the hubcaps off cars."

He hung up and Vicktor clutched another dead phone in his white-knuckled fist.

Gracie fumbled with the ropes that bound Evelyn's wrists. She couldn't look at Evelyn's ashen face.

Evelyn's body lay at a contorted angle and her head had lolled back to reveal a jagged cut just below her chin. Gracie kept her gaze on the rope. Her fingers were slick, her eyes flooding. "It's almost loose, Evelyn," she soothed, as if her glassy-eyed friend could hear.

When the knot slid free, Evelyn's still hands remained a sickly gray, the blood refusing to flow into the gnarled fingertips. Gracie wrapped her arms around her waist and rocked. Her breath wheezed through dry lips.

"What happened?" she moaned. Her heartbeat thundered in her ears, her body shuddering with shock. "What happened?"

She heard a wail, and with horror realized it was her own. "Oh God, help me." She covered her head with her hands, scraping up control. Her breath came in hiccups, hard, fast.

An eerie silence invaded the room. Gracie's skin chilled. What if the murderer still lurked nearby? Fear drove her to her feet.

She had to call the police.

Her head spun as she wiped tears from her face. The phone. Stumbling to the desk, she picked it up and dialed 9-1-1.

The dead tone buzzed in her ear. Fool! Russia didn't use 9-1-1. For the first time in two years Gracie dearly wished she lived in America. She held the receiver against her forehead. "God, help," she whimpered.

Her eyes latched on to the phone list. *Andrei*. She left a trail of red on the number pad. "Be there!" she demanded, sobbing. She slammed down the receiver on the tenth ring, then grabbed up the telephone, shaking it. "Be there!"

*Larissa*. Gracie grabbed the handset. Crumpling to the floor, she pulled the phone into her lap and dialed. She hugged her knees to her chest as she closed her eyes and listened to the ring.

"Aeroflot Travel. This is Larissa Tallina. Hello."

"Help."

"Gracie, where are you?"

Thank the Lord, Larissa recognized her voice.

"Help. Evelyn…" Gracie's voice sounded reed thin, unrecognizable. Her head spun. Acid pooled in the back of her throat.

"Are you hurt?" Larissa's voice held panic.

Gracie shook her head.

"Are you at home?"

Gracie shook her head again, beginning to tremble.

"Gracie, talk to me! Where *are* you?"

*Focus*. Gracie steeled herself, inhaled deeply and formed speech. "Evelyn…was…murdered." She felt a sob roiling to the surface.

Larissa gasped.

A floorboard creaked; the refrigerator hummed from the kitchen. "Larissa, don't leave me! Are you there?"

"*Da, Da, Da.* I'm here." Larissa's voice sounded pinched, perhaps with grief. "Stay right where you are. I'm calling the police. Stay put."

Gracie's plea lodged in her dry throat and surfaced in a ragged whisper. "Don't hang up." The dead tone buzzed in her ear. *Oh please, Lord, no. Please don't leave me here all alone.* She pushed the phone receiver into her cheek and blew out, fighting the panic clogging her mind.

"*Yea, though I walk through the valley of the shadow of death, I will fear no evil; for Thou art with me; Thy rod and Thy staff they comfort me.*"

Gracie curled into a ball, ignoring the comfort that could be hers, covered her hands with her face, and wept. Her sobs echoed through the flat and drowned the rasp of the steel door as it eased open.

# Chapter Four

The Wolf had grown to like the alias. He liked to think of himself as a hunter. "Where is it?" He slammed his hands down on his desk and leaned forward in his rickety chair. The flimsy piece of laminate trembled, as did the weakling sitting in the straight chair across from him.

"I don't know." The man's face paled. He turned up his fraying collar.

The Wolf saw the quiver in his hands, and rolled his gaze up to the ceiling. The ceiling fan swirled the stale air through the tiny office. Dust rose from the matted red rug and mixed with the sour smell of mold clinging to the walls of the cement and log building. The place should have been destroyed years ago. Someday it was going to come down, but he hoped to be long gone before then.

He rose, rounded his desk and leaned against it, folding his hands on his lap. His stress was beginning to manifest itself in the flesh of his knuckles. His fingers screamed as dry skin cracked and bled. He needed a bottle of Smirnoff and a good massage. But not here, not now. Pleasure would have to wait until he'd finished what he'd started. That's what commitment meant. Putting off 'til tomorrow the delights of the flesh, staying the course until the job was complete.

That much he'd learned over the thirty years of his virtual imprisonment.

He watched the man fidget, play with his leather key chain. Idiot. The man had all the markings of a new Russian—cocky on the outside, kasha for stuffing. Flighty. Uncommitted. Men like the one before him made the Wolf physically ill. They had no idea what it meant to sacrifice for the *Rodina*, the Motherland. Men like him were like a virus, infecting the motherland with greediness and a lust for westernism. He despised the leather jacket, the black shoes, the clink of keys to a fancy Japanese sedan.

He despised the next generation. Their idealism, their selfish dreams. The Wolf smiled. He'd shattered some of those illusions today.

He let the kid sit in silence, watched a line of sweat drip down the angular face.

"It's your own fault."

The younger man looked up, eyes lined with red. "How's that?" The tough tone was belied by an edge of horror.

"If you'd dug deeper, none of this would have happened."

"He didn't have it. He knew nothing!"

*Weakling.* "He knew."

"He died rather than tell you?"

"Yes."

The man rose and went to the window. "I feel sick."

The Wolf knew just how the kid felt. He remembered the day not so long ago, when everything he built his life on dissolved like salt in water.

He'd been left to drown.

The Wolf clamped a fat hand on the chauffeur's shoulder. The younger man jumped. Outside the grimy window, a group of blue-gray pigeons wandered through the garbage of an overflowing Dumpster, picking at juice cans and hard bread. The wind blew a plastic bag through the rutted dirt yard. It caught in the branches of a budding lilac.

"Find what I need and you'll feel much better. I promise."

In the wake of Gracie's sobs, the whine of the steel door on its hinges ignited her adrenaline like tinder.

Someone was here.

Gracie held still, letting the saliva pool in her mouth. She heard nothing but the whistle of a draft from the outside hall, yet she felt a presence slink toward the bedroom. Gracie drew in a slow, noiseless breath, trying to ignore the sound of her pounding heartbeat. The presence edged closer. Clamping down on her trembling lower lip, she moved the telephone to the floor. It jangled.

Gracie froze.

Glancing around the room for a weapon, her heart sank. The Youngs had nothing more dangerous than a couple of oversize pillows in their room. Her slaughtered body would be found clutching a feather pillow like a shield. Revulsion sent an unexpected streak of courage into her veins. She wasn't going to let Evelyn's murderer kill her without a fight.

Her eyes fell on the crystal vase Dr. Willie had given his wife for Christmas. Gracie eased to her feet and grabbed the vase. The faux flowers went airborne, scattering the potpourri Evelyn had tucked inside.

Gracie heard a brushing sound, as if the intruder had skimmed his jacket along the wallpaper. She gritted her teeth, willed her pulse quiet, raised the vase.

The door cracked open.

Gracie wound up.

A fuzzy white paw clawed at the invisible.

The vase crashed.

Gracie's heart nearly rocketed out of her open mouth. Shaking, she sank onto Dr. Willie and Evelyn's double bed and wheezed deep breaths.

She'd nearly killed a cat. What if it *had* been the killer? What was she supposed to do, bean him with a pot of flowers? The absurdity of her defense sent heat into her face. She was a fool. And she might be in danger.

Glancing at Evelyn's butchered body, she pushed a hand against her pitching stomach and released a shuddering breath. "I'm sorry, Evelyn. I have to get out of here."

Gracie grabbed her satchel from its landing place near the door and stepped out into the hallway. Nothing but shadow and the *plink* of water from the kitchen sink. On noodle legs, she ran to the door, just daring someone to leap from the kitchen or the living room. She'd send him out of the window and into the next country.

She stepped into the hallway, strode to the landing and started down the stairs. One step at a time, skipping two, then three, feeling the hem of her dress catch as she hung on to the rail and flung herself down every flight until she stumbled, breathless through the entrance and out into the clear, blue-skied day.

Her gaze landed on a babushka, still attired for January, sitting on a bench near the door. The old woman scrutinized her with a slit-eyed stare. Gracie stalked away, her strides not nearly long enough for the speed she needed. The cacophony of sirens, horns and car engines on the street played her tension like a drum.

Footfalls streaked up behind her. She ducked her head. Panic made her stiffen, yet she glanced up.

A teenager ran past, his backpack slapping against his hip. He frowned at her as he whizzed by. She lowered her eyes and repositioned her satchel on her shoulder, increasing her stride.

Color caught her eye. Dark red. She slowed and examined her hands.

*Blood.* Her breath stuck in her throat. Blood welled in the creases of her palms, smeared her hands, stained her shirt-sleeves. It saturated her denim skirt, lined the hem of her trench coat.

She'd held her head in her hands, wiped her tears…*Evelyn's blood streaked her face.*

Gracie felt another howl begin in her gut and fought it. She wanted to retch on the sidewalk.

*Run.*

Light-headed, she stumbled to an alleyway. Threading between metal garages, she found a niche between two blue, peeling units and sank down next to a pile of vodka bottles.

Hiccuping in horror, she wrapped her arms around her body and rocked as Evelyn's pale face ravaged her memory. And Gracie was covered in her blood. The world spun; she forced herself to breathe. Battling for sanity, she spoke aloud.

"Get home. Get clean. Get out of Russia."

Yes, get out of Russia. *Now.* Gracie climbed to her feet. Bracing an arm on the garage, she forced herself to formulate a path home.

She'd cut through the garages, around the park, along the alley and behind the bread kiosk, then make a frenzied dash to the front door.

Ducking her chin, she raced toward her apartment.

"We're not as free as you think, Vita, that's all." Yanna didn't look at Vicktor. She stirred her cold tea, pushing the tea bag into a wad at the bottom of her cup. The beverage had long since sent off its last wisp of steam. Vicktor's stomach churned as he watched her twirl her spoon. Something was eating at her, something bigger than tonight's tournament.

Vicktor kept his voice low. "Could you be more clear?"

Yanna sighed, dropped the spoon and flicked her hair back. It shone rich mahogany in the well-lit cafe. She crossed her arms over her chest, wrinkling leather and appearing exasperated. "*Nyet.* Just keep our little online friends a secret. Don't breathe names, or even connections. Chat rooms are not private, even encrypted ones like ours. *Ponyatna?*"

"Yeah, I got it." Annoyance plucked his nerves and he felt a faint ripple of fear. He wasn't under any illusions that the Internet, and even his e-mail, couldn't be monitored. That was why they used nicknames and chatted in English, why Preach had set up their private, encrypted chat room. Vicktor rubbed his thumb along the handle of his coffee cup. Post-Communism residue soured his stomach.

"Is it lunchtime yet?"

Yanna's face lit up. "Roma!"

Vicktor stood and locked hands with Roman, who grinned. "I got a tidbit for you that will make your day."

"You're on Evgeny's case," Vicktor guessed. It gave him pleasure to see his friend's smile droop.

"How did you know?"

"Malenkov. Chewed my ear off this morning for not calling him on his day off."

Roman turned a chair around and straddled it, joining them at the round table. He eyed Vicktor's beverage with a grimace. "Vicktor, why can't you drink tea like every other Russian?"

Vicktor ignored his sour stomach and took a long, loud sip of his coffee.

Roman put two hands to his neck and squeezed, mimicking choking. Vicktor nearly choked for real with laughter when a waitress hustled up, and looked at the COBRA captain like he had a disease.

Yanna shook her head.

Roman cleared his throat, becoming, instantly, the counter-terrorist Red Beret who knew how to defuse a tense situation. He smiled, nicely. "Got any borscht?"

"I'll see," the waitress snapped. She whirled and headed for the kitchen.

Roman gave an exaggerated shiver. "Oh, how I love Russian service."

Vicktor gulped his laughter. Roman didn't need any outside encouragement.

"So, you already know my big news." Roman crossed his arms and waggled his eyebrows. "Well, I'll bet you don't know this…"

Vicktor gave him a mock glare.

Roman glanced at Yanna. "He's grumpy, huh?"

She smirked.

"Roman," Vicktor warned.

"Keep your shirt on, Vita. Some of us got to asking how the comrade major found out about Evgeny. I mean, Arkady certainly didn't roust him out of bed with the news, did he?"

Vicktor leaned forward, his heart missing a beat. "Who told him?"

"Actually, we're not sure."

Vicktor's eyes narrowed.

"But we do know the call came in early this morning on one of Major Malenkov's private lines, right after he came in to work."

Disbelief almost stole Vicktor's voice but he forced out the words, "The comrade major's phone is tapped?" He glanced at Yanna, whose eyes were wider than her teacup.

Roman held a finger to his lips.

Vicktor gasped. "Why?"

Roman's smile vanished. "Listen to me, Vita. Everybody's phone is tapped at HQ. Fourth Department knows all."

The Fourth Department. Internal Affairs. Shock turned him cold. Why would the Fourth be investigating Comrade Malenkov?

"The call came in on an ancient number we've been monitoring for years." Roman leaned forward for emphasis. "It's been out of use for a decade, but the comrade major himself requested the tap."

Vicktor's mind reeled. Why would the major ask to have one of his lines tapped?

"Why hasn't the number been used for so long?" Yanna rested her elbows on the table. "Shouldn't it have been reassigned?"

"It used to be Comrade Major Ishkov's line. I guess they thought leaving it open might lead to his murderer."

"Murderer?" Vicktor said, and three heads turned from a nearby table.

Roman shot him a cross look.

"Sorry," Vicktor mumbled. He schooled his volume. "Ishkov was one of the heavyweights, mentored under Khrushchev. I didn't know he was murdered." He pushed his coffee away, his appetite gone. "I thought he had a heart attack. I remember him. He was a legend. I never did figure out why he didn't retire."

"They needed him around to keep the old spies in line. Ten years ago, the plants from the old KGB were still working the system. Ishkov was assigned to reel them in and send them to pasture. He bought it before he could finish the job."

"So Malenkov kept Ishkov's number open to see if he could tempt some of the old goats in from the cold, in case they called to report?"

"Maybe." Roman fingered his soup spoon.

Yanna steepled her fingers and rested her chin on them. "So, you're saying an old agent, or an informant, called in on Ishkov's old number, got Malenkov, and reported Evgeny's murder?"

Roman pointed at her. "*Tochna.*"

"Who would know enough about Evgeny's murder to call Malenkov, and why?" Vicktor asked.

Roman gave Vicktor a steely look. "One of Arkady's boys? Disgruntled?"

Vicktor scowled. "Hardly. His men are more loyal to him than their own wives." Still, the image of a scaly-skinned tech at Evgeny's clinic flashed through his memory. He pressed his thumb and forefinger to his eyes and pinched the image away. "I don't know."

"Food for thought," Roman commented, and crossed his arms over his chest.

Vicktor chuckled to himself, spying Roman's captain bars glinting gold on the collar of his COBRA uniform. Although clad in black jeans, boots and a black leather jacket, Roman never could stray far from the reminder of his rank. Roman had fought for his bars—Vicktor didn't blame the guy for wearing them every waking moment. He supposed it kept Roman focused on his end goals, and his mind off his losses.

"Ah, food for the famished!" Roman smiled broadly at the waitress skulking back to them. She balanced a bowl of borscht on her tray.

Ignoring him, she plunked the borscht down on the table. "Twenty rubles."

Roman peeled a bill off a wad from his pocket. She snatched it from his grip and marched back to the kitchen.

A tendril of steam curled from the borscht like a ribbon and Roman made a show of sniffing. The smell of dill clawed at Vicktor's taste buds, but he doubted he'd ever have an appetite again after Roman's news.

The cell phone trilled in his coat pocket. Vicktor dug it out and flipped open the case. "Shubnikov."

"Get over here, and don't ever say I never did you any favors."

"Arkady?"

"That's still *Chief* Arkady to you. I'm at Kim-yu-Chena Street, apartment twenty-three, sixth floor. You'd better hurry if you want to beat the rest of your three-letter cohorts here and get a piece of this."

"Piece of what?" Vicktor asked, wadding a paper napkin in his fist.

"You're in luck, hotshot. The Wolf has struck again."

# Chapter Five

Gracie's keys shook as she fought with the bolts of her steel door. Flinging herself inside her apartment, she slammed the door shut behind her.

Fatigue buckled her knees and she crumpled hard onto the floor. Sweat poured down her face, into her eyes, down her chest and back. Hiccuping breaths, she fought with her buttons, then shrugged out of her coat and left it in a heap.

*Get clean.* The thought pushed her forward, beyond exhaustion. Toeing off her shoes, she unbuttoned her dress, let it slide off and left it in a ring. Stumbling down the hall, she whipped her turtleneck over her head and pitched it into the corner. She slapped on the bathroom light, then reached for the faucet and cranked the water on full, hoping the city hadn't turned off the hot water yet. She ripped off her socks and underclothes and shoved her hands under the spray. Dried blood loosened, dripped off her. *Evelyn's blood.* She felt her stomach convulse.

*Keep it together, Grace.* She fought the shakes as she climbed into the tub, unwilling to wait for the water to warm, and grabbed her soap.

The water turned her skin to ice. Blood edged her fingernails, lined the creases in her hands. She scrubbed until her fingers were raw and wrinkled. Her eyes burned as she watched the water pool red at her feet.

*Evelyn. Oh, Evelyn.*

A howl, hot and painful, began at Gracie's toes. By the time it had worked into her chest, she was shaking.

Gripping the sides of the tub, Gracie sank into a ball and wept.

Evelyn deserved better than this. After everything Evelyn had done for God, didn't that guarantee her some safety? It felt as if Gracie had been kicked in the chest. "Is *this* how You protect those who serve You?"

What did it mean to be a Christian if she couldn't count on the Almighty for the one thing she needed from Him—protection? Why had she poured out her life for a God who so obviously didn't care?

Gracie curled her arms over her head, kneaded them into her wet hair and rocked. Evelyn's face, white and horrified, stared at her. She pressed her fists into her eyes. She heard herself moan, and gulped it back.

If Evelyn's sweet life devoted to God couldn't protect her from a brutal murderer, then where did Gracie, a soiled failure, stand in God's eyes?

Memory hit her like a fist and she heard laugher.

Tommy's laughter. She pushed away the feeling of his hands on her body, his roughness. Had she seriously thought that an escape across the ocean might free her from the nightmares?

She got out of the tub, toweled off and grabbed a robe. Shivering, she realized she'd come full circle.

She was alone. Just as she had been the night three years ago when she'd gone home with the campus jock.

No wonder God had abandoned her. What a farce she lived.

Better than anyone, she knew she didn't deserve God's forgiveness, let alone His protection.

She pulled the robe tight, trying to warm herself, but it was quite possible she'd never be warm again.

The ringing phone sliced through her despair. Gracie's heart stopped. Who knew she was here?

*No one.*

The only people who would call her now were…dead.

She dried her hair with the towel and dashed to her room, panic making her muscles pulse. She tugged her sweater over her head and was pulling up her jeans when the ringing finally stopped, leaving an eerie silence in its wake.

Gracie abandoned her apartment moments later, to the sound of the murderer—she was sure it was him—again ringing her line.

Vicktor flipped on the siren. Somehow the rhythmic whine slowed his heart beat and enabled him to sling his car safely around traffic toward Leningradskaya Street.

The Wolf had returned. Vicktor's knuckles blanched white on the steering wheel as he tried to corral his racing thoughts. The implications of the Wolf appearing again after nearly a year meant he hadn't moved on to Moscow, as informants had speculated. Vicktor's pulse hammered in his ears.

Maybe he could finally put right what went wrong and atone for his mistake. And it all hinged on him finding a woman covered in blood, stumbling around Khabarovsk.

How hard could that be?

Vicktor screeched onto Leningradskaya, nearly dropping his cell phone. "Yanna, you still there?"

"We just got the file from Passport Control, Vicktor. It's loading. Hold on to your shirt."

Vicktor slowed and turned into the rutted courtyard of Grace Benson's apartment. *Please, please let her have returned home.* He'd spent the last hour walking through the crime scene with Arkady, reliving every crime that bore the Wolf's mark. The

Wolf's first victim had been a girlfriend of a KGB colonel. Ten years hadn't erased from Vicktor's memory her glassy eyes, or the wound across her throat. No forced entry, no obvious struggle. Medical Examiner Comrade Utuzh had dubbed the killer "the Wolf," like the Siberian dogs who stalked their prey, then pounced without mercy. This was a lone wolf, however—cruel, maybe desperate.

And an American woman might be Vicktor's only lead. While Vicktor scoured the scene with Arkady, Yanna had pulled the FSB file on the victims—Dr. and Mrs. William Young. Evidently, they had one emergency contact, a woman who just might match the description offered by the local neighborhood watch, an elderly babushka sitting outside the apartment building. Vicktor had tracked down the American's address, and after calling her flat three times, he'd had to concede that Miss Grace Benson was not going to answer.

But…maybe she was holed up inside, hiding. He eased his car over a pothole as he struggled to think like an American.

"Yanna?"

"The file is still loading," Yanna snapped. "That's what we get when the government siphons funds for parades instead of equipment."

Apparently Yanna still nursed wounds over the city's penchant to re-do the streets every time Putin came to town, leaving her with ancient paperweights for computers. No wonder she did so much of her work at home.

Vicktor softened his tone. "I'm sorry, I'm just in a hurry."

"Blond, five foot two, green eyes."

"Thanks, Yanna. You're a prize."

"I forgive you."

Five minutes later he was leaning on the American's doorbell. "I know you're in there," he muttered to the closed door. "I see the footprints." Her steps were outlined in mud, and a wad of fresh dirt stuck out from a groove in the metal door. She'd scuffed her shoes stumbling over the frame.

No answer.

He buzzed the neighbor. A wide-faced babushka cracked open her door and peeked her nose over the chain.

"Did you see your neighbor come home—an American lady?" Vicktor asked.

The babushka ran a wary gaze over him. She shook her head. Vicktor leaned close and lowered his voice. "Did you hear anything?"

"*Nyet.*" The woman slammed her door. Vicktor tried not to kick it and sucked in a hot breath.

*Think, Vicktor. Preferably like an American.*

Vicktor ran down the stairs two at a time to his car. What would an American do when faced with the murder of a friend? What would David do?

Call the cops. Americans believed in their judicial system and their police force. In the absence of cops, she would call soldiers, or maybe American friends in town.

Or the U.S. embassy.

Vicktor climbed into his car and slammed the accelerator to the floorboard. The *Zhiguli* screeched out of the courtyard, scattering a flock of pigeons.

The nearest American consulate was in Vladivostok. She'd have to take the Okean train. Vicktor checked his watch. He had forty minutes before the next train left.

The *voxhal* teemed with travelers toting children and suitcases. The Trans-Siberian Railroad remained Russia's best and most efficient method of transportation, especially after the fall of communism when the ruble plummeted to new, despairing depths. People could barely afford bread, let alone an airline ticket. The train, however, could transport a person to Vladivostok and back for the price of a McDonald's Happy Meal.

Vicktor flashed his ID and hustled past vendors hawking wares in the dank underground passageway that burrowed under the train tracks. Ascending to the platform for the Okean train, he squeezed past a soldier holding an AK-47 and surveyed the crowd.

No blond American. He fought frustration and strode through the crowd. She had to be here. The train had rolled in and layered the air with diesel fumes. Vicktor wrinkled his nose and tried not to sneeze. A baby began to wail. The crowd murmured as it shifted toward the tracks. Vicktor backed away, took a deep breath and stared at their shoes.

Americans could always be identified by their footwear—sensible, low, padded and expensive. Russians wore black—black heels, black loafers, black sandals, black boots.

He spotted a pair of brown hiking boots and trailed his gaze up. Smart girl. The American had wrapped her head in a fuzzy brown shawl like a babushka and now clutched it as if a hurricane were headed in her direction. She held a nylon bag in the other hand, a black satchel peeking through a tattered corner.

She joined the throng and shuffled toward a passenger car. He clenched his jaw—he had to get her before she boarded that train. Pushing through the crowd, he worked toward her, but the passengers tightened and packed him in. He felt an elbow in his side, didn't search for the owner, and plowed forward. The crowd split into two lines and he suddenly found himself propelled toward a car entrance. He scanned the other queue and glimpsed the American handing over her ticket.

*Gotcha!*

Stepping up to the conductor, he flipped open his identification, weathered her annoyed expression, and took the train steps in two strides. Taking a left, he edged into the car and peeked over the tops of embarking passengers until he saw Miss Benson's fuzzy, shawl-covered head duck into a compartment.

Vicktor pushed past a family stowing suitcases and reached the *Americanka*'s door just as it was sliding shut. He rammed his foot in the gap and curled a hand around the door, intending to slam it back.

Her boot crunched his loafer. "No!"

Pain speared up his leg. He yanked his foot back, unable to stifle a grunt.

"Get away!" she yelled, and started to yank the door shut.

He wedged his arm into the crack, banged it open and plowed into her compartment. She stumbled back, clutching her bag.

"Get out!"

Her startled, fearful look stopped him cold. Rattled him.

She flung her satchel at him. He caught it. What was her problem?

She gasped and scurried back into the corner, looking as if he were going to eat her alive. "Get out!"

Okay, he could concede he might be a bit scary—big man, no identification. He reached into his pocket, scrambling for English.

She nailed him in the shin with her boot.

He winced and couldn't keep frustration from contorting his face. "Calm down!" he ordered. Yes! His language skills hadn't defected.

Only… "Get away from me!" she shrieked. Her face blanched, as if his English had stunned her.

Shoot. He didn't want to scare her, but most of all he wanted to get off the train before it started rolling.

"Are you Grace Benson?"

Her eyes went wide.

Bull's-eye. He smiled at his sleuth work. "I'll take your silence as a 'yes.'"

Fury filled her green eyes. She glanced past him, into the hall, as if hoping for reinforcement.

He had to make her understand. "I've been searching all over for you."

Oh joy, she went white.

He turned and slammed the door shut behind him. He didn't need an audience, and he had a feeling she wasn't going to go quietly. Sighing, he weighed his options as he ran a hand through his hair. Now what? An ugly picture of him throwing her over his shoulder, fireman style, and hauling her from the train filled his mind. No, bad idea.

Turning back, he caught the warning expression on her face a millisecond before she went berserk. She pounced on him, clawing at his face.

What was *wrong* with her? He grabbed her forearms. "Stop it! Please. I'm not going to hurt you, trust me."

She ripped her arms from his grip and sat down, hard. Her breath came in gusts.

"*Perestan!*" he hissed, both to her and his thundering heartbeat. "My name's Vicktor. I'm with the KGB and I'm trying to help you!"

# Chapter Six

Shock turned her numb. Gracie drew her legs into a ball and stared at the officer. He blinked at her and smiled, as if suddenly he'd solved her every problem. He was a *KGB* officer?

"Is that supposed to inspire confidence?"

His smile dimmed.

"I mean, the KGB isn't exactly a foreigner's best friend. So, excuse me for my hesitation."

His eyes darkened, and she called herself a fool for her sassiness.

"Actually, it's the FSB now," he said, "and you'd better start to trust me. I *am* trying to save your skin. You're not leaving Khabarovsk until you answer some questions."

"Spit it out—the train has already whistled," she retorted with false bravado. Behind her sassy mouth lived a coward whose brain was screaming, *Run!*

His jaw dropped like he'd been slapped. She saw shock flicker in his blue eyes, then he stepped up to her and held out a hand. She stared as if it were a bomb.

"C'mon. We're not having our chat here."

"I—I'm an American citizen," she stammered. "I want a lawyer."

"Why? Do you need one?"

Gracie's heart slammed into her ribs. "No," she squeaked, swallowing hard. His hand remained outstretched.

"I could stay on the train. You can't make me get off."

A muscle tensed in his jaw. His presence filled the compartment—wide shoulders, thick arms that strained the material of his jacket. He was tall enough to scrub his head on the door frame, and he looked as fit as a soldier and in no mood to argue. His eyes latched on to hers and sent a streak of fear into her bones. She raised her chin, hoping to appear strong and defiant.

"I could make you get off, but I won't." His tone was low, calm. "If this train moves, however, I stay here, in this berth with you all night until we get to Vladivostok." He paused. "Your choice."

Gracie ignored his outstretched paw, stood, grabbed her bag and brushed past him just as the train lurched. She felt his presence closing behind her as they wobbled down the corridor. The train had already begun easing forward. She paused at the door, watching pavement glide by.

He touched her elbow. "Jump."

She shot him a glare and made the easy leap to the platform. He swung down right behind her. His hand again curled around her elbow.

"Unless I am your prisoner, please unhand me," she snapped.

He withdrew his hand, but stayed close enough to rein her in, obviously to ward off any impulses she might have to ditch him in the tunnel back to the parking lot.

Gracie seethed all the way through the station, refusing to make room for cold fear.

The KGB. She didn't know what was worse. Being chased by a killer or interrogated by the KGB. Where was a decent hiding place when a person needed one?

They climbed into his greasy rattletrap of a car and Gracie huddled on the smooth vinyl seat, shooting a glare his direction. He ignored her. Motoring into traffic, he said nothing.

"Some interrogation," she muttered.

He kept his eyes forward, but she noticed his whitened grip on the steering wheel.

"Where are we going?"

"Back to the scene. We need you to walk through what happened with us."

"What? No!" She grabbed the door handle. "Let me out! I'm not going back there." She began to shake, her composure unraveling. Tears bit her eyes. Where was Miss Sass and Courage when she needed her?

He pulled over and she braced herself, poised to fly out of the car and run until she hit the Chinese border, or beyond. Let him try to catch her. She didn't care if they had to run her down with a tank—she wasn't returning to the scene of her friend's murder.

He grabbed her arm, reached across her and held her door shut.

Was she that transparent? "Get away from me."

"Don't be afraid, Miss Benson. I'll be there with you."

She stared at him, at his eyes and the way they looked so incredibly blue, surprisingly tender for the situation, and suddenly, hot tears were running down her cheeks. "I don't even know you." Agony stretched her voice thin. "I just want to go home."

He continued to hold her arm, but loosened his grip on the door. "I know," he said. His words were a salve on her raw emotions. Oh, how she wanted to unravel into a puddle of pain.

"I know you don't know me. But I mean you no harm. All I want to do is find your friends' killer."

His voice had turned soft, and even with the accent, she could hear a man trying to soothe a woman's fears. He might have tried *that* approach when he was breaking into her train compartment. She looked away from him.

"You must have been horrified to find them. I'm sorry you had to see it," he said.

"Them?" she croaked, then realized he meant Dr. Willie. So…Evelyn's kind, handsome husband had also been murdered. A moan ripped through Gracie, and she covered her face with her hands.

The cop put his hand on her shoulder. Warm, strong, a presence that she should probably shrug off. But it seemed so…kind. She just closed her eyes and let herself cry.

The sounds of her anguish filled the car. She didn't even think to be embarrassed; she just let her grief spill out. The cop didn't move, didn't pull her into an awkward, polite embrace, but didn't remove his hand, either. Somehow that balance felt comforting.

She finally pressed her fists into her eyes, trying to stem the tears. "I didn't know Dr. Willie had been killed."

"I'm sorry."

His tone went straight to her battered soul.

Okay, so maybe she'd misjudged him. Or, more likely, she again was falling victim to her own abysmally bad judgment.

She glanced at him. He didn't betray any inkling that she might look a mess, with blotchy skin and bloodshot eyes.

Raising dark eyebrows, he smiled sadly. "Ready?"

She shook her head, then nodded, completely confused.

"Okay." He eased the car out into traffic and they rode in silence until he pulled up to the Youngs' apartment building. Gracie felt emptied. The front door hung open and she recalled with pain the suspicious gaze the old babushka had sent her when she had tumbled outside.

Of course. She'd been covered in blood. No wonder the old woman had gaped at her. Thankfully, now the bench outside the building was empty.

The FSB agent—whatever his name was—got out, came around the car and opened the door. He held out his hand, and after a second she took it. He held it a second longer than was necessary, it seemed, to help her out of the car.

"Thank you…"

"Captain Vicktor Shubnikov."

He smiled, and the warmth in his expression helped her rally.

"Ready to go up?"

She nodded.

They rode up the lift. Dread pushed down on her with every passing flight. The doors bumped open on the sixth floor and she shuffled out, Captain Shubnikov on her tail.

The Youngs' door hung open. She heard voices inside—gruff, angry Russian.

"This way," Captain Shubnikov said, and pointed to Evelyn's kitchen.

Gracie obeyed, greatly relieved not to have to enter the room where her best friend lay murdered.

"She's not there." Larissa hung up the telephone and sat back in her office chair, folding her arms over her silk blouse. "Are you sure she's not at the Youngs'?"

Andrei fiddled with his car keys and shook his head. "I went up there, peeked in. The place is a cop circus. She's nowhere to be found."

Larissa had never seen her cousin so…shaken. She knew he was in love with the American, but Gracie's disappearance had him unglued. His hair was mussed, his jacket hung on slumped shoulders. Had he even shaved today? His jingling car keys frayed her nerves.

Where was Gracie? Larissa chewed her lip. They had to find her, fast. Before the FSB got to her. The last thing Gracie needed was a day with the FSB to force her back inside her turtle shell. The poor thing was just getting used to taking public transportation. The sooner she was out of Russia, the better—for all of them. Even if it did rip a hole through Larissa's heart. She'd come to truly care about the American with the obsession about God that matched that of the rest of her mother's family. Religion was the opiate of the masses. Of the Tallin family, for sure. Look what it had done to Andrei.

Larissa stood up and crossed to the front of her desk, grabbing Andrei by the collar of his coat. "Find her. Make sure she's safe. Bring her back to her place and I'll meet you there later."

Andrei's brow furrowed. "You're not coming with me?"

She circled back to her desk chair, pausing for a moment to give him a frown. "I have work to do."

Vicktor strode in behind Grace Benson, feeling sorry for the lady every step of the way. It seemed utterly unfair that she should have to face the horrific scene twice in one day. That had never seemed clearer to him than in the car when she nearly shattered before his eyes. *Oy,* he had to admit, he'd never seen a woman so completely wear her feelings on the outside of her body. And when she looked at him with so much fear in her eyes, well, he'd had to fight the weird desire to pull her into his arms.

Her wounded expression had reached out to him in the train and turned him into some sort of cream puff.

He felt like a jerk for suspecting her, but that was his job. He shoved his hands in his pockets and fought to harden the soft places she'd touched in his heart.

Grace crossed her arms and stared out the kitchen window. Her erect posture gave her dignity, but Vicktor had seen the slight quake of her shoulders and the two deep breaths she'd gulped as she entered the kitchen.

"Ask her what she knows," Arkady said, following them both into the room.

Vicktor shot a look at him. The chief leaned against the counter, watching the American's body language like a psychiatrist. After a moment, he turned his gaze to Vicktor, a hard edge to his brown eyes.

"*Zdrastvootya,*" he said with a biting tone, "you can still speak English, right?"

Vicktor glared at him. "Miss Benson, could you please tell us what happened here?"

She breathed a sigh of palpable sorrow, but she tucked a stray blond hair behind her ear and lifted her chin.

"I came this morning to check e-mail. When I arrived, the doors were open."

"Both of them?"

"*Da.* Sounds familiar, doesn't it?"

She nodded. "It was creepy. Evelyn is very careful about keeping her doors locked, so I knew something was wrong. I never guessed…" Her voice plunged to a whisper and Vicktor fought the urge to take a step toward her. His face must have revealed pity, however, for Arkady shot him a scowl.

Vicktor fisted his hands in his pockets. "Where did you find her?"

"The bedroom. I checked the house and decided to do e-mail before I left."

"Do you often check your e-mail here?"

Her eyes sparked. "I don't have my own computer."

He couldn't imagine life without his laptop. Odd for an American.

"What did you do when you found her?"

Gracie's shoulders shook, but her voice emerged steady. "I untied her hands. Then I called my friend Larissa. She told me she would call the police."

Vicktor translated her answer for Arkady, who lit a cigarette. "Ask her why she took off."

"Why did you leave, Miss Benson?" He wanted to cringe at the sight of her red-rimmed eyes.

"I was afraid. I thought the murderer might still be in the flat."

"Smart," he said, and was instantly glad when he saw one side of her mouth tug up.

Arkady scowled at him. "Did you ask her what these Americans were doing here? What organization were they with? Did they have any enemies?"

Vicktor waved him quiet. "This doctor and his wife—what did they do here?"

Her eyes aged before him, and he found himself wondering how old she was.

"They were missionaries. Dr. Willie worked mostly with the leaders of the church, but sometimes he would help out a few doctors he knew." She shook her head as if anticipating his next question. "No, I don't know any names. It seemed like Dr. Willie knew just about everybody, but I can't tell you whom."

"Did they have any enemies?"

Her eyes locked on his. "No."

He turned to Arkady. "She doesn't know anything."

"Tell her to stick around."

"She's headed for the border, Chief. I pulled her off the Okean to Vladivostok."

"Take her into custody." Arkady let the ash from his cigarette fall to the ground.

"Right. And have the U.S Consulate hound me for the next decade? No thanks. She doesn't know anything." Vicktor glanced at her. "Let her go home."

"She's hiding something." Smoke puffed out of Arkady's mouth with each word. "Did she see anyone? Ask her again."

Vicktor shot Arkady a crippling look. "Is there anyone else that could have come here today?" he asked in English.

She frowned, as if the possibility hadn't occurred to her. Then she closed her eyes and rubbed her index finger between her pinched brows. The gesture seemed so forlorn, it made him want to take her home, lock the doors and *dare* the Wolf to come hunting.

The Wolf. He'd nearly forgotten that these weren't just any murders—these were Wolf attacks.

"Please, anything," he said, flinching at the earnestness in his voice.

"Well, maybe," Gracie replied.

He raised his eyebrows, fighting hope.

"My driver, Leonid, didn't show up today, and I thought maybe he would come here." She scowled and shook her head.

"But probably not. His car wasn't here, and he hasn't been very dependable lately."

"This Leonid…what's his full name?"

She gave him a pitiful look. "I don't know. We call him Leonid the Red."

Vicktor frowned.

"His hair. It's red."

Gracie's wretched answer sounded hollow even to herself. She was useless. She turned back to the window before the captain could see her crumple.

It didn't help that the other cop studied her as if she were evidence. She crossed her arms and glowered at him over her shoulder. Let him try to push her into a corner. She might be a foreigner, but she was still an American citizen. She knew her rights. She watched him wrap his fat lips around his foul-smelling cigarette, and she wrinkled her nose in disgust. The cop glared back at her as if she had the answers and was hiding them.

If it hadn't been for Captain Shubnikov's presence, she would have been afraid. The captain's voice bolstered her courage. She had the oddest feeling she was safe with him in the room.

Behind her the two cops argued in Russian, probably about her. Then, strangely, they left her alone in the kitchen with only a cloud of smoke as a reminder of her showdown with the KGB. That and the quiver she'd somehow managed to hide. But she hadn't collapsed. That counted.

Where were Andrei and Larissa? Four hours had passed since her phone call. A horrifying thought struck her—what if the murderer had already pounced? How much danger were they in? She shuddered, remembering the eerie phone call unanswered in her flat. Five days left on her visa suddenly seemed like an eternity.

Gracie rubbed her eyes with her thumb and forefinger and scanned her memory for anything that might help Captain Shubnikov find the Youngs' killer. It was doubtful that anything she learned in Russia would be valuable to anyone with an ap-

petite for murder. Her memories were of sweet children singing praise songs, the weird advice of well-meaning babushkas
and friends laughing over tea. Nothing in that batch seemed suspect.

She heard a knock at the door. More cops, then a Russian
voice calling her name. She turned, and in strode Andrei. Worry
knotted his face.

"Gracie?"

He hesitated before her, as if suddenly unsure what to do.
Tears rimmed his eyes.

Then, wordlessly, he held out his arms.

"Oh, Andrei, it was just so awful," she whispered, and
walked into his embrace. She rested her head on his shoulder,
wrapped her arms around his waist and let herself cry.

His arms tightened around her. She'd never been so grateful for his friendship.

After a few moments, he put her away from him, scanned
her from head to toe. "Are you okay?"

Gracie managed a shaky smile, not sure how to answer.

"*Kto eta?*"

Blue-eyed Captain Shubnikov stood in the doorway.

Andrei answered in English. "Andrei Feodorvich Tallin." He
hesitated, then stepped forward and extended his hand, eyes
wary. "I'm a friend of Gracie's."

Shubnikov fired off a question in rapid Russian.

"Speak English, please," Gracie muttered.

The investigator ignored her.

Andrei looked at Gracie as if confused. Then he replied in
an even quicker staccato.

What was Shubnikov's problem? The shift in his demeanor
astounded her. Only moments before, he'd seemed a friend.
Now she'd been sucked back to the Cold War.

"What does he want?" Gracie asked, and frowned at him.
He met her gaze with cold eyes that felt like a slap.

She'd been duped by the KGB. She should have kicked him
harder.

From this angle, he looked every inch KGB menace. His neatly clipped army-style haircut did nothing to soften high cheekbones that slanted to his square, pure tough-guy jaw. A hint of dark stubble punctuated otherwise smooth skin and he had folded his arms across a sturdy-looking chest, rumpling his sports coat. Arrogance in his dark blue eyes gave him a dangerous look. He started to drum his fingers on his arm, as if waiting for an answer.

Andrei leaned over and translated. "He says he has to ask you more questions."

"What? We've already talked. You tell him whatever he has to ask, he'll ask it now." Wait, who was she kidding? Mr. Games knew how to speak English. She glowered at him.

Andrei closed his eyes and grimaced. She waited for him to translate, but instead he breathed wisdom into her ear.

"Gracie, he's with the FSB. They don't understand the word *no.* They're like your FBI—above the law."

"The FBI is *not* above the law."

Andrei shrugged. "Believe what you like, but here the FSB doesn't answer to anyone."

Gracie dug her fingers into Andrei's arm. "Don't you dare tell him where I live."

"He probably already knows."

Gracie felt like a child with a giant name tag around her neck, the type they gave her in kindergarten to help her find her school bus. She had absolutely no control over her own life.

Acting like she didn't exist, Andrei and Investigator Shubnikov talked a moment longer. Gracie turned away and sulked.

Andrei finally settled a hand on her shoulder. "He'll call you if he needs anything. You're supposed to stay in town. I think we can leave now."

She shrugged off his touch. Oh, sure, she'd stay. Long enough to pack a carry-on for her trip south. "I need to get Dr. Willie's computer." She whirled and leveled a piercing glare at the two-faced captain. He blinked as if shocked, but she jutted her chin and brushed past him, hoping her cold shoulder sent him frostbite.

Gracie bumped past the cops dusting the room, kept her gaze off the sheet-draped body and walked over to the coffee table where the black laptop hummed. With a jerk, Gracie unplugged the computer from the wall. It died with a gasp. She was putting her hand on the cover to push down the screen when a hand clamped her wrist.

"Let me go!"

"That's evidence, we need it." Shubnikov's English seemed fine now.

*Games, games, Mr. KGB.* So very typical of all men.

"I need it. I have to write to America, tell them what's happened."

"Call them."

Gracie snatched her arm out of his grasp. She tugged her coat around her and knotted the sash. "When can I have it?"

His gaze roamed over her face. She felt it burn, but kept her expression neutral. He turned and barked at one of the techs, who mumbled something in return.

"Tomorrow."

The air puffed out of her. "What?" She licked her lips and scrambled for an answer. "Well. Fine. Tomorrow, then."

For the briefest moment she thought she saw him smile. Arrogant jerk. Brushing past him, she joined Andrei standing by the door. Her satchel dangled from his hand.

"Take me home, please."

Andrei hung the satchel over her shoulder, then crooked his elbow. She slid her arm through his and left the Youngs' apartment for the last time.

# Chapter Seven

A muscle knotted in Vicktor's neck as he watched Miss Benson leave with her chauffeur. But he didn't realize his teeth were clenched until Arkady sidled up behind him.

"She's a looker, eh?"

*Yeah, looks like trouble.* What was with her sudden about-face in demeanor, as if he was the one who'd dragged in reinforcements? He didn't lead her on with a smile. He'd been warm, kind, supportive.

She had all but kicked him in the teeth. So much for his feelings of pity. Vicktor turned, and nearly plowed into Arkady behind him.

Arkady smiled. "She got to you."

"Not a chance." Vicktor stalked past him to the bedroom.

"You know what this means," Arkady called after him. "You've just inherited problems. You know Americans can't keep their noses out of anything."

Vicktor stopped. "She's got other things to worry about. Her boyfriend, for one."

Arkady drew in on his cigarette. "Chauffeur."

"Yeah, right. I saw the grip he had on her, and from the expression on her face, I don't think she minded."

Arkady's cheek twitched in another smile.

"I gotta work," Vicktor mumbled. He strode into the bedroom, Arkady's chuckle ringing in his ears.

The faster he solved this crime and washed his hands of the blond American, the better. Arkady had her pegged. If Grace Benson were anything like Mae or David, he'd have to beat her away from the investigation with a stick. Americans never let anything lie.

The woman's body had been outlined and bagged. Two techs were taking blood samples from around the room, from the comforter, the carpet, a nearby bookshelf and even the hallway. A scant trail of brownish red led from the bedroom to the front door. Vicktor stared at it, rubbing an irritating whisker on his cheek.

"Why did he kill the two separately?" Arkady's question voiced his thoughts.

Vicktor glanced at him and watched Arkady blow smoke from his nose like a medieval dragon.

"Why didn't he just tie them both up and torture them until they got what they wanted?"

"Maybe he came in, killed the husband and then surprised the wife. Or vice versa," Vicktor suggested.

"What about motive? If it were a burglary, the computer would be gone."

"Seems that way." Vicktor cupped the back of his neck with one hand and leaned his head back, stretching his taut muscles. Two Americans, from all outward appearances living like their Russian neighbors, here on goodwill visas, victims of a Wolf attack. Why would the Wolf murder missionaries?

The Wolf always attacked key players—FSB agents, informants, even mafia brass. But missionaries? *Tyomnaya Delo.* They had to be up to their elbows in something nasty. Vicktor strolled around the bedroom. He stopped at the tall bookshelf next to the door, squinted at dusty books, Bibles and commentaries, and nearly pulled out an English version of *The Last of the Breed,* by Louis L'Amour. On the night table sat a photograph of a small boy wearing a cowboy hat. Cute. Chubby cheeks and blue eyes, with a patch of tawny brown hair.

He lifted the edge of the bedspread and found dust balls, sunken suitcases, a broken pencil and a pair of crumpled black dress socks.

Rubbing a thumb and forefinger over his eyes, he tried to recall what Grace had said. *They were missionaries. Dr. Willie worked with a few doctors in town, but I don't know who.* Oh, that was helpful. Then again, that was during the cooperative stage of the interrogation. Perhaps she hadn't been worth the effort of yanking off the train. His shin began to throb. Next time he had to apprehend her, he would wear his hockey gear.

Next time? No, thanks.

Stepping over the woman's corpse, he crossed the room and noted a pair of glasses, a thin book and a medicine bottle on the floor next to the bed. Sighing, he pulled back the lace curtains and stared out the window. Outside, children ran in a wild game of tag, their school backpacks propped against rotting wooden benches. Laughter and games. Life skipping by while inside the building that shadowed their play, two human beings lay slain, their lives spilled out like spoiled milk.

Senseless. He wondered whom the victims had left behind.

An angry and frightened blond *Americanka* for one.

He was about to let the lace fall when he noticed a curling photograph, covered with a translucent film of dust, wedged between two ceramic pots of blooming African violets. He pulled it out. A tanned and smiling version of the victim in the family room stood in the middle, his arms draped around the shoulders of two men. On the left stood a Russian with a wide face, a bushy salt-and-pepper goatee and a mustache. Set against steely gray eyes, his smile could have been a wince.

The other man was not Russian. He was small with straight dark hair, brown eyes and a bright smile. Vicktor guessed Korean.

Vicktor turned over the picture, hoping for identification. Nothing. Disappointed, he slid the photograph into his pocket.

"Vicktor!" Arkady hollered from the family room.

Vicktor found Arkady standing beside an opened sofa.

"A storage drawer," Vicktor said starkly. "With contraband?"

Arkady snapped on surgical gloves and lifted a piece of manila paper. "Empty visa forms from the Russian embassy." He handed Vicktor a black metal box. "Look in here." His expression betrayed his knowledge of the contents.

Vicktor found a black inkpad and two rubber stamps, one with the Russian seal and the other from the DPRK—Democratic People's Republic of Korea. *North Korea.*

He felt as if he'd been kicked in the gut.

"It seems our American missionaries were into something a little more 'humanitarian' than just preaching the Bible," Arkady muttered.

"*Tyomnaya Delo.*" Vicktor slammed the cover down. He just hoped he wouldn't have to be the one to tell Gracie Benson.

Gracie sat with her back propped against her living room sofa, the phone between her feet. She wound the cord around her finger as she listened to the line ring.

"No one?" Larissa asked.

Gracie shook her head.

Taking off her glasses, Larissa rubbed a red spot on the bridge of her nose. "You would think they would give you the director's home number."

Grace set the receiver back in the cradle. "Dr. Willie probably has…had it. I'm just a missionary peon. Dr. Willie and Evelyn were the team leaders." The caretakers. The winners-of-souls. The missionaries who mattered.

And God had let them be slaughtered, like sheep.

The low sun striped her brown rug with the hues of twilight, and the chill of a spring evening crept into her noiseless flat. Sitting on the sofa, Andrei looked dazed, and his occasional deep, agonized sighs did nothing to assuage her grief.

God had so vividly abandoned all of them, and she had not one word of hope to offer her friends.

"We should call your Pastor Yuri," Larissa mumbled. Andrei gave her a sharp look.

Gracie cringed at her oversight. Of course Pastor Yuri should know. He was Dr. Willie's coworker and friend, and the closest thing she had to a supervisor. "I'll call him."

Andrei put his hand over hers as she grabbed the receiver. "Wait, Gracie. Is there anyone else in the States you could call? Your brother? Anyone else from the mission? How about your mother?"

Gracie eyes burned. "No, I can't call her." A lump balled in her throat. "She doesn't need to worry." Her mother would only panic and send her brother, or worse, her cousin and all his FBI buddies, after her. No, she had to keep this horror close to her chest until she disembarked from the plane. Then, she'd hide in the safety of her own bedroom overlooking the harbor on Skyline Drive in Duluth. They'd have to pry her out with a two-by-four. "No," she repeated.

"I think someone in America should know what happened." He glowered at Larissa, and Gracie scowled at the obvious tension between the two. "For her own good."

"I have you two, and Pastor Yuri," Gracie said. "Later tonight, when it is morning in America, I'll call Headquarters and talk to our missionary director. He'll know what to do."

Larissa flattened her lips and nodded.

Andrei slid off the sofa. His arms wrapped around her shoulders and she sank against his wide chest, welcoming his familiar leather and cologne smell. Andrei was safe. Honest. As opposed to the game-playing Mr. FSB she'd met today. And to think she'd actually thought she'd seen kindness in his eyes.

He was probably laughing at her naiveté over a shot of vodka at that very moment.

"Gracie." Andrei's voice was low. "I have to ask you. Do you know why the Youngs were murdered?"

Gracie mouth opened. She felt as if she'd been slugged, and jerked away from him. "No, I don't."

"They didn't give you anything or mention anything that seemed out of place lately?"

"No, Andrei. I have no idea who would kill the Youngs, or why." Her voice shook.

"Okay," Andrei said, and reached for her.

She backed away from him. "Not okay." She glanced from Andrei to Larissa. "Do you think I'd keep that from you? Or worse, maybe you suspect *me?*"

Larissa's mouth dropped open.

"*Davai,* Gracie. Of course we don't suspect you." Andrei actually looked angry, his brown eyes glittering. "I just wanted to know what you thought. If you knew *anything.*" He looked away, and his expression made her wince.

She stared in shame at the betrayal written on her friends' faces.

"We'll talk about it tomorrow, when things have had a chance to…calm down," Larissa said. "Right now I think you need some sleep."

Oh, sure, so she could dream about Evelyn's chalky death expression? She'd probably never sleep again. She whisked tears from her cheeks. "No. I'm okay. I'm sorry. I'm just a little…yeah, maybe tired." She suddenly wanted to curl into a ball and just stay there, perhaps under the covers, forever. Never. Wake. Up.

Larissa returned the smile. "Let me tuck you into bed, Gracie. I'll sleep on the sofa and Andrei will guard the front door."

Larissa silenced Gracie's protests with a look. "In Russia, friends watch out for each other."

Oh, now she felt like a real give-me-a-prize-for-my-insensitivity type. She so obviously didn't deserve these friends. She nodded, unable to speak.

Andrei helped her to her feet. Tucking an errant strand of hair behind her ear, he stared over her head, toward Larissa. "I'll call Pastor Yuri."

Larissa didn't answer as she guided Gracie from the room.

Vicktor braced his elbows on his knees. The arena seat felt like it had been constructed with razor blades. He'd forgotten how long these matches were. Next to him, Roman waggled his fist.

"Oh-Rah!" he shouted.

From the court, Yanna looked in their direction and returned the fist-up victory gesture. Her spike had just landed her team another point, and they were well on their way to cleaning up the two-out-of-three game match. Vicktor watched them set up for another serve and tried to focus on the game.

"Want a soda?" Roman asked.

Vicktor shook his head.

"I heard about the missionaries. Ouch." Roman made a face. "Don't jump to conclusions too quickly, my friend. You know the Wolf. If it is him, he kills good guys just as often as bad."

"These missionaries had fake passports and visas. I wouldn't call that your usual missionary paraphernalia."

Roman stared straight ahead, but Vicktor saw a muscle pull in his jaw. It had to stab his friend's Christian pride to discover that one of his own had been found treading on the dark side. It didn't make Vicktor happy to see his friend suffer. He respected Roman's, David's and Mae's religion, even if he didn't agree with it. It had certainly changed Roman from a womanizing hooligan to a straight-shooting hero of the state. If anything, Roman's Christian beliefs made him a better friend and soldier. Probably a better man.

"Don't worry," he said quietly. "If your missionaries are clean, I'll clear their name."

Roman's gaze didn't waver from the game, but Vicktor saw his slight nod.

"Hey, check out the redhead in the corner by the south entrance." Roman didn't point, but angled his head slightly.

"I knew you wouldn't stay single long," Vicktor said as he squinted in the direction of his friend's gaze.

"Look closely, Vicktor. I wouldn't dream of chasing this one."

The small arena was packed, a sea of people jammed hip to hip up to the nosebleed bleacher section and elbowing one another in the doorways. He scanned the entrance, and when he spied a familiar curly mass of red hair he couldn't keep from grinning.

"You saw her," Roman confirmed.

"What is she doing here? I thought she was sequestered at the base?"

"Want a Coke?"

Vicktor followed Roman down the row, pausing only a moment to *oh-rah* when Yanna went airborne and blocked a spike from the opposing team. Vicktor winced at the sound of the ricochet off her arms.

They hit the arena floor at a jog, scuttled into the corridor and ran around the stadium to the opposite side. It felt like their college days, when a short skirt and a saucy smile had them fighting for position. Roman shot him a cocky grin.

They dodged a woman selling programs and skidded to a halt near the entrance to the arena where Mae had been standing.

"Do you see her?" Vicktor asked, hands on his knees.

"You're breathing like you've run a marathon." On tiptoe, Roman peeked over the shoulder of a man in a Bulls sweatshirt. "Don't see her."

Vicktor stood up, disappointment slowing his pulse. "Are you sure it was her?"

"Are you?"

"Point taken," Vicktor acknowledged. "Okay. Where would she go?" He searched the crowed. Traffic thinned now and again as people streamed in and out of the arena, on their way to refreshments or facilities. Vicktor stepped aside to let pass a babushka toting a toddler by his collar. From inside the arena, ecstatic fans erupted, fanning the flames of victory for the Khabarovsk team.

Roman raised his hands and shrugged.

"Excuse me, sir?"

Vicktor whirled and nearly upset the popcorn of a young boy. The kid's eyes widened with fear.

"Are you talking to me?" he asked, catching a few kernels.

The boy nodded and held out the popcorn. "This is for you."

"For me?"

The boy shrugged. "Some lady asked me to give it to you." Vicktor took the popcorn and noticed a slip of paper nestled between dry kernels. He grabbed the paper. "Here, kid," he said, handing back the popcorn.

"So? What does it say?" Roman breathed over his shoulder.

Vicktor opened the note. "'Shadow, 2:00. Springtime, 11:00.'" He glanced at Roman and they exchanged grins.

"I'll get the shadow," Roman said, and turned on his heel, heading for a stout-looking solider in plainclothes hovering near a potted floor plant at two o'clock on an imaginary clock face. Vicktor so wanted to linger. The soldier had no idea he was about to be dressed down by a Red Beret captain, on loan to the FSB COBRAs. But Vicktor had to find out why Mae had risked her stripes trying to contact them at Yanna's volleyball match.

Vicktor strode northeast, toward eleven o'clock and Mae Lund/Springtime. As he passed a cotton candy vendor, a hand snared his arm and yanked. He stumbled into the shadows of an unlit doorway, whirled and fell into the laughing embrace of Mae Lund.

"What are you doing here?" he whispered, holding her tight. She always smelled so fresh and clean, and he noticed her hair had grown longer, below her ears. Pulling away, he held her at arm's length. Tall and wiry, she still came only to his shoulder.

"Major Ward loves volleyball. He and Commander Belov are in a private military booth on the north end of the arena."

"Then what are you doing here?"

She grinned. "Picking up pointers for our team. You know the commander's daughter is on my squad."

"You amaze me."

Her hazel-green eyes sparkled and her nose wrinkled, blurring the array of freckles dotting it. "I'm supposed to be using the facilities. But I saw you and Roman, and you looked so down, I just had to see you. I missed you at our last online getaway."

Vicktor felt something unravel inside him and he glanced away. Mae could always read him like a book, and despite the fact they hadn't seen each other in nearly two years, she knew how to peel away his defenses and peek right into his soul.

"Are you okay?" she asked, smoothing the collar on his leather jacket.

"It's been a tough week."

"It's Monday," she said, but sadness ringed her eyes.

It sent him back five years, to a time they'd been stuck in her car in Alaska, waiting for help in a whiteout. She'd nearly convinced him to surrender to her God that day. Thankfully, help had arrived and he'd come to his senses.

"Yanna told me about your finding your friend murdered." Her voice was so tender it made him flinch. "I'm sorry."

"*Da*. And today we found two missionaries murdered in their flat," he said quietly.

Her mouth opened a long second before she asked, "Missionaries—how?"

Vicktor shoved his hands into his pockets and peeked around the corner. Roman had the shadow turned and staring at his shoes. Good boy, Roma. "We think it was the Wolf. Typical Wolf M.O.—stealth entry, as if he knew the folks, and jagged knife wound across the neck."

"Oh, Vita. I'm sorry."

"Don't be. He's back and maybe I have a chance to catch him this time."

Mae's eyes flickered with worry. "Be careful."

He kept his voice light, dodging the significance of that warning. "Of course."

"Any leads?" Mae ducked her head around, snagging a glimpse of Roman and her Russian guard. A smile tugged at her mouth.

"No, but there is an American missionary who found them. I had to pull her off a train to Vladivostok this afternoon."

Mae's eyes widened. "An American missionary," she repeated. "A lady?"

Vicktor flattened a pile of dust into the cement floor with his foot. *"Da."*

"She's cute."

His gaze darted up and he scowled at her smirk.

"I recognize that particular shade of red on your face." Her eyes twinkled, sweet like fresh-cut grass. She folded her arms across her chest. From the arena, a thunderous roar signaled another point won by Yanna's Dynamo team. "What's her name?"

Vicktor considered Mae, testing for any shred of romance left in their friendship. It seemed awkward to discuss women with a lady he'd once dated. That had been nearly a decade ago, however. Since then she'd dated other men and been quite vocal about it. Just because he hadn't moved on didn't mean she still lingered in his heart. Vicktor saw sincerity written in Mae's eyes and released a sheepish grin. "Grace Benson. She's blond, but feisty just like you."

Mae raised her perfectly plucked eyebrows. "She'd better be more than feisty, if she wants to outwrestle your pride."

Vicktor's smile dimmed. "Is that what went wrong between us, Mae? My pride?"

Mae touched his cheek with her hand. "You're a tiger, Vicktor. Stalking alone in your private forest. There was no room in your world for another tiger, even a mate."

"From what I remember, you didn't want to be a part of my forest."

Mae shook her head. "I had my own worlds to explore. Still do. But God has a woman out there for you, Vicktor. Just don't let your hard crust keep her from the marshmallow inside."

Before he could respond, she stood on her tiptoes and kissed him on the cheek. "See you online, Stripes." She glanced at Roman, then turned back and winked at Vicktor. "Tell him that he'd make a great spook."

Then she shot off, quick-stepping toward the military section of the arena.

# Chapter Eight

❧

"So you think these people were spies?" Nickolai Shubnikov asked. The early morning sun fell at his feet, dappling the painted burnt-yellow floor and highlighting a layer of dust.

Vicktor scraped a greasy Russian pancake from the cast-iron pan and tossed it onto the top of a hot buttered stack in front of his father. "No, not spies, but maybe smugglers." He smeared butter over the *blini*. It melted through and dripped over the edge. "Whatever they were into, they crossed the Wolf, and he killed them for it."

His father digested the news with harrumphs and mutters. Vicktor tapped the spatula on the side of the pan, watching the next pancake bubble and spatter. The memory of the Wolf and his bloody trail drenched the room in silence.

"Are you sure it was the Wolf's handiwork?" his father finally asked.

Vicktor blew out a breath. His stomach tightened as he squinted at the old cop. Nickolai had washed, slicked back his gray hair and shaved off the night's whiskers, as if he were heading to the office, but his ratty brown bathrobe and worn cloth slippers betrayed the day's events: *Santa Barbara* and maybe a dose of *Dallas* reruns on the side. And, if he was lucky, a documentary on World War Two.

"Arkady thinks so," Vicktor answered.

A muscle tensed in Nickolai's jaw as he turned and stared out the grimy kitchen window.

Grease smacked and spattered in the cast-iron pan, layering the air and the pumpkin-orange wallpaper with sunflower oil. Vicktor wrinkled his nose against the pungent smell and turned back to his work, trying to ignore his father's drooping shoulders.

It irritated him that plaster curled from the ceiling and the lace curtains appeared more gray than ivory. His mother never would have let it decay like this; she gave the ceiling a fresh coat of paint every year before Easter, and re-wallpapered often enough to keep up with the trends. This year it would have been a mint green. He made a mental note to pick up some paint, soon, and to sweep before he left today.

Vicktor flipped the skinny pancake. They weren't his mother's, but the texture seemed okay and it was definitely a tasty alternative to the stale bread his father had been about to slice up when he walked in the door. Toeing off his running shoes, Vicktor had tossed his cap on a bench and shouldered past the old cop with a bag of eggs in one hand and a bottle of milk in the other. Surprise, or perhaps relief, flickered in the old man's eyes before he dropped into a chair. Vicktor had stirred up the familiar batter and muttered generalities about his new case.

Forking the last *blini* onto the stack, Vicktor slathered on more butter. His father continued to gaze out the window, his face vacant.

Vicktor poured them each a cup of tea and found two spoons in the sink. He wiped them clean and placed one before his father. No reaction. He stood there for a moment, wondering if he should interrupt. Was the old man in mourning, thinking about the *blini* his wife would have created, or merely wishing he still had a career?

"I think you need to find that chauffeur." Nickolai's voice held a spark of the old days when he had talked his cases through late into the night with Antonina.

"What? Why?" Vicktor covered his shock by piercing a *blini* with his fork, folding it twice and sliding it onto his tea saucer.

His father mimicked his action. "These are too thin."

Of course they were. Vicktor stared past him and listened to street traffic suggest the time.

"Because he was there," Nickolai answered, talking with his mouth full.

"How do you know that?"

"No forced entry. The doors were open, both of them."

Vicktor turned the *blini* over on the saucer, pushing it through a puddle of butter. "It could have been anyone—a neighbor, a friend. Or maybe they just forgot to shut the door."

"*Nyet.* Think it through, son."

Vicktor's mind scrambled for an answer while Nickolai forked another *blini* and sipped his tea, all the while unsuccessfully hiding a smile.

"Okay, what?"

Nickolai leaned forward, one elbow on the table, his eyes alight. "The Wolf knew these Americans. They let him in. More than that, when they did, they didn't bother locking the steel door behind him. As if they weren't expecting him to stay. What type of visitor doesn't stay when he calls?"

Vicktor grimaced. "A driver."

"This chauffeur fella didn't show up for his morning appointment, and for some reason the girl expected him to report to the Youngs. Maybe they were his boss, or scheduled his appointments. Whatever the reason, I think he *did* go there. They let him in, expecting him to leave in a moment…and, well, there's your perpetrator. Find the chauffeur and you'll find the Wolf."

"Oh, that's too easy. The chauffeur had to know we'd suspect him."

Nickolai fingered his teacup. "You didn't."

*Thanks, Pop.* Yet another reminder that he would never fill the shoes of the cop who sired him. "Well, I would have, in time."

"But maybe not before he hid himself in some remote village. You haven't found him yet, have you?"

"We just started looking. I don't even know if Arkady put out a warrant for him."

Nickolai stabbed his fourth *blini*. Vicktor wondered what he'd eaten for dinner last night. Maybe a can of sardines.

Vicktor swallowed the last of his tea. "I gotta go." His appetite had disintegrated.

Nickolai shrugged. The spark in his eyes died to an ember.

Vicktor pushed his stool away from the table.

"By the way, what were these Americans doing here?"

Vicktor ran tap water over his plate, the water beading on the grease. "Besides smuggling?"

Nickolai harrumphed.

"They were missionaries. Working with the Russian church."

Nickolai stared at him for a moment before he blinked and looked away. "Be careful, Vicktor."

"So, I called Yuri and he said he'd call your organization. He told me to tell you not to worry." Larissa sat cross-legged on the living room floor watching Gracie pace the room, clutching socks in one hand and a Grisham book in the other.

"Funny they haven't called yet," Gracie said. But to have to talk about it, explain the story, voice the words—"*The Youngs have been murdered.*" No, maybe it would be better to hop on a plane and do the explaining in America. Far, far away from the crime scene, the memories, the failures...

"Have you heard from the Consulate? Are they sending someone?"

Gracie shrugged, staring first at the socks, then at the empty suitcase. "I don't know. I figure the cops will call the Consulate." Did it really matter who they called? It certainly wouldn't change reality.

Evelyn and Dr. Willie had been murdered.

"You have to pack something, Gracie. You can't go home naked." Larissa's cat-eye glasses slid down over her nose, making her appear a disapproving schoolmarm. She sounded like one, as well. "Pack the socks and give me the book."

Gracie plopped both in Larissa's lap.

"I don't care what I bring home…everything I care about is here." *Was here.*

Larissa stared at the socks.

Gracie cringed at her words. What was wrong with her? Here, Larissa had taken the day off to help her and Gracie had the sensitivity of a lizard. She sat and squeezed Larissa's knee. "I'm sorry."

Larissa's eyes glistened. "I understand."

Tears stung Gracie's eyes. She bit her lip and forced them back.

"I need to pack the mail, at least." Gracie crawled over to her satchel and pulled out the plastic bag of letters Evelyn had given her only two nights before.

*"Can you mail these for me? It'll take a decade from Russia. I'm terrified of the Russian mail service."*

The irony made Gracie's throat tighten. Evelyn had certainly known real terror in the last moments of her life.

Gracie wrestled the thought into captivity lest it consume her, and flipped through the letters. One to Des Moines, the Youngs' daughter and son-in-law, two to relatives in Georgia and one to a son in college in Ohio. The last was an oversize bright blue envelope, addressed to "Cowboy Tyler" and his parents, from Grandma and Grandpa.

Sorrow tightened like a fist. The Youngs had lived a good life—honest, hardworking, devoted to serving the Lord. They both deserved to die in their sleep after another forty or so years. Life had been cruel, or maybe God had been cruel. She didn't want to hash out her theology now. She wanted to blame someone. To hurt them. It was un-Christian, unforgiving and she knew it. Still, someone had to pay.

As if they ever could.

She put the letters aside and fingered a manila envelope protruding from the bag. It was thick, bulky and taped three or four times, with a veritable ribbon of stamps pasted in the top right hand corner. Gracie read the address, written in black marker—Karin Lindstrom, M.D., c/o University of Minnesota Cancer Center, and an address in Minneapolis. No one she knew. Gracie gathered the envelopes into a pile and tucked them between two sweatshirts in her suitcase.

"There. That's done. Now, what else?"

"How about this stuff?" Larissa gestured to a stack of Russian memorabilia—birch-bark pictures, *matroshka* dolls, blue and white painted *zhel* china.

Gracie grabbed a sock and tossed it into Larissa's lap. "Start wrapping."

Two hours later, Gracie closed the second of her two suitcases, gritting her teeth as she worked the zipper. Grabbing the weathered handle, she muscled the bag off the sofa to the floor. "This thing weighs a ton. They'll never let me on the plane."

Larissa tested the other suitcase. "You'll have to buy an extra ticket."

Gracie stepped back, her hand on her hips, and scowled.

Larissa pushed her glasses up on her nose. "I know, let's call Andrei. He can come and get us and we'll weigh these at my office. Then you'll know whether you should give me that Irish wool sweater and your Gap jeans."

"Wouldn't it be easier just to buy a bathroom scale and bring it here?"

"And risk having to dump out your bags in the middle of check-in? You want the other passengers to know you travel with a worn teddy bear and a bottle of Pepto-Bismol?" Larissa reached for the telephone. "Aeroflot has accurate scales." She gave a chuckle. "The last thing you need is Customs Control rifling through your baggage while you try and repack."

Why not? The FSB had her phone number. Why shouldn't Customs know the color of her socks? Gracie rubbed her temple with her thumb and forefinger, aware suddenly that she'd glanced at the telephone one too many times today.

FSB Shubnikov hadn't called. Good riddance.

Except, of course, when he came to her in her rebellious dreams, concern in his blue eyes and his comforting hand on her shoulder. Had she completely forgotten that he'd treated her like a suspect? *Wake up and see the bright interrogation lights in your future, Gracie.* She shook free of Mr. FSB's tempting memory.

"Yes," she said. "Let's call Andrei."

Vicktor leaned against the door frame, steeling his stomach against the rancid odor of formaldehyde, and watched Medical Examiner Vladimir Utuzh prod a gray cadaver. Utuzh's assistant, a bald, spiny man named Shiroki, scurried to the coroner's side, utensils in hand. Another man sat on a high stool, bony knees poking out between the buttons of his lab coat, taking notes in Russian shorthand.

Vicktor purposely ignored the various body parts floating in the jars lining the back wall. He had been wise to take only one semester of forensic science at the Academy. Medical Examiner Utuzh had been his teacher, and as well as making his skin crawl, he had embedded in Vicktor a healthy respect for the *Sydebno-Meditsinskaya Ekspertiza*—Khabarovsk Coroner's Office. Feeling more queasy than he wanted to admit, Vicktor cleared his throat.

Utuzh glanced up, a scowl knitting his bushy blond eyebrows. Six foot four, with the girth of a small grizzly, he already had white streaks in his blond beard and his unruly hair spiked upward despite obvious attempts to make it behave. Vicktor offered a smile. Utuzh paused in his monologue, stepped away from the victim and snapped off his surgical gloves.

"What brings you to the 'Last Stop,' Vicktor Nickolaiovich?" He extended his hand, his brown eyes friendly.

"Following up on a couple of your projects." Vicktor glanced at the two assistants and jerked his head toward the hall.

The click of the door echoed like a gunshot down the long sterile corridor. Fluorescent lights scattered shadows into oblivion and the dank smell of whitewashed cement accented the gruesome aura of Utuzh's stomping grounds.

Vicktor braced a shoulder on the wall. "I'm the primary on a case involving a couple foreigners by the name of Young—"

"Did 'em early this morning."

"So, was it the Wolf?"

Utuzh combed his beard with two fat fingers. "The wound pattern seems to indicate a similarity to the Wolf, but there are a number of peculiarities."

"For example?"

"Bruises on the man, in the back, near the kidneys…in the shape of a boot. Not typical Wolf M.O. He doesn't beat his victims."

The conversation was starting to turn Vicktor's breakfast sour.

"And the woman had skin under her fingernails, like maybe she got in a few good swipes."

Vicktor winced.

"Or—and your pal Arkady was especially fond of this one— how about paper wadded in the nostrils?"

"Both of them?"

"*Da.* Sounds familiar, doesn't it?"

Vicktor crossed his arms and leaned his head back. The cement felt cool on his scalp. "Too familiar."

"I think the paper rules out a Wolf hit. Arkady said mafia."

"Korean. It's a signature." Vicktor sighed, frustration rolling through him. "What do you think? Three murders, within two days, all with the mark of the North Korean mafia."

Utuzh smoothed his bushy mustache as his brow edged skyward in thought. "*Neznaiyo*. If it wasn't for Evgeny's murder, and the wadded-paper signature, I could sign off the Americans as smugglers involved in a mafia land war and ship them off in crates to America. But something doesn't feel right. It's too easy. Visa stamps, the mafia signature. There's no effort to hide any of it. I don't think it's the mafia."

Vicktor looked at the floor, squinting at his shoes and running Utuzh's words through his mind.

"My instinct tells me your vet was in cahoots with these missionaries and it got them all killed."

"Or perhaps one was really a mafia hit and the other a ruse? To throw us off the scent?"

"Maybe they all knew a few too many secrets." Utuzh cracked open his lab door. The smell of death leaked through the opening. "All I want to know is if this is the end of the body trail…or the beginning."

## Chapter Nine

~~❦~~

Vicktor nearly tripped over the door frame, seeing his elusive office-mate, Maxim, slouched in his desk chair sifting through messages. His scruffy brown hair scraped at his shirt collar, and the guy had forgotten to shave, again. Vicktor glimpsed a Snickers bar clenched in his left paw.

Maxim glanced up. *"Privyet."*

"Hello," Vicktor replied. He shrugged out of his coat as he took in Maxim's sagging face and drooping shoulders. His rumpled brown polyester suit coat hung over his chair. "You okay, Max?"

*"Da,"* the younger man confirmed, his gaze glued on his sea of paperwork. Vicktor saw him drop the candy wrapper on the floor and kick it into the pile under his desk.

"You got a message, by the way. The Consulate is sending a representative. Said they'd call when they got here."

*Oy, oy, oy.* That would be fun. Vicktor hung up his coat and grabbed his mug. The samovar glistened through the steam. Vicktor poured hot water into his mug and stirred his coffee and cream to a sandy brown.

"And Chief Inspector Sturnin called," Maxim said without looking up. "About an hour ago. Said to have you call him back."

Vicktor speed-dialed the number.

The secretary answered. "Chief's out." Her syrupy tone hinted that she was currently between beaus. "Any messages, Vicktor?"

Vicktor could see her gliding one sleek leg over the other and grinning into the phone, a gleam in her brown eyes.

He bristled. "*Da*. Tell him, 'Chauffeur.'" He hung up, chuckling.

He flicked on his computer, then dialed the in-house computer department. Something inside him wanted to keep his promise to Grace Benson and give her the computer today— after copying all pertinent files, of course. Certainly a doctor would keep some sort of record of his daily activities. He just hoped the American had been high-tech enough to do it on his laptop.

The phone rang in his ear for an eternity while he picked up his e-mail messages. Nothing from Preach or Mae. Dread inched into his thoughts—Mae hadn't been caught last night, had she?

Taking his coffee with him, he headed toward Yanna's office, reminding himself that Mae most often used his personal address at home. He threaded through the maze of junior investigators, their heads bowed over mounds of paperwork. A road two meters thick could be laid from Vladivostok to Moscow from the paperwork the FSB generated in one year.

The Electronic Surveillance Department sprawled nearly the entire third floor and was filled with young men with big eyes glued to computer screens, scanning the millions of letters beaming over the Internet within and around Russia each day. They had their "tags"—people they suspected in international espionage, smuggling or industrial crimes, and a small division devoted to reading the mail of diplomats, businessmen, cultural exchange students, and humanitarian aid workers. Vicktor laid good odds that they would have a file on the Youngs.

He entered the reception area and strode toward an office of specialized technicians. The room hummed at a high-pitch as he stalked past cubicles and stopped behind the chair of Artyom Bartnyk. Vicktor grinned. The hacker was in a chat room, and from the looks of the icons on the screen, it wasn't work related.

"How you doing on that computer I gave you, Artyom?"

The kid jumped. *Ha*. Artyom whirled in his chair, his face the color of a beet. He scrambled for words as his Adam's apple bobbed.

"How's Natasha?" Vicktor asked, enjoying this more than he should.

"Fine," Artyom croaked, then spun in his chair to close out the chat screen. "It's the only time she can chat that doesn't cut into her study hours."

"And the only time she doesn't have Arkady listening in." Vicktor clamped the kid on the shoulder, noting the horror in the man's eyes. "Don't worry, Artyom, his bark is worse than his bite."

Vicktor laughed as Artyom's mouth gaped open. He'd be a little nervous, too, if he were dating Arkady's only daughter. "Don't worry, Natasha's as savvy as her old man. If you can sweet-talk her, I'm sure you'll have no problem with Arkady."

"I hope so." Artyom closed out the chat. "I'm thinking about asking her to marry me."

"That's a pretty big step…"

Artyom smiled, and a dreamy look crossed his eyes.

"O-kay," Vicktor said, seeing the battle lost. "How are you doing on that laptop I gave you?"

"Just getting started." Artyom scooted his chair toward his PC. The Youngs' computer was connected to a parallel port on his desktop IBM by a thick black nulmodem cable. He typed in the proper keystrokes and suddenly Dr. Willie Young's welcome page flashed on the monitor. Ten or so icons dotted the picture of the young cowboy Vicktor had seen in their bedroom.

"What do you want to see?"

Vicktor set his coffee on the desk, drew up a stool and draped his arm over Artyom's chair. He studied the screen. The icons represented a regular bouquet of high-tech American culture.

"Can you read English?" Vicktor asked.

"Enough to understand Windows and the installation instructions on my favorite games."

"How about this one?" Vicktor pointed to the icon entitled "My Documents."

Artyom clicked on it. A dialogue box opened and asked for a password.

"*Tochna*. That's where we'll start." Vicktor whacked Artyom on the back.

Artyom grimaced. "Gimme all you got on this guy. It might take a while."

An hour later, Vicktor thought he might send the machine through the third-story window if it beeped one more time. "Artyom, you're supposed to be some sort of wizard. Can't you find a shortcut to get past this thing?"

Artyom scowled at him.

"I told their American friend she could have the computer back today." Not like he'd had a choice, with her glaring at him. Okay, so he had had a choice. The fact was, he'd had a hard time not offering to bring the computer back to her himself.

Artyom gazed at the screen and wiggled the mouse.

Vicktor watched the cursor dart, flicking from icon to icon.

"Are you bothering my staff again, Vicktor?"

Vicktor leaned back in his chair and grinned up at Yanna. She'd pulled her long brown hair into a clip, and in a black blazer and skirt, she appeared every inch the director of her Electronic Surveillance Department.

"Sorry, Captain Andrevka. Your hacker here is totally inept." He saw the glare from Artyom and grinned. "Evidently everything is password protected."

"Not a bad idea," Yanna said, rubbing her chin with her forefinger, as if thinking. "Laptops are stolen every day in Khabarovsk."

She glanced at him. "So, did you have a good time last night?"

Vicktor smiled, swept up by the twinkle in Yanna's eyes. He nodded. "Good game." Obviously Mae had made it back to base without hassle. He didn't want to imagine the late-night conversation she might have had with her partner-in-crime, Yanna. Next question would be about the American he'd cornered on the train.

"Oh, I'm an idiot." He shot a look at Yanna, who raised one groomed eyebrow. "Don't go there. It's just that I'll bet Miss Benson can get into this thing. She wanted to take it with her."

Artyom leaned back in his chair. "I doubt it. Passwords aren't the kinds of things people share, even with their best friends."

"Still, I'll bet she knows something." He pulled out his notebook and reached for the phone. It rang more than ten times before he concluded she wasn't home.

"Maybe I should pay her a visit," he mumbled, as if testing the idea.

Yanna nearly yanked him to his feet. From her bemused expression, he knew his guesses about Yanna and Mae's late-night gossip had been spot-on. *Great.*

"Go see her," Yanna said, grinning. "I'll stay here and see if I can help my *inept* hacker find a back door."

Vicktor ignored Yanna's wink and stalked out of the office.

The sound of the telephone ringing, for the billionth time, shredded the last of the Wolf's nerves. Especially when he saw Sergei reach for it. He rounded on the kid behind him. "What. Are. You. *Thinking?*"

Sergei yanked his hand away, shock on his face. "Sorry. Reflex."

"Idiot." The Wolf was growing weary of Sergei's appearance, as well as his stupidity. His shiny black leather coat was the only non-repulsive part about him. Bags of gray hung under the kid's eyes, and whiskers layered gaunt cheeks, parting around a scar along his jaw. Brains were obviously an overrated attribute in this new era. The hoodlum made the Wolf wince. "Just... hurry."

Sergei shrugged, and crunched through the shards toward the kitchen.

The Wolf's mouth filled with curses, words he hadn't thought or said for over two decades, so meticulously had he created his façade. Even now, his tongue stumbled over them, and he said them again, finding a particular satisfaction as filth spewed into the room. He'd sacrificed so much of his life. Finally, he would reap what he'd sown.

He clenched his fists and stalked into the bedroom. A scatter of balled socks littered the bed, like snowballs on a brown wool blanket. Dust mites, raked out from under the bed, caught in the afternoon sun, swirling in an illuminated swath along the wooden floor. He knelt, lifted the blanket and came up sneezing. More curses.

He was keenly aware of the sound of glass breaking in the kitchen, and decided not to chase after it. So the place got roughed up. He'd send a message; one he hoped would command attention.

He was tired of not being taken seriously. The Koreans had actually laughed at him.

He'd show them.

Sergei appeared in the door. "It's not here."

The Wolf swept an arm across the nightstand and sent crashing to the floor an alarm clock, a container of acetaminophen, and a five-by-seven framed photo of Dr. and Mrs. Young. He stepped on the picture. The glass cracked in a web of jagged lines.

The Wolf smiled for the first time in days.

Vicktor gripped the steering wheel, the memory of the ringing phone in his ear. *Please, Miss Benson, don't be on the train again to Vladivostok.* Relief felt thick and hot in him when he turned into her courtyard and spied her climbing out of a blue Toyota Corolla.

He pulled in across the lot and watched her. The sun lit her blond hair a dull gold and she appeared tired, lines creasing her wan face. It was hard to discern if she was thin like the Russian girls under her baggy dress and sloppy trench coat, and she was wearing those silly boots again. Yet, her face had a molded softness. And, as she gritted her teeth, prying at the trunk latch, Vicktor decided she was pretty. Not in a chic European way, like Yanna, but more like the Lands' End models he had seen pasted on the covers of the catalogs on his friend's table in Oregon—welcoming, casual and friendly.

Then Andrei, her protective chauffeur-maybe-boyfriend jumped out of the car. Vicktor bristled. He absently rubbed his shin, calling himself a fool to be duped by her simple appearance, again. It would do him well to remember how her warm, needy demeanor had vanished the minute her hero driver darkened the door. Vicktor steeled himself and climbed out of the car.

Recognition flickered in Andrei's eyes and he barely masked a scowl. He leaned down and whispered something into Grace's ear. She glanced up at Vicktor. Oh boy, did she have green eyes—and he felt just a little sick when they clouded.

"What do you want?" Grace's voice trembled.

Did he still think her pretty? He studied her—her hands perched on her hips, jeweled eyes glinting with suspicion. Yes, spunk only made her cute.

He jingled his car key as he wandered toward her. "I need to talk to you," he said in English.

Andrei slid his hand onto Grace's shoulder and narrowed his eyes.

"I have nothing to say to you," Grace said.

"If you want to find your friends' killers, you need to help us."

Mistrust in her eyes, her stance told him she'd been briefed on the reputation of the FSB. He tensed with offense. Not every

Russian cop abused his power and lived above the law. More and more, with western ideas, that theology was dying a slow death. But, as he read the skepticism on Grace's face, the stigma felt like a slap.

"All I want to do is talk."

Grace frowned. Vicktor added a one-sided smile. He could almost see her shuffling between her instinctive trust of cops, and her fear. He actually heard his heart beat in his ears when her expression gentled.

"What do you want?" she asked.

"I have your computer."

"Where?" She stared pointedly at his empty hands.

"At the office. I need your help with it."

"What kind of help?" She looked him up and down, as if searching for a gun, or a bowie knife hidden under his jacket. What did she think—that he was going to haul her into HQ and put her in shackles? This wasn't a Bond movie.

"I'm stuck on the welcome page. Our hackers can't crack the password, and I've been unable to read any of his files."

She froze and squinted her eyes. "What are you doing snooping around in Dr. Willie's files?"

Andrei tightened his grip on her shoulder. She shrugged out of it.

*Yeah, that's right, she doesn't need you, Boris.* Vicktor stifled a grin. "Well, we're not trying to beat his solitaire record. I'm hoping we can find some clues—"

"I'm not helping you break into the Youngs' computer, and if you had any sense you'd spend your time finding the murderer instead of stealing files from Americans," Gracie snapped.

Vicktor's good humor disintegrated. "*Tiha,* sweetheart. We *are* searching for the murderers. But we have some serious questions about evidence we found in the Youngs' apartment."

"Evidence?" Grace raised her brows at Vicktor, as if waiting for him to explain himself, much like a teacher responding to an unruly student.

Frustration strummed a tense neck muscle. Well, *that* hadn't gone well. Obviously, prying the password from her would take a little more finesse. Vicktor scanned the courtyard. Babushkas on benches leaned forward on their canes. Children, in the bread queue near a dilapidated kiosk, stared at them, mouths agape. Vicktor pointed at the car trunk.

"Can I help you?"

Grace stared at him as if he'd spoken French.

"Let's have this conversation inside." He tried the smile again. "Please?"

Grace paused, then slowly stepped aside while Andrei opened the trunk. Inside, two bulging suitcases lay like fat carcasses, jostled from a back-road journey. Andrei heaved one out. Grace grabbed the other. Vicktor moved up behind her and gripped the handle, covering her hand. She stiffened.

"Let me help you," he said gently. Uh, where had *that* tone come from?

Grace turned, her face only inches from his. She smelled good. Clean and fresh and pretty and he suddenly felt like a stray next to her. Something that sniffed the garbage and slept under Dumpsters.

*"Ladna,"* she mumbled, using the Russian term for *okay.*

She turned toward the building, and he stumbled after her, hating her ability to throw him off balance. Thankfully she didn't glance back to watch him scrape himself together.

The bag thumped against Vicktor's leg as he followed Grace and Andrei down a small hill and into the darkened entrance of the apartment building. The third step had eroded from the cement staircase. Grace stepped over it with practiced grace. The old, cranky lift groaned as it plummeted down nine flights, and Vicktor gave thanks he lived on the fourth floor.

"Okay, what do you want to talk to me about?" Grace stepped back. The dark corridor eclipsed her expression.

He hesitated, wishing for privacy. "I found some…contraband at your friends' flat."

Grace folded her arms across her chest.

"I found visa papers," he continued, his voice low, "forged visa papers and a counterfeit Korean stamp." Even in the dim light, he saw her brow crease. He knew he shouldn't be telling her this—not when she might still be considered a suspect by Arkady. And certainly not in the middle of the hall, regardless of how he pitched his voice. This should wait until they were inside her flat. Where he could lock Andrei in another room and grab a pillow for his shins.

But maybe giving out a morsel of information would earn her trust.

Vicktor took a deep breath and braced himself. "We think they were, uh, smuggling something into or out of North Korea. Maybe even people."

"That's a filthy thing to say."

So much for earning her trust. The elevator arrived. Grace stomped in and the small box trembled. Andrei and Vicktor squeezed in behind her. They stood inches apart in the dim light as the lift shuddered upward. Silence pulsed between them. Vicktor couldn't remember the last time he'd had so much fun.

The doors opened, and Andrei purposely hip-checked him into the wall. Vicktor glared at him as Gracie worked the lock to the steel door.

"What's *wrong* with this door?" Gracie gave it a kick, obviously unraveling.

"Let me try." Vicktor touched her shoulder, intending to nudge her aside. She jerked away and gave him a look that should have knocked him out. Except that a tear had caught in her lower lash.

There went his voice. Abandoning him on the battle line. He felt like an idiot.

"What do you want?" she demanded, her voice tremulous.

Vicktor took a deep breath and looked away from her, unable to see her pain. It unnerved him that she had the ability to make him feel like he'd personally screwed up her life. Not to mention her ability to make him *feel* in the first place. "I want to help."

"Then find their killers."

"I'm trying, Miss Benson. I'm not your enemy…"

She sucked in a breath.

"…contrary to popular belief." He glared at Andrei as he said it.

Vicktor fished around in his coat for the picture he'd picked up at the Youngs' apartment, unable to figure out what else to do, hoping he wasn't making it worse. "Do you possibly know these men?"

Grace tucked her hair behind her ear, and accepted the picture. She studied it. Her nod gave him the first flicker of hope of the day.

"The Russian is Yuri Mikhailovich, the head pastor of the Russian Church in Khabarovsk. The other man is Pastor Paul Yee, head of the Korean Church in town." She lifted her chin. "Maybe the Youngs smuggled *him* in."

"Maybe."

Okay, that only made her mad. She glowered at him and shoved him the picture. "Leave me alone." But her voice shook, just enough to make him pause, stare hard.

Her eyes had turned deep green, and the haunted look in them skimmed under his defenses and clipped his heart.

The woman was more than afraid. She had secrets. And demons.

He knew all about nightmares haunting the dark places.

She yanked her gaze away.

He released the breath he'd been holding as she turned the key in the lock.

Stepping back as she yanked open the door, he braced himself for more fun once they got inside.

She froze, staring inside. "Oh, no."

Vicktor peered over her shoulder and winced.

# Chapter Ten

Larissa fingered the gold chain at her neck, absently running the tiny gold cross along the links as she clicked on the search engine results for "Bali." Just the sound of the word sent a tremor of delight running up her spine. She angled her computer screen away from the door and clicked on the "Tour of Bali" welcome page. Palm trees and coconuts, backlit by a rich orange and cranberry sunset, filled the screen. The scenes sent warmth through her. She clicked on the accommodations page and lost herself for a few moments inside luxury suites and alongside pools so vivid she could nearly feel the water gliding over her sun-baked body.

Soon. Thankfully her cubicle didn't have a window, but the lingering image of crusty gray snow, black puddles of mud, the streets lined with paper, plastic bags, cigarettes and the byproducts of animals, made her nose curl.

The sooner the better.

She checked her watch, counting down the hours she had yet to put in at this dingy office. Boris would be waiting for her when she got home. Maybe sitting in his Moscovitz, his hands drumming the wheel as he watched her stroll up the street. Perhaps he'd have a bunch of purple chrysanthemums or white dahlias wrapped in florist's paper lying on the seat.

She saw right through his pitiful advances. It wasn't hard to recognize a ploy when he stepped into her office six months ago, asking her to arrange a flight to Moscow, something he could do in the lobby, or over the telephone. When he "bumped" into her two nights later, at a disco, she knew. And played along.

The first few weeks, she wondered why he'd picked her. Boris was doting enough, tolerable. He tried to hide his age, his obvious paunch, his cynicism. She allowed it, curious and bored with the men who fancied her. He was a puzzle, but smart. She knew that from his eyes. Dark brown, always watching. She could practically see the gears working in his head, especially in his unguarded moments. Finally, after she'd fielded his questions—coyly, of course—she realized.

The Youngs. The man was after Dr. and Mrs. Young. Briefly, she considered her loyalties.

Then she saw beyond the present into the future. Her future. Whatever he was planning, she'd extract some promises. Gently, subtly. She'd reel out information, play with his ego until the hook was planted. Then she'd give it a good jerk.

Bali. He'd suggested it, but it sounded fine. Anywhere outside the former Soviet Union would work. She could ditch him at any time, as long as she had the cash.

It only took a little emotional nudge, and some external prodding, for him to unwrap his plans. He needed her, and she'd gladly agreed. It was a partnership forged in greed, but she didn't care about the motivations. She wanted results.

If she had to sacrifice a friend, she'd do it. Perhaps with sadness. But she'd done her time. Bali and the rest of the globe awaited.

Her hand closed over the cross. The gold bit into her hand as she logged off the Internet.

* * *

"I'm okay!" Grace stuttered. "Let go of me!" She put two hands on his chest and pushed.

He'd grabbed her. Instinctively, of course, to keep her safe. "Let me go in first." He looked beyond her, into her apartment. *Ouch.*

She started to move forward. He swept out his arm. "I'm not kidding. Stay here."

Vicktor took his Makarov pistol from his shoulder holster. She stared at the weapon with wide eyes. Andrei didn't look any better, pale and frozen behind her. Some bodyguard. Vicktor stepped into the flat.

Destruction pervaded the apartment. Clothing spewed into the hallway; the pieces of a shattered mirror glinted like droplets of water on the brown carpet. Stillness embedded the walls. Vicktor's skin prickled. He stepped farther in, crunching glass under his loafers.

"What happened to my apartment?" Grace whispered from the hall.

*"Tiha!"* Vicktor snapped. He strode down the hall, stopped briefly in the family room, and continued to her bedroom. Bedclothes, the contents of her closet and upended drawers littered the floor. Someone had stepped on a framed photo of the couple murdered yesterday. Vicktor listened for the sound of breathing.

Nothing.

Turning, he slammed open the bathroom door, flicked the switch. Light scattered shadow from the room. Only a flimsy shower curtain. Adrenaline poured out of him as he whipped it back.

"Okay, come in." He sheathed his weapon and returned to the doorway.

"This is unbelievable," Gracie said as she tiptoed inside.

Vicktor stepped over an emptied box of medicines and knickknacks. Behind him, Andrei lugged in the suitcases and propped them against the wall in the hall. The guy looked like he'd been punched.

Grace pushed past Vicktor and stood in the center of the room. "It looks like a robbery," she said. "But I don't have anything of value to steal." She had begun to sway, like a drunk. She braced her hand on the sofa, then sat down hard.

Vicktor looked away before the expression on her face made him do something really stupid, like pull her into his arms.

Her chauffeur crossed the room and sat beside her. "It'll be okay, Gracie," he said.

Vicktor wondered what Andrei meant by "okay." Because he felt pretty sure that *okay* wasn't going to be a part of her vocabulary until she put Russia a couple billion kilometers behind her.

Broken glass from the wall unit crunched under his feet. "Was this locked?" he asked, pointedly not glancing at the couple.

"Yes," Grace said.

Vicktor dug out his cell phone, then grimaced when the battery light died. He dropped it back into his pocket and paced the room. Kicking aside a pillow, he found her telephone, smashed.

"Do you have another phone?"

"In the kitchen." She pulled away from Andrei.

Vicktor suppressed a smile.

The contents of her refrigerator covered her linoleum floor in a swampy brew that included pickles and mashed potatoes. He found the telephone receiver in the sink, the rest under a plate of greasy fried cabbage he uncovered with his toe. Rubbing his chin with the back of his hand, he returned to the family room.

Grace was on her knees, gathering the remains of a bottle of vitamins. Andrei stood sentry behind her. He glared at Vicktor when he returned. What? Was it his fault that she had a knack for finding trouble?

"Miss Benson, do you know why anyone would want to rob you?"

She sat back on her heels and gazed up at him, her expression morose. She looked emptied, as if someone had reached inside her and torn out her heart. He swallowed, hard, and tried to push away the feeling that somehow he'd failed her.

"I don't know," she answered weakly.

Running a hand through his hair, he turned away and blew out a breath. His gut said this wasn't the act of a thief. Someone had entered Grace Benson's flat looking for something, and when they didn't find it—rage.

What if she had been here when the thief broke in?

Oops, he shouldn't have entertained that thought.

"Who did this?" she asked, her eyes moving from her chauffeur to Vicktor and back.

"I don't know." He hated his answer. Crouching before her, he hung his arms over his knees. "Do you have any enemies? Anyone who would want to hurt you?"

"I am a *missionary,*" she retorted. "I work with the Church, the poorest people in Russia. What enemies would I have?"

He schooled his tone. "Well, obviously someone doesn't like you."

Her eyes widened as his words sank in. The medicine slid from her hand. "I have nothing of value here…and no enemies…that I know of."

Andrei crouched beside her. "You can't stay here, Grace." He put a hand on hers. "Come with me. You can stay with my parents in their village."

Vicktor pinched his lips. The chauffeur was right, of course, her flat wasn't safe, but the man couldn't simply tuck her away in some little hamlet. And, aside from the fact she was Vicktor's prime witness, she was also a victim and a target.

"*Nyet.*"

"Why?" Andrei's eyes darkened.

Vicktor pounced to his feet a second before the chauffeur. He took in Andrei's clenched fist and narrowed his eyes.

"Watch yourself," Vicktor growled in Russian. "Just give me an excuse to pull your license and make you hitchhike for the next ten years."

Challenge flickered in Andrei's eyes. Andrei obviously wasn't afraid of him. That meant he had a *kreesha*, someone with pull who stood behind his words and actions. Mafia? Yet, something had definitely rattled the guy when he'd seen Gracie's flat.

Who was Andrei and what was he doing hanging around a missionary? "Can you protect her?" Vicktor asked.

Andrei's mouth drew into a fine line. "Better than you can."

Now was probably a good time to reinforce all those reasons why the civilian population should quake when the FSB walked into the room. Civil rights were definitely overrated.

Except...he shot a glance at Grace. She looked stricken, and it spiked his heart. She needed a friend, and unfortunately, she felt more comfortable with her driver than with the FSB. He took a calming breath. "Can you bring her into the office tomorrow?"

Andrei nodded stiffly. He reached out for his charge. "Let's go."

"I'll call in a team to sweep the place for evidence," Vicktor said as the pair brushed passed him.

They didn't acknowledge him. Grace retrieved her satchel from the floor and slung it over her shoulder. Andrei stalked out the door.

Gracie suddenly stopped, one hand on the door frame, and turned. Her gaze lifted to Vicktor's and held it. Intense and needy, it implored him with an unspoken request. "Thanks," she finally said.

Then she whirled and followed her chauffeur.

Vicktor watched her leave, listening to his heart make all sorts of promises he wasn't sure he could keep.

Gracie cupped her hands over her face and willed herself not to cry. Her eyes burned, her face felt chapped. She was tired of tears. Fury churned inside her. Who had done this? And what was he after?

*God, where are you?* The thought rose, unbidden, and she deliberately forced it away, unable to face the answer.

"Gracie, are you okay?" Andrei's hands gripped the steering wheel, and his voice was low. Gracie nodded, glancing at him. He appeared tired, drawn. She'd seen him toe up to the FSB captain, and gratitude swept through her for his faithful protection. Whatever they had said, obviously he'd won.

Nevertheless, as she closed her eyes and leaned her head back against the rest, the image of Captain Vicktor Shubnikov—his pensive blue eyes, his face twisted in worry, and the smell of his clean, spicy cologne—uh-oh, should she be noticing that?—filled her mind. So she liked him. Was that a crime to admit? He wanted to help, she felt it in her gut, despite his poking around the Youngs' computer.

Maybe she shouldn't have treated him like vermin.

Especially when she could hardly suppress a smile, remembering the feel of his arms around her, holding, protecting.

"That cop is worthless. I'll bet he's searching your place for cash right now."

Andrei's derisive tone spliced her thoughts. She frowned at him. "I don't think so, Andrei. He seems nice." *Too much information.*

Andrei shot her a dark look. "He's *not* nice. He's FSB. Of any person you might meet in Russia, he's the dead last person you should trust."

Gracie nodded, but she was remembering the captain's eyes and the look he'd given her as she left. It spoke to her in a way that she couldn't ignore. He *cared* what happened to her. No matter what Andrei said.

Which was probably a sign that she was already in deep trouble.

"You don't know cops like I do," Andrei mumbled.

She hoped she wouldn't get to, either.

"Goal!" Roman pumped the air with his hockey stick, rolling in a circle on his blades.

Vicktor skated to the curb and dug the ball out of a gutter. Sweat streaked between his shoulder blades and down his back, saturating his sweatshirt. Flipping the ball toward Roman, and ignoring the look of triumph on his opponent's face, he skated to a bench and grabbed a jug of water.

"That's three to one, Vita. Your mind's not on the game."

Vicktor grabbed a towel from his gym bag and swabbed his face. A scant wind hissed through the trees, ruffled his hair and raised gooseflesh on his clammy skin. Twilight slung long shadows across the paved boulevard in Lenin Park. Beyond the Amur River, a fiery red sun painted the river in cinnamon hues. Vicktor palmed his lower back and stretched.

"Give me a second to focus, Roma," he said, frustrated that he couldn't unstick Gracie Benson from his brain. Where was she, and was she safe?

Roman sat down on the bench, tugging out his own bottle of water.

Vicktor skated backward, flexing his new skates. His feet had started to burn. "Any leads on Evgeny's murder?"

Roman draped the towel around his neck. "We're talking to a couple of the pet owners, but other than a babushka mourning her Persians, nothing."

Vicktor retrieved the ball and began batting it with his hockey stick.

"Might have something on your American missionaries, however."

Vicktor nearly drove the ball into the trees. "What?"

"Malenkov brought us the case this afternoon."

Vicktor peered over Roman's shoulder at two children on swings in the playground. The swing set squealed in irritating rhythm. "Then, despite my report and Utuzh's opinion, he doesn't think it's the Wolf."

Roman hung his arms over his knees. "Sorry, Vita. He's sticking to the mafia leads."

Vicktor skated over and sat on the bench, feeling the last shreds of hope unravel. "Maybe the Wolf's gone, moved to Moscow."

"Maybe."

The breeze washed through the trees, carrying remnants of Siberia's winter smells. Vicktor grabbed his leather jacket. "So, what do you know about the missionaries?" He tried to keep his tone light, knowing anything Roman uncovered would stab at his convictions.

Roman unsnapped his skates. "Malenkov got another call."

Vicktor froze. "On Ishkov's line?"

"Keep this close to your chest, Vicktor, but there's something nasty going on. Someone called yesterday…right about the time you were pulling your American off the Okean, gave the Youngs' address and hung up. As if they wanted us to find the Youngs, and maybe even your American woman."

Silent questions hissed on the nippy breeze. "They're linked," Vicktor said tightly.

Roman nodded again, his face grim. "Your missionaries were murdered by the same guy who took out Evgeny."

Vicktor leaned over and also worked off his skates. He rubbed his foot for a moment before sliding it into his cold loafer. "Could be the perpetrator."

"Could be," Roman agreed. "But whoever killed the vet and the missionaries is searching for something. He seems almost desperate. I think somebody who knows what he's up to is calling the old number, hoping we'll nab him."

Vicktor moaned, leaned forward and rubbed his eyes. "I hope Grace Benson isn't next on his list. She was their friend."

Roman's face darkened.

"I have no idea where she is."

"Stripes," Roman said, shaking his head, "this might be a good time for you to think about getting religious."

Vicktor eyed him quizzically.

Roman pointed skyward. "Pray."

Gracie sat on the bed, tucked her chin into her drawn-up knees, folded her hands around her ankles and shivered. Evening bathed the tiny bedroom in shadow. A yellow, lopsided moon sent pale streaks through the grimy window and across the wooden floor. The barren bedroom smelled of mold and coal soot, its damp cement walls useless in preventing fear from seeping into her soul.

Outside the bedroom door of the tiny wooden house, in the main room, she could hear Andrei pulling out a sofa bed, and his mother clucking in Russian about her unexpected visitor. Aleksandra Tallina had been kind enough, pulling Gracie into her ample bosom when they'd arrived, but somehow Gracie couldn't shake the idea that she'd dragged evil with her into their home. Aleksandra's smile didn't quite make it to her wrinkled brown eyes, and Gracie wondered how welcome she truly was in Andrei's family home.

A chill bit Gracie's skin. Outside in the muddy yard, a cat screeched on its nightly prowl. Gracie tensed against the cold and tucked her legs closer. Lumps in Andrei's paper-thin mattress irritated her.

What was she doing here?

Bitterness filled her throat. Her life had turned inside out in a matter of twenty-four hours. She could count her friends on the fingers of one hand.

"Oh, God, where are you?" she moaned. "I'm so sorry I turned away from You. I need You more than ever. Don't abandon me!" Gracie gritted her teeth. She might not deserve God's protection, but it couldn't keep her from asking.

*"Yea, though I walk through the valley of the shadow of death, I will fear no evil."* Psalm 23. For the second time, the Psalm filled her mind. This time she allowed it to find root. David had been pursued. Chased. Abandoned. Afraid. His best friend had been killed. She grabbed her satchel and dug through it for her Bible and a flashlight.

Flipping through Psalms, her eyes fell not on Chapter 23, but on Psalm 22. "'My God, my God, why have You forsaken me?'" She trembled as the words embedded themselves in her heart. These were Jesus' words, spoken as he suffered on the cross. Even God knew what it felt to be alone and afraid.

"'Do not be far from Me, for trouble is near.'" Gracie repeated the verse in a whisper.

"God, I'm terrified. I know You can save me, but will You?" Gracie surrendered to the burn in her throat, tears filling her eyes. "What do I have to offer You? I don't deserve Your love. I've failed You so many times."

She bit down on her trembling lower lip. Leaning back, she clutched the Bible to her chest. What did she have to offer God? Why should He protect her? She wasn't like Evelyn or Dr. Willie, leading people to the Lord. She was on the run, from her past, from her guilt. She was the one who deserved to die. A sob shuddered through her, and she clamped a hand over her mouth, stifling it.

Remember David.

Gracie's rapid breath stilled. *David.* Her eyes widened and a she wiped her sodden cheeks. Of course. David, the King, the anointed one, the favored of God. David, who killed a man to hide his sins with Bathsheba. David, the man after God's own heart. Why did God love David?

Gracie laid the Bible in her lap and scanned the verses in Psalm 22 with her flashlight. Verse twenty-three nearly screamed her name. "'Ye that fear the Lord, praise Him.... For He hath not despised or disdained the suffering of the afflicted; neither hath He hid His face from him; but when he cried unto Him, He heard.'"

*Cried unto Him.* David called on God. Not because he deserved it, but because he needed God's salvation.

Gracie flipped to Psalm 51, David's prayer of repentance. "'Have mercy on me, O God, according to Your unfailing love.'" Her mind sorted through the words. David called on God's mercy and unfailing love. God had not only forgiven him, He'd restored him, and protected him. David's faith and his need for God, instead of his triumph as a king, earned him a place in God's esteem. Not because he was perfect. But because he wasn't.

"'Yea, though I walk through the valley of the shadow of death, I will fear no evil; for Thou art with me.'"

Gracie let the words sweep through her. Could it be that God hadn't abandoned her? Maybe, in fact, *she'd* just been ignoring *Him*. If her understanding was correct, it was those who needed Him that found Him. Maybe she didn't have to be a stellar missionary, or even someone deserving of forgiveness to receive it. She could be like David…a person whom God loved, despite her mistakes. "Oh, God, please forgive me," she whispered. "I know I don't deserve Your love, but because of Your mercy, save me. Protect me. Deliver me home."

She drew a shaky breath as warmth flooded her. Although eerie gray shadows filled the room, and the air was nippy, the warming peace swaddled her.

Why had it taken a trip across the ocean and the death of her friends for her to see it? She closed her Bible and curled up on the bed. Tucking the Bible next to her, she rubbed it gently. Fingers of moonlight streamed across her hand, and she imagined it was God caressing her hand with His own.

# Chapter Eleven

⁂

The Wolf leaned against the chipped cement building, the cold sneaking in under his flimsy gray trench coat. What was he doing, depending on someone else, again? Had thirty years as a pawn taught him nothing? He watched a young couple stroll by. She laughed, her head back, bleached blond hair streaking into the wind, skinny legs in slinky black hose, her leather jacket longer than her skirt. The young man beside her smoked a cigarette and the smell curled around the Wolf like a snarl, taunting, mocking. He bristled.

He missed those days. Youthful days when desperation didn't know his name.

What was *taking* her so long?

Farther down the street, the statue of Lenin cast a dark shadow across the newly tiled Lenin Square. The old boss's arm stretched out, finger pointing up to the future. The Wolf couldn't bear to look at it anymore. The Grandfather of the Glorious State would weep to see her today.

A stiff wind, carrying the odor of mud and old snow, slogged down the street, scraped up candy wrappers. A dented can rattled toward him. The Wolf felt grit clinging to his eyes, nose.

The phone rang. He snatched up the receiver, nearly ripping the wire from the base. *"Slyushaiyu."*

"He just called. They went to his parents' home."

*"In Berozivka?"*

*"Da."*

He hung up. Gray, tired eyes watched him cross the street. The window of a rusty *Zhiguli* came down halfway.

"It's about time," the Wolf said as he climbed in.

Vicktor wrestled with his bedclothes as the dream took possession of him. He had the faint impression that perhaps, if he could just focus, he could alter the events, but the force of memory drove the nightmare unchanging through his mind.

*"Viktor, wait." The voice sounds as if it is in a tunnel.*

*Vicktor's skin prickles as he enters the gutted apartment building. The moon creases the cement in splinters of pale light and eerie shadows embed the crumbling walls of former habitation. He wades deeper into the darkness, steps echoing.*

*Outside, sirens mourn.*

*The Wolf is here. Vicktor knows it. He feels the Wolf's presence like fingers on his clammy skin. Somewhere in the back of his mind, he hears screaming.*

*The smell of fresh rain upon cement makes his nose wrinkle. He stills. Strains to hear beyond his roaring pulse.*

*He knows the pain will come before it splinters his head. But he's too slow, caught in the mire of subconscious regret. He falls to his knees. Another blow and his cheek slams into the floor. He rolls, scrambling to evade his attacker. A kick to the jaw, and his head rings. Blood fills his mouth.*

*"Here I am," a voice snarls.*

*Vicktor blinks, scrabbling at the fog, the layers of pain.*

*Metal glints in the Wolf's hand. "No!" He hears himself, and another voice behind his thought pulses....*

*Wake. Up.*
*Then footsteps, swallowed by the darkness.*
*No!*
*A shot. He feels his chest burn as a scream rends the air.*
*Sweat bathes his body. It's dark. The scream forms, becomes his name. Then moaning. Over, and over.*
*He's in the street. Light shining at erratic angles, and he sees.*
*Nickolai. Writhing. His dark eyes pin Vicktor.*
*"What have you done?"*

Vicktor cried out, and awoke to the bedsheets clutched in his fists, one leg outstretched as if he'd tried to leap from the bed. He threw off the covers. The sweat layering his body chilled in the crisp night air. *What have you done?* Only the dripping of his kitchen faucet remained of the voice, but guilt had him by the throat.

His impulsiveness had destroyed his father's life.

He got up and padded over to the window, bare feet turning to ice on the wood floor. Early morning had colored the cityscape deep purple. Across the street, the lights from two windows pushed against the morning shadows. His stomach tightened. Somewhere out there, an American lady was hiding for her life. And he had no idea from whom.

*Time to get religious.* Roman's voice echoed in his head. He gritted his teeth, wishing for once he had something to hold on to—not God, perhaps, but hope in a power beyond himself that might turn the tide in his favor. He scraped a hand through his hair. Perhaps that was the appeal of God—someone to turn to when life felt out of control.

Vicktor left the window and sat back on the bed. The frosty air prickled his skin, but he made no attempt to cover his bare chest. He knit his hands together and rested his forehead on them.

What did Grace Benson have to do with the Youngs' Korean smuggling connection? Was she a part of the ring of thieves? He blinked and saw her eyes—pure, naive, beseeching him.

Sure, the woman had *violent murderer* and *thief* written all over her.

He shook his head, stalked to the kitchen. Lighting the stove, he put a kettle of water on to boil.

He had to admit, the whole thing made him slightly ill. In a small way he relied on people like David and Roman to fill the world with some kind of hope and light. To balance the darkness and despair.

When the pot hissed steam he fixed himself a cup of instant coffee and sat down at his tiny kitchen table. His gaze fell on his black laptop. He'd forgotten to ask Miss Benson about the password. He scrubbed a hand down his face and groaned. Keep this up and his new career would be chipping ice off the sidewalks. Or trash duty in the park.

Then again, sometimes it felt that way already.

The telephone rang. Vicktor jumped to his feet, sending the chair over, and strode to the phone. *"Slyushaiyu."*

"Wake up," Arkady barked.

"I'm up."

"Get dressed and come over here."

Vicktor leaned against the wall. Cold streaked down his arm. "Where are you?"

"Utuzh's office. We have a surprise for you."

"What kind of surprise?" Vicktor rubbed his chin and dragged the phone toward the hall mirror. Red, cracked eyes stared back.

"We found your chauffeur."

Vicktor's breath caught in his chest. "Is he…?"

"Yep, a clean, ear-to-ear smile right below his chin. Been dead for at least a day."

Vicktor groaned. "Are you sure it's him? There're a lot of chauffeurs in town."

"It's him, all right, Leonid the Red, remember? This guy has a mop redder than the Kremlin."

Vicktor's head pounded as he went for a cold shower.

\* \* \*

By seven a.m. Gracie couldn't ignore the barnyard ruckus any longer and pried herself from the bed. Her matted, greasy hair felt like a wig and chunks of mascara had wedged in the corners of her eyes. As she stared into Andrei's tiny desk mirror, her shoulders slumped at the sight of the person in the wrinkled denim dress.

Rifling through her satchel, she unearthed a hairbrush and attempted to construct a greasy braid. Oh, she was a real prize this morning. Wiping the mascara smudges from under her eyes, she sighed and surrendered to homeliness. Quickly smoothing Andrei's bed, she sank beside it, clasped her hands and bent her head. "Oh, God, protect me this day." She stilled, waiting for peace, and found it in the rose-hued dawn that poured through the window.

Silence bathed the living room as she cracked open the bedroom door. Andrei's sheets were folded neatly on the made sofa bed. She padded to the kitchen and paused in the doorway. Aleksandra stood at the table, cutting bread. She appeared ages older than her fifty-some years with her hair tied back in a handkerchief and a hand-knit wool sweater covering her worn housedress.

"*Dobra Ootra,*" Aleksandra said. A slight smile wrinkled her face.

Gracie returned the smile, inflecting apology. She couldn't dodge the idea Andrei had put his parents in danger by dumping her on their doorstep like a stray.

Aleksandra pointed to a chair. Gracie wrapped her arms around herself and watched Aleksandra cut bread. A teapot gurgled on the stove.

"Where's Andrei?" Gracie asked, fumbling in Russian.

Of what Aleksandra answered, Gracie only understood the word *soon.*

They fell into an uneasy silence. Gracie stared out the window. In the backyard, laundry flapped in the May breeze, a handful of chickens pecked, and the pig rooted through his food.

Andrei emerged from the door of the tiny barn at the far end of the yard. He threw a mound of hay clamped in a rusty pitchfork into a tall, decaying pile of manure, eggshells, potato peelings and bones.

Gracie grabbed her trench coat, hanging on a hook near the door, and pulled on her hiking boots. The wooden door thumped as she closed it behind her. "Andrei!"

He turned from the entrance of the barn. A wide grin formed on his unshaven face. *"Dobra Ootra."*

Gracie wrinkled her nose as she stepped into the barn. Ooh, the smell of manure instead of breakfast. "What are you doing out here?"

Andrei hefted his pitchfork. "Chores. Want to help?"

"Sure, I can bat away the flies while you…um…what are you doing?"

"I just finished milking." Andrei threw his pitchfork into a mound. He looked decidedly Kansan this morning, sweat running in a long trickle down his face and meshing with an array of coffee-brown whiskers. He reached for the pail. It brimmed with creamy milk.

She reached for the bucket, and with it between them, they started toward the house.

A *crack* shattered the crisp air. Gracie jumped. Milk sloshed into her boots. Another *crack* and Gracie felt Andrei's hand snake around her neck. "Get down!" He slammed her into the ground, splashing the milk, covering her body with his. His hot breath steamed in her ears.

"What?" She could feel his heart beating through his chest. Milk seeped into her dress. "Is that a gunshot?"

"Stay down," he hissed.

Another *crack*. Gracie's ducked her head. "Are they shooting at us?"

"We have to get out of here!" Andrei iron-clamped her arm and yanked her to her feet.

Panic stripped every rational thought, and she could only obey.

Andrei dragged her through the muddy yard. She stumbled behind him, numb. "Why are they shooting?"

He shoved her through a gap in the back fence. *"Bwestra!"*

Gracie ran headlong through the yard, scattering chickens. More shots ripped the air.

"Oh, God, help!" she gasped, legs pumping. She slammed open a gate and nearly flew over three steps that led into the street.

She landed on her ankle, went down hard and rolled into the mud.

Andrei's hands hooked under her arms. "Get up!"

Pain made her woozy as she fought her way down the street.

An odd stillness followed in their wake as they rounded the next corner and sprinted. Gracie heard only the sound of her rasping breath and the whoosh of feathers as they startled pigeons.

Andrei grabbed her elbow and yanked her into an alcove between a rusty metal Dumpster and a rickety wooden fence. His hands gripped his knees. He hauled in heavy breaths, horror paling his face. "They found us."

Her voice was thin when she asked, "Who found us?"

"I'll get the car. You stay here and wait for me."

She nodded, but her heart froze in her chest when he left her there, crouched between a crushed soda bottle and a pile of decaying paper.

# Chapter Twelve

❧

Vicktor stared at the death mask of Leonid the Chauffeur, turned a waxy yellow by the overhead lights, and winced. Did his father always have to be right? Frustration frayed his emotions as he walked a circle around the last known link between the Youngs, their killer, and Miss Grace Benson.

"You're sure it's him?" Vicktor's gaze strayed from the gray lips to the shock of bright red hair. The corpse lay on the long metal table, a red line down the center of his chest, coarsely stitched by Utuzh sometime in the wee hours. The indignity of it turned Vicktor's stomach. It coupled with the pungent odor of formaldehyde and, for a moment, the room pitched.

Vicktor slammed his hand on the metal table to steady himself, then yanked it back when it touched cold flesh. He'd had more than one nightmare about turning up on this table, naked and gray, with a seam parting his rib cage. Vicktor fisted his hands in his pockets and glanced up at Arkady.

Arkady nodded without meeting his gaze. "He had identification." Fatigue etched craters into the Bulldog's face and even the rumpled raincoat couldn't hide the caving of his shoulders.

Vicktor frowned at the obvious exhaustion. "Did you go home last night?"

"What, and miss all the fun here?"

A smile tugged at Vicktor's mouth.

"Your father called me."

Vicktor narrowed his eyes. "Why?"

"Seemed to think we're after the Wolf." Arkady rolled the cigarette between his thumb and forefinger. "Don't get him worked up, Vicktor."

"Hope is all he's got. I haven't told him yet we were wrong." Vicktor studied the corpse, the blackened wound across the man's neck. "Maybe I should. What do you think, Utuzh?"

"Still trying to figure that out." Utuzh shuffled out of his office, a shadowed cave in the corner of the room.

Okay, someone needed to tell these guys to take a day off and bathe. Utuzh smelled like day-old roadkill and looked worse. Chubby bags hung under his eyes and his beard looked combed by a mammoth bone. His stained lab coat nearly sent Vicktor into the hallway. Someone would have to remove his stomach—and his olfactory glands—before they made Vicktor work in the M.E.'s office.

"No signs of struggle," Utuzh said, obviously unfazed by his appearance. "I doubt the chauffeur realized what was happening until his voice box was severed. Wolf handiwork, without a doubt."

Vicktor's pulse rocketed. "The Wolf. Are you sure?"

Utuzh bushy brows pinched together. "Do I look like an amateur to you?" He shot an annoyed glance at Arkady, who shrugged as if he'd toted in a kindergartner.

"Where'd you find him?" Vicktor asked, ignoring the obvious scorn of his elders.

Arkady fished around in his coat pockets. "Down by the river. Last night. A couple of unlucky kids kicked their soccer ball under his car."

Vicktor scuffed his toe into the mottled cement. "Pop said, where you find the chauffeur, you'll find the Wolf."

Arkady harrumphed and pulled out a crumpled pack of Bonds.

Utuzh tugged a sheet over Leonid the Red's remains. "We have some sort of nasty *mokraya delo* here, boys. This is the mark of someone trained to kill. And this is the fourth victim I've seen with the same signature."

"The fourth?" Vicktor frowned.

"Leonid had a wad of paper shoved up his left nostril."

Vicktor rubbed his eyes with a thumb and forefinger. Evgeny, the Youngs, and Grace Benson's chauffeur. A veterinarian, two American missionaries, and a driver. Were they all in league with the mafia? What had they done to trigger a Wolf attack?

Vicktor checked his watch. Seven-thirty a.m. "Do you think they were related? I mean, maybe Leonid just picked the wrong guy to give a ride to." He realized the stupidity of his own question even before it left his mouth. The same style of murder, the paper in the left nostril, the only remaining unaccounted connection between Gracie and the Youngs. Arkady shot him a disgusted look and Vicktor felt like a rookie. He shrugged as if trying to deflect the rebuke. "I gotta get going. Thanks for calling, Chief."

Utuzh crossed an arm over his barrel chest and combed his beard with his paw. "One more thing you should know, Vicktor. This guy's missing a few organs."

"Organs?"

"Spleen, half his stomach and a rib."

Vicktor scrutinized the now sheet-draped corpse. Tall, over six feet, and nearly eighty kilos, by rough guess. He remembered a hairy stomach and padding around the midsection. "He looked healthy enough."

"He's got a nine-inch surgical scar from his stomach to his back. I'm going to petition his medical records and see what that's about."

Vicktor turned to Arkady. "Identification?"

Arkady indicated with his cigarette a metal table along the wall. Vicktor crossed to the table and fingered a leather wallet, car keys and pocket change. Flipping open the wallet, he took out the license and examined an unforgiving shot of the stiff on the table, his height and weight. He copied Leonid's home address in his notebook.

"That makes four in a week for the Wolf," Arkady murmured. Smoke puffed out of his mouth with each word.

Vicktor turned and met his gaze. "New record."

Utuzh arched his brows. "I wonder who's next?"

Gracie peered out the dirt-streaked passenger window at the greening spikes of field grass, feeling numb.

Someone had tried to kill her.

She thought she just might be ill. Instead, she clutched the shoulder band of her seat belt and held on as Andrei swerved around potholes on his way to Khabarovsk.

He'd said nothing. Which screamed just exactly how he felt about her dragging danger to his parents' front door.

In fact, here he was, trying to save her life while his parents might be bleeding to death.

Yes, definitely, she was going to be sick.

"Andrei, pull over."

He glanced at her. *"Nyet."*

Okay. She turned toward the window, swallowed hard and tried not to cry.

They rode in constricted silence for the better part of an hour. As they neared the city, cement housing projects hurled ominous shadows across neighborhoods of dilapidated *domicks*. Gracie watched an elderly woman pump water from a street pump into a dented metal container on a cart. A small child slammed the door to a peeling outhouse and ran up a dirt alleyway. A sudden gust of river wind bullied the tarpaper off roofs, and snared the slightest wisp of coal smoke spiraling skyward. Gracie wrinkled her nose against the odor of burning coal and diesel, and closed the car vents. Sometimes she had a hard time believing Russia had put a man in space.

She glanced again at Andrei. His stark expression chilled her to the bone. He still wore the faded leather work coat, threads dangling from the cuffs, a distinct contrast from his usual suit pants and crisp black leather jacket.

She touched his arm and he spooked. "Are you all right?" She still hadn't figured out how he'd retrieved the car without getting shot. Perhaps that's what had turned his face ghostly white. He looked at her, his brown eyes hard, wary.

"I'm fine."

Gracie's eyes burned at his clipped response. "Oh, Andrei," she rasped. "I'm so sorry. This is all my fault."

A frown creased Andrei's face. Gracie bit her lip and turned away from him. She couldn't bear to see the accusing expression.

Andrei turned onto Karl Marx Street.

"Where are we going?" Gracie asked. She didn't know the town well, but she felt pretty sure that her apartment was in the opposite direction.

Andrei didn't answer.

She swallowed, hard. "We're going to see that cop, aren't we."

He barely nodded.

Gracie rubbed her forehead with her hand, despair cresting over her. Andrei was washing his hands of her, dropping her into the grip of the FSB.

She could hardly blame him.

FSB Headquarters lived up to its ominous reputation. The mustard-yellow building encompassed a full city block and a freshly painted iron fence surrounded it like a prison barricade. *Oh, God, give me strength.*

Andrei gave his name and destination to the gate guard and received a pass to Inspector Shubnikov's office. He drove into a parking space, cut the ignition and stared at the building, mute, face blank.

Gracie fought tears. How quickly their sweet relationship had crumbled. She took hold of the door latch. "Thank you," she choked, then scrambled out of the car.

She headed for the front entrance door on legs of rubber, her heart pounding through her chest. Please let her gut feeling about Mr. FSB be right.

Two workmen were sweeping the sidewalk with bundled twigs. As she leaped up the wide marble steps, she scattered a flock of blue-gray pigeons.

In forty-eight hours, she'd lost nearly every friend she'd made in Russia. Thank the Lord, she still had Larissa. She shivered, feeling hollow.

A hand closed around her elbow and she nearly shot through her skin.

"Are you going without me?"

Stumbling, she caught her balance and whirled to meet Andrei's tight expression. She mumbled a negative reply.

His brown eyes softened and, for a moment, with some relief, she saw the old Andrei, the one who had once proposed. "We have an appointment to keep." He pulled her by the elbow up the stairs.

Except, he didn't let her go. Not even when they entered the front doors and stopped at the administration desk. She felt like Joan of Arc being led to the pyre.

Andrei presented identification to a chubby, uniformed woman who looked wider than she was tall. She nodded and pointed across the marble floor to a shiny new elevator. Clean. Efficient. Honest.

Yeah, right.

It would behoove her to remember she was entering the belly of the KGB, no matter what the golden plaque on the door now called the place.

Her mother would have a coronary on the spot. Gracie's chest tightened with each step.

The lift opened to a yawning, red-carpeted corridor. Above the chair rail, oils of distinguished officers with stoic faces and beady eyes followed her down the hall. Andrei stopped in the doorway of a noisy inner office. Suited FSB agents bent over piles of paperwork or scurried between desks. Phones buzzed and pockets of quiet conversation made the room hum. Gracie swallowed a lump of terror. Yanking her elbow from Andrei's grip, she wiped her sweaty palms on her jean dress.

Andrei conversed with the sentry at the door. The uniformed man pointed to an inner office.

The room screeched to silence as she threaded her way to Shubnikov's office. Heads turned, and her face flamed, a ghastly addition to her unpainted face, her greasy hair, her hiking boots and her rumpled jean dress. She looked like a hobo. Just the impression she wanted to make…

Shubnikov sat at his desk, a phone glued to his ear. He thumbed a coffee mug in one hand as he talked. His eyes flickered recognition when she appeared in the door, and he raised his mug to her, beckoning her inside. Another man, overweight and slouching at a messy desk, glanced up and gawked at her, as if she were a dancing poodle. No, wait, at least then she'd be pretty and groomed.

She tried to ignore him and marched up to Shubnikov's desk. Andrei shuffled in behind her.

Shubnikov's Russian was crisp and neat. The language rolled off his tongue, and the commanding tenor of his voice sent shivers up her spine. She put a hand on his desk and fought to hold herself together.

F.S.B. *Federal Scare Bureau.* She couldn't keep the nickname from searing her brain as she watched Shubnikov, his dark blue eyes, his close-cropped black hair, his matching black turtleneck and jeans.

No wonder Russians had a hard time distinguishing the good guys from the bad.

He set the receiver down on the cradle and met her gaze with brittle, red-rimmed eyes. Then he smiled kindly, like he had in the car when she'd crumpled in tears.

"*Dobra Ootra.*" He stood and indicated a chair.

Gracie returned the greeting. So he looked like an overworked thug this morning. He smelled good. Very good.

She tried not to think about her own delicious odor.

First thing she would do when she got home, before cleaning her flat, was take a shower. Maybe two.

"Good morning, Captain," she returned as she sat in a straight-back chair.

"I have some…disturbing news," Vicktor began before she could open her mouth.

She couldn't help notice that he looked suddenly bone weary, despite his freshly shaved, angular face. Like he'd spent the night at the office. Hopefully he'd been working on the case of the murdered missionaries. Still, Gracie wondered what news could be more distressing than her own.

"We found Leonid." Vicktor paused, sighed and set down his coffee cup.

Gracie braced herself. His gaze caught hers, as if trying to comfort.

"He's dead. Killed just like the Youngs."

"What?" Gracie clutched her chair seat with a white hand. Closing her eyes, she forced herself to hear his words.

"We found him last night. In his car, by the river. He hasn't been dead long."

Gracie felt Andrei touch her shoulder.

"Wh-what now?" she stammered. She glanced at Andrei. He was a ghost beside her, fear in his expression.

"We need to get you undercover, somewhere safe—"

Gracie read worry in Shubnikov's face.

"I don't know what they are after, or why, but I do believe you're in danger."

Gracie nodded, her heart a stone. Her plane left in two days. She prayed desperately that she'd be on it.

# Chapter Thirteen

The Wolf paid the hot-dog vendor seven rubles and took the paper-wrapped lunch.

"Ketchup?" the uniformed lady asked.

"*Nyet.*"

He turned, and found himself, as always, staring in momentary surprise at the beautiful woman waiting for him. She sat on the steps of the central fountain in Lenin Square, the wind brushing her short hair. Hair he loved to touch. She had her eyes closed. He could trace the outline of her face in his sleep.

He felt suddenly young, his heart beating wildly in his withering, flabby body. He'd never expected the rush of emotions their partnership had created. To think he planned his day, his weeks around these moments.

A fine mist hung in the air as he approached her. The sun turned it a kaleidoscope of hues. Pigeons picked around the square, eating seeds and other edible garbage left by tourists. A monkey on a leash beckoned visitors to take their picture with him.

She opened her eyes and smiled at him.

He felt a knife slice through his chest.

He already hated her at times, for what she'd done to him. For making him feel, for making him want. For that very reason, he couldn't take her with him. She didn't know it yet, but he saw liability in those beautiful brown eyes. Liability and heartache.

He wasn't a fool. He knew he'd lost his appeal years ago. She'd find another man, old or young didn't matter. She cooed sweet promises, but that would only make the pain unbearable.

He smiled and sat next to her. Her leg touched his, and he felt warmth ripple through his body. "It wasn't in her apartment," he managed to say.

"No, *Tovarish?*"

She used the old Russian term for *comrade* on purpose, because he liked it.

"And it's not in her bag." He'd searched it twice, then ripped it apart after Sergei delivered it from the village.

She chewed her lip, looking pensive. He narrowed his eyes. She knew the stakes as well as he. Had been with him when he'd made promises he couldn't break to men who knew how to make a liar suffer.

He turned his face into the wind. The breeze cooled the sweat dappled along his balding scalp. "It's up to our friend, then."

"Yes," she said, and there was worry in her voice.

He threw away the rest of his hot dog. It was already beginning to rot in his stomach.

"Gracie isn't going anywhere with you," Andrei growled from his perch behind Grace Benson. The chauffeur clamped one hand on her shoulder. The other he made into a fist.

Vicktor dragged his gaze off Grace's terrified face. He was in trouble. It wasn't just that she looked wrung out and tired, but the way she gazed at him, with the slightest edging of hope, had ignited all his protective instincts. For the first time he cared, momentarily, more about getting Grace safely out of Russia than nabbing the man who haunted him.

Vicktor narrowed his eyes at the dark expression on the chauffeur's face. "Miss Benson is in danger," he said in Russian. "Sorry, but at this point neither you, nor she, has a choice. She stays in my custody."

The glimmer of hate in Andrei's eyes struck Vicktor's weary nerves. "Listen, we have four dead bodies in the morgue, three of whom knew Miss Benson." He glanced at her, took in the way she stared at him trying to understand their conversation, and his voice turned hard. "I don't want her to be next."

"I don't, either," Andrei retorted, but indecision lurked on his face. The guy appeared ragged this morning, not the same chauffeur who had bared his teeth at Vicktor yesterday. Dressed in a faded, fraying leather coat and grimy work pants, he reeked like a farm animal. Fatigue etched furrows around his eyes, and a scowl creased his brow.

Vicktor held up a hand as if to offer peace. "How about some tea?" he suggested in English.

Suspicion tinged Andrei's expression, but he released his grip on Grace's shoulder. Grace's gaze roamed between the two men as she nodded.

Vicktor glanced at Maxim, who did a poor job of hiding in his paperwork. "Let's go to the conference room."

Vicktor led them through the office. In the corridor, he stepped aside and let Grace catch up. "Is this your first time in FSB Headquarters?"

The look she gave him made him long to crawl back to his office and hide under his desk. "Right. Sorry." He pointed to the oil paintings. "These are our generals."

"So I gathered."

Even he could admit he sounded like he was in junior high. He could use a little of Roman's legendary charm. Stopping at a thick oak door, Vicktor knocked twice, then stuck his head in. "In here, please."

The unsmiling portraits, the wood-paneled room and the flame-red carpet crushed any hint of welcome. Hello, Communism. Vicktor fixed a smile and indicated chairs at the oval oak table. Grace sat down and folded her hands in her lap. Andrei remained standing.

"Sit," Vicktor ordered. "Please," he added for Gracie's sake.

He turned to plug in the samovar, and heard the creak of leather as the chauffeur complied.

"The way I see it, Miss Benson is the last link between the Youngs and the Wolf," he began.

"The Wolf?" The tone in Grace's voice made him turn.

She'd gone ashen. He took a steadying breath and continued.

"The Wolf is a serial killer we've been tailing for nearly ten years. He's sly and he always kills with a hunting knife and without a struggle, which means he gets close enough to his victims to make them believe he's their friend."

The color had returned slightly to Gracie's cheeks and she feigned composure by tucking her hair behind her ears. "So, you think this Wolf killer knew Dr. Willie and Evelyn?"

"And Leonid, your chauffeur."

"*Their* chauffeur," she corrected.

"Their chauffeur," he repeated, shooting a look at Andrei. The man's arms were folded over his chest, his feet set wide on the floor, as if any moment he'd pounce. His rock-hard expression read *dubiousness*. If the Youngs' chauffeur was anything like Grace's, it was difficult to believe the Wolf had gotten near enough to kill them.

Unless Leonid had been an accomplice. The thought hit Vicktor and for a second, he just stared at the pair.

"So you're saying, maybe I know this Wolf?" Grace's question yanked him back.

He gave her kudos for guts. Knowing she was a possible target had to be unnerving.

Vicktor leaned a hip against the table and nodded.

"And you're going to keep me safe?"

The way she said it—doubtfully, but somehow thick with hope—made him wonder if he'd read her wrong. He managed another nod.

The samovar bubbled, steam coating the silver exterior. Vicktor listened to the thundering beat of his heart. "Tea?"

Grace smoothed her skirt. "Do you have instant coffee?"

Vicktor smiled. "I do."

Then she smiled. A real, here-comes-the-sun, I-sorta-trust-you smile, and he knew he'd run to Colombia to get it, if need be. "Can I trust you two to stay put while I go to my office?" He flicked a wary glance at Andrei.

Grace looked at Andrei, then back at Vicktor. "You can trust me." She leaned back in her chair, crossed one leg over the other and folded her hands on her lap. "I'll be here when you get back."

Yes, he could definitely say he liked her. She was brave, and something about the honesty in her expression drew him.

On the other hand, he'd like to send the chauffeur headfirst through the window.

"I'll be right back, then."

He dashed to his office, grabbed his mug and his container of instant coffee, and was out the door before Maxim even looked up from his desk.

Sprint-walking back down the hall, he saw two figures hovering near the conference room door, their backs to him.

"Spies, both of you!" he hissed as he approached. "What do you want?"

Yanna turned to him, looking sharp in a black skirt and white blouse. "She's in there, isn't she?"

Vicktor hid the coffee behind his back. "She came in to be questioned."

His friends exchanged looks.

"There's a killer after her, folks. What did you expect, that she would hide out in her village and cross her fingers?"

"You know," said Roman, "Americans have this thing. As soon as they're in trouble, they run right to the FSB for help. It's a real epidemic." Roman arched one eyebrow.

"I asked her chauffeur to bring her here today so I could question her. The Wolf, or somebody, ransacked her place yesterday and she was simply too shaken up to talk about it. She's not a suspect, and she needs protection."

"Your protection?" Yanna asked, and one side of her mouth tweaked up.

Vicktor frowned at her. "Yes." Definitely. "She just may be on his hit list, and I don't want any more dead bodies, especially hers."

Yanna stepped up to him, and peeked behind his back at the goods. "Well then, Stripes, I guess you need to protect her."

Roman leaned close to him. "She's cute. Need any help?"

Vicktor tossed him a sharp look. "When did you see her?"

"We watched from our stakeout position in the hall when you made riveting conversation about our respected leaders," Roman said, unsuccessfully concealing his grin.

Vicktor winced.

"It took about three seconds for the entire building to know you had an American in custody," Yanna said, smiling.

"She's not in custody."

"You might want to rethink that. It might be the best thing for her to spend a few days under FSB lock and key."

"Over my cold and rotting corpse."

Even Roman remained speechless.

Vicktor shook his head. "I can protect her my way, without scaring her further."

"I see," Roman said. "I hope you know what you're doing, pal."

Vicktor let himself linger on Roman's words, weighing them against his memory of the expression of trust on Gracie's face. "Me, too. Listen, I have to get in there before the chauffeur sneaks her out the window."

Yanna moved aside. "By the way, you're not thinking of taking her back to your place, are you?"

"Yes." Vicktor frowned at her. "It's safe, and the last place the Wolf would look."

Warning lit in Roman's eyes. "Think, buddy. She's not just an American woman, she's a *missionary*. There's no way she's going back to your flat. The impropriety alone would send her into fits."

"I don't think she's the type to have fits," Vicktor retorted, but his throat tightened. Good thing Roman hadn't been on the train. No wonder his threat to ride with her to Vladivostok had worked.

Roman raised his hands in surrender. "The point being, she's not going to stay there with you…alone. Trust me on this one."

Vicktor studied his two cohorts. "Why?"

Even Yanna looked astonished. "Vicktor, not to put it too bluntly, but according to Mae and David, Christians don't like to have their honor compromised. Even *I* can figure that out."

"I wouldn't even think of it."

"I know that, but she doesn't." Yanna flicked a glance at Roman, then smiled, the corners of her eyes crinkling. "How about a chaperone?"

Vicktor squinted at them.

"What if Yanna and I come over tonight, just to keep tabs on you two?" Roman suggested.

"I sense a conspiracy here."

Roman and Yanna exchanged expressions of horror.

Roman clamped him on the shoulder. "Vicktor, I'm on your side. You want to keep her safe? What's better than having three trained FSB agents hovering over her? And she'll feel better with another woman around."

Yanna nodded, apparently enjoying the moment.

Vicktor shook his head but couldn't suppress a smile. "You should both be working for Black Ops, the way you blindside your targets."

They laughed.

"See you tonight," he said as he entered the conference room.

Gracie cupped her hands around the hot mug of coffee, blew on the steam and let Vicktor's kindness wash over her. Offering her a cup of coffee, running down to his office to fetch it, then giving her his mug seemed such a simple act. But the generosity of it warmed her to her bones. Although the instant coffee was a poor imitation of fresh-brewed beans, with each sip, courage seeped into her spirit.

Next to her, Andrei fingered his teacup, muttering to himself. What was his problem? Wasn't it his idea to drag her here in the first place?

Gracie didn't know what to think about her chauffeur, but as sun cascaded into the dark room, turning the carpet rose-red and polishing the oak table, her fear of FSB Captain Vicktor Shubnikov was dying to an ember.

Vicktor sat next to her, a finger circling the brim of his cup, also filled with coffee. She noticed, as he entered the room, a fresh smile on his face. It ignited a strange feeling inside. She had the very unnerving, and completely delectable feeling that Captain Shubnikov might just be a good bodyguard indeed.

The thought widened her eyes and she gulped her coffee down. *Way to go, Gracie. Look at his blue eyes and muscles instead of his heart.* Had she learned nothing two years ago? Except, she felt as if she *had* gotten a glimpse of his heart...and something about it made her feel just a little...safe.

"First thing we need to do is change your appearance."

"Change my appearance?" Now that suggestion hurt. What was wrong with her that he didn't like what he saw? Or rather, why did she always let her heart make the decisions for her brain?

Vicktor ran his gaze over her, head to toe and back. Gracie cringed under his scrutiny, knowing she looked like she'd slept in an alley. "Why?" She smoothed her skirt. "What's wrong with how I look?" Oh, there was way too much vulnerability in that question.

His expression turned apologetic. "Nothing." He ran a hand over his cropped hair, his gaze darting away from hers. "You just look so...American."

Gracie frowned, then kicked out her feet and surveyed her hiking boots, her thick white socks and her ankle-length dress. A hand went to her greasy, unkempt hair. "Okay, you win. But I'm not dyeing my hair."

He looked up at her, smiling. His eyes twinkled. "I wouldn't even think it."

So maybe she'd been just a little hard on him.

Vicktor squinted into the rearview mirror. Time to lose the chauffeur. The guy was like a bulldog. He not only bristled at the suggestion that Vicktor take Grace shopping, but now he drove so close, he'd ram right up their tailpipe if Vicktor touched the brakes. Vicktor bit back his irritation and answered Grace's question.

"I learned my English at Moscow University."

"You're very good. Barely an accent. I can hardly tell you're Russian."

"Is that so bad?"

"No, I didn't mean that at all." She cringed, and he felt like a heel.

But still, it was telling. Maybe it wasn't a strike against him to be Russian.

By her blush, he knew she was sorry. "No problem."

She twisted her hands in her lap. "No, really, I like Russia, and Russians. I couldn't be here if I didn't. I have a lot of Russian friends, I like Russian food..."

He suppressed a grin, and without thinking, reached over and touched her hand, silencing her explanation. "It's okay, Miss Benson. I'm not offended."

She sighed, and he was achingly aware of the softness of her skin. He yanked back his hand, feeling it tingle. The rumble of street traffic and the tick of his ancient engine invaded the sudden silence.

"Please, call me Gracie," she whispered.

*Gracie.* Yeah, he liked that. "And we can dispense with the Captain Shubnikov." He drummed his fingers on the steering wheel while they sat at a red light. "My name's Vicktor."

"I remember," she said, staring out the window.

He wondered if she also remembered his arms around her, protecting her in the doorway of her apartment. He surely did. That and her smell, and the way she let her emotions unravel in the car...

So maybe a chaperone or two this evening *was* a good idea.

He parked in front of *Dom Adezhda*—the House of Clothing. In what had once been the state department store, a hundred budding capitalists hawked their recent clothing finds, from Italian leather to Chinese polyester, in aisle after aisle of crammed kiosks.

Gracie jumped out of the car and Vicktor opened the front door for her. He gritted his teeth as Andrei scooted in behind her. On their heels, Vicktor felt like a tagalong.

The latest in European fashions stretched across modern silver mannequins, and ebony boots, in softened leather, lined glass showcases at the end of each long row of kiosks. Thankfully, the store was still empty, but Vicktor soon realized their liability. Vendors trailed them like hungry puppies, barking out sales pitches, prices and fresh deals as they wandered up and down the aisles.

Gracie seemed to be in no hurry, stopping now and again to examine skirts. Andrei strolled beside her, translating quietly into her ear, hands shoved into his coat pockets. Vicktor pursed his lips, annoyance building with each step.

Gracie halted, staring at a wall of long, straight black skirts. She pointed to one, and the clerk took it down, then pulled it open to reveal an attractive side split. Gracie wrinkled her nose and shook her head.

Vicktor sighed. The skirts were either too short, or too long, or too tight. He would have liked to see any of them on her.

He sidled up to her and grabbed her elbow. She stiffened.

"Sorry, I didn't mean to startle you."

"That's okay," Gracie said, but fear had leaped into her eyes.

He softened his voice and leaned close, noticing the whisper of floral scent skimming her skin. "Anything would look good on you. Please, hurry."

She suppressed a smile. He was pleased to see her blush, but hoped his words hit home. The longer she clomped through the store in those painfully ugly hiking boots, the more dangerous her world became.

She continued to meander down the aisle. Vicktor buried his hands in his trench-coat pockets and followed her with as much patience as he could muster.

Two fruitless stops later, worry pushed him to his limit. Ignoring Andrei's stinging glare, he placed a hand on the small of her back and maneuvered Gracie toward an unmanned kiosk.

"Pick something out, please."

The expression on his face must have startled her, for her eyes widened.

"I don't wear these kinds of clothes, Vicktor. I don't know what to get."

He liked the sound of his name on her lips. "I'll help you." Scanning the aisle he made eye contact with a clerk. She hustled up to the booth.

"We'll take that," he said, pointing to a short black dress with a flared skirt.

She handed it to Gracie and motioned her toward a dressing room. Gracie screwed up her pretty face, unsure.

"Just try it on."

She disappeared into the booth, looking doubtful.

Five minutes later she was grinning at herself in a long mirror.

Vicktor barely disguised his delight. Oh yeah, hidden under all that denim was a woman that just might kick up his heart rate if he wasn't careful.

Who was he kidding? He could already feel the pulse in his ears.

The black dress skimmed her curves, flaring out just above the knees, conservatively longer than the latest thigh-high fashion but short enough to reveal some seriously shaped legs. Gracie wrapped her arms around her body. Vicktor stepped up behind her and pulled them down, revealing her figure. He could admit he wore his heart in the gesture, but he couldn't help himself. She needed this dress.

"I'm getting this for you." He pulled out his wallet and fingered two hundred-ruble notes.

"No, Vicktor, I can pay—"

"Now, boots and some stockings," he said, and pointed to a pair of slender ankle boots under the glass countertop. The salesgirl handed them, and a pair of packaged black hosiery, to Gracie.

Gracie took them, but said, "I don't know, Vicktor. They aren't me. They're too…Russian."

Vicktor met her eyes. "That's the point. Trust me, I won't let it go to my head, even though it'll be difficult." *Liar, liar.*

Gracie blushed and fled into the dressing room, followed by the salesgirl.

Vicktor ignored Andrei's glower.

Giggles, then Gracie emerged.

How he loved it when he was right. His breath caught in his chest. She'd swept up her hair, the color of creamy butter against the overhead lights, into a loose inverted bun, fastened with a gold clip provided by the inventive clerk. Her eyes sparkled and she wore a delicious expression of delight. Vicktor could barely swallow past the lump in his throat. He moved forward, intending to indulge her with a well-deserved compliment, but Andrei beat him to it.

"Wow."

Vicktor couldn't tell if Andrei was impressed, or disturbed by his new Russianized girlfriend, but Gracie smiled, pleased by his comment.

Vicktor dredged up his voice and suggested lunch at a local cafe.

"I thought we were to stay undercover," Andrei said.

"We are." Vicktor gestured toward Gracie. "Who is going to recognize her? A little red lipstick and she'd pass for my cousin from Moscow."

"No red lipstick, please," Gracie said, laughing.

Andrei frowned. "I don't think that is a good idea. You never know who could be watching. Maybe they followed us into the store."

"Who followed you?"

Gracie glanced at Andrei. Guilt darkened their faces and Vicktor felt as if he'd been punched in the chest.

"We were shot at this morning in the village," Andrei admitted in a low tone.

"Excuse me?" Vicktor clenched his fists to keep from turning this idiotic chauffeur inside out. "Why didn't you tell me this before?" He glowered first at Andrei, then at Gracie. She shrank before him. So much for the trust.

Gracie's face conveyed her feelings of regret. "I'm sorry. When you told me about Leonid, well, I was so upset, I just forgot."

"You *forgot* to tell me you were shot at?" The sarcasm in his voice was so biting, she winced.

He turned to Andrei and spoke in low, staccato Russian. "If you want to help your girlfriend stay alive, I suggest you start trusting me. I don't want to hurt you. I just want to find the killer and keep her out of trouble. You have nothing to fear from me."

Andrei hooded his eyes. "*Da,* right, I've heard that before."

*What?* Vicktor frowned, but before he could reply, Andrei grabbed Gracie's arm and pulled her out of the booth and down the aisle, leaving Vicktor to pay the eager salesgirl.

# Chapter Fourteen

❧

The Wolf's knuckles whitened on the steering wheel. His jaw muscles ached and sweat pooled in the etching around his right eye. They'd been inside for nearly an hour. He certainly hoped his little spy hadn't conjured up any rash ideas about ditching him. The noon sun was beginning to bake the Moscovitz, the odor of dusty leather irritating his already raw nerves. Two days they'd been chasing the girl and the closest they'd gotten to her was a parking spot thirty feet from the local department store where she was shopping.

That was about to change.

The words of a man greater than he rang in his ears. *"Death solves all problems. No man, no problems."* He should take Father Stalin's advice and apply it to Sergei. The ineptitude of the man soured the Wolf's empty stomach. He glowered at the entrance, willing her to appear.

Grace came barreling out of the double doors first, then, on her tail, her chauffeur, appearing pensive and annoyed. Relief washed over the Wolf and he felt the blood flow into his clenched fists. He fixed his attention on Gracie and felt a smile on his face. What had happened to the missionary? The woman was a looker in that sculptured black dress and ankle boots. Except, who was she trying to fool? Without a hint of makeup, she was a walking Stars and Stripes. No Russian woman under the age of fifty in her right mind would leave the house without a thick layer of makeup.

The Wolf licked his lips and his stomach growled. He watched her stop on the sidewalk and talk with her driver. She seemed angry, her face screwed up in frustration. He wished he were close enough to catch her words.

A second later, the FSB agent joined them, pouncing into their conversation like a tiger. The Wolf couldn't help but smile. Vicktor Shubnikov still couldn't rein in his anger. That fact had worked to the Wolf's advantage on at least one occasion and he hoped it would make Vicktor sloppy now. He was counting on Shubnikov to deliver Grace Benson safely into his arms.

"How can you expect me to protect you if you won't trust me?"

Vicktor's accusation stung and Gracie flinched. He raked a gaze over her, then turned away, kneading the back of his neck. Remorse rushed through her.

Next to her, Andrei glowered at Vicktor. Leather squeaked as he folded his arms across his chest. The set of his jaw turned Gracie cold.

Andrei *hated* Vicktor. She placed a hand on Andrei's arm. His eyes warmed slightly when they reached her.

"We should have told him," she murmured.

"Why?" He leaned close. "Haven't you learned not to trust Russian cops?"

Gracie drew a breath, unsure if she was being naive or acting in faith. "I think we can trust him, Andrei. There's something about him..." She peeked at Vicktor, and blushed when she saw his gaze on her. What was it about Mr. FSB

I'm-full-of-surprises that drew her like a campfire, flickering yet dangerous. And the look in his eyes when he'd seen her in the dress… She liked that far more than she should, probably.

She met Andrei's glacial stare. He pursed his lips and looked away.

Vicktor's eyes were on her. She shifted, feeling a blaze start at her toes and rush clear to her ears. "I really am sorry, Vicktor," she said. "I didn't mean to deceive you. It was truly an oversight. I'll trust you from now on."

Raw shock flickered in his eyes so briefly, it could have been a blink. Still, Gracie saw it and it rocked her. Her trust meant something to him.

Beside her, Andrei harrumphed.

Silence stretched between them. Vicktor cleared his throat. Gracie drew her coat around her. Andrei glared at traffic.

"How about some lunch?" Vicktor offered a wry smile, and she saw in it forgiveness. And the smallest beginning of friendship. Oh no, she should not, should *not,* unlock her heart for this man.

Even if he did make her feel beautiful, greasy hair and all.

Gracie nodded and followed him to his car, aware of the steam rising off Andrei. She hoped he followed them.

Vicktor opened her door as she climbed in, then shut it behind her. Gracie clasped her hands in her lap. He slid into the driver's seat and tossed a bag into the back.

"What's that?" Gracie asked.

"Your American outfit."

"Oh," Gracie said, realizing she'd completely forgotten to pick up her clothes when Andrei dragged her from the store. "Thanks."

Vicktor shrugged, but she saw him smile. So, he was thoughtful, too. And taking her out for lunch.

*And a KGB agent.* Where was her voice of reason when she needed it?

It was behind her, closing in on their rear bumper, a look of fury on his face. Gracie turned around and waved, hoping that Andrei wouldn't think she had ditched him. Despite her chauffeur's caustic behavior, she was still grateful for his hovering. She wasn't quite ready to be abandoned into the hands of a Russian cop, regardless of the fact that she felt a thousand times safer with him around.

And with her less-than-stellar history with men, how strange was that?

Gracie buckled herself in and fiddled with the shoulder strap.

"So, do you have any idea who might be following you?"

"Not the faintest."

Vicktor picked up his cellphone and dialed. "I'm going to send someone to check on Andrei's parents." She heard him fire off rapid Russian, grateful he'd moved past anger to action. He closed his phone and slipped it into his pocket. "How would the Wolf know you were in the village?"

"Are you sure it's the Wolf?"

Vicktor glared at the Moscovitz in front of him and did a quick lane change. "No, but we have some pretty strong evidence pointing to him."

Gracie smoothed her skirt. Every nerve in her body pricked. *The Wolf.* What a horrible label. *Please, God, don't let this Wolf be after me.*

Vicktor drove down Karl Marx Street, past hot-dog vendors and babushkas selling barely-lavender lilacs. He turned toward the wharf. "I know a great little lunch spot."

Gracie cracked her window open and the fresh smell of the Amur River spiced the air. Her stomach growled and she pressed the palm of her hand against it.

"I don't know how such a small person can have a growl that large."

Gracie blushed, aware that his sweet words tugged at her defenses. He was going to make her enjoy his company despite herself.

"Let's see if we can silence that monster."

The street opened up into a scenic parking area. A wharf, with an ancient ferry moored at the end of a cement pier, took center stage. Thick ropes hung from post to post, ringing the parking area and protecting the boardwalk that meandered along the riverfront.

Down the beach, beyond a cluttering of fishing boats and ferries, smoke spiraled from a shish-kabob vendor's grill. A slight wind scurried off the river and brushed the willows and evergreen standing sentry on the hills above the river port.

Vicktor pulled up to a stone wall pushing back a grassy hill at the far end of the lot. He got out and moved around the car and opened her door.

Gracie frowned, searching for a restaurant. "Where are we eating?"

"You'll see."

Gracie couldn't help but warm to his smile. He stuck out an elbow.

"Protection."

She nodded, but her pulse skipped as they walked close, her hand resting on his arm, his hand cupped over hers. Her edginess calmed under his protective stance, and, as they walked up a set of wide stone stairs, she twined her fingers in his trench coat. Oh, he smelled good. She barely felt like the same, grimy girl next to him.

Okay, that wasn't quite true, but she did like the dress. And with her hair up, she didn't look so pitiful. In fact, on his arm she felt nearly ethereal, and not at all like she'd been dodging bullets in a farmyard earlier that morning.

It hadn't escaped her that maybe, just maybe, God was answering her prayers for protection in a six-foot-something, muscles-and-grins Russian cop. And wasn't *that* a surprise?

They walked on a blacktop path, along a cliff high above the river. The breeze nuzzled the shoreline and the sun sifted through the forest to their right, winking from behind the trees in dazzling explosions of light. Springtime fragrances—lilac, jasmine and honeysuckle—saturated the air. As they walked in silence, Gracie felt her anxiety slough off her. She sighed, long and deep.

"Are you okay?" Vicktor asked, casting her a worried look. Grace met his eyes and nodded.

His gaze lingered on her face, searching. He smiled. "You really do look incredible in that dress."

She grinned, and something passed between them that made the little hairs rise on the back of her neck. No, she should not like him this much. Not when she was on the next plane out of Russia, never to return.

Maybe.

"Where are we going?" Gracie asked.

"My friend runs a little cafe overlooking the river. He'll give us a private room for lunch."

Gracie couldn't ignore the lurch in her stomach when he said "private." Obviously her demons hadn't quite died. A chill washed through her and her smile faded. "Sounds great," she squeaked. Peeking over her shoulder, she was horrified to see Andrei nowhere in sight.

"Where's Andrei?" she asked, fighting the tremor in her voice.

Vicktor glanced behind him, then shrugged. "Maybe he decided to trust you to my care."

Right, when the moon turned blue. "Maybe," she murmured. She couldn't help wonder, however, if FSB Agent Vicktor Shubnikov had ditched her poor chauffeur.

She loosened her hold.

They climbed a small rise and ambled toward a lighthouse. Vicktor led Gracie around the front, to a walled lookout. On the beach below, the cheers of volleyball players dressed in sweatpants and jackets drifted up and mingled with the caw of magpies and crows. Ships dotted the river, which stretched like a blue ribbon into the far horizon. On the far bank, she glimpsed tiny *dachas* nestled into the trees—garden homes of

Khabarovsk's city dwellers. Larissa's *dacha* sat somewhere among them. Sadness thickened her throat. A nippy breeze whistled off the river and she shivered.

"Ready for lunch?" Vicktor asked.

Gracie forced a nod, wishing she didn't have a past to haunt her, to push against the pleasure of being in this handsome man's company.

Vicktor turned and opened a little door tucked in an alcove of the lighthouse.

"It's in the lighthouse?" Gracie asked in surprise. Vicktor smiled, his blue eyes twinkling. She walked past him and stood inside as Vicktor met a maître d' and shook his hand. The thin maître d', dressed in black pants and a sailor's jacket, led them through the cafe.

Gracie's boots clicked on the white tile floor as she passed aquariums of neon fish and baby sharks. She identified strains of Bach's Brandenburg Concerto drifting on hidden speakers. Vicktor took her elbow and guided her down a set of spiral stairs toward a tiny room. Nestled inside, like a ship's cabin, was a booth nudged up to a floor-to-ceiling picture window. Gracie gulped a deep breath and slid into the private alcove. All grins, Vicktor slid in opposite her. He took the menus and the maître d' closed the door behind him.

They were alone.

Together.

Gracie folded her hands on the table, battling to still them. She swallowed her irrational fear and forced a smile.

Vicktor laid a hand over hers. "Don't worry, Gracie. The Wolf won't find you here. You're safe."

At the moment, it wasn't the Wolf she feared.

Her hand was ice. Vicktor studied her vain attempt to conceal her fear and his heart sank. If he didn't know better, he'd wonder if she was afraid of…him.

Oh no. He cleared his throat and withdrew his hand. Burying his attention in the menu, he scanned the choices without seeing them. A smart man would have noticed the way she tensed up after noticing Andrei's absence.

And here he thought she actually *trusted* him. In fact he'd thought…no, it didn't matter what he thought. "Do you know what you want?" *Women*. Every word he'd spoken to Roman suddenly seemed gut-wrenchingly true. "They have great salmon steaks here."

Gracie's eyes went to the window. "Sure."

He set his jaw and thumbed the menu. Silence ripened between them. What an idiot he was to—

She sniffled.

What? He stared at her. A tear hung on her lash and another streaked down her face, despite her clenched jaw.

"Gracie. What's the matter?" He couldn't keep the worry from his tone at seeing her come apart. Not Gracie, the woman who had kicked him black and blue in the train car. Unable to stop himself, he reached across the table and thumbed away a tear. "What did I do? I'm…sorry."

A smile came to her face. She met his eyes. The look in them only made his throat thick. Just when he decided she was hiding something, she had to go and be…vulnerable.

"You are a kind person."

His breath staggered. "Not usually."

She squinted at him, taking in his words. He withdrew his hand and tucked it under the table, hiding a sudden annoying tremor. The piped-in strains of a concert violin drew out a mournful and sad note.

"Maybe you bring out the best in me," he said, wanting it to be true.

Her eyes widened. "Oh. Wow. That's…" She looked out the window.

"Please, Gracie, tell me what's wrong." *And please, don't let it be anything to do with Andrei*. Like suddenly missing him.

Sadness colored her expression. "It's nothing. Just something that happened a long time ago. Occasionally it creeps up on me."

"I see." His mind conjured a number of horrid scenarios that made him wince. "I'm sorry if I caused it." Boy, was he sorry, especially when he'd wooed himself into really enjoying this unplanned lunchtime escape. He'd wanted that smile, those green eyes, maybe even her laughter all to himself.

But, honestly, he hadn't been trying to ditch Andrei. Not once.

Gracie scanned the room. "It is a safe room, isn't it?"

Vicktor frowned, nodding.

She laced her hands on the table, playing with her thumbs. "Do you come here a lot?"

So they really were changing the topic. Okay, he wouldn't push. Not yet. He shook his head as he answered, wishing he could lie and ignite a spark of jealousy. The truth was, however, he'd never been here on a date…if he could call this a date, which he couldn't. "My buddy Roman has money in this place. He helped a mutual friend fix it up after the FSB ran out the local mafia."

She looked impressed. "It's nice. Cozy." She reached for the menu. "Have you been with the FSB for a long time?"

Her voice stayed light, but he wondered what his answer would mean to her. Could a missionary trust a man who had dedicated his life to an organization that sent thousands of Christians to their deaths during the Communist reign?

He cleared his throat, thankful he could answer honestly. "No."

She interrupted her scan of the menu and caught his eye. "But you seem so…practiced."

He couldn't help but smile at her search for the right word. He hoped she meant *capable* or even…*brave?* "I've been a cop for over ten years. Before that, I was a soldier in the Russian army for a number of years. I even served in Special Forces." He liked the interest written on her face. Usually cops scared the general Russian population into deep freeze. He appreciated a woman who didn't bristle at the sight of militia.

"Do you enjoy it?" She folded the menu, eyes glued on his face, her concentration chipping at his walls of privacy.

"Yes." He shrugged out of his suit coat. Honeyed light dappled the white table through lace curtains and the white rose in the center of the table perfumed the room. Maybe it was a date, after all.

Leaning forward on her bench, her body language spoke anticipation. "Yes?"

"I never thought I'd be a cop." That felt good to finally admit. Her wide smile reeled him in and he felt himself relax. "I always enjoyed detective work, but since my pop was a cop, I didn't want to live a cop's life."

Her eyebrows arched in silent question.

"Because he couldn't shake the darkness. It rode him home every night and seeped into his moods."

A shadow fell across her face, her eyes.

"No, he wasn't ever abusive or anything. He's a pretty good guy, and a great cop." He fixed his gaze on his drumming fingers. "It's just that he couldn't shake the frustration of seeing lives shattered and killers escape." He met her piercing gaze and attempted a wry smile. "I guess I inherited his indignation."

"Or his sense of justice." She reached across the table, cupped her hand over his.

Hers was remarkably warmer. He stopped his drumming.

A knock at the door made them both jump. Gracie yanked back her hand. Vicktor grabbed the menu. The waiter entered the room, surveying them like choice cuts of meat.

"Decided?" Vicktor asked, ashamed at his rocky voice.

Gracie peered at him, her head lowered. "Whatever you're having."

He noticed the tinge of pink on her cheeks.

Vicktor frowned. "Gracie, can you read the menu?"

She shrugged.

He held up a finger to the waiter. "One minute, please."

"Gracie," he said gently. "How is it you've lived in Russia for three years—"

"Two—"

"Two," he corrected. "And you haven't learned to read Russian?"

She fingered a rebellious hair that had fallen from her hair clip. "I was only here short term, so I never learned. I had a translator and fumbled my way through."

He leaned back in the booth, watching her smooth her hair, then her skirt. She smiled at him, her eyes rich and sweet.

He was suddenly thankful that Roman and Yanna would be at his apartment to chaperone. Maybe he wasn't quite as trustworthy as he claimed.

She shrugged. "I know how to say, 'I don't understand.' I use it a lot." She wiggled her brows.

He had to admire her for the pluck it took to live and work in a country where she could barely buy bread.

"How did you survive?"

"The grace of God, I guess. He always gave me the right charades and lots of bilingual friends."

She reminded him of Roman and Mae, with her faith in God. He felt a pang of emptiness, and he stared at the menu, seeing nothing. A woman like this didn't just wander through a man's life without turning it inside out. If he kept hanging around Gracie Benson he'd either have to dodge her faith or slam right into it.

He felt her hand on his arm and nearly jumped.

"A salmon steak and fried potatoes sounds good."

"I'll go tell the waiter," he said, scrambling for a quick escape.

Gracie watched him leave and blew out a shredded breath. He certainly had a way of wheedling inside her good graces. She had nearly cracked when he touched her cheek and placed the blame for her fears on his shoulders. Poor guy. She'd had to restrain her tattered emotions and construct a hasty defense. Thankfully, he didn't press her. The last thing she needed was to dissolve into tears, reliving the horror of her nightmare with Tommy.

She couldn't tell Investigator Shubnikov that she'd been… raped. By a man she'd been dating. Yeah, that would make their relationship take off with a roar. Either he'd peg her into a category…or he'd never touch her again.

Relationship? Touch? Just because she felt somewhat safe in his protection didn't mean she was going to give away her heart.

And… She was leaving. *Pay attention to your future, Gracie.*

Except, he had the most intriguing, nearly transparent blue eyes. And a voice that made her tingle. And he *was* kind, despite his offhanded compliment meant to give her the credit. True, it had delighted her, but the guy had a history of kindness…even when she'd aimed for his jaw with her boots on the train. He could have just as easily handcuffed her and hauled her away.

Instead, he'd let her cry, without criticizing.

He'd fetched her coffee.

He'd bought her a dress…a dress that made her feel beautiful. Or was that due to the appreciation in his eyes?

And didn't that feel good.

Her face grew hot as she realized how much she enjoyed his ministrations. Someone better write it on her hand, and fast, that he was a Russian cop. More than that, she barely knew him. Most of all—and this was something that should make her get up and run for the border—*he wasn't a Christian.* She closed her eyes. "Oh, God, please give me wisdom and help me to think clearly. Help me not to fall for him."

The door handle clicked and Gracie added a hasty "My heart can't take another disappointment." She opened her eyes.

Her breath caught in her chest.

"I've found you."

# Chapter Fifteen

❧

What was Andrei doing here?

Larissa set down her cup of tea. "I thought you were with Gracie."

Andrei sat on the edge of Larissa's desk, rattling his key chain, picking out each key and examining it.

"She's with the FSB. The agent took her out to lunch."

Larissa grabbed the keys from his hand. "The FezB? Andrei, are you crazy? You're supposed to protect her from people like the FSB."

"Maybe he can do a better job." His voice was tight. "We were shot at today."

She saw the streaks of red in his eyes and knew she was in big trouble.

"Andrei." She came around the desk and touched his arm. "Are you okay?"

He covered his face with his hands. "She's going to get hurt. I can feel it. This FSB guy says the Wolf is after her. *The Wolf.* That can't be true, can it?"

She stepped back, his expression scaring her. "The Wolf is a myth." They'd all heard the stories—who hadn't?—about a serial killer who eliminated people who betrayed the *Rodina*. People who acted for themselves in this new era, people who didn't give a second glance at history and sacrifice and everything Russia stood for.

Russians had to band together to survive change, like dogs in a pack. Survival ran in the Russian blood, but some had to be reminded of it. The Wolf myth did that—reminded, and led by example. It was a lesson from the era of the NKVD—"terror is power." She could understand why the FSB might use the power of the Wolf on Andrei. The death of foreigners, especially missionaries, would have to be dealt with delicately, quietly, domestically.

But why scare Gracie?

Unless the FSB was after something. Something they thought Gracie knew, or *had*.

"You need to get her away from him."

"What?" Andrei grabbed up his keys. "She's safer with him. Wolf myth or not, they're shooting at us. They almost killed Gracie today. I'm not going to let her die."

"I think she's safer with you."

Andrei's eyes hardened, and for a moment it rattled her. She could do this. She had to do this. She put a hand on his arm. "If you love her, you must keep her safe."

He whirled, stalking toward the door. Then he stopped. "She'll only be safe when she's out of Russia."

Larissa fingered the necklace at the base of her throat. *Won't we all.*

Gracie pressed her hand to her chest as recognition washed over her. "Pastor Yuri, you nearly scared the life out of me!"

Pastor Yuri closed the door behind him, his smile crinkling his eyes and turning up the corners of his steel-gray handlebar mustache.

"Sorry, Gracie, I didn't mean to startle you." He extended a fleshy hand to her.

She took it, noticing it was slightly sweaty.

"I'm so glad I finally found you. Are you okay?"

"What are you doing here?" Gracie fought the urge to wipe her hand on her skirt.

Yuri grinned at her. His thinning gray hair glistened in the sunlight. He appeared grossly unkempt today, nothing like the Sunday-morning spit-and-polished pastor who spoke from the pulpit. His white shirt bunched loosely at his waistline tire, a black tie hung slightly ajar, and his face was red. If she didn't know better, she'd accuse him of drinking.

Gracie indicated the opposite bench. "Sit down, please. How did you find me?"

"I saw you at the riverfront. I was just coming out of the orphanage across the street."

So that's why he was red-faced. If she knew Yuri, he'd spent the last hour playing tag with a group of gangly, parentless ten-year-olds.

"We've been worried sick about you. We called your flat but there was no answer."

"I've been…hiding." She lowered her eyes, ashamed she'd been so irresponsible as to not call him. "But I think I'll be safe now. Thank you."

He shook his head. "I'm afraid we have a problem. Your mission needs to speak to you. You need to come to my office and call them."

"What about?"

Yuri gave her a pained expression. "They are afraid for your safety."

Of course. Guilt tugged at Gracie. She should have called them. Her oversight had been inexcusable.

He reached out to her. "I'm sorry. Can you come now? I think we should call immediately."

Gracie fumbled to sort her thoughts. She felt Yuri's hand on her arm. "Yes, of course. But I have to tell Vicktor."

"We can tell him on the way out."

She slipped from the booth. He opened the door for her. "Can you wait while I find him?"

"Of course." He took her elbow, practically marching her toward the stairs.

At the top landing, she scanned the open room for Vicktor. "He's not here." Yuri was pushing her, gently, toward the door. "Wait, Pastor, I must tell Vicktor. He'll worry."

"Why don't we leave a message with the maître d'?"

"I understand, but really, I'm sure Vicktor will be upset. Please, just wait, let me find him—"

"Find who?"

Gracie whirled, and relief flooded her as she spied Vicktor striding toward her from across the room. Except, he had a darkness in his eyes that sent a shiver down her spine.

"Vicktor! I was looking all over for you!" she exclaimed, a little too brightly.

He scrutinized the man behind her. "Sorry, I was at the bar, trying to get you a soda."

"I bumped into Pastor Yuri and he said I need to go to Headquarters and call my mission. Evidently, they're worried for my safety."

"As they should be," Vicktor replied, but Gracie heard the edge in his voice. "Were you going to leave without telling me?" His gaze never left Pastor Yuri.

She shook her head, feeling suddenly uneasy.

Pastor Yuri stuck out a hand. "Yuri Visilovich Mikhailovich. Glad to meet you."

A muscle pulled in Vicktor's jaw as he took Yuri's hand. "We're having lunch right now, Pastor. Can it wait? I can assure you I'll keep her safe."

Gracie knew Vicktor well enough to know it wasn't a request.

"Sure," came Pastor Yuri's easy reply, as if he hadn't nearly hauled her, feet tripping, up the stairs.

Gracie stared at him, frowning as he smiled at her.

"See you later, Gracie," he said.

Gracie could only nod, and watch him as he left.

Vicktor put a hand on Gracie's lower back. When he finally met her eyes, his expression had changed.

She wondered, with a streak of fear, just what exactly he'd meant when he said, "keep her safe."

"How did he get in here?" Vicktor asked after he settled her back into her side of the booth. His heartbeat was about to betray him and he fought to keep his voice schooled. Didn't she listen to anything he said? He turned away from her, wanting to hit something, hard. Why couldn't she just cooperate?

"He just came in. He was at the orphanage across the street. He said my mission board was trying to contact me."

Vicktor forced a calm tone. "But what if he were the guy trying to kill you. You just got up and would have left with him! See, that's why I want you to listen to me."

She stared at him with a stark expression. "He's the pastor of the church, Vicktor. Don't be so suspicious."

"My job is to be suspicious. Besides, one near miss a day isn't enough for you? Trying to go double or nothing?" He looked away from her. "With a serial killer out there, I'm the *only* person in Russia you should trust at the moment. Please, in the future, don't go anywhere without me."

Silence answered him. When he turned back he noticed she'd folded her arms across her chest, and now stared out the window. Yeah, well, he felt the same way. So much for their "date."

He flipped open his cell phone and dialed Yanna. Glancing at Gracie, he spoke quickly. "Yanna, find me everything you can on Yuri Visilovich Mikhailovich. He's a pastor."

Gracie didn't spare him a glance. Probably, hopefully, she hadn't understood his words.

Moments later, the waiter brought their salmon and potatoes. She ate in silence. He pushed around his food, his appetite soured by frustration.

He refrained from taking her hand as they walked back down the boardwalk. The fresh breeze shifted through his hair and he heard laughter from the beach below. A kite lifted above the trees, its red tail dancing in the wind. Vicktor walked with his hand on the small of her back, his gaze scanning their path. Maybe locking her up at HQ was exactly what he should be doing.

He hated how the wind reaped a delicious scent from her skin. "Forgive me, Vicktor. I know you're only trying to protect me. Yuri would never hurt me, but I will listen to you. I *am* trying to trust you."

He slanted her a dubious look. Her green eyes caught his, and he couldn't deny she delivered apologies with convincing sincerity. The breeze played with rebellious golden wisps that had escaped from her hair clip, feathering the strands across her face.

He stopped, and couldn't believe it when he caught her hair, pushed it behind her ear. So maybe her words meant more than he would admit.

"Okay. No more fast escapes and I'll forgive you."

She smiled, and it was so sweet, he couldn't help but smile back. Yes, this was much better than locking her up at HQ.

The sight of Andrei leaning against his car, wearing an expression that could curdle blood, made Gracie yank her hand from Vicktor's arm. She gulped and marched up to him.

"Where have you been?" he growled.

Vicktor answered in a tone rippling with anger. "Lunch. Where were you?"

"Waiting."

Gracie took a deep breath. "Sorry, Andrei."

"Sure you are." He whirled and climbed into his car. He slammed the door and sat behind the wheel, refusing to look at her.

"C'mon, Gracie. Let's go." Vicktor touched the small of her back.

She acquiesced, sank into her car seat and fumbled for the belt.

"He was my best friend," she murmured.

A half hour later, she was standing in front of Vicktor's building, praying Andrei had forgiven her.

"I am not going to your apartment, Vicktor." She crossed her arms. "Not. Not. Not. Are we clear?"

For the third time, Vicktor rolled his eyes, as if trying to figure out what he'd done to scare her. "Listen, I understand, I really do. I promise everything will be fine. I'm not lying when I tell you my apartment is safe."

Yeah, from whom? He had no idea she'd heard those words before—with a disastrous outcome.

"No."

Vicktor braced a hand on the hood of his car. Gracie glanced at Andrei, sulking in his car across the street, and silently pleaded with him to get out and help her.

"I have chaperones coming, I promise. But they don't get off work for two more hours."

"You arranged for chaperones?" What kind? Drinking buddies? Only, Vicktor didn't seem the kind to get soused down at the local pub and then bring it home to her.

Then again, neither had Tommy.

Still, he used the word *chaperone*. Like he was aiming for…propriety. "Who?"

"My friend Yanna. And my buddy Roman. You'll like him. He's a Believer."

A Believer? So that's where he got his ideas about a chaperone. And a woman, too. Maybe…but… "Still, until they get here…no thank you."

He winced. "What about Andrei? You trust him, right? He can come up."

Gracie considered her chauffeur. Andrei sat hunched over in his seat, his eyes shooting daggers at Vicktor through his grimy car window. "I don't think he will."

Vicktor squinted at him, then gave a wry nod. "I don't think so, either. He doesn't like me very much."

"That's an understatement."

He made a face.

"Why do you suppose that is?"

Vicktor pocketed his hands and shrugged. "Most people have had run-ins with the KGB. Many of them got pretty shredded, if not destroyed. Especially in the old regime."

A shadow fell over her heart. Had Andrei been scalped by the Russian police force? She shuddered and cast her friend a look of pity. Poor, dependable Andrei. "Let me talk to him."

"I'm right behind you."

Andrei wouldn't even crack open the window.

"C'mon, Andrei, please, let me talk to you."

He drummed his fingers on the steering wheel.

"I need you," she pleaded, ignoring Vicktor's sigh. "Please, open the door."

The door opened. "Get in." Andrei unlocked the back door.

Gracie hopped in, ignoring Vicktor's frown.

"What's the matter?" She leaned forward in her seat, wrapped her arms around the headrest and propped her cheek on the seat.

Andrei floored the gas and the car squealed out into the street.

"Andrei! What are you doing?" She turned and spied an enraged Vicktor racing for his car.

"Andrei, stop! What are you doing? Stop the car!"

"Why? So you can run back to him?" His caustic words stung and she recoiled into the seat.

"I'm not running to anyone."

His hands clenched on the steering wheel.

"He's just trying to protect me."

"That's *my* job."

Her heart fell. "No, that's not your job. I almost got you killed this morning."

"That wasn't your fault." He careened around a corner. Gracie heard the motor rev high as he pushed the pedal to the mat.

She searched for the seat belt. "Slow down!"

He ignored her. She clipped the seat belt, planted her feet. "Andrei, stop right now! Vicktor is only trying to protect me. And you can't. I nearly got all of you killed today. If I hadn't been there, your parents' home wouldn't have been attacked."

He went silent. She caught a glimpse of his face in the mirror and was startled by the fury in his eyes. She clawed his shoulder. "Stop the car!"

"No. I have to get you away from him."

"Vicktor isn't going to hurt me."

"You don't know that!" The intensity in his voice shook her. "You don't know what men like him will do."

*Men like him?* "Why did you bring me to him if you didn't want his help?"

He clenched his jaw. But, thankfully, he slowed.

They drove in wretched silence while Andrei wove through Khabarovsk. The wharf skimmed by, as did Lenin Square, and finally they left the city limits behind in a cloud of dirty smoke.

"Where are we going?" Dread stretched her voice thin. Andrei had completely snapped. Vicktor was going to kill him— and her. For all Vicktor knew, she'd tried to ditch him, again.

Andrei turned onto a dirt road, wound his way down to a lonely beach and cut the motor. The only sound was the lapping of the river.

"Can I get out?"

Andrei turned and hooked an elbow over the seat. "You're not my prisoner. I just wanted to get you away from him."

"Why?" Gracie searched his face.

Suddenly, he reached out and cupped her face with his hand. "You mean so much to me, Gracie." His voice shook.

What had she done to deserve him? Her heart ached, knowing that she had stronger feelings for a man she'd met only two days ago than she did for the man who had been her chauffeur for two years. Why couldn't she love him? "I'm sorry, Andrei. For everything."

"Just let me take you away from here. Somewhere safe."

"Where?" she whispered.

"I don't know." His eyes shimmered. "I am so sorry I got you into this. But I swear I won't let him hurt you."

Vicktor, hurt her? What had the KGB done to Andrei that drove him now?

Was he insane? Or was he...the voice of reason.

A lonely siren spliced her thoughts. "Vicktor," she breathed.

Andrei dropped his hand and scanned the horizon behind her. "He is determined," he muttered.

Gracie touched the door handle. "I'm going with him."

The pain in his expression made her heart twist. She lifted her chin, her eyes pleading with him. "Thank you for trying to protect me. I will always be grateful for your loyalty."

He closed his eyes.

She hopped out just as Vicktor skidded to a dusty halt. He sprang from his car and scrambled toward her. It made her blood run cold to see the stripped expression on his face.

Vicktor feared for her life, just as much as Andrei did.

In fact, it made her wonder suddenly if Andrei was high on Vicktor's short list of murder suspects.

And then, in a move that completely undid her, Vicktor crushed her to his chest. She felt his breathing rumble through her.

"Are you okay?" he asked, and his voice was rough with emotion.

She was in his arms. And it felt way, way too good. She gulped and pushed away from him, nodding and hiding the sudden, stupid, rush of emotions. It was only a hug. Probably an I'm-so-glad-you're-okay-and-I-don't-have-to-call-the-Consulate type hug. A wise girl wouldn't read anything into it.

But she couldn't help but enjoy it when he didn't let go of her but inspected her from head to foot. "Are you sure you're okay?"

His voice even shook, just slightly. She nodded, words deserting her.

His face darkened. "Where is that snake?"

"Let's go." Gracie clutched his arm. Oh, hard muscles and they weren't yielding. She felt like a rag doll trying to hold him back. "No, Vicktor. He was just trying—"

"It's okay, Gracie." He stopped, and the calm in his eyes emptied her. "Trust me."

Gracie went cold as she watched Andrei climb out of the car. His face was set in an angry mask. His fists were clenched and his chest rose and fell.

She felt Vicktor tense beside her. And when he stepped away from her, she couldn't help but wonder just exactly what she was supposed to trust him to do.

# Chapter Sixteen

"Are you trying to get her killed?" Vicktor demanded in Russian. No one but he had to know he'd gone cold when Andrei kidnapped Gracie. And that, as the suspicion sifted in that Andrei might be her stalker, he'd imagined her blood-splattered body on the pavement.

Seeing the chauffeur's face, however, Vicktor realized that Andrei wasn't a killer. At least, not Gracie's. He might, however, be happy to take out Vicktor.

Because the chauffeur was so obviously jealous.

Every nerve in Vicktor's body knotted, wanting to uncoil in fury at this reckless driver who had no thought in his head but his own broken heart. Only a touch of empathy kept Vicktor from burying his fist in Andrei's snarl. That, and the fact that if Vicktor hoped to get Gracie inside his flat, even with chaperones, he'd have be on his best behavior.

Andrei didn't answer. Instead he pinned him with a look of hatred. *Ouch.* Vicktor had seen that look too many times.

Vicktor stared back. "Don't do that again," he threatened in Russian.

Andrei blinked at him, obviously expecting something more. Appearing weary and rumpled in his scarred leather coat, his eyes went to Gracie, then back to Vicktor. Then his shoulders slumped. His fists loosened and he turned away, staring out into the river.

Dirty foam lined the shore, broken only by tidbits of trash washed ashore during the thaw—wood, old tires, wire and metal scraps. The crisp wind hissing off the river reeked of rotting fish. Vicktor peeked at Gracie. She was shivering, her face slightly chapped. He fought the urge to wrap his arm around her. Probably not a great idea, especially in front of Andrei.

But *oy,* did she feel good in his arms.

"Just don't get her killed." Andrei's voice was nearly a mumble, stretched taut by surrender, but Vicktor caught it.

This, they could agree on.

"Of course not."

Andrei followed him back into town at a reasonable distance, never straying from Vicktor's rearview mirror. Gracie sat beside Vicktor, worrying her lower lip. She'd stopped shivering, but hugged her waist in a death grip, staring out her window at the greening countryside. They passed a field of red and blue painted *dachas*. Shoots of tiny green potatoes formed long rows in the rich black earth.

"Are you okay?" Vicktor asked.

Gracie rubbed her hands on her upper arms. Vicktor drummed two fingers on the steering wheel.

"You're really scared, aren't you."

The question hit him hard. He hazarded a glance in her direction and saw her eyes on him. He nodded.

She reached over and kneaded her fingers into his coat. "Then you'd better take good care of me, huh?"

His pulse notched up at her words. He covered her hand with his, and forced speech through his dry mouth. "It would help if you would cooperate."

They rode that way until he pulled up in front of his flat, his heart still hammering.

He nearly cheered when he saw Roman and Yanna standing by his apartment building holding bags of food. Although, hearing their raucous sniggering as he climbed out of the car, he suddenly wondered if Andrei would make better company than this pair of mischievous matchmakers.

"So this is your missionary!"

Gracie took Vicktor's hand, climbed out of the car and searched for the feminine voice. Vicktor turned to a sleek brunette with eyes the color of glimmering opals and hair that cascaded over her shoulders and shimmered like mink in the sun.

Gracie felt instantly dowdy, despite her tailored black dress. She'd give nearly everything she owned—and that was quite possibly not enough—for a hot shower and a pair of warm sweatpants, fuzzy slippers and a good book. What she got was a hug from Vicktor's dazzling friend.

"This is Yanna, one of my coworkers," Vicktor said in explanation.

Gracie smiled meekly.

"And I'm Roman," came a tenor voice in English.

Gracie peered way up into the twinkling blue eyes of a wide-shouldered cop. Seeing his short tawny brown hair, square chin, reddish five-o'clock shadow and a smile big enough to hide inside, she found herself instantly warming to Vicktor's friend as she met his grip.

"Our 'chaperones'?" she asked Vicktor. He shrugged, but with a smile.

Roman clasped Vicktor's shoulders, leading him toward the building, the two of them huddled in conversation. Gracie strained to hear their words. Not that it would do any good— they spoke Russian.

Yanna curled her arm around Gracie's waist. "How was your day?" she whispered in English.

Gracie scrambled for a reply. What, exactly, was Yanna referring to? The way her life had spun out of control over the past three days, or the fact that she'd met a guy who made her feel…worth saving? To her profound relief, Andrei pulled up to the curb and honked. She disentangled herself from the brunette's grip, hustled over to Andrei's car and opened the passenger door.

"I'll be back in the morning," Andrei said, barely meeting her eyes. "Don't leave without me."

Her knees nearly buckled. "You're leaving?"

Andrei looked away, out the opposite window. "I have to check in at work. I have a job, you know."

Guilt cascaded over her. "I'm sorry, Andrei. Of course you do." She glanced at Yanna, who stood a meter away, a warm smile on her face. Gracie shot her a tentative grin. "I think I'll be okay."

Andrei met her gaze with hard eyes. "You call me if you need me."

Her throat felt raw. "Thank you."

He nodded. She shut the door and he roared away. Her protector. Her last link between her old life and this new surreal existence in the company of the FSB. Gracie shook her head in disbelief as Yanna called her over.

"So," the brunette said as they climbed Vicktor's stairs. "You have four flights to tell me everything about your afternoon, and I'll spend the rest of the night telling you why you should fall in love with Vicktor, hard and fast, and never let him go."

"What?"

"Vicktor. He's single, and wonderful, and you have to admit…cute."

Gracie's startled expression seemed to make Yanna smile.

"Okay," Gracie whispered, leaning close and stunned that she was even acknowledging it. "He does have the most gorgeous blue eyes I've ever seen."

Yanna nodded. "See, I knew you had good taste."

Gracie's face flamed, but it felt good. She hadn't noticed an attractive man for years. Scars did that to a woman. Yes, Vicktor was dashing, strong and brave. His looks turned heads and she liked being tucked under his arm. But more than that, he made her feel safe. As if she mattered.

"Did he take you to lunch?" Yanna asked as they climbed the stairs.

Gracie nodded. "The lighthouse."

Yanna gaped at her. "He said he'd never be caught dead in that dainty place."

Gracie shrugged. "Showed me around like he owned the place."

"Men." Yanna rolled her eyes.

"I know you women would like to keep your gossiping a secret, but you'll have to find a place other than an echoing stairwell to do it."

Yanna and Gracie exchanged horrified looks as Roman bounded down the stairs and grabbed the bag of groceries from Yanna.

*Oh, wonderful.*

Roman leaned close. "Don't worry, fair maiden, he didn't hear a word."

He flashed a sly look at Yanna, then back to Gracie. "You see, Miss Benson, you're in the middle of an FSB plot."

If the plot included a shower and dinner, she was all for it.

An hour later, Gracie stepped out of Vicktor's shower, feeling like a new creature. Two days of sweat and grease pooled in the tub floor. Her hair squeaked as she ran a towel over it. Yanna had graciously brought her a pile of clothing in a bag, but she doubted she would fit into any of the shapely beauty's attire.

Yanna had excellent taste in clothing. She'd left a pair of track pants and a baggy Alaska University sweatshirt and had even remembered a pair of woolen socks. Gracie fingered them and thanked the Lord for providing for her.

She wiped a splotch of steam from the mirror and stared at her reflection, wishing for a comb. Her satchel! She'd have a comb in her bag. Pressing her forehead with her index finger, she groped through her foggy brain for its whereabouts.

The village. She'd left it at Andrei's mother's house. Groaning, she sank down on the edge of the tub. Her passport and visa were in the satchel. Without them she hadn't a prayer of leaving Russia, at least not anytime soon. She winced, imagining the arctic reception Andrei's parents would surely give her. She felt ill knowing they had been terrorized. Thankfully, Vicktor's contact in the village had called with an update. The Tallins had been shaken up, but not hurt.

In fact, she should be praising God that none of them were hurt. At least physically.

She knelt on the tiled floor, feeling moisture pool around her bare legs. She didn't care that she was shivering, dressed in only a towel, wet hair dripping in streaks down her back. She folded her hands. "Dear Lord, thank You. You've protected me and brought me to this safe place, despite my fears. I asked You this morning for safety. Though I was shot at, kidnapped by Andrei and dropped into the lap of the FSB, You kept me safe. And soon, comfortable and warm."

She raised her eyes, tasting salt as tears dripped into her mouth. "I have trusted in You, and You have not disappointed me. You have been near to me through Vicktor and Andrei. I owe You my life. Even though I don't deserve this." She sighed. "I know I've asked You this before. But I truly want to be of some use to You, Lord." Her throat burned. She wished, for once, she could repay God for all He had done for her.

A tap on the door brought her to her feet.

"Gracie, it's me, Yanna. Supper is nearly ready. How are you doing?"

Gracie wrapped a towel around her head and squeezed the excess moisture from her hair. "Be out in a minute."

She threw on the pants and sweatshirt, did her best to comb out her tangles with her fingers, hung up the towels and padded out holding her socks.

A dog the size of a mule buffaloed her into the alcove by the door.

"Vicktor!"

Pouncing near her, the dog's huge jowls dribbled white foam and his brown eyes perused her as if she were a piece of liver. Gracie held both hands up in surrender. "Vicktor!" The brute sniffed her legs. She resisted kneeing him. "Help!"

Vicktor appeared in the narrow hallway, a dishrag over his shoulder, dressed delightfully casual in a pair of black jeans and an untucked denim shirt. It did magic things to his blue eyes.

"Your horse likes me," she said.

"Alfred! Back, boy!" He grabbed at the dog's collar and wrestled him into an adjoining bedroom. "Sorry about that," he said, closing the door against the whine of his canine roommate. "He's friendly."

Gracie hid a smile. "I'd say. Not much of a watchdog."

Vicktor squatted and reached into a cupboard. "No, he's a good watchdog. He'd take your leg off if you weren't cute." He handed her a pair of worn slippers.

Now, wasn't that sweet? Sirens blared in the back of her head. She tried to ignore them as she sat in a leather armchair. It welcomed her with a creak. "Maybe it's because I smell like Yanna?" She tugged on Yanna's warm socks. Heat flooded to her toes.

"I doubt it. Yanna doesn't spend too much time here."

And hearing that felt good, too. It must have shown, for he smiled and his blue eyes sparkled. "C'mon, Roman and I made you ladies a scrumptious supper."

Gracie took his outstretched hand. "Really? What?"

"Smoked salmon and sauerkraut."

She made a face.

He laughed. "No, just kidding. How about fried potatoes, meat cutlets and a carrot salad?"

"That sounds better," she said, her stomach roaring to life at the smells drifting from the kitchen.

The galley kitchen was roughly the size of her hatchback now in storage in Duluth. Yanna sat at the tiny folded table, nursing a soda. Roman, like his pal, Vicktor, wore a dish towel over his shoulder and flipped julienne potatoes sizzling in sunflower oil.

Vicktor pulled out a chair and Gracie squeezed past Roman's bulk. Vicktor reached around his friend, extracted a glass from the cupboard and poured her a drink from the cola bottle sweating on the table.

"How do you get around in here?" Gracie asked, seeing Roman nearly catch his shirt on the gas blaze as Vicktor shoved past him.

"I don't usually have guests." Vicktor grinned, but Gracie guessed he was embarrassed by this truth.

"That's because he doesn't like to clean his house," Roman jabbed.

Vicktor glared at him.

Yanna leaned close. "Don't believe Roma. Vicktor is the most domestic guy you've ever seen. Irons his own shirts, bakes his own bread, even makes his own jam."

Vicktor tried to swat her with his towel, but she ducked.

"I've even known him to dust!"

Gracie peered at Vicktor, catching Yanna's infectious mirth.

"Lies," Vicktor rebutted.

From the pristine white curtains and the way the milk-glass light fixture sparkled, Gracie suspected Yanna spoke the truth. She bit back a grin.

"Give me a break, please, gang?" Vicktor turned away to wash out a glass in the sink.

Gracie watched him work, muscles rippling down his wide back, the five-o'clock shadow he'd yet to shave darkening his face. Yes, it felt good to notice a good-looking man. She tore her gaze away and focused on Yanna.

"Have you known each other long?"

Yanna and Roman exchanged a look. She thought she saw Roman shrug.

"*Da,*" Yanna confirmed. Her eyes lost their mirth. As she reached across the table, taking Gracie's hand, the set of her mouth told Gracie the games were over.

"Want to know how we all met?"

Vicktor bathed a fried potato in ketchup and listened to Yanna as the tale unfolded. He remembered that first meeting so clearly, from Yanna's terror-stricken pasty face to David's overbearing indignation. He'd no idea a night of horror would usher him into friendships dearer than life.

*"The symphony was beautiful tonight, wasn't it?" Yanna's bright smile had yet to lose the glow of wonder. A girl from a village wouldn't have a hard time being awed by Moscow, he supposed. Vicktor turned up his coat collar, wondering if he'd have time to cram for his English exam, cursing himself for succumbing to his mother's pleas. "Yanna is new in town. She needs a friend. Take her to the Bolshoi." Needs a babysitter was more like it.*

Glancing at her now, Vicktor found it difficult to believe Yanna had been a mild-mannered village girl with a flimsy backbone.

*The moon hung as a sliver of gold in the sky, surrounded by millions of winking stars. A greedy wind gusting off the Volga River snared his hat and sent it skittering over the shimmering red cobblestones toward Lenin's Mausoleum. "Stay here," Vicktor said as he shot out after it, his feet echoing across the square.*

*When he turned around, she had vanished.*

"I don't know what I was thinking, running away from Vicktor." Yanna separated a long strand of hair and examined it, splitting it into smaller strands. Her breath came out in short bursts, unsteady. "All I knew, one minute he was there, the next, he'd disappeared."

Vicktor's appetite died, remembering Yanna, a crumpled mess, crying, terrified.

*A scream rent the night air. Vicktor's adrenaline spiked. "Yanna!" Where did that girl go? "Yanna?" The Kremlin stretched out in shadow, like a phantom, hiding everything in darkness. Another scream. Vicktor bolted toward the State Department Store on the opposite end. His breath burned in his chest.*

"Roman, and his American buddy David Curtiss were coming home from some kind of meeting—"

"A Bible study," Roman interjected.

"They caught the attacker mid-grope." Yanna's eyes darkened as she said it.

"While I was kicking my hat around the graves of Stalin and Khrushchev, David was running down one of Moscow's most wanted." Vicktor's voice was low. There were just some things a person shouldn't be forgiven for.

*"Yanna?" Vicktor found her holding tightly to a man in a suede jacket, and landed two punches before another man locked his arms behind him. Yanna's shouts registered. "Vicktor, stop! They're trying to help!" She grabbed the man holding Vicktor in a vice. "Please, let him go."*

*A moment later, Roman turned and decked him. "Don't you know better than to leave a woman out alone, in Moscow?" Vicktor let the indictment stand. And never forgot the lesson.*

Vicktor noticed Yanna was much kinder in her explanation. Vicktor shared a look with Roman as she told it.

"Roman and David just appeared out of the night, scared the guy away and took off after him. Vicktor ran up a second later." She flipped back her hair and spread her hands on the table. "It was the beginning of a beautiful friendship."

Gracie sat still, as if rolling the story around in her head.

Roman put an arm around Yanna. "Once we figured out what happened, David and I decided *not* to turn Vicktor into mashed potatoes—and became friends instead." He cast a glance at Vicktor. "Actually, I already knew Vicktor. We'd competed against each other in club hockey."

Gracie angled him a look of amused interest. "You play hockey?"

Vicktor liked the way the light glittered in her eyes and turned them to jewels. He nodded.

"David, my American friend, and I became friends through an off-campus English Bible Study," Roman explained.

Vicktor laced his hands behind his head and leaned back into the chair. "David also plays hockey, but nothing like Roman, who can skate us into knots."

Roman didn't spare him a glance, but leaned toward Gracie, working his story. "Vicktor started hanging around us." He nodded at Vicktor as if in understanding. "Probably because we had all the girls."

Vicktor rolled his eyes.

Gracie giggled.

"Soon we formed this little group—me, David, Yanna and Vicktor and another American named Mae."

Roman looked pointedly at Vicktor. "Yes, there was also Mae."

"Mae?" Gracie echoed.

He reached for his soda.

Yanna covered Gracie's hand with her own. "She was Vicktor's first introduction to stubborn American women."

"And a painful introduction it was," Vicktor mumbled.

Gracie raised her eyebrows.

Yanna chortled. "Mae is still a dear friend. My best. But she was and is, headstrong and independent. She flies C-130s for the Air National Guard." She flicked a mischievous glance at Vicktor. Vicktor begged for mercy with his eyes.

"Vicktor had it in his head he would never let anything happen to another woman friend, so he started shadowing her."

"Protecting," Vicktor interjected.

"Hovering," smirked Roman.

Vicktor glowered at him.

"It turned out okay," Yanna said. "He saved her from a mugging one night. But she caught on to his little obsession and told him to back off."

Gracie grimaced playfully. "Does he still have an issue with shadowing?"

Yanna leaned close, staring at Vicktor but speaking to Gracie. "You tell me."

Vicktor nearly fell backward off his chair. "Enough!"

"No!" Gracie said, her shoulders shaking. "Tell me about Mae. Did she ever forgive him?"

"What's not to forgive?" Vicktor asked.

Roman shook his head.

"Yes, she forgave him. Made him walk at least ten feet behind her for about six months, but yes." Yanna tilted her head at him. "But I'd say he still has a thing about protecting American ladies. Wouldn't you agree, Vicktor?"

He smiled weakly and wished the earth could open up and swallow him whole.

## Chapter Seventeen

❧

Larissa watched Boris in the dim evening light. Twilight was his kindest hour. It softened his hard eyes, gave his paunchy body angles, erased the wrinkles, darkened his hair.

It helped.

She picked up the shot glass and let the vodka flame her throat. Warmth crept through her body and dulled her disgust. Yes, she could do this. She fingered her necklace, then padded up behind him and put her hands on his shoulders. She kneaded the muscles, bunched tight under layers of flesh. "Have faith, *moy Tovarish.*"

It was good to call him Comrade. He needed it. And it had the right connotation. They were partners, yes. However, no more than that, despite the hunger in his eyes. He was usually so gentle with her, as if afraid of the power she held. And she *did* hold power.

But not enough. She let the images of Bali, and perhaps a house on some warm shore, swell in her mind. She'd never return to Russia, to cold and gray. She massaged his shoulders, not too hard. *Don't anger him.*

She'd seen his anger, once. It was enough. She dragged the tips of her fingers across his sweaty flesh, gently calming his heated nerves. "Andrei is with her, right now."

"I am afraid, my little *shpeon*, you don't know quite as much as you think."

Boris turned, his dark eyes sharp like knives. His gaze fell to her neck, fastened on the necklace. "I thought I asked you not to wear that around me."

He reached out and tore it off with a snap.

<Logging on to network>

Vicktor wiggled the computer mouse, watching the cursor flit across the message displayed. The modem hummed, then buzzed as he connected to the Internet. *C'mon, Preach, be online tonight.*

Roman yawned from his post on the sofa. "He's probably asleep at this hour." He checked his watch. "Seven a.m. East Coast time."

"I doubt it." Vicktor turned and hung his elbow over the back of his chair. "He's probably doing his last round of stomach crunchers."

<Preach Online> announced a pop-up screen on his chat menu.

"Score." Vicktor turned and typed quickly.

<Stripes> Preach, got a moment?

He drummed his fingers on the mouse pad, waiting for David's reply.

<Preach> Yeah.

Vicktor sent him an invitation and the dialogue box opened.

Preach's name appeared on the lower box, while Vicktor's on-line name identified his box.

\<Preach\> What's up?
\<Stripes\> I'm in big trouble.

Vicktor threw a hasty look at Roman, who had propped his smelly feet on the sofa and now mindlessly scratched Alfred's spiked ear. His eyes were closed. Good.

\<Preach\> What's up?
\<Stripes\> An American missionary by the name of Grace.
\<Preach\> You're full of surprises.
\<Stripes\> I need to keep it quick. Redman is on the sofa just itching to read my mail.
\<Preach\> Go ahead.
\<Stripes\> What are my chances?
\<Preach\> What, you want to date her?

Vicktor wiggled his fingers over the keyboard for a second before he typed.

\<Stripes\> Maybe.
\<Preach\> You should know the situation better than I do.
\<Stripes\> You're the Christian.
\<Preach\> Right. Well, if you're asking if I'm giving you per-mission to date a sister in Christ, I'd have to say no.

Vicktor turned cold. David and his principles.

\<Stripes\> Why?
\<Preach\> Unequally yoked, friend. She's a princess of the King of the Universe.
\<Stripes\> So, she's off-limits because I'm not a part of the club?

If Vicktor didn't respect the guy so much, he wouldn't have asked. Still, David's reply cut deeper than Vicktor wanted to admit.

<Preach> It's not a club. It's a family. But until you surrender to God, you aren't a part of it, as much as it hurts me to say it.

Vicktor narrowed his eyes at the screen. A family. People to trust, to belong to. People that depended on one another. People to turn to when trouble slithered into a man's life. *Thanks, Preach, for your unconditional support.*

<Stripes> So you're saying hands off unless I join the family?
<Preach> I'm saying don't do anything to break her heart. What's she doing hanging around scum like you anyway?
<Stripes> She's under my protection.
<Preach> Oh, that's a great way to keep your distance.
<Stripes> Very funny. Yanna and Roman are here, playing chaperone.
<Preach> Wise. So, what happened?
<Stripes> She could be the Wolf's next target.

The pause was either a glitch in his modem line or David absorbing that information. Vicktor kept typing.

<Stripes> I think the Wolf killed her teammates, and my pal Evgeny. There's a third body in the morgue, her chauffeur.
<Preach> Sounds like a woman who attracts trouble.
<Stripes> Not intentionally. You'd like her, she's blunt and honest and she's got guts. And she's really pretty.
<Preach> You're in trouble, pal.

Vicktor shot a look at Roman. The guy was staring at him as if reading his mind.

&lt;Stripes&gt; I know.

He heard Roman shift off the sofa and move toward him. Roman's breath swished past Vicktor's ear.

&lt;Stripes&gt; Redman is snuffling through my mail.

"Pretty?" Roman read aloud. Vicktor elbowed him.

&lt;Preach&gt; Hi Redman.

"Tell him hi," said Roman, rubbing his gut and backing away. "Tell him you're in prime tiger form tonight."

&lt;Stripes&gt; Hi back. I gotta go.
&lt;Preach&gt; I'm praying for you, Stripes. You know God isn't done with you yet.

Vicktor cast a look toward his closed bedroom door.

&lt;Stripes&gt; Thanks. TTFN.

He closed his dialogue box before David could respond. He didn't need a long-winded chat with Preach about the needs lurking in his heart. He knew better than anyone the demons he battled.

He closed the laptop and drummed his fingers on the case. He just wished one of those demons wasn't hot on Gracie's tail.

Yanna tossed her a pillow. Gracie caught it with one hand and tucked it into a crisp white pillowcase. "Is this pillowcase *ironed?*"

Yanna grinned. "Told you he was domestic."

"The perfect catch." Gracie couldn't believe she had said that. Emboldened, she plowed ahead. "So, is he dating anyone?"

"No. Not for years." Yanna gathered her hair and snapped a band around it. Gracie tried not to be jealous that the woman looked good even in ragged yellow sweats and a green army T-shirt. At least Gracie's hair now felt clean and dry, bouncing slightly from its natural curl. She laced her fingers through it.

"Thanks for staying here, Yanna. You and Roman are good friends to Vicktor."

Yanna shrugged. "We love him like a brother." She fixed her eyes on Gracie's and they darkened. "And we don't want to see him hurt."

Okay, copy that. Gracie managed a smile and shook her head. "I leave in two days. Don't worry, I can't start anything."

"I think you already have."

Gracie frowned, scrolling back over her day, seeing Vicktor's face when Andrei kidnapped her, his smile when he bought her the dress, his chagrin tonight at Yanna's chiding about his friend, Mae. And why, exactly, did the thought of another woman in his very capable arms, even for the purposes of protection, start a slow burn in the center of her chest?

So maybe something *had* started, for both of them. Gracie shook her head. "No, for personal reasons, I can't make him any promises." Like, for example…he wasn't a Christian. Not that she'd asked, but somehow, she could see it in his eyes when he'd told her Roman was a Believer. Vicktor didn't put himself in that category. And that fact alone should make her post a Do Not Enter sign on her heart.

Unless he had already snuck inside. She tried not to scowl.

"Vicktor needs more than promises, I'm afraid," Yanna said with a wry smile. "He doesn't trust easily."

"Why not?"

Yanna stretched out on the double bed, crossing her feet at the ankles. "It comes with the territory. He's a cop. He's seen too much. His faith in human nature is so low it's negative." She tugged off her socks. "Still, I think you might be just what he needs to soften that calloused heart."

Gracie blushed. "You're presuming a lot. How do you know Vicktor is even interested?" She sat on the bed and dipped her feet into a pool of lamplight illuminating the orange carpet.

"Women's intuition. Besides, I haven't scrutinized his very rare relationships for nothing. The man's mush with you." Yanna climbed under the blankets and tucked the covers up to her chin. "Turn off the light, please?"

Gracie switched off the lamp. Wrapping her arms around her waist, she padded to the window. Outside, lights from opposite apartments glowed orange and yellow and a pale moon skimmed the rooftops on its heavenly ascent. A mild breeze brushed unseen trees. Gracie leaned her forehead against the cool glass and chewed Yanna's words. She'd never turned a man to mush. Well, maybe Andrei, but he had never turned *her* to mush.

Not like Vicktor. Gracie shut her eyes. *God, I've made a big mistake. Please, don't let me fall for Vicktor.*

Not only shouldn't she give away her heart two days before she left Russia. But especially not to a non-Christian. Folly loomed before her as she considered Vicktor's blue eyes and megawatt smile. Folly and heartache.

"I'm getting a drink of water," she announced to Yanna. The woman answered with a hum.

Gracie opened the door and peeked out. In the dark living room, she spied Vicktor lounging on the sofa, an arm slung over his eyes. His friend Roman had obviously departed. Holding her breath, she tiptoed past the living room and into the kitchen. Fumbling in the milky darkness, she found a cup and opened the refrigerator for a bottle of filtered water. Light washed over her, she blinked and squinted in the glare.

A hand touched her arm.

"Can I help you?" Vicktor asked. "Hungry?"

Gracie felt like a burglar. "No. I wanted a drink of water."

He reached past her and grabbed the bottle. "Let me help you."

"Thank you," Gracie said as he filled her glass.

He closed the door and the night bathed them in velvet. He stood so close she could smell his skin, the scent of his cologne, and feel his breath on her neck. She tensed. He must have felt it, for he stepped back. She started to move past him.

"Gracie, why did you come to Russia?"

She turned and studied him. The moonlight fell across his face, and his eyes gleamed. Goose bumps peppered her skin, but she made up her mind. If she was going to earn his trust, she'd have to give him the truth.

She fingered a loose hair, then tucked it behind her ear. Silent, she leaned against the door frame and ran her eyes over him. Illumined by a fragment of moonlight from the living room, she appeared pale and frail. An illusion. He hoped it was the only illusion about her life.

"I don't know," she finally answered.

She ran her fingers through her drying hair, and Vicktor was momentarily distracted by the moonlight turning it gold. She gazed past him as she spoke.

"I used to think I came here because I wanted to share the gospel. Because I wanted to spend my life telling people about Jesus." Suddenly, her eyes fixed on him, intense. It raised the fine hairs on his neck. Made him squirm. "And I do. Without Jesus, without Him paying for my sins and giving me a new life, there is no hope. I know that as well as I know that I must breathe each day." Her gaze gentled. "But I think I really came to prove something to myself, or maybe earn something...." Her voice quivered. "No, rather, God sent me here to teach me something." She peered into her glass, sipped water, then held the cup in both hands.

Vicktor frowned. "That's it? That's why you came here? To learn something?" He folded his arms and a knot formed in his stomach. He'd hoped for more, something profound, life changing. Something he could cling to. "You mean you spent two years here and it was just to learn a lesson?"

Hurt shadowed her face. "I think this lesson affects every part of my life, Vicktor."

"So, just what is this lesson?"

Gracie rubbed her thumb along her glass. Then she pushed past him, walking toward the window. He ran his eyes over her outline, the tilt of her head, her angular face, the curve of her body filling out Yanna's clothes better than Yanna did. He tore his eyes from her and stared at the floor.

"I think the lesson has to do with needing God. With Him looking past my sins to give me grace."

Vicktor came up to stand behind her at the window. He placed his hands on her shoulders. She stiffened.

"Are you afraid of me?" he asked, feeling the silky softness of her hair on his hands. The smell of her clean skin was making his head spin.

She began to tremble, as if...as if she *was* afraid. He stared at her, horrified. He wanted to groan, but it stuck in his throat. As if they were poison, he yanked his hands off her shoulders and stepped away.

"I'm sorry," he said, his voice thick. He hadn't meant to frighten her. "Oh man, Gracie, I'm really sorry. I just thought..." What had he thought? He didn't know what he had expected, but that afternoon she had been so inviting, so beautiful in her new dress. And with her playful attitude, her teasing smirks at dinner...he'd seen signals. "You looked so nice today and I..."

No, that wasn't what he meant at all. Her dress and Russian makeover had nothing to do with the way his heart practically jumped up and galloped when she walked into the room. No, his pulse rate had more to do with her rapt attention, her smile...those eyes needing him.

Only, obviously it had all been an act. She didn't trust him. Why? Was he a monster? Obviously, from the way she'd stiffened, practically repelled by his touch, he'd offended her. His chest burned and he couldn't figure out if it was from shame...or frustration.

"Gracie," he started, trying to figure out a way to apologize—

She turned. Thick tears plowed down her cheeks.

Oh no, *now* what had he done? He felt like a jerk. "Gracie," he began again. She held up a hand, stopping his fumbled apology.

"Don't. It isn't your fault. You did nothing wrong." Her lip began to tremble and she bit it, wiped her tears and continued. "You don't know anything about me. You think you do. You take America and everything you think you know about it and you make assumptions. Then you put me in that pretty dress and think that I'm Russian. But I'm neither, Vicktor. I'm a Christian. I'm a unique package, designed for unique, eternal purposes—only God knows about. Each and every lesson I learn is to help me become that creation, His creation." She swallowed and her voice gathered strength. "To answer your question, I think the lesson God sent me here to learn was that I don't need to prove anything to Him to earn His love and forgiveness. I just have to need *Him*. He does the rest."

Vicktor blinked at her. Scrubbing a hand through his hair, he stared beyond her, out into the dark street. It didn't seem right, or fair. Forgiveness had to be earned. If it wasn't, then how could a person accept it?

"I have to admit, that wasn't what I was expecting. But... thanks." He turned, and noticed that she was smiling. Her green eyes shimmered, reaching out in acceptance. It moved him and again he battled the urge to weave his fingers into her hair, pull her to his chest and hang on tight.

Only, it was more than just her sweet smile and genuineness that drew him. It was something she had. A feeling. A countenance. A strength.

Peace?

He rubbed the burning in his chest with the palm of his hand.

"Thanks for the drink, Vicktor." Gracie brushed past him. "Good night."

Vicktor forced a good-night past the lump in his throat. David was right.

Gracie could never belong to him. And Vicktor was in big, big trouble.

# Chapter Eighteen

❧

Hot, slimy breath gusted across her face, and the odor of hair and flesh poured into her nostrils. Gracie snorted, opened her eyes and screamed.

Alfred licked her across the face.

"Vicktor! Your dog!"

Brown eyes stared at her and drool hung from his floppy lips. Gracie slid toward the center of the bed, praying the animal wouldn't jump in next to her.

The door slammed open and Vicktor careened into the room.

"Help?" she pleaded weakly, eyes on the brute.

Vicktor scrambled around the bed. "Alfred, you hooligan! Get out of here!"

The dog dodged him, scooting toward the nightstand. The lamp wobbled and a tiny alarm clock fell to the floor with a crash. Gracie bit her lip, stifling a relieved giggle. Vicktor lunged for the animal, which fled across the bed, narrowly missing Gracie's stomach. She ducked and pulled the covers to her chin. Vicktor threw a shoe at him. It banged against his bedroom door.

He turned to her. "Are you okay?" The sweet concern in his eyes made her laugh.

"If that's your idea of an alarm clock, I promise I'll never oversleep again."

"No, he just—"

"I'm kidding, Vicktor." She longed to enjoy the look of horror in his eyes, just one more second, but the guy looked wrung out and just a little out of sorts this morning. She glanced toward the open door, and the aroma of frying bacon nearly made her leap for the kitchen. "Where's Yanna?"

"Eating breakfast."

"Save me some. I'll be out in a second."

"Aye, aye, captain," Vicktor said on his way out, and closed the door behind him.

Gracie pulled the covers over her head. *Great*. Just how she wanted to present herself—sleep-tousled and late. She scrambled out of bed and pulled on the black dress and hose. Shaking out her hair and twisting it into a bun, she vowed to buy a hairbrush before the day was out.

Her satchel. She'd meant to tell him that she'd left it in the village at dinner last night, but enveloped inside the easy banter of his friends, well, she had completely forgotten. Or maybe it had been more than that.

Maybe she'd simply wanted to escape. To hide inside this altered reality that made her feel at once reckless, and yet so safe.

She and Andrei would have to call the village today, maybe drive down and pick up her bag. She made a mental note to mention it to Vicktor.

She ran a tongue over her teeth. They felt covered in wool. She'd also pick up a toothbrush. She ran a hand over the bedclothes, folded Yanna's clothes. Then, feeling like something the cat dragged in, she padded from the bedroom.

Sunlight washed the kitchen in orange and gold. Roman stood at the stove, frying bacon with the movements of a master chef.

"Hey there," he greeted as she halted in the doorway. He looked comfortable in a pair of baggy blue sweatpants and matching sweatshirt.

Yanna sat at the table, sleek and refined in an olive suit coat and black skirt. Her hair was pulled back and her face made up to subdued perfection. She fingered a morning newspaper, her eyes on a front-page article. Gracie fought chagrin and joined her at the table.

"Coffee?" asked Roman.

She nodded. "Sorry I overslept."

Roman set down a cup of coffee before her and she curled her hands around the mug. The rich scent fed her spirit.

Yanna smiled warmly. "You snore."

Gracie paled. Yanna laughed, her brown eyes glinting in amusement.

"Uh, where's Vicktor?"

"In the shower," Yanna answered.

Gracie glanced at Roman. "I thought you went home."

Roman handed her a plate with two slices of fresh wheat bread, a scrambled egg and bacon. "Yep, but I just couldn't stay away...Vicktor shouldn't get all the girls."

Yanna kicked at him. He dodged but looked sufficiently rapscallion-like as he turned back toward the stove.

Breakfast had never tasted so good before. Gracie devoured the meal. Usually she had a pickle or a piece of dry bread for breakfast.

Vicktor entered the kitchen, looking crisp and dapper in a pair of pressed black suit pants, a white oxford and teal diamond tie. She caught the enticing aroma of cologne and turned quickly back to her meal. Yikes, he sure could clean up when he wanted to. Then again, she liked the late-night, moonlit, rumpled look, too.

Danger, *danger!*

"Good morning, ladies."

Gracie pushed a bit of food past the lump in her throat, cleared her head with a sip of coffee, then turned to him. "I forgot to tell you something."

He poured himself a cup of coffee. "What?"

"I left my satchel at Andrei's house." Gracie dabbed at her mouth with a napkin and wished for a breath mint. "I need to go and get it this morning. It's got my passport and visa, and I'll need them to fly out tomorrow."

Vicktor shook creamer into his coffee. "You're not flying out tomorrow."

The room went icy silent and only the sound of spitting bacon grease fractured the air.

"What do you mean?" A chill rippled up Gracie's spine as she stared at Vicktor.

He looked at her, his face dark. "I mean we need to decide if it's safe for you to go. The killer may try and follow you to America and, well, I can't protect you across the ocean."

*Protect me…across the ocean?* Gracie gaped at him. "You really think some Russian murderer is going to get on a plane and follow me to Minnesota? I seriously doubt it."

"It's not your decision."

Okay, his refined thug look was very, very convincing.

Gracie shot a help-me look at Yanna. She met Gracie's gaze with a feeble shrug. Gracie's heart turned leaden. There would be no backup from the other female in the room.

"I can't stay in Russia forever."

Vicktor said nothing, but stared at her, his eyes boring into hers, with fury…or desperation?

She refused to shrivel under his scrutiny. "Listen here, Mr. FSB," she said, forcing a cool tone. "I am going home and you can't stop me."

Vicktor glanced at Roman. Gracie followed his gaze. Roman's grim expression widened her eyes. "You all truly believe that a killer would follow me all the way to America?"

Vicktor shrugged.

Panic pitched her voice high and ragged. "*No.* Sorry, I don't believe it. Listen people—I am going home tomorrow. You can't hold me hostage!"

Vicktor's look was hooded, dark. Then, quietly, he said, "Watch me."

Gracie felt the blood drain from her face and reached for the back of her seat.

Vicktor's stony expression slackened and for a second his face muscles struggled for control. "Listen, that didn't come out right." He shook his head. "Gracie…trust me."

"Yeah. Right," Gracie whispered.

He stared at her, and she tried to ignore the look of pain that flashed in his eyes. She gritted her teeth against a rush of regret. If he thought he was going to keep her off that plane tomorrow—

The doorbell chimed.

Vicktor whirled and headed for the door.

She cast a look at Roman. "He can't make me stay."

He raised his eyebrows, suddenly looking one hundred and twenty percent like a Russian solider. Hard. Unfeeling.

She grabbed her plate and cup and rinsed them in the sink, too furious to speak.

"Are you okay, Gracie?" Andrei's voice came from behind her.

She turned, nodding, and hid a flare of alarm. The man looked freshly flogged. Bags hung under his brown eyes, he wore the same rumpled leather jacket, reeking of the barnyard, and his face had aged ten years since the night before. He seemed worn-out and…afraid.

She longed to tuck herself inside his protective embrace. To wrap herself in their easy friendship and know nothing had changed. Except, they couldn't rewind time, and yesterday had changed everything.

"Thank you for coming." She noticed Vicktor standing behind him, his eyes pinned to her every movement. She fixed her gaze on Andrei. "We need to go back to the village today. I left my satchel at your mom's house."

His eyes settled on his scuffed loafers.

"Your satchel isn't there. I called my mother today and she told me it had been stolen."

Dread filled Gracie.

Now she *was* a hostage in Russia. Maybe she shouldn't have been so rash with her words.

Vicktor snapped the lead on Alfred, turned and locked his steel door. Whirling to catch up to Gracie and his other house-guests, he nearly slammed into Roman.

"Hold on, Stripes," Roman commanded, his voice low.

Vicktor heard footfalls echoing from the stairs below, dying as the women and Andrei headed outside.

"What?" he asked. He had had enough of Roman's teasing after last night's chat with Preach. He'd finally sent the joker home, and after his pulse-jumping encounter with his American houseguest, he'd spent the night trying to figure out how to keep Miss Gracie Benson, feisty blonde and all-around distraction, alive.

He couldn't have Gracie. He knew that. But he wouldn't let the Wolf get her, either. Even if it cost him his life. He met Roman's steely look with silence.

No hint of tease remained in his friend's voice. "I don't know what you are thinking, pal, but maybe her best bet at safety is in the States. I don't think the Wolf would follow her there."

"What about Valentine Timofeovna?"

Roman winced and leaned against the stair rail. Memory stretched the silence taut between. Colonel Valentine Timofeovna, FSB agent, slain while on vacation in Bali. A crime yet to be solved, but popularly attributed to the Wolf.

"Don't underestimate this guy," Vicktor said, both to himself and Roman.

Roman folded his arms across his chest. "Still, I can't help but wonder if it would be best if you shipped her out on the next flight home."

"And just how am I going to protect her from Russia?" His tone emerged harder than he had wanted it to be. And a little too desperate to ignore.

"Maybe you'll have to trust her to a Higher Power," Roman said quietly.

Vicktor turned away, shaken by the urge to clock his best friend. "You just don't get it, do you." He felt himself fighting for control. "This is real life, Roman, not games. You don't wish danger away and you don't just hope that some unseen hero is going to save your skin." He slapped his chest with a flat palm. "It's up to me. I have to keep her alive. And no fairy tale is going to help me."

Roman didn't blink. "God is using you to keep her alive, Vicktor. But He can do it without you, also."

Vicktor glared at him, hating Roman's steel grip on his childish religion. "What if she dies? What if the Wolf follows her home and kills her in her own backyard?"

"Then she's still safe."

"How do you figure that?"

"That's what Christianity is all about. Safety in this life, and beyond. God doesn't always protect our lives, but our *souls* are safe forever in His hands."

Vicktor threw his hands into the air. "Who cares about eternity when there is *now* to deal with?"

Sadness, or something like it, darkened Roman's eyes. "That's the point. Our lives here are but a blink compared to eternity. That's why Gracie is even here, risking her life. To tell others to care about eternity, about their souls." He leaned close to Vicktor, his face grim. "Gracie's not only safe in God's hands, she's ready for whatever the Wolf dishes out." His voice softened. "Are you?"

Vicktor clenched his teeth. He looked down at Alfred, who sat watching them with a mild expression. "I have work to do."

Roman clamped him on the shoulder. "I wonder. Maybe you don't want her to go because you need her more than she needs you?"

* * *

Gracie stood beside Vicktor, watching him pace in the tiny corridor, feeling like an intruder. Crouching beside his dog, she ran a hand down Alfred's long, sleek back, and waited for Vicktor to tell her what had his face screwed up in frustration. The smell of old cigarette butts and orange peels filled the stairwell and only a shaft of morning light from a shattered window illuminated the dismal hallway.

Vicktor couldn't have been more clear about his feelings if he'd stood on the hood of his car and screamed with frustration. He didn't want to babysit her any more than she wanted to be toted around.

Maybe she should have told Andrei yesterday to floor it. What an idiot she'd been to be suckered by Vicktor's warm smile, beguiling concern, rugged looks.

*Pay attention to your history, Gracie.* A smart girl would be glad he was tired of hanging around her.

Okay, that hurt.

Suddenly, as if at the pinnacle of his courage, Vicktor marched up to a metal apartment door and shoved a key into the lock. Alfred immediately jumped to his feet and lunged for the door, nearly ripping Gracie's arm from the socket. As Vicktor eased the door open and Alfred plowed past him, Gracie searched Vicktor's face for an explanation. But his expression was stone, his eyes distant. Mr. Cold and Gray.

She wanted to cry.

He held out his hand, motioning her to enter.

The tiny flat smelled old, of worn leather shoes, stale grease and ancient dust. Vicktor made a face, which she wasn't sure she was meant to see, and closed the door behind her.

"Pop," he hollered. Moving past Gracie, he left her in the corridor and strode toward a back room. Alfred had already settled himself on an indented, fraying green sofa, nudging himself into a worn afghan at one end.

Gracie leaned against the door frame, her heart sliding into her knees.

The muffled sounds of voices reached her ears and a moment later an elderly man shuffled out of a back room, leaning heavily on a cane. Vicktor was on his tail, rubbing a hand over his neck, a sign she'd come to interpret as meaning he was stressed. Her heart twisted for him and she called herself a fool. Had she forgotten in the space of thirty seconds that he didn't want her around?

She forced a smile. "Who's this?"

Vicktor glanced from her to the old man, then sighed. "Okay. I have work to do at the office, and I don't feel good about putting you in a holding cell, so…" He pulled in a deep breath. "My pop is going to protect you."

*Holding cell?* She didn't feel so good about that, either. Still, looking at the old man, she wondered just how badly Vicktor wanted to dump her. Gracie swallowed and forced a breezy tone. "Your pop?" The old man, although tall and broad shouldered with a mass of muscles stretching his green army shirt, was…*crippled.* Who, in fact, was going to do the protecting here?

She started to shake her head. Vicktor held up a hand. "It's just until lunch. I'll be back soon and your pal Andrei said he'd be back even sooner, so it's probably for an hour at the most."

No wonder Vicktor had appeared relieved when Andrei suggested he sit with her after he reported in to work. It would have been nice if Vicktor had made those intentions known *yesterday,* before she burned her bridges with Andrei.

"My pop is one of the best cops on the force," Vicktor went on. "Well, I mean *was* one of the best on the force." His eyes darted away when he said it.

What was that? Pain, flashing across his face? She stared at him, her heart stepping to attention. And when he forced a smile and met her eyes, she saw something that made her want to cry. Remorse.

"Gracie Benson, this is my father, Nickolai Yacovich Shubnikov."

She held out her hand. "Glad to meet you."

The man took her hand and smiled. *"Zdrastvootya."*

Russian? "Vicktor, does your father speak English?" she whispered, keeping the smile firmly planted on her face. Her eyes met Vicktor's and she hoped he read her panic.

Vicktor smiled. "Not yet. Maybe you can teach him some words."

"Oh sure. Great. Thanks." She kept pumping Nickolai's giant hand and noticed it was warm and strong. His brown eyes scanned her up and down and she wondered what Vicktor had told him.

Vicktor said something to his father, who nodded. Moving past her toward the door, Vicktor stopped and breathed into her ear. "Better yet, maybe you can learn some Russian."

She half glared, but noticed the playful glint had returned to his eyes. She gritted her teeth. *Don't. Be. Nice.* Still, warmth lit in her stomach.

Nickolai said something. Vicktor snapped his gaze to his father and she saw shock in Vicktor's eyes. When he turned back to her and smiled, the look on his face turned the warmth to an inferno.

Oh, she was downright pitiful. So much for her attempts not to like him.

# Chapter Nineteen

❧

Vicktor breezed past bowed heads and ringing phones, toward the dark cave of his office. He felt a billion times lighter—not only was Gracie in safe hands, but his father had thanked him for trusting him.

*Thanked him.*

After Vicktor's mistakes, he had to admit, he'd never dreamed of hearing anything but anger or disappointment from his old man.

*Thank you, son.*

In a way, he owed it all to Gracie.

He noticed a shape in Maxim's chair, feet up, head lolled back, mouth half open. The heavy breathing sounds of slumber told him the body wasn't dead. Ready to shake Maxim for his laziness, Vicktor flicked on the overhead light. Arkady sputtered to life, wincing in the abrupt fluorescence.

"What are you doing here, Chief?" Vicktor plugged in the samovar and shrugged out of his coat. Arkady harrumphed, righting himself in the chair.

"What kind of cushy hours do you keep, rookie? I've been here since daybreak like a real cop."

Vicktor rolled his eyes.

Arkady patted his pockets, mumbling.

"No smoking here," Vicktor reminded him.

The chief's red-rimmed eyes nearly cracked from the pressure of his glare.

Vicktor hung up his coat, grabbed his coffee mug and plunked another in front of his old boss. "Coffee. It's better than smokes. Not much, but at least it won't turn your lungs to pitch."

"Just your teeth," Arkady retorted, but grabbed the mug.

Vicktor leaned against his desk. "You look like you spent the night in a Dumpster."

"I can leave anytime. It's your favor I'm doing."

Vicktor held up a hand in surrender. "Just an observation. Don't get edgy. I'll be nice."

The samovar steamed, and Arkady held out his cup. "Black. Very black."

Vicktor filled it and stirred in a generous helping of instant coffee. "So, what's so important that you slept in my office last night?"

Arkady began to sort through Maxim's papers, as if he'd left something behind. "Utuzh got Leonid's hospital records."

Vicktor sat down at the desk, turning on his computer. "And?"

Arkady shook his head, patting his coat again. "The guy should have been dead a year ago, maybe even longer."

"Yeah, why's that?" Vicktor grimaced, seeing the Bulldog had struck pay dirt and unearthed a wadded pack of Bonds.

"He had cancer, that's why. Stomach cancer."

"The scar."

"Right, and the missing parts, like his spleen. He had surgery over four years ago."

Vicktor drummed his fingers on his desk. His welcome page opened on his computer and he logged on to the Internet. "So, why didn't he die of natural causes?"

Arkady lit his cigarette. "That's a good question. Utuzh said the guy didn't have a trace of cancer left in his body. As if it just disappeared. Strange, *nyet?*"

Vicktor rubbed his chin with the back of his hand, humming in thought. He clicked on to his account and found no new mail. "Dr. Young. He was a medical doctor, right?"

Arkady kept wading through the flood of paperwork swamping Maxim's desk. "What a slob. Yeah, the good doc was a medical physician. But although he donated nearly 20K worth of equipment to the hospital, nobody seems to remember him practicing medicine. He certainly didn't have surgical rights or hospital clearance. Advisor-only status."

Vicktor logged off and closed his screen. He pressed his temples with a finger and thumb. "How do you suppose he knew Evgeny?"

"*If* he knew him."

"And how did Leonid the Red get cured of cancer?" The question swirled through Vicktor's mind and hit him in a soft place near his heart. If only he'd known about this magical cure a couple years ago...

Maxim's chair groaned as Arkady pushed it back on two legs and threw his feet on Maxim's pile. He dangled the cigarette from his lips, letting it bob as he smoked. "So, where's the girl?" A smile teased his lips.

"At Pop's."

"He tells me you spent the night with her."

Whoa, Vicktor had never felt *that* emotion before—the one that made him glare at Arkady. It rattled him. "It's not like that."

Arkady rolled the cigarette between two fingers. "I figured you'd come out of hiding sooner or later, but I never figured it being with an American. I guess missionaries aren't worth their reputation."

Vicktor's roll chair slammed into his file cabinet before thought could catch up to action. "Get out."

Arkady's face darkened. "Don't get your shirt in a knot."

"We were chaperoned. Yanna spent the night. And Gracie is due every bit of her reputation."

Arkady drew deeply on his cigarette and held the smoke in his lungs. "You got it bad, rookie."

Vicktor shook his head, realizing he'd probably taken out his heart and pinned it to his sleeve. "Listen, I have one hour to break into Dr. Young's computer and figure out what he was up to, so if you'll excuse me…"

Striding past Arkady, he listened to the cop's laughter trail him down the hall.

The sun streaked through the grimy window, sliding across the carpet in streams of gold and orange. Gracie sat on the sofa, Alfred's giant mug in her lap, twirling the dog's spiked ear between two fingers and listening to Vicktor's father spin tales about his son.

If only she could understand one word of what he said.

Nickolai's face danced with expression. He traced the air with gestures that illustrated his story and his voice infused the tale with emotion and meaning.

She nodded, smiled and prayed for Andrei to show up.

Nickolai leaned close, his brown eyes illuminated with some sort of fascinating mystery, and asked, *"Da?"*

*"Da."* Gracie agreed, wondering what she'd just acquiesced to.

The old man clamped his hands on his knees, looking satisfied, got up and shuffled to a bookshelf. Gracie followed his movements with curiosity. Why had Vicktor left her in the care of a man who couldn't protect her from a wandering roach, let alone a serial killer? The question knotted her mind. Nickolai seemed strong, the way his biceps squeezed out of a T-shirt, and his lean face showed years of street-toughening. And the way he probed her gaze with a look of age-old wisdom, she couldn't help but surmise Nickolai knew something about her. All she could do, however, was watch in befuddled amazement as the old cop shuffled around the room, and pray Vicktor knew what he was doing.

Nickolai pried a worn, fat book from its resting place between two leather-bound volumes, hobbled over to her and plopped it on her lap. Gracie fingered it while he settled next to her. Then he took the book and opened it between them. Delight arrowed right to the soft parts of her heart. A photo album. Obviously the *family* photo album, judging from the boy on the first page. Vicktor as a preteen, on skates, posing with a hockey stick. A familiar, determined look glinted from his dark eyes. The black-and-white photo curled from the page, the old glue crumbling from the backside.

"Vicktor?" she asked, pointing. The man nodded, his eyes gleaming.

He turned the page. Another yellowing picture, this time of Nickolai, a young woman and a baby between them. It reminded her of a picture of her grandparents. Neither adult smiled. The baby was dressed in a christening gown, chubby and drooling.

Gracie tapped the picture. "Vicktor?"

Nickolai nodded. His finger moved lightly over the photo, along the woman's profile. A shadow crossed his face. Gracie pointed to the woman. "Is this your wife?"

His mouth stretched tight, nearly a flat line across his face. He turned the page without meeting Gracie's eyes. Father and son wore that same look when they wanted to avoid a topic.

The next few pictures showed Vicktor as a child, at the beach, taking a bath, beneath a Christmas tree. Gracie examined each one. *Vicktor, what made you such a serious child?*

Pride lit Nickolai's expression as he pointed to each picture and illuminated it with an explanation. Gracie longed to understand his words.

She paused at a picture of Vicktor in a uniform—full-dress Russian army—taken in the middle of Red Square. St. Basil's Cathedral loomed in the background. She bit back a chuckle at Vicktor's high and tight crew cut. Still, however, that driven look lurked in his eyes. It haunted her. She glanced at Nickolai, wondering if he noticed it. The man's dark eyes scanned the picture. He ran a finger gently over the soldier's form.

Gracie glued her eyes to the book, chewing over questions about the history of these two men. What was it that made Vicktor burn with intensity in these photos and out of them? What was the sadness that washed across Nickolai's face when he stared at his son and his young wife?

The sound of metal grating at the door shattered her thoughts. Nickolai jumped to his feet. Gracie barely caught the book in her lap. Hobbling to the door, Nickolai peered out the hole. Beneath her hand, Alfred's body stiffened. His lips drew back to reveal canines. A low growl rumbling at the base of his throat made her skin prickle.

"It's just Andrei," she said, as if Nickolai could understand her. She patted Alfred. At least now, she might understand Nickolai's stories. If she could get Andrei to translate.

Nickolai turned, and his expression sent a chill up her spine.

"What?" She stood and watched Nickolai hobble to the telephone. He lifted the receiver to his ear only to slam it into the cradle.

Gracie went weak.

Nickolai stared at her for an eternal second, frowning, something gathering in his eyes. Then he hobbled over and motioned her into his bedroom.

"No, what is it?" Gracie fought him as he pushed her toward his room. Hadn't Vicktor told his father that Andrei was coming? She yanked out of his grip, started for the door.

The sound of the metal door groaning on its hinges made her freeze.

Nickolai grabbed her arm. *"Bwestra,"* he said softly.

*Quickly?* Gracie's heart reacted and landed in her throat. "What—?"

*"Bwestra!"* he hissed.

*Oh no, not again.* Gracie's head spun as she whirled and beelined to the bedroom.

She stopped at the door, turned, and fear sucked the moisture from her mouth. Nickolai sat on the sofa, feet wide, back stiff. In his hands he gripped a…gun?

Gracie dove into the bedroom, slammed the door, fumbling with a flimsy hook-and-eye latch, and scanned the room for escape.

Trapped. The room smelled of old cotton sheets and dust. Dark shadows lurched from a closet door. On the other side of the room, a breeze snagged the grimy green floor-to-ceiling drapes.

The metal door screeched again.

She slouched against the door. Covered her ears with her hands. *God, please protect Nickolai!*

A hammer against metal. The entire building shook. Gracie ran to the window. Throwing back the drapes, she spied a narrow balcony door. She yanked it open.

Three flights down. It felt like thirty. She turned back to the room. Nickolai was yelling.

*No, no!* Terror forced her to the edge of the balcony.

"Oh, God!" she moaned, not able to complete her plea.

Her slick hand clawed the balcony rail as she threw her leg over. *What. Am. I. Doing?* She angled the other leg over and hung from the edge. Below, the dirty alley glinted glass. A flock of pigeons clustered around a spattering of garbage. Her stocking toes dug into the rough cement. She'd left her shoes by Nickolai's front door, per Russian custom.

Her hands were slick with moisture.

For a second, the idea of surrender crossed her mind. She didn't have anything of value—perhaps they would let her and Nickolai go. She was nothing more than a Sunday School teacher on her way home.

The memory of Evelyn's pale face drove the suggestion from her mind.

She inched down. Felt with raw feet for the balcony below. Her foot scraped on a metal grate. Pain spiked up her leg, but relief rushed through her body.

The neighbors downstairs had enclosed their balcony with ironwork.

She shimmied down like a monkey, shredding her nylons, snagging her skirt on a jagged piece of curled metal. Sharp edges sliced her hands. Her knees scrubbed against bricks, leaving skin. Gritting her teeth, she closed out Alfred's barking from the apartment above and let her feet dangle from the next balcony. Thin air and a drop of over fifteen feet.

A gunshot, and a scream.

Pigeons scattered in a flurry of wing and claw.

Gracie fell backward, flinging her arms, screaming.

# Chapter Twenty

Vicktor sauntered into Artyom's cubical and found the hacker peering into the grimy dark screen of an ancient laptop. Green letters flashed in neon as Artyom scrolled down and analyzed the DOS language.

Vicktor scanned the cubical and spotted the Youngs' computer folded and tucked onto a stool under the tech's desk. Irritation stabbed at him. He cleared his throat. "Hey, Artyom, got any good news for me?"

Artyom jumped, knocking into Vicktor's coffee hand.

"Arrgh!" Vicktor jigged around, spattering liquid, wincing when the scalding beverage hit his pants leg. "There goes my suit."

Artyom scrambled to his feet. "Sorry, Vicktor Nickolaiovich, I'll get you a towel."

A moment later he returned with two paper towels and Yanna on his heels.

"I thought I heard you here. It's about time. I think by now your father and Gracie have run out of topics." She tapped her watch. "It's been two hours. I'm shocked you're able to stay away from her that long."

Vicktor scowled. "I promised her she'd get her laptop back before she left town."

Yanna's eyebrows rose. "Is she leaving?"

Vicktor wiped the bottom of his mug, then set it on Artyom's desk. Dabbing at his pants leg, he looked over at Artyom. "What are you working on?"

"It's Gregori Strakhin's notebook. They brought it in last night. It's encrypted."

"Gregori Strakhin—Customs director?" Vicktor braced an arm on Artyom's cubical wall and glanced at Yanna. "We've been watching him for years. The guy is clean."

Yanna shook her head. "The COBRAs picked him up last night. Part of a smuggling ring—Korean mafia."

"Really." Vicktor picked up his cup. "I wonder if he knew the Youngs."

Artyom turned in his swivel chair. "I don't know about Strakhin, but I know someone else who did." The hacker smiled like the cat that caught the canary.

"Who?" Yanna demanded.

"My girlfriend."

"Natasha?" Arkady's daughter knew the Youngs? "How?" Vicktor asked.

"Evidently, Dr. Young did a presentation in her academy class on first aid."

He looked at Yanna, then back at Vicktor. "We started talking about the case, and you know Arkady—"

"Nosy."

"Let's say inquisitive," Artyom corrected. "He is going to be my father-in-law. Anyway, he told me a little about the case and…" He threaded his fingers together and flexed them.

"And?" Yanna demanded.

"And," Artyom answered, reaching for the Youngs' laptop, "see what I found."

Vicktor set down his cup.

"I don't suppose you got the password?" Artyom asked off-handedly as he plugged the machine in and turned it on.

Oh yeah, the password. Wasn't he just on his game these days? Vicktor shook his head.

Dr. Willie Young's welcome page filled the screen. Artyom moved the track ball until the cursor settled on the "My Documents" icon and clicked. The dialogue box appeared, requesting the password. Then he rolled back from his desk, nearly knocking Vicktor in the knees.

"Type in, L-e-o-n-i-d."

Vicktor froze for a moment before he typed in the name.

Artyom's chair creaked as he leaned back and laced his fingers behind his head. "Impressed, huh? When Arkady told me about your recent corpse, well, I guessed, but…" He waved a hand as the computer began to whiz, its electronic brain churning. "Wait 'til you see what he's got tucked away."

"Which one? My Docs or Personal Journal?" Vicktor asked, reaching for the mouse.

"Click on the journal."

Yanna's perfume edged close as she leaned over Vicktor's shoulder. "Leonid's Cure," she whispered as he opened it.

A list of dates. Randomly, Vicktor picked one. February 10, 2001. "Leonid took the first of the two Shtumm vaccines today."

Vicktor scowled at the screen. "What is it?"

"I think it's a history of treatment," Artyom said.

Vicktor popped open the file for March 27, 2001. "Today began air purification treatment. Leonid submitted to two hours of air therapy with Aleon 132 Lystra machine."

"I don't get it. What did Dr. Young have to do with Leonid's cure?" Yanna said. "He didn't have hospital privileges, or a license to practice in Russia. He wasn't allowed to give shots or dispense medicine."

"Maybe because Russia's health care doesn't allow for individual treatment." Vicktor remembered, too well, the wall-to-wall beds in the cancer ward, the expressionless doctors who offered hopelessness. The smells, the moans, the faces of death.

No, he had no trouble at all understanding why Leonid might turn to an American for help in the area of medicine. He scrolled down the screen.

"Read June 12, 2001." Yanna tapped her finger on the screen.

"Began second cycle of vodka and oil diet. Schedule as follows: two parts vodka: two parts pure sesame seed oil, three times daily for ten days. No sugar."

"Yum," murmured Artyom. Vicktor threw him a dark look.

Vicktor took a step back and rubbed his neck. "Evidently this Leonid must have been desperate for a cure and thought Dr. Young could help him."

"But how? For all practical purposes, the man couldn't practice medicine here." Yanna leaned a hip on the worktable.

"What about this vaccine thing?" Vicktor leaned over and scrolled down the screen. "Here's another one. 'Gave Leonid second dose of Shtumm vaccine after positive ultrasound and X-ray (see cr: April 10, 2002).'"

Vicktor clicked on the entry for April 10. "Second series X-rays today revealed a stall of the cancerous tumor growth in Leonid's stomach. No noticeable growth since January 2002."

"No noticeable growth," Artyom echoed.

Vicktor stepped back, absorbing the information. Artyom grabbed the mouse.

"Go to the last entry, Artyom. Read it." If Dr. Young had been practicing medicine, perhaps he was also smuggling in illegal drugs. He recalled the fake Korean documents. Drugs from Korea? He frowned. The North Koreans barely had enough money to eat, let alone research new medicines.

"Here it is." The tech's mouth hung open as he scanned the screen.

"Read it."

"Leonid is in complete remission. Fourth series ultrasound and X-rays reveal a decrease in the mass of the cancerous tumor."

Vicktor cupped his cheek, absorbing the information. Utuzh had said Leonid's corpse was cancer free. *Cancer free.* Whatever

Dr. Young had smuggled in and used on Leonid the Red had worked.

Vicktor reached for the back of Artyom's chair. Yanna grabbed his arm.

"Vicktor?"

Words deserted him as he stared at Yanna's ashen face. He fought for breath. Leonid had been cured—*cured.* Fury reached up and grabbed him by the throat. He opened his mouth, but nothing emerged.

"Come with me," Yanna urged softly.

Numb, he let her lead him to her office. She settled him on a straight-back chair, then closed the door. The room hummed with technology—Yanna's specialty. One of the first female communication specialists in the FSB, Yanna had made a name for herself by helping write software to intercept and read Internet files during transmission. It earned her captain's bars and a director's position over the hackers' department.

"Can I get you a drink of water, Vita? You're scaring me."

Vicktor buried his face in his hands, shook his head and fought for a steady breath. Yanna crouched beside him, her hand on his back.

"Talk to me."

Vicktor closed his eyes. "My mother died of cancer."

"I know."

"Two years ago."

Yanna nodded.

He looked at her, blinking back the sting in his eyes. "A year after Leonid was cured, Yanna. An entire year. What worked for him could have worked for her." His voice caught in his parched throat.

Yanna's eyes glistened. "Maybe. But there are many types of cancer. You don't know it would have worked."

"I have to find out what Dr. Young was doing and why." He scrubbed his hands over his face, feeling close to losing it completely.

He clenched his teeth, willing himself to pull together. "A cancer vaccine. That's what the Wolf's after, I know it." He turned to Yanna. "Think of it. A vaccine against one of biggest killers across the globe. It would be worth a fortune. It would change the world."

"If it worked, yeah."

"According to Utuzh, it worked." Vicktor kneaded his temples. "It's so unfair." Rising, he paced the room. "I don't know who this Leonid person was, but I know my mother did not deserve to die the wretched, painful death she did."

He pinned Yanna with a dark look. "God should have given the cure to my mother. She deserved it."

"You know I'm not the one who can answer those questions. You need to talk to Preach…" Yanna raised her gaze and the tears in her eyes made him hear her words. "Or your friend Gracie. Maybe she can tell you why your mother died."

"Yeah. Maybe. Or maybe Gracie Benson isn't everything she appears, either, just like Dr. Young. Maybe she knows more than she's saying."

"Vicktor, I don't think she's keeping anything from you. She's no doctor. How would she know anything about a cancer treatment?"

"Well she knows something. And someone's trying to kill her for it."

Yanna held her hands palm up and shrugged.

Vicktor turned, one hand on the door handle. His voice dropped to a whisper. "If Gracie Benson is hiding something, it's gonna kill me."

"I know," Yanna said.

Gracie hobbled down the sidewalk. The cement chipped into her bare feet and she ached to her toes. She ducked her head at the gawks of two overdressed babushkas in wool coats and headscarves. Running her tongue over her throbbing lip, she tasted blood.

She needed to hide, and fast. For all she knew, the killers had finished off Nickolai and had turned their sights on her.

Glancing over her shoulder, she saw only blue sky and green parkway.

No, gun-wielding killers. No maniacs with hunting knives. *Think, Gracie!*

Her right arm felt numb down to her fingertips, except for a white-hot burning in her elbow. Clutching her wrist, she tucked the injured arm close and speed-walked toward the Aeroflot office, her closest link to safety.

Beyond hiding inside Larissa's office, she hadn't a clue what she would do. Someone needed to get help.

*Please, Lord, don't let Nickolai be dead!*

Her feet felt like chunks of ice as she climbed the cement steps. Head down, she scuttled through the lobby and nearly broke into a run on the way down the hall to Larissa's office.

Larissa looked up. "*Oy.* What happened?" She rose to her feet.

"Do I look that bad?"

Larissa rushed around her desk and Gracie let herself sag into her friend's embrace. "Oh, Larissa..."

"What happened?"

Gracie pulled away, took a deep breath. Two wide-eyed women goggled at her from across the hallway. "I'm in trouble," she said in a low voice.

Larissa frowned, pinched her red lips into a line and hooked her arm around Gracie's waist. Gracie fought a wince as she limped with Larissa down the hall to a tiny, windowless office. Larissa closed the door and turned on the overhead light, filling the room with fluorescence.

"Where's Andrei?" Larissa led her to a chair.

Gracie sunk into it as every muscle screamed. "I don't know."

Larissa wore a look of horror as she knelt before Gracie, examining her wounds. "Were you attacked?"

"I'm...in a bit of trouble." Gracie sank her head into her hands. "Since I saw you last, my flat has been destroyed. I've been shot at. I've had my bag stolen. I've spent the night in two different beds. I'm in the custody of the FSB, and just now, I think a man was killed trying to protect me."

Put that way, it sounded a billion times worse than Gracie had ever realized.

"I think someone is trying to kill me." Gracie blinked back tears as the truth slammed into her.

Someone was trying to kill her. Why, oh why, hadn't she listened to Vicktor? Believed him? Gladly taken the holding cell deep in FSB HQ?

Or maybe…only Vicktor knew where she'd been in the village, or at the restaurant, or even today. And had been conveniently absent each time. Could the FSB somehow be behind the murders?

Vicktor wouldn't kill his own father, would he?

*Lord, please, give me wisdom!*

"Larissa, I need a place to hide. I can't leave Russia because my passport and visa have been stolen. I need a place to stay, a place no one knows about."

"How about my *dacha*? You can go there. You know where it is and no one would think to look there."

Gracie kneaded her eyes. Yes, maybe Larissa's summer cottage, a small two-room shack in the middle of a fenced garden plot, was just the forgotten hideout she needed. "Are you sure?"

"I'm sure, Gracie." Larissa scowled. "But first let's get you into some decent clothes and a pair of shoes."

Vicktor stood in front of his samovar, holding his empty cup, tapping it in one hand. Leonid's million-dollar cure. Dr. Young. Gracie. Evgeny. How did they fit together? And who wanted them dead? He would have bet his life on the Wolf twenty-four hours earlier, but now? Was the Wolf a smuggler? Or were the Youngs smuggling in experimental cancer drugs?

The samovar steamed, hissing. Vicktor unplugged it with a yank and filled his mug. Two heaping spoonfuls of instant coffee turned his water to mud. So maybe his mind was on other topics. Or maybe he needed the double jolt to help his brain unravel Gracie's mess.

Vicktor set the mug to cool by the computer and opened his mail program. Shooting a look toward Maxim, he turned his screen away from Max, put the keyboard on his lap and logged on to the Internet. Typing in the address of an e-group chat room, he entered a password and left a message. Then he accessed his private electronic mailbox and sent a letter. "Please, Preach, check your mail tonight," he breathed, then quickly closed out his program and logged off.

His telephone buzzed not ten seconds later. *"Slyushaiyu!"*

Shots fired. And the address given to him nearly made him retch.

# Chapter Twenty-One

Larissa rooted through her wooden locker, located in a small changing room down the hall from her office. "Aha!" she exclaimed and pulled out a pair of black polyester bell-bottoms and a velour leopard-skin patterned shirt.

"Oh…I don't know…" Gracie stared at the outfit.

"Compared to the little number you've got on, this thing is tame." Larissa draped the shirt over Gracie's body.

"Where do you wear this thing after Halloween is over?"

Larissa gave her a look of mock offense.

Gracie wiggled out of her ripped black dress and let it fall in a heap to the floor. Larissa picked it up with two fingers, as if it were something the cat dragged in.

Gracie pulled on the shirt, gingerly working it over her injured elbow, hating how it molded to every curve. Just what she needed to make Vicktor notice all her attributes except her morals and ethics.

Not like she'd ever let him get that close again.

The memory of a dog whining and a voice calling her name

echoed in her ears as she tugged on the bell-bottoms. "I think it might be against my religion to wear something like this."

"You look fabulous! No one would ever guess you're a missionary."

"That's what I am afraid of."

"I'm just trying to help you out here. The idea is to blend, right?"

"I think my mother had an outfit like this when I was about three years old."

"Sandals?" Larissa held out a pair of stiletto high-heeled sandals.

Gracie made a face. "Thanks, Larissa, but maybe it would be easier to go barefoot."

Larissa held up the sandals like they were earrings. "They're my favorite pair."

Gracie slipped on the shoes. She rose three inches higher and wobbled. "I don't want to know how I look."

Larissa urged her toward a full-length mirror. "Oh yes, you do."

Gracie groaned as she hazarded a look. Her hair fell around her gaunt face in an unkempt mess, shadows bagged under her eyes, and a muddy scratch ran along her cheekbone. She traced it, noticing tinges of purple. "I didn't realize I'd hit my face when I fell."

"Fell?" Larissa echoed.

Gracie didn't elaborate. And she had to concede that, despite the war-torn additions, she looked little, if anything, like the woman who'd fled the Youngs' flat only three days ago. Was that a good thing or a bad thing?

She unpinned her hair and attempted to gather it. Larissa scrutinized her injury for a moment, then retrieved a brush from her locker. Gracie swept back her hair, turned it into an inverted ponytail.

"Now some mascara."

"Wow, clothes and makeup, too. What is this, Larissa's Beauty Salon?"

"Close your eyes. Pretend you're reading a good book late at night in bed and you're fighting to keep your eyes open."

"Right." Gracie lowered her eyelids and felt Larissa layer her lashes with mascara. A moment later, Gracie smiled at her new, groomed reflection. The throb in her elbow seemed to lessen.

"I don't know how to thank you," Gracie said, pulling Larissa into an embrace.

"You just be careful." Larissa's voice thickened with emotion. "Here, take this." She pressed a wad of rubles into Gracie's palm. "I'll come out tomorrow to check on you."

Gracie nodded. "Oh, can you call Andrei and tell him where I am? He'll be worried."

"Of course. What about the FSB?"

The FSB. The Formerly Safe Bureau. The Federation of Spies and Bad Boys. Gracie's jaw tightened. "I'm on my own now."

She left the Aeroflot office and sauntered down the sidewalk feeling like she was on exhibit. Noting the curious glances from old women, a blush heated her face. No one would guess she was American missionary Gracie Benson. For the moment, her leopard-skin patterned shirt protected her.

Her injured ankle began to ache and the high-heel shoes pitched her at an unfamiliar angle. She longed for a pair of faded jeans and her hiking boots, but they felt as far away as America.

No passport, no visa. No clothes, little money. Gracie hobbled to a bench and sank onto it. "Lord, I really need Your help here."

The wind picked at her hair and sent chills up her spine. She should have borrowed a jacket, too.

The smell of fresh bread called to her empty stomach, and it groaned. The boulevard traffic had picked up—women walking dogs, children scampering home from school for lunch. Gracie watched a group of boys jostling one another, playing, laughing. Carefree.

Her chest burned and she swallowed the acid creeping up her throat. Once she got to Larissa's *dacha,* what would she do? Her list of friends shrank daily. Even Andrei had seemed standoffish, annoyed this morning. And if Vicktor found her…he'd probably throw her in the clink until he could send her packing.

If he didn't have other plans for her… She let her fears settle into one painful truth—precious few people knew where she'd been this morning and the glaring majority had been FSB agents.

Someone had leaked her whereabouts.

First sign of Mr. FSB and she would kung fu him and run for the hills. The thought brought tears to her eyes. What had she been thinking, throwing herself into the arms of the FSB? She shuddered. Andrei had known better. Fear had uprooted her common sense and tossed it hither. The FezB had a reputation that made the average Russian shudder, not to mention what it would, no *should,* do to a foreigner. Vicktor was the last person she should trust. His blue eyes had obviously charmed away her brain cells.

She pushed to her feet, swayed on legs of rubber, then gritted her teeth and set out for the train station. In an hour she'd be tucked away at Larissa's *dacha.*

Someplace where the FSB, or Vicktor's so-called Wolf, would never find her.

Vicktor screeched up to the curb, nearly crunching Arkady's black Moscovitz. He scrambled up the three flights to his father's flat, his heart rocketing through his chest. If he were a praying man, he'd have been making serious promises.

He nearly collapsed when he saw Roman hanging out near the doorway. His friend braced two hands on Vicktor's shoulders, barring his entry to the flat. Vicktor's breath caught in his throat. "No, Roman, don't tell me—"

Roman's eyes locked his. "He's fine."

Relief washed over Vicktor. Wrenching out of Roman's grasp, he doubled over and gripped his knees, his breath ragged, his chest tight. "The dispatcher said shots were fired."

"Your pop got him."

Vicktor stood up. "The Wolf?"

Roman again palmed his chest to stop him. "We don't know. There were two of them. One of them got away."

Vicktor pushed Roman's hand away. "What don't you want me to see?"

Roman grimaced. "He's okay, Vita. The paramedics are patching him up."

"What about Gracie?"

"She's gone."

Vicktor sprinted past him. He nearly fell over the bloody corpse sprawled in the hallway of the apartment, but didn't stop.

Nickolai sat on the sofa, surrounded by medics, blood-smeared cloths layering the floor. Vicktor braced his arm on the wall, feeling weak. "Pop? You okay?"

Blood ran down the side of Nickolai's face, dripped off his chin and pooled in his shirt collar. Vicktor knelt before him. "What happened?"

Nickolai raised his gun. "Still a crack shot."

"But you're hit." Vicktor reached up and peeked under a thick gauze bandage wrapped around Nickolai's head.

"It's a scratch."

Vicktor frowned at him.

"Alfred did it when he jumped off the sofa. Upset your mother's shelf. The vase I gave her for our last anniversary nearly did me in." He pointed to the shattered remains of Antonina's vase. Relief poured out of Vicktor in a hot breath.

Nickolai's expression darkened. "Your girl got away, Vicktor. They tore off the door coming in. I popped the first one while she went out the window. Alfred took after the other one. She's got guts, that American. I don't know how she got off that balcony. But she's scared and running. You need to find her, fast."

Vicktor climbed to his feet and strode to the balcony. Outside, the wind picked up just enough scent to suggest spring. The sun winked overhead as if betraying a secret. Vicktor clutched the rail and peered over.

A fragment of black material flapped from the neighbor's ironwork below. His throat knotted. "Where are you, Gracie?" Squinting at the ground, he couldn't make out blood, but he winced as he imagined her falling. He closed his eyes as indictment curled around his soul. He'd done it again: had let the Wolf get his father. What had he been thinking bringing Gracie here?

Roman's presence behind him made him hang his head.

"I shouldn't have left her here."

"Yes, you should have. She's alive because your pop is a better cop than he believed, and you knew it."

Vicktor met his gaze. "I have to find Gracie."

Roman nodded. "You find her. Keep her under your wing and let us hunt down the Wolf."

"I'm not sure it's the Wolf we're after."

Roman frowned.

"I can't explain now. Just do me two favors. Go talk to a guy named Strakhin. The COBRAs arrested him last night."

"One."

"Then check our chat room at eight p.m."

"Got it."

As Vicktor brushed past him, he felt Roman's hand on his arm. "Watch your back. I'm not here because of your pop, Vicktor. Malenkov got another call on Ishkov's the private line. This time, the voice on the other end warned us of a crime."

"The crime?"

"The murder of an American woman and a Russian cop," Roman said quietly. "I think someone besides you is trying to keep Gracie alive."

"Or maybe it's someone who needs her alive, instead of dead." Vicktor stalked out to the family room.

"You said there were two of them?" he asked Nickolai, who was busy giving his statement to a rookie crouched at his feet. Vicktor noticed stars gleaming in the rookie's eyes. He shot a look at Arkady, who leaned against the doorjamb. Arkady met his gaze with a tight expression.

Nickolai nodded. "Bigger than you and wearing a dark leather coat." In his brown eyes Vicktor saw an old spark ignite.

"Thanks, Pop," he whispered.

"And find my dog, too, son."

Gracie fingered Larissa's wad of rubles as she approached the bread factory, hunger clawing at her stomach. Perhaps a loaf of bread would stave off the growling beast that seemed determine to broadcast her presence.

Cutting a path toward the factory, she ducked into a long line winding out from a weathered blue kiosk. Ten minutes later she emerged with two fat loaves of hot bread. Yes, yes, yes, the best things about Russia…crusty bread and the smell of lilacs in spring. Her mouth watering, she picked her way back toward the boulevard.

She noticed the shadow a second before a body slammed into her. "Ahh!" Her breath was jolted from her. She stumbled and dropped one of the loaves of bread. Alfred scooped up the loaf and bounded off with it, saliva dripping over his prize.

"Alfred!" Relief made her stagger to a tree, where she braced an arm and scowled at the thief. Alfred dropped the loaf between his paws and appeared apologetic, blinking those brown eyes. Gracie sighed. "C'mere, you big oaf." She patted her knees and the dog swaggered toward her, his fat rump twisting with the sway of his whip tail.

Crouching, she embraced his wide head and scratched the flat place between his ears. "I was afraid you'd been shot…"

Her heart went cold. "If you're out here, then what happened to Nickolai?" She grabbed the dog's ears and buried her face in his head. "Oh, please, Lord, no."

Alfred licked her on the face and she wiped her cheek. She painfully sifted through her options. Responsibility and Christian love would send her back to Nickolai's, but respect for his sacrifice would push her to the train station. She felt sick, but climbed to her feet. Scratching Alfred's snout she murmured, "Say goodbye to Vicktor for me."

\* \* \*

Vicktor sprinted along the boulevard, feeling lost. Frustration welled up in the pit of his stomach. "Where are you, Gracie?" he asked, turning a circle.

He felt as if he'd pushed her off the balcony himself. Roman was wrong. He *hadn't* been sure his old man had the pluck to defend her. He'd been desperate, and while he had hoped Nickolai could handle the job, he hadn't seriously thought anything would happen.

Overconfident. Reckless. The accusations burned into his mind.

Vicktor stood, arms hanging at his sides, directionless. He'd just scared the skin off a young woman in a black coat and blond hair.

Shoving his hands in his pockets, he shot a glance heavenward. It was the third time in two days he'd considered praying. Scowling, he shook his head. What was it about Gracie that made him feel so helpless, so...panicked? The thought of her terrified and wounded made him ache.

Good thing Roman wasn't here to see worry turn him to befuddled mush.

He'd find Gracie, throw her into a safe, as-comfortable-as-he-could-make-it holding cell and keep her under sentry until he could find a way to fly her home. Roman was right. The best idea was to send her safely away, quickly and quietly. And he'd let Roman pray the Wolf didn't tag along.

His hands in fists, Vicktor marched down the boulevard toward his father's flat. It was time to call in reinforcements. He'd find Gracie even if he had to alert the entire FSB force from here to Moscow. "Sorry, Gracie."

The sound of a dog's bark stopped him. He whirled, searching for the animal. "Alfred?"

The dog bounded toward him from across the boulevard, near the Svezhee Bread Factory. Vicktor ran to him, never so grateful to see his father's mutt in all his life. His heart almost pounded through his chest. He caught the dog, who jumped up on Vicktor like he was a poodle. Vicktor wrapped his arms around Alfred's girth. He didn't even grimace when the animal slobbered on his face.

"I'm glad to see you, pal," Vicktor said into the dog's fur. "Where have you been?" He pushed the dog down and Alfred ran in circles. Then Alfred barked once and lit out for the bread kiosk.

"Come back here!" Vicktor yelled.

Gracie cast a look back and broke into a jog. "Alfred," she growled, anger fueling her steps. Just when she thought she was safe, Alfred the Wonder Dog had to alert the world to her presence. She peeped behind her and her heart fell. The fool animal was following her and barking!

"Alfred!"

She heard Vicktor's voice a second before she saw him, running with his coat open, his expression furious looking, hollering at his disobedient mutt.

If only he know how obedient his police dog truly was. Gracie gritted her teeth, whirled and attempted an escape. Hobbling ungracefully, she fought the urge to rip off Larissa's blasted sandals and run full out, barefoot.

Alfred bounded in front of her, barking as if he were herding sheep.

"Shoo!"

Alfred wagged his tail. Gracie glared at him.

"Alfred!" Vicktor yelled, then let loose a string of Russian words.

Gracie ducked her head, praying her disguise worked.

Vicktor's dark form whipped past her as he lunged for the dog. Alfred dodged him, but Vicktor had practiced aim. He snaked a hand under Alfred's collar. Gracie scooted past him, not daring to look.

*"Izveneetyeh!"* Vicktor called, asking her pardon in Russian. She held up a hand, waving her acceptance, and kept her eyes forward, praying she wouldn't turn her ankle in Larissa's stilettos.

\* \* \*

Alfred lunged for the woman, ripping out of Vicktor's grip. He nearly knocked the lady off her heels. She turned to push him away.

Vicktor's heart turned inside out with relief. "Gracie!"

She shot him a look, one he'd seen before, outside her apartment. It hit him squarely in the gut. *I. Don't. Trust. You.*

Not that he expected better, but still, the fact he'd failed her so abysmally only turned like a knife in his heart.

"Are you okay?"

Her green eyes were steel hard. "Yes." She turned and stalked away.

"Wait!" He raced after her and grabbed her elbow.

She cried out in pain and doubled over.

"You're hurt!" Vicktor knelt beside her, sick. Her beautiful face twisted in agony. "Gracie, what happened?"

She looked away.

He blew out a frustrated breath. "I want to help you."

"You want to kill me."

He recoiled as if he'd been slapped. "What?"

Her voice was low and sharp. "Someone tried to kill me." She fixed him with a gaze that arrowed clear through him. "I don't know who to trust."

"I understand you're afraid, but you can trust me."

"Can I?" She pulled her wrist close to her body. "How do I know you're not living up to your reputation?"

"Reputation?"

"KGB? You don't exactly have a pristine history."

It would have hurt less if she had kicked him in the teeth. Vicktor fixed his eyes on the bread kiosk as he scrambled for an answer. "That's not fair. I'm trying to keep you alive." His tone was irritated. "Besides, I'm not the only one with secrets."

Gracie scowled at him.

"Your Dr. Young discovered a cure for cancer, didn't he."

Either she was a consummate actress or she had no clue about her coworker's activities. The look of suspicion dissolved from her expression and left only shock. "What are you talking about?"

Vicktor considered her, watching the wind play with her hair, the rebellious gleam in her green eyes. Her body language screamed defiance; he felt way too sure she would stride right out of his life without glancing back.

"Your doctor friend discovered a cure for cancer, and he used it to heal Leonid Krasnov."

Gracie frowned at him. "No. No way. How could he?"

Vicktor shook his head. "I don't know. But we found his personal notes, and they chronicled Leonid's cure."

Gracie again shook her head. "I don't believe it. A cure for cancer would be worth… Well, is it even possible?"

"Someone thinks it's worth killing over."

"Maybe the KGB thinks it's worth killing over."

He flinched. "Gracie, I promise, my only agenda is protecting you." Well, sorta. Because if he read the churning feelings in his chest correctly, she'd gotten under his skin, and just maybe he wondered what it might be like to take her in his arms, to kiss…

"I don't know who to trust." Her admission came out quietly, yet had the power to make him moan.

"Trust me, Gracie. Please."

She looked at him. The beautiful green eyes, staring right through to his heart. His soul. *Trust me.* He tried to let his eyes speak the truth.

Gracie sighed and allowed the smallest smile. "I'd like to get out of Russia in one piece, okay?"

*Oy.* When she said it like that, all her hopes and fears in her voice, laying her life at his feet, it was all he could do to breathe, let alone answer.

He nodded, and knew he was definitely in over his head when he ran his thumb along her chin, near an ugly scratch. "I'm sorry you fell."

As she leaned into his hand, he noticed her leopard-skin out-fit. "Where did you get that getup?"

"A friend," she said with a smile. "I do have a few, you know."

"Well, it looks ridiculous."

She edged up her chin and smiled again. "Perfect."

Oh, how he wanted to strangle her. That, or crush her to his chest. Okay, so that was probably a bad idea. He indicated her arm. "Did that happen when you jumped off the balcony?"

"I fell." For a second, right behind her eyes, he saw the terror of falling from three stories. The image emptied him. Then her face paled. "Your father—is he—?"

"He's fine."

"I heard a shot."

Vicktor nodded. "Pop has good aim."

She closed her eyes as if letting that information take root. "He saved my life."

Vicktor had nearly lost her. For the first time, his brain wrapped around that reality.

It shouldn't hurt this much, should it? He'd only known her for two days.

Except, it felt like a small, wonderful lifetime. He shoved his hands into his coat pockets, fighting the urge to scoop her into his arms and run for the border.

"Want to see my father?" he asked, hating the ragged edge to his voice.

"Please."

Gracie peeled back the layer of gauze protecting Nickolai's wound. "A vase?" She glanced at Vicktor, who shrugged. "You're not trying to hide something from me, are you?"

His wide-eyed, innocent look made her giggle, and when he smiled, she felt it clear through to her marrow.

How had she ever thought she might escape Russia without his help?

They'd passed a slow-moving ambulance on the way to Nick-olai's apartment. Vicktor had watched it with a stony expression.

Nickolai's face filled with relief when he saw Gracie. His gaze lingered on her new attire just a moment longer than needed, and he topped off his assessment with a translatable "Wow."

Gracie blushed.

Over a lunch of bread, Edam cheese, lemonade and boiled meat dumplings, Gracie explained her plan to Vicktor. "Larissa's *dacha* is only an hour from here by train. I can hide there until you can get me a passport. Then I'll race for the plane and fly home." She tore her cheese into little bits as she talked. "The Wolf won't have time to find me. I'll be out of your hair and his sights."

Vicktor twirled his spoon in his bowl, pushing around cold dumplings. "It's a good idea," he said, "but I'm going with you."

"No." Gracie saw him gathering his arguments. "You need to stay here. I can get there by myself." She glanced at Nickolai for reinforcement. The man was hungrily downing a third bowl of dumplings. He grinned at her.

Vicktor leaned toward her. His smell, safe and strong and masculine, curled around her and his face was so close she could see the fine etch of worry lines around his eyes.

"I'm not letting you out of my sight again," he said softly.

If she thought her heart had jump-started when he ran his hand down her wounded cheek, wincing, it was nothing compared to the way his voice, tinged with accent, rocketed her pulse. Vicktor made her feel dangerously alive in a place she had thought dead. She felt the heat of another blush and ducked her head.

"How are you going to solve the case living out in the country with me?"

"This case is not just about your friends, the Youngs. We now have a body count of five."

"Five?"

Vicktor touched her hand. "There's one you don't know about. The day before the Youngs were murdered, I found a good friend of mine killed in his lab."

"I'm sorry." Gracie turned her hand over and held his. He had long fingers, clean, strong hands.

"Someone is after something they think you have. It's not in your flat. It's not in your bag, so they think it's on you. Which, as anyone can see—" his eyes traveled over her tight uniform "—it's not."

Shock sent Gracie's chin downward. Then he winked at her. Secretly delighted, she pursed her lips in a mock glare.

He sat back in his chair, but kept his hand over hers. "They're after you, Gracie, and so far they've been able to find you. Someone needs to protect you. I'll send someone to watch your flat while I watch you, at Larissa's *dacha*. I'll bring a cell phone along and we'll be safe there until your flight."

Gracie fought to hear his words. He was rubbing his thumb absently over hers, sending warmth coursing through her veins. Keep it up and she'd turn into a pile of cooked kasha. And then wouldn't it be so very, very easy to scrape herself away from him when she left?

Back up. She *shouldn't* be enjoying holding hands with a man who didn't even have a relationship with God, let alone serve Him. Oh, she was courting trouble. She swallowed, disentangled her hand.

"Pop will keep in touch with my friend Arkady, who will then let me know what is happening. It's a good idea and the only one we've got right now."

Alone, at a *dacha,* with Vicktor? Gracie fought the panic rising in her chest. "I think you should be here, trying to find the murderer. Besides, I can take care of myself. No one can find Larissa's *dacha*…it's hidden in a forest of other tiny summer homes."

She picked up the crumbs of her cheese, polished them off. "Andrei knows where I'll be and will probably come out and check on me, so I'll be protected."

*Andrei*.

"He was supposed to meet us for lunch," Vicktor said slowly. His expression darkened.

Gracie stared at him. Worry squeezed her voice to a whisper. "What if they found him?" Sweet, patient Andrei, shot, bleeding, or even dead? Her stomach lurched. Vicktor took her hand. So much for trying to distance herself. It didn't help that she liked his touch oh so very much.

"Maybe he's not here because he's the one who sent them," Vicktor said quietly.

*What?* So much for romance. Gracie yanked her hand away. "How dare you? Without Andrei I would have drowned here. He protected me and listened to me and translated for me. He's the truest friend I could ever have." She narrowed her eyes and pointed at Vicktor, ignoring the way his jaw tightened and the warning that flashed in his icy blue eyes. "Back *off,* Vicktor. Andrei is my Christian brother. I can trust him with my life."

Vicktor's voice was harsh. "Tell me, Gracie. If Andrei is the only one besides me who knows where you are, how is it trouble always finds you?"

# Chapter Twenty-Two

Vicktor braced himself as he climbed aboard the passenger train. The soupy fog of body odor, the gray-blue haze of old cigarette smoke, and the endless sets of prying eyes that followed him and Gracie as they bumped down the aisle, set his teeth on edge. He wished for his *Zhiguli*. A car would be easier, and safer. But he wasn't sure the auto barges were running yet, and a short train ride followed by a little hike was the only way they were going to get to Larissa's *dacha* in a hurry.

Vicktor sighed and tried to relax against the molded wooden seat. He glanced at Gracie. Stubborn to the core, she'd refused to change clothes, and had barely spoken two words to him as they hightailed it to the train station.

If only she knew how hard it was for him to focus on the blue-haired babushka in front of him. Gracie's outfit did everything to accentuate all her formerly hidden features and he knew, by the way she tugged at the hem of her shirt, that she was all too aware of it. He knew better than to offer her his coat, however, despite the fact he'd dearly love to see her hidden inside it. She'd probably take his head off at the mere suggestion, judging by her board-stiff posture and furrowed brow.

Vicktor rested his head against the wooden seat. Gracie sighed in frustration. She stared out into the train yard—a muddy, rutted plaid of tracks and wire—and twirled a tail of golden hair between her fingers.

Vicktor closed his eyes and thought about Andrei. Her precious Andrei, her Russian boyfriend, her closest friend…. A muscle knotted in his neck. The creep hovered between them like a bad odor, even when he was absent. Vicktor shifted in his seat and stretched out his legs, knotting his arms over his chest. The look in the chauffeur's eyes had been downright conniving when he'd kidnapped Gracie yesterday. Vicktor didn't doubt, had he not lit out on Andrei's tail, that her overzealous driver would have her halfway to Moscow or hidden in the wilds of Siberia.

Maybe that wasn't such a bad idea. He heard Gracie blow another thunderous sigh and he winced.

Drumming his fingers on his arms, he opened his eyes and scrutinized the wood-paneled ceiling. He had to admire her loyalty for her friend, but he couldn't shake the feeling Andrei couldn't be trusted. Take Andrei's so-called communication with his mother in the village…even Vicktor knew villagers didn't have personal telephones. How then did Andrei so easily know Gracie's bag had been stolen?

Then again, perhaps his mother had called, or he'd called the *stansia*—the central phone station—and asked them to fetch her.

But what about the thugs who'd assaulted Nickolai? Had Andrei led them to Nickolai's flat? Maybe they spent the night on the street, then followed them to that morning. Except, if the attackers *had* watched Vicktor's flat in the night, why didn't they strike sooner?

Vicktor's head throbbed. The train coughed and lurched into gear, the wheels squealing. "How long to Larissa's *dacha?*"

"One hour," Gracie snapped.

He hazarded a look at her. She seemed tired, her shoulders sagging. His heart twisted in pity. "How's your elbow?"

She ignored him.

Vicktor stared past her out the window. The train rolled past a dingy, lifeless factory. A few forgotten birch trees dared to show buds and an azure sky hinted at the countryside beauty. Anticipation swept through him. He, *not Andrei,* was here with Gracie. It was up to him to sweeten the fragrance of the day, especially after he'd so horrendously bumbled her protection that morning. He reached over and pushed the errant strand of hair behind her ear.

"I'm sorry, Gracie. I didn't mean to upset you."

Her lips parted, but no words emerged. Her eyes glistened as she ducked her head, but her body relaxed and turned slightly away from the window. He slid a hand over the back of the seat, behind her shoulders. "I just want to keep you safe."

Those words lifted her gaze to his. Searching his eyes, she finally gave a small nod. "Okay. I forgive you." Then one corner of her mouth curved in a smile, and for a second he wondered what it might be like to kiss that sweet mouth. The one that could send his pulse rate into overdrive just seeing a quirk at the corner.

He swallowed the impulse and let his hand settle on her shoulder. And when she didn't flinch, but turned into the pocket of his embrace, he decided it was enough.

Maybe, just maybe, he'd work up to a kiss later. At the *dacha.* With the sweet breeze off the river and the moon lighting her pretty face.

*Think, buddy.* She's wasn't just an American woman, she was a missionary. There was no way she was going back to his flat. Roman's words thundered behind his thoughts. *The impropriety alone would send her into fits.*

Except, that was yesterday. And she didn't seem to be throwing fits, did she? Or…he scrolled back to the way she'd gone white at the table, when he'd suggested he accompany her to the *dacha,* and suddenly he felt sick.

Maybe he wouldn't be kissing her in the moonlight.

Still, she was here, with him, without her chauffeur, and Vicktor would use the time to rekindle her trust. Vicktor indulged himself in the scent of Gracie's hair. Maybe, in fact, he'd jumped to conclusions about Andrei. Crabbiness didn't indict a person. Somehow, over the last twenty-four hours, the killer had become a sullen Russian chauffeur who knew English.

Vicktor was losing his focus. Gracie's easy laughter, and the magnetism of her beautiful green eyes had snarled his investigator's sixth sense into hard knots. He spent more time ridiculing her outfits than he did devising her escape plan. That had to tell him something…what, he didn't want to explore. But if he didn't pull himself together, the Wolf would walk right up to them and tap him on the shoulder.

And then he'd not only scuttle his career, but he'd lose Gracie.

He wouldn't admit to himself which was worse.

The train settled into a rhythmic harmony and Gracie's head bobbed onto his shoulder. Perhaps a day in the country was just the escape they both needed—blooming lilac sprinkled the air and the birds sang from budding plum and mountain ash trees.

Maybe at Larissa's *dacha* he could gather his wits and figure out a way to save Gracie's life. Maybe even earn her trust.

And then what?

Vicktor caught sight of the conductor swaying toward them, asking for tickets. He let go of Gracie and reached inside his coat. Pulling out two passes, he leaned close to Gracie. "Don't say anything," he breathed. She nodded.

So she'd been listening when he'd briefed her. Without a passport, no conductor worth her salt would allow an American out of city limits. Worst-case scenario would be an ugly scene with him flashing his ID and sabotaging their disguise.

Gracie turned toward the window.

Vicktor stared ahead, face blank, eyes on the conductor. Dressed in a gray polyester dress that just barely contained her folds and wrinkles, she looked as if she had eaten a few of the passengers for dinner—and enjoyed it. She ripped off the stubs of the couple in front of them, then approached him. Weariness draped her dark eyes. Vicktor kept his face bored and handed her the tickets. She raked a gaze over him, then glanced at Gracie. A smirk flickered on her pudgy face.

Vicktor kept his face stoic, didn't meet her eyes.

She ripped the tickets and handed Vicktor the stubs. Vicktor reined in his sigh of relief until she was two rows past them.

He glanced at Gracie, then grimaced. Shrugging out of his jacket, he tucked it over her.

"What's this for?" she asked.

Vicktor curled an arm around her and pulled her close. He couldn't bear to tell her she'd just been mistaken for a prostitute.

The Wolf paced the room. The clock on the wall ticked out the minutes, seconds he had left to produce an excuse—and a good one. He rubbed a hand over his head. It came away wet.

The door opened and a large man—too large for the Wolf's comfort level, with a shaved head and hard eyes—beckoned him in.

The Wolf entered the adjoining hotel room, feeling for the first time as if it might have been better to run when he'd had the chance.

Smoke hung in the stale air. The odor of vodka told him business had already been conducted. He hoped favorably. He sat down on a fraying armchair the color of old blood, and pinned on a face that he'd learned aeons ago. No fear. The *pero* strapped to his shin helped, but it suddenly burned, and he crossed his legs, hiding the blade.

"Minksy is waiting. He says he has a potential buyer for you." The man in the opposite chair was ten years younger, but had the eyes of age. He rolled a Marlboro between his fingers, staring at the glowing red embers. "Don't let him down. He's not a man who enjoys embarrassment."

The Wolf rubbed his hands on his pants legs, fighting the urge to carve a line across the man's neck. How dare he threaten him? The man had forgotten who he was.

They all had.

*He* nearly had, for that matter.

Still, this was a new age, and that meant new tactics. He smiled. "I'm having some difficulty obtaining the package."

The crackle of burning cigarette paper was all that broke the silence.

"But I'll get it." His heart thumped and he cursed this sudden show of cowardice. Yeltsin and Gorbachev had done this to him. He hated himself for becoming the kind of man he despised. After thirty years, he'd expected something more.

A medal, maybe.

Weakness had led him to this moment. Weakness of the people. Weakness of his leaders.

But strength would lead him to the future. "I'll get it," he repeated.

A deep indigo sky streaked with fading cirrus canopied them as Vicktor and Gracie strolled down the pebbled dirt road toward Larissa's *dacha*. Gracie swung a bulging plastic bag filled with bread and canned items they had purchased in a nearby village. She breathed the scented air, letting it fill her lungs. There was peace here. She could feel it. Outside the city, spring had already revived the wild plants and kissed the trees. Pollen hung heavy in the air. A melody of twilight crickets began to sing, a welcome replacement to the symphony of honking cars, screaming children and hissing trains from the city.

Gracie exhaled, feeling fear rush out with her breath. The road behind them was empty, clear for at least a mile before it fell over the horizon. *God, please make this a safe place.* She shot a look at Vicktor. *In every way.* She'd spent the last hour tucked under the safety of his arm. And, despite the fact common sense occasionally rose up to knock her upside the head, she had loved it.

But a train loaded with onlookers was one thing—a secluded *dacha* in the country a completely different story. She licked her dry lips and set a smile on her face.

Beside her, Vicktor also carried a plastic bag, stretched thin with bottled water and a jar of mayonnaise. Gracie couldn't help but notice his rigid jaw and pensive expression. His dark mood had surfaced right after they'd disembarked from the train and had been slowly seeping out of him as they distanced themselves from the village.

She didn't want to guess at its meaning.

They crossed a side road and startled a pheasant. Gracie glanced down the road at the *dacha* houses lined up, one after another, a quiet audience to their journey. One-room huts, sometimes equipped with a bed, or a stove and sink, and painted sky blue, or jade green, they seemed grim and cold, waiting with dark eyes for summertime activity. Some already evidenced life, in the spaded soil and green potato shoots peeking from black earth.

"I've never been here in the spring," Gracie said, hoping for conversation. She pictured the flowering lilac trees, the current and Saskatoon bushes climbing into the sky, peering over fences. "It seems dead."

Vicktor stared straight ahead. Gracie bit her lip. The guy was in knots.

"Do you have a *dacha*, Vicktor?" It suddenly occurred to her that they could have gone to his place so he could protect her on his home turf.

"No. My pop didn't like gardens and Ma was too busy with her job."

"What did your mother do?" Gracie asked, thankful to see a spark of life in his stony face.

"She was a nurse. She worked for thirty years in the Khabarovsk hospital. Retired three years ago." His tone warped with bitterness. "She died of cancer a year later."

Gracie heart wrenched. "I'm so sorry, Vicktor."

He shrugged.

The breeze shifted as they drew closer to the river. It lifted the hair from her neck and chilled her ears. Gracie shivered slightly, wishing for a jacket. At least she had decent shoes—she'd traded in Larissa's horrendous sandals for her ankle boots when she left Nickolai's.

"So, do you think there's a heaven?"

Gracie stopped and stared at him. He dodged her gaze.

"Yes, absolutely, Vicktor."

"How can you be so sure?"

Her heart thumped in her chest. "Because I believe the Bible. And the Bible tells me that it is so."

He turned his incredible blue eyes on her and the intensity of his gaze speared her. "And how do you know the Bible is true?"

God picked *now* to let her witness? She dug through her memories, and prayed for the right answer. "A part of it is faith, Vicktor. Faith says there is a God and that He made us, and gave us His Word so that we can know Him. The Bible is the record of His activities with the kingdom of Israel, and of who He is, in the personage of Jesus Christ. But consider this—if the Bible isn't true, or only parts of it are, how are we to know which parts are accurate and which aren't? You either believe it in one gulp, or dismiss it outright. It can't be pieced out."

Vicktor wrapped a hand around his neck. She had the urge to massage that tense muscle for him. "So, why does it matter if the Bible is true, or not?"

Gracie felt his question more than heard it. Why did it matter? So what, there is a God. Why did it matter to anyone what God thought?

"I guess it only matters, Vicktor, if you consider life beyond this earth. The Bible talks about heaven. It also mentions an unimaginable, eternal hell. Two forevers. One incredible, the other horrifying."

Vicktor began to walk, speaking into the breeze. "Why would a God who says He loves us send someone to hell?"

"He doesn't *send* people to hell. He gives us a choice. But if we do nothing with that choice, we're making a decision. We're choosing indifference. For the present, without thought for our eternal tomorrow. We have to take the step to ask to be saved."

"I thought he was God. Can't he just save us? I mean, what's an all-powerful God for if He can't just do it?"

Okay, it was conversations like these that made her feel like a failure. The words always felt stilted, even desperate. "He did. That's the point. Listen, God is a Holy God, which means that, while He is merciful, He is also just. He can't just absolve us of the punishment for sin. Someone has to pay. Which is why Jesus died, in our place. Our sin is what keeps us from God, not God's choice. On the contrary, he chose to make a way to save us, through Jesus Christ. Now we just have to accept it. But God demonstrates His own love for us in this—while we were yet sinners, Christ died for us. It's a verse in Romans, but it pretty much sums up the Bible."

Vicktor went silent. Then, said starkly, "I have a few sins."

Something gave way inside her at his words. "Oh, Vicktor, we all do." She reached out, wanting to stop him, her heart already halfway there, longing for him to understand—

He whirled, fury in his eyes. "But my mother didn't have any sins. She was good. Kind. She spent her life taking care of sick, worthless people, and in the end she died their deaths."

Gracie tried not to wince at his grief.

"Is she in heaven, Gracie? Did God save her? Or did her sins send her to hell?"

Gracie's mouth went dry. Why, oh why, did she always find herself feeling like she had to defend God?

Psalm 22 flashed through her mind. "For He hath not despised or disdained the suffering of the afflicted; neither hath He hid His face from him; when he cried unto Him, He heard."

God didn't ignore the sufferings of people—that much she'd learned over the past two days. And this hope she could offer Vicktor, without knowing the answer. "Vicktor, I can't judge your mother. I didn't know her, and I'm not God. Only God sees the heart, sees the soul. But I believe God hears the mourning of our hearts. And maybe He met your mother in her darkest place." Her answer registered on his face in a scowl. "I do know, however, that for you, if you don't ask forgiveness for your sins, the Bible is painfully clear about the consequences."

Vicktor stared at her for a long moment, then stalked off.

Gracie's heart plummeted, and all she felt was the ache of emptiness where it had once rested. She had failed God. Again. Why couldn't she get it right?

Ten minutes of silence unfurled as they trudged down the road. It narrowed, then turned along the riverbank, becoming a two-lane rut of dried tire tracks. Larissa's *dacha* appeared at the end of a long row: a yellow two-story cottage surrounded by a thicket of lilac trees and wild roses. The gate was closed, but as they walked closer, Gracie saw that the vegetable beds in the back had been worked and black soil waited for its seeds.

It was a forlorn, barren place without the greenery of infant plants, but Gracie had seen the fruit, knew its potential, and in her memory she saw the paunchy red tomatoes, the emerald cucumbers, the violet eggplants.

"Not much of a place," Vicktor commented.

Gracie sighed as they stepped through the gate. She wanted to curl into a ball and weep for the barrenness and pain in Vicktor's soul. Swallowing her disappointment, she walked up the skinny path to the front door.

It was unlocked.

Gracie had expected that, and pushed it open. Larissa never locked her door. She said that whoever felt they needed to steal the chipped cups and the stained plates needed them worse than she did. Gracie stood in the doorway, rubbing her arms against the winter chill still lurking in the whitewashed walls. Vicktor went over to a tiny iron stove, opened the door and peered into the yawning pitch.

"I'll get a fire going."

Gracie nodded and reached for his bag. He handed it to her and she plopped the groceries onto a table shoved under a wide window. She stared at the lifeless garden. She'd forgotten that from the *dacha*, they couldn't see the street.

But no one would find them here, right?

Was that good or bad? Especially when she glanced at Vicktor, his strong arms stacking wood into the stove, his handsome whiskered face, his beautiful eyes that had the capacity to reach down to her heart.

Reaching into the bag, her hand closed on a soft bag. Coffee. Gracie stared at it for a moment, wondering how Vicktor had bought it without her noticing. The unexpected kindness, despite his frosty demeanor, tugged at her heart. *Give me another chance, Lord, to help him see the Truth.* She couldn't give up, had to keep reaching out to him. Because the thought of going back to America knowing Vicktor was back in Russia, demons prowling his heart, was a thousand times worse than being caught by the Wolf. At least she had eternity.

Vicktor had nothing but darkness.

# Chapter Twenty-Three

"Andrei, I'm so glad I caught you!" Larissa leaned back into the sofa. Her head throbbed and she kneaded her temple as she pressed the phone to her ear. "Where are you?"

"Pacing the floor of my kitchen."

She imagined him in the one-room dump where he lived. Wood floors, a green fraying pullout sofa, the smell of sunflower oil and fried potatoes clinging to the gold wallpaper. He had so little ambition. No wonder Gracie had refused to marry him.

"I'm worried about Gracie," she said.

"She's with that cop. I'm sure he'll take good care of her."

She didn't miss the strain in his voice. After all was said and done, she couldn't accuse her cousin of acting out of anything but love.

She could use that.

"Andrei, she needs you. I can't believe you'd abandon her."

"I didn't abandon her. She's safe."

"She's *not* safe."

Silence. "What are you saying, Larissa?"

"Have you forgotten everything? Need I spell it out? *F. S. B.*"

The pause from him echoed with pain. She hoped she hadn't pressed him too far. His nightmares could be helpful, but not if they paralyzed him.

"I'm sure Mr. FezB will try, but c'mon…think. Who made up the Wolf myth in the first place? The three-letter boys." Her voice dropped. "Go get her. She's at my *dacha,* waiting for you," she soothed. "Then bring her to the airport. I'll make sure she gets on the plane and gets home. Safely."

He sighed, and she knew he was reliving the past, weighing her words against his own memories. She'd won. "Tomorrow, at the airport."

"What about her passport and visa? She can't leave the country without them."

Larissa took off her glasses and rubbed the bridge of her nose. "I'm a travel agent. You let me take care of that. You just go get Gracie." She hung up before he could argue.

"Are you happy?" Larissa asked, smiling sweetly to the man next to her.


The fire snapped and chewed at the dry kindling, its light scattering the creeping shadows, bathing the cottage in a warm glow.

Vicktor crouched by the fire and wiped his grimy hands on a rag. Out of the corner of his eye, he saw Gracie moving at the small kitchen table, chopping, humming. She'd thrown a blue denim work shirt over her leopard-skin top and looked delightfully comfortable, at ease for the first time all day. Vicktor watched the fire, wishing he felt her peace.

An angry fire, as hot as the one flickering in the stove, burned inside him. Why had he brought up her religion?

Answers. For some reason, grief had slugged him in the gut today, and, like Yanna had said, maybe Gracie knew why God had picked on him. Unfortunately, her bluntness had drilled him in the chin. It had taken all his tenacity not to turn and leave her and her merciless faith alone to fend for themselves. Surrender to God or hell. The choices hurt.

Except, could it be that simple? Tired, Vicktor hung his head in his hands. Roman was forever dogging him to trust in the unseen God. Roman simply didn't understand that Vicktor would never be worthy to receive forgiveness. Sorry, but he just didn't buy this "free gift" stuff. Sins had to be punished. Christianity seemed too easy. Where was the justice? More than that, how could he trust a God that had no reason to save him? Surely the God of the universe would have a few prerequisites for acceptance into His kingdom?

"Do you want coffee or soda?"

Vicktor snapped his gaze to Gracie, who stood with one hand on her hip, holding a teakettle. Her face shone, her eyes sparkled; no trace of fear remained. It was balm to his heart to see her change in demeanor after her horrific morning.

"Yes," he answered in a thin voice.

Gracie laughed. "Okay." She plunked the kettle on the one-burner hot plate and cranked it up. Then she turned back to the table and began slicing bread.

Vicktor swallowed a lump in this throat. "Why aren't you angry at me? Obviously I don't agree with you."

She angled him a frown, but softened it with a smile. "No, you don't. But that's okay. I'm hoping, though, that you'll learn to trust me, like I trust you."

Oh. He looked away, not ready for the sudden rush of feelings. What was it about her that made him feel…clean? She had a transparency that sucked him in, that made him feel alive, even at peace.

He sighed and sat down in a worn armchair. Peace was the last thing he should feel if he hoped to keep her safe. Peace was the last thing he deserved after *his* mistakes.

"Suppertime." Gracie's cheery tone threaded through him and produced a smile.

"I'm sorry, Gracie. You've been working so hard, I should have helped." He gestured to the bunk she'd made up for him. "I take it you're sleeping upstairs?"

Gracie smiled, but he spied a tinge of embarrassment rise in her eyes. He took the plate. "It's a great idea. The last thing I want is for you to spy on me while I sleep." He smiled, hoping it eased her discomfort.

And was rewarded with a grin… Oh, he'd have to be on his best good-boy behavior tonight if he hoped to be worthy of that smile.

She returned to the table and Vicktor set the plate on a towel she'd spread out on the swept wooden floor. Her resourcefulness and spunk in the face of terror had bolstered his respect for her.

Maybe, in fact, her words about God hearing her mourning and meeting her in her darkest place had some merit. A believing man might admit that her God had plucked her out of a few painful tussles the past few days.

Gracie returned with two glasses of soda. The fire crackled, spicing the air with the pleasant scent of birch and oak. Vicktor pulled up two armchairs. "Your table, milady."

"Thank you, sir."

And how was he supposed to concentrate on eating when she wore that delicious smile?

Where were Roman and Yanna when he needed them?

"Let's see what is on the menu tonight." Vicktor lifted the plate. "I see salmon sandwiches, and a dill and cucumber salad."

"Only the best for my bodyguard." Gracie's eyes were turned toward his, curious, delighted.

The look on her face made him weak. Hastily, he continued. "So, um, do you want to pray?"

She gaped. "Pray?"

"Roman likes to pray before we eat. I just thought—"

"I'd love to." She bowed her head. "Lord, thank You for this supper. Thank You for this *dacha* and the safety it offers. Please surround us with Your angels and protect us this night." She paused, and her voice turned hoarse. "Lord, thank You for my friends—for Larissa, and Nickolai and especially Andrei. Please protect him, wherever he is. Keep him safe and fill him with Your wisdom."

Vicktor's eyes flickered open, but Gracie's head stayed bowed, her fingers clasped tightly on her lap.

"Lord, thank You for Vicktor. Thank You for his patience and his protection. Please help him to find the Wolf or whoever killed Evelyn and Dr. Willie. Please give him wisdom to help me get home safely." Her voice dropped to a whisper. "And please, Lord, help Vicktor to find the answers he is searching for. Amen."

Vicktor's mouth went dry. He tore his eyes off Gracie and stared at the plate of sandwiches. She'd prayed for him, been thankful for *him*. Asked God to help *him*.

Okay, that round hit way too close to his heart. Gooseflesh raised on his skin. He didn't know what rattled him more— that Gracie would pray for him, or that God might answer.

Gracie picked up a salmon sandwich, contemplative as she peered into the flames.

"That was a nice prayer. Thank you," he said, feeling like a spiritual idiot.

Her expression didn't change when she turned to face him. He suddenly felt vulnerable, and grabbed a sandwich. "This is delicious."

She grinned, but he wondered if she could see right through him to the terror inside.

"Thank you. My friend Larissa taught me."

It just felt way too good to have someone care…that much. And it felt about a billion times different than Roman's or Mae's spiritual nudges.

This one nearly brought tears to his eyes.

And wouldn't that be great? A FSB cop breaking down into a soggy mess in front of the woman he's supposed to protect?

He suddenly wondered just who was doing the protecting.

His cell phone jangled. Vicktor scrambled to his feet and reached for his coat. He wrestled the phone from the pocket and flipped it open. *"Slyushaiyu."*

"You were right," Arkady's tired voice barked from the other end.

"Come again?" He felt Gracie's eyes on him and regretted having to speak Russian in front of her. Invariably, she would think he was hiding something.

Arkady chuckled. "Sending Roman to interrogate Strakhin."

Hope filled Vicktor. He turned and smiled at Gracie, whose eyes lit up. "And?"

"The Youngs may have been framed. Strakhin has never even heard of them."

"What about the signature—the wad of paper up their noses?"

"It's textbook Korean mafia, but the COBRAs ran Kim Jung and his gang back to the border over a month ago and Strakhin says the hit looks like a copycat."

"Still, maybe the Youngs were into something *tyomni* and simply escaped the COBRA net. Maybe they got cocky with Jung gone and he decided to take them out?"

"The passports and visas were plants. I showed Strakhin the stamp. He gave it the once-over and pronounced it fake."

"Fake?"

"*Da.* This guy's a real class act—he's smuggled in everything from drugs to females, but he knows his paperwork."

Vicktor watched Gracie as she picked up her empty plate and brought it to the tiny table. He had the sudden desire to pull her into his arms.

"Our unfortunate missionaries couldn't have gotten a dog license in Korea with that stamp, let alone smuggle drugs across the border," Arkady said.

Vicktor turned decisively away from Gracie, wincing in his effort to focus. "So it was a setup."

"Looks that way." Arkady sounded tired. "Now what, hotshot? Our Russian smuggler just flushed our leads."

Vicktor grimaced. "I don't know. Gracie's flight leaves tomorrow. I guess I'm going to get her to the airport and put her on the plane, and then maybe I can sort this thing out." He rubbed his forehead with his palm. "I hate to ask, but how did you squeeze all this information from Strakhin?"

Arkady's tone chilled. "Just be glad that in this country, the laws are still gray."

Vicktor cringed. Arkady's methods of interrogation weren't pretty, at best. "Watch out for my pop, Chief."

"I'm eating cutlets with him at the moment."

Vicktor managed a slight smile. "I'll be in touch. Thanks." He closed the phone and turned back to Gracie, tapping the unit against his leg. She stood beside the stove, holding the teakettle.

"Who was that?" Her cheery tone eased the dread fisting his stomach.

He smiled at her, masking the bad news. "One of my men, following up on a lead." He sat back down in his chair. "Evidently your friends, the Youngs, weren't smugglers. The visa kit we found was a fake."

He couldn't miss the triumph that lit Gracie's face. He allowed her the moment, unutterably glad she'd been right. Somehow it restored his faith in the salt and light of society.

But now their only lead had shattered. Whoever killed the Youngs, Evgeny and Leonid was after something, and although it had been unlikely, the possibility of the Youngs' involvement in some kind of drug smuggling had been the perfect solution. Somehow, with them as cohorts in their own death, Vicktor could argue away the idea that someone wanted Gracie. He could coerce himself into believing the attacks on her had been random. That she didn't have the Wolf tracking her.

His appetite died. He rubbed his forehead, fighting despair.

"Are you all right?" Gracie's victorious look had evaporated, replaced with one of genuine concern.

"Yep, just thinking about how you were right."

Gracie smiled again and handed him a hot cup of coffee. "Well, then, this is your reward for seeing the truth."

Vicktor cradled the cup in his hands. Steam spiraled from the surface and soothed his fraying nerves.

"*Pravda*," he mumbled as he blew the steam away.

"Truth," she translated as she sat on the armchair.

He met her eyes and their warmth melted another layer of his defenses. "*Da,* truth. It seems a bit beyond my reach, as if it's out there but I just can't seem to grab it."

"Vicktor, you know the truth—you just need to believe, to open your eyes and see it."

Vicktor frowned slightly, confused, then chuckled wryly. He sat back in his chair. "I was talking about the case."

"Oh," Gracie said.

"But," Vicktor continued, drawing a breath for courage, "I am curious about something you said. Why would God choose to save us? I mean, you're—well, yes, I can see him wanting someone like you. But me, I'm not…" *Oy,* this was harder than he had thought, especially with her staring at him, compassion in her eyes. "I'm not a saint." He looked away "I've made mistakes. Mistakes that cost lives."

Silence.

He hazarded a glance at her and winced when he saw Gracie's eyes glistening. She looked stricken, as if he'd wounded her. He was right; he read it on her face. God wouldn't want a sinner like him in heaven. His sins were too terrible to forgive. A fist closed over his heart and for the first time in his life he hoped he was wrong.

A tear slipped down her cheek. She didn't bother to wipe it away, just stared at him, her eyes darkening to a deep green.

He felt like crying, too. He focused on the fire. So it was all for naught. There was no salvation for him.

But then she was on her knees before him. She took his coffee from him, then held his hands in hers.

"You listen to me," she said softly. "No one lives a life without mistakes and sin. And God knows that. But he has chosen to love us, to demonstrate just how deep and wide his love is. You can't out-sin God's grace."

Vicktor frowned. "Grace?"

"Getting what you don't deserve. As opposed to mercy, which is not getting what we do deserve. God's really good at both. In fact the entire point of the Bible is that we don't have to get it right. Because He already did." Her voice fell. "All we have to do is need Him. To ask for salvation."

He wondered if she could see right to his soul, to the darkness, the nightmares and regrets. Yes, he needed forgiveness. Maybe even salvation.

Her voice dropped to a whisper. "Do you want to ask for it?"

Oh man, for the first time in his life, he wondered. He chewed her words, feeling as if his were trapped in his chest. Why couldn't he just reach out and grab on to this God that Roman and David and Mae and Gracie seemed to embrace?

Because, on the other side of surrender was discovery. Despite Gracie's words, Vicktor knew that once God got a good look at the things buried deep inside him, well, redemption just wasn't available for a guy like him.

Vicktor slowly shook his head.

Sadness crept into her eyes. "Okay, Vicktor." She moved back to her chair and stared into the fire.

Despite the warmth, Vicktor shivered.

Gracie wrapped her arms around her waist and wandered out into the barren garden. The moon was a perfect sphere in a velvet sky, spilling a carpet of light upon the coal-black dirt. Gracie listened to a sightless breeze rustle the half-clothed branches of a nearby pear tree and raised her eyes to heaven. "Why, oh Lord? What keeps Vicktor from embracing Your grace? What am I doing wrong? He seems so close, so open."

Gracie closed her eyes, fighting the tears burning her eyes. "Why can't he trust in Your love?"

"My God, my God, why have You forsaken me?" Gracie saw the words of the psalm in her memory. "O my God, I cry out by day, but You do not answer." Hadn't she cried out, wanting God to forgive her? She saw herself, tattered, broken, dirty, clinging to the shower stall in the bathroom, crying.

Gracie's throat thickened. "All who see me mock me." Yes, she'd mocked herself. Let herself believe condemnation. "I am poured out like water, and all my bones are out of joint." She'd felt poured out, emptied. Useless.

"For He has not despised or disdained the suffering of the afflicted one; He has not hidden His face from him, but has listened to his cry for help…" But God had heard her cry for help. Over and over.

And provided.

"The poor will eat and be satisfied. They who seek the Lord will praise Him—may your hearts live forever."

Gracie opened her eyes as the words settled. Had she truly let herself be satisfied with God? Or had she spent all her time feeding herself on what she thought might taste good to her impoverished soul? Had she truly let God satisfy her?

Probably not. She'd spent a lot of time trying to satisfy God, instead. Just like Vicktor, perhaps, trying to work himself clean of his sins. It was time for that to change. "Lord, I want to seek You. I want to let You satisfy me. Show me what that means."

She stiffened, suddenly aware of a warm breath behind her.

"Cold, Gracie?"

"No, not cold, Vicktor. Just…thinking." She half turned to face him. The stars lit his beautiful eyes and a blanket of emerging whiskers darkened his square, stubborn chin. He smiled, a crooked, white grin, and it sent a shiver of delight down her spine. She noticed he'd left his jacket inside, and his unbuttoned shirt pulled slightly against his chest and through the arms. In the light of the romantic moon, he was deliciously, dangerously handsome.

"Thinking about what?"

She swallowed. "God. How He's protected me. Through you."

He frowned. "I…I'm trying." He sighed. "I hope so."

The breeze whispered through his hair, caught his cologne, sent it to her. He made her feel so…safe.

That thought landed in a soft place in her heart. God had sent her to a man that made her feel safe?

Vicktor ran a finger down her cheek. "I still can't believe you took a flying leap off my father's balcony." His eyes caught hers and she saw something soft flicker in them. "You scared me."

"I'm—" She opened her mouth, but the look on his face stopped her. His eyes caught hers, he touched her face. And then he kissed her. His touch was sweet, soft, unhurried.

She closed her eyes. *Vicktor.* For a second she leaned into him, needing this moment, wanting to sink into his protection, forgetting completely who she was and where she'd been. *Vicktor.*

She felt him tremble, as if holding in emotions. And he tasted so good, of coffee and tenderness, and it made her want to wrap her arms around him. But something tugged in the back of her brain. Common sense or…reason…or…

He cupped her face in his hands, pulled away and searched her face. "I was hoping, but this was more than—"

"No, Vicktor, please." Her voice emerged too quickly, too high. She backed away from him. Probably the other side of the world wasn't far enough away to keep her from feeling his longing, or hers, radiating between them. *Lord, help me not fall for him!* Only, she had the wretched feeling it was too late.

"What's the matter?" He looked stricken. "Did I hurt your elbow?"

Gracie felt a fool. She hadn't panicked when Andrei had hugged her.

But this was different. Andrei hadn't kissed her. And the fondness she had for Andrei couldn't begin to scale the mountain of emotions she felt for Vicktor. The man who had just admitted that she'd scared him when she'd disappeared this morning.

*Scared* him. Imagine that. She moved back another step, trying to ignore the hurt on his face. "It's not my elbow." She shook her head. "Vicktor, I can't…"

"Oh." The soft look in his eyes vanished. "I'm sorry I offended you." He turned and ran a hand through his hair. A breath shuddered out of him. "I don't know what I was thinking."

At his defeated tone, tears nipped at her eyes. She couldn't look at him. One sweep of his blue eyes and she'd be back in his arms.

And would that be a great souvenir of her missionary trip to Russia? A broken heart? She would not, would *not* be someone who dated a non-Christian in hopes he would get saved.

Besides…outside this moment, their future had zero chance of success. Especially after he discovered she wasn't the person he thought.

*Used goods.* The old taunts landed just a little too close. She stared at Vicktor, at his wide back, his tensing muscles. She couldn't let him think this was about him. He'd been more than a gentleman, over and over. Yes, she couldn't date him. But there was more.

She touched his arm. "I'm sorry, Vicktor. It's not you. It's…well, I'm afraid."

He turned, and something like disappointment ringed his eyes. "Gracie, I would never hurt you." His voice dove to a whisper. "I want you to trust me."

"Listen to me." She shortened the gap between them. "Something happened to me…years ago…"

Vicktor frowned. *Oh please, Lord, do I have to?* But, if she didn't, Vicktor would never know how much she felt like God had plucked him out of the landscape to teach her to trust.

That thought rushed through her. God, teaching her to trust a man?

"I do trust you." Her own words burrowed deep into her heart. "I'm not afraid of you," she repeated, and the look in his eyes took her breath away. Vulnerable, hoping. A wall cracked open and behind it she glimpsed an ache so deep it made her want to cry.

"Years ago, I was attacked by a man I trusted."

A frown formed on his face. *Oh no, wait, Vicktor. I can't do this if you freak out.* She licked her lips and looked away, toward the rustling pear trees. She thought of Yanna's story, the laughter and friendship that had been carved from a near tragedy. Her own memories were so different. How she wished a man like Roman, or Vicktor or even this David person had been there the night she'd wrestled Tommy for her honor…and lost.

She tried to speak through the sudden crunching of her chest. "He raped me."

Nothing.

She looked at Vicktor.

His eyes were closed, his jaw tight. He wore a sick expression.

What had she done? She felt like an idiot and it was all she could do to stand there and not howl. "I'm sorry, I shouldn't have—"

"Oh, Gracie." He opened his eyes and the agony in them made her tremble. He swallowed, and when words emerged his voice sounded tight, even close to tears. "I'm sorry."

She hadn't expected this. "Vicktor, I'm okay. I mean, yes, it was horrible, and it's taken me a few years to get over it. And probably I'll never really be over it, but I know that I'm forgiven—"

"You, forgiven?" He gave a harsh laugh. "I should probably be asking forgiveness for the thoughts I have right now. Like, wanting to track down this jerk and…well, you probably don't want to know." He was shaking. "But the thought of someone doing that, to you." He blew out a breath. "You've nothing to be forgiven for."

She stared at him, feeling her emotions pile up against her heart. "I sorta felt like I…had caused it. Because he was a friend. Someone that I dated. And I went back to his dorm room."

Vicktor's eyes widened and he stared at her with horror. "You thought that I…" He held up his hands. "Oh, Gracie, I am so sorry. I promise, I would never, ever—" He turned, stalked away. "I'll sleep outside tonight."

No, that wasn't what she'd wanted to tell him at all.

She ran to catch up with him, caught his shirt. "Vicktor. Calm down. I told you all that because…because I know I can trust you. And I wanted to tell you why I was sort of—"

"Jumpy?" He turned and shook his head. "Of course you were. And for good reason. I feel like a brute. I forced you to stay in my apartment—"

"—and provided chaperones."

"And now you're here all alone with me."

"Of my own free will." She stared into his beautiful eyes. "And, while I might not kiss you, I'm telling you, Mr. FSB, that I trust you."

He stared at her, his emotions right there for her to grab.

She tried to deflect his gaze, but it sent tingles down to her toes. "I still want you to stand guard near the door, to protect me. I'll be upstairs."

His grim expression softened, and he broke out in a smile. "Of course." Then, he cupped her neck, wove his fingers through her hair and leaned close. She froze, suddenly realizing how very badly she wanted him to kiss her. *Lord, I'm so weak.*

But, he kissed her on her forehead. The touch of his lips brushing against her skin sent a trail of heat to her toes. Then he caressed her face with his eyes roving over her eyes, her nose, stopping at her mouth. Her lips parted.

*No.*

The command came from inside, from the places beyond desire.

*No.*

She closed her mouth, her gaze on him, and shook her head.

Without warning, Vicktor turned around and pushed her behind him. She gasped, stumbled and hung on to his arm.

"What?" She squinted into the shadows.

*"Kto tam?"* Vicktor yelled.

Someone was out there?

"Don't shoot!" Andrei walked into the moonlight, hands raised.

Vicktor continued to hold her behind his back. "What are you doing here?"

"It's okay." Gracie pushed away from Vicktor. "I asked him to come."

Andrei lowered his arms. "We have to go." Even in the dim light, his face looked pale. He called out again and his tone froze Gracie to the bone. "They know you're here."

## Chapter Twenty-Four

❧

"How do you know that?" Fury started in Vicktor's gut and surged white hot through him. He didn't wait for an answer. Rage possessed him and he hurtled himself at Andrei. The chauffeur threw up an arm in defense, but Vicktor dodged it and angled an uppercut at Andrei's jaw. Pain exploded in his fist.

Andrei grunted and staggered backward. Vicktor leaped on him, landed on his chest, hit him in the face. Andrei's head jerked to the side. Blood spattered from his nose.

"Vicktor, no!"

Gracie's voice splintered the wave of anger. Vicktor hesitated.

Andrei cuffed him across the face.

Tasting blood, Vicktor fell back, taking Andrei with him by the neck of his shirt. Andrei's eyes darkened. A snarl built into Vicktor's next blow. He whipped back his arm—

"No, Vicktor! Stop!"

Vicktor's fist skimmed Gracie's shoulder as she jumped between them.

"Agh!"

Her cry of pain shook him and he staggered backward. "Gracie! Get away!"

She turned, her face knotted in horror. "Why, so you can finish the job?" She turned to Andrei. "Are you okay?"

Shock rooted Vicktor to the ground. "Did you hear what he said?"

She looked at Vicktor, eyes blank. "Yes. That we need to get out of here." Andrei swallowed and scooted back, putting a healthy distance between them. "Andrei, what's wrong?" Gracie asked, frowning.

Vicktor leaped to his feet. He closed the gap in two steps and grabbed Andrei's worn leather jacket. "Repeat what you said for Gracie, please."

Andrei glowered at him.

"Do it now or I'll empty this into your rib cage."

Andrei glanced down as Vicktor screwed his pistol into the driver's stomach.

"That's not necessary. I'm trying to save her life," Andrei said in a tight voice.

Gracie stood a foot behind them. "Vicktor, what are you doing? Leave him alone!"

"Elaborate," Vicktor growled.

Andrei glanced at the gun.

Vicktor shook his head.

The anger drained from Andrei's face with a sigh. "Please, we have to leave now. I'll tell you in the car."

Vicktor squinted at him. Gracie's hand settled on his coat. Her pale face spoke confusion.

"Get our things, Gracie," he said quietly. "We're leaving. Now."

Vicktor had her locked in the back seat of Andrei's Toyota Camry like a child. Gracie shivered, despite being wrapped in Vicktor's coat.

Seeing Vicktor, the man she had nearly given her heart to, hold a gun on Andrei, her best friend, had turned her colder than she'd ever been, even staring at Evelyn's corpse. And the expression on Vicktor's face now did absolutely nothing to calm her ragged nerves.

She wouldn't be surprised if, should Andrei even look at Vicktor the wrong way, she'd have to hurtle over the seat to stop Vicktor from pummeling Andrei. Her shoulder still hurt from where his fist had grazed it.

She bit her lip and gazed at Andrei in the rearview mirror. His expression lodged her heart in her throat. Andrei's fists were tight on the steering wheel, and from the way the car was spitting up rocks on the gravel, he was serious about their getaway.

She reached for her seat belt. "Vicktor, please, put your gun away." The look he gave her made her shrink into her seat. "You're scaring me."

His expression softened, but he didn't lower the gun. "Sorry."

"What's the matter with you?" she asked Vicktor. He was taking this protection thing over the top. Muscles streaked up his forearms and his back was against his door. He looked like he was taking target practice.

"Ask your friend."

"Andrei?" Gracie leaned forward in her seat.

"Pull over," Vicktor said quietly.

His tone made Gracie wince. "Vicktor, don't hurt him. Please."

He glanced at her. "We need to hear what Andrei has to say and I don't want to get us killed while we're having our conversation."

Gracie stared at him. *Killed?*

Andrei pulled over. Moonlight bathed them in an eerie pale glow.

Vicktor took a deep breath, his eyes on Andrei. "Gracie, did I ever tell you that I spent six months in America, working with the Seattle police force?"

Gracie frowned. *Now* he wanted to chat about his past? "Um, no."

"Yeah." He switched his gun to one hand, pushed the gear shift into park. "I loved it. Not only did I refine my English, but I made a few good friends. And I learned something."

She swallowed the lump of dread in her throat.

"I learned that I also liked being a Russian cop. You see, Gracie, American cops are handcuffed by rules and paperwork." He narrowed his eyes at Andrei. "But here, we're not so fussy. The law has shades of gray."

"Vicktor, there are no gray areas in this car. Andrei is my friend. And you're overreacting."

A sigh rumbled from Vicktor's chest. "Andrei, don't make me sorrier that I didn't arrest you two days ago. And remember, I'll do what I have to, to save Gracie's life."

"*What?*" Gracie felt her world shift on its axis.

Vicktor's eyes never left Andrei. "Gracie, sit back and don't say a word."

Andrei's gaze searched for hers in the rearview mirror. "I'm sorry, Gracie."

He turned to Vicktor. "I didn't have to come. I could have stayed in Khabarovsk. I could have let him get her."

"Who?" Vicktor said it, but Gracie's mouth parted, breathing the question. *Him?*

Andrei shook his head.

Vicktor raised the gun.

"Listen, I'm just trying to keep her alive. This is bigger than you, Shubnikov. I can't tell you."

"I'm listening."

Andrei swallowed loudly. "They're after something they think Gracie has. I figured it out as soon as I saw her apartment. I should have said something before they shot at us. I'm sorry for that." He glanced at the rearview mirror.

Gracie felt her chest spasm.

"Who shot at you?" Vicktor's hand clenched on the gun handle.

"Two men. I recognized one of them—and that's when I knew."

"Knew *what?*" Gracie blurted.

Andrei turned toward her. His face contorted with sadness. "Knew they'd tracked Dr. Willie's information to you."

Dr. Willie? "What are you talking about? I don't have any information."

"The cancer vaccine," Vicktor said coldly.

Andrei nodded. "That's why the Youngs were killed. And now they're after Gracie."

Gracie opened her mouth, dredged up words. "I don't know anything about this so-called cure."

"Did you know Leonid had cancer?" Vicktor asked Andrei.

He nodded.

"So Leonid became his guinea pig."

Gracie cringed at his words.

"No, actually, it was the other way around," Andrei said. "Leonid got cancer. He got his hands on an experimental drug, but wanted Dr. Willie to follow the treatment. Dr. Willie refused, but Leonid said he'd do it even without Dr. Willie's help, so the doc monitored his progress."

"Dr. Young didn't design this drug?"

Andrei shook his head.

"How did Leonid get it?"

"Some doctor doing experiments in his back-door lab. That's why it wasn't legit."

Vicktor's gun hand shook slightly. "A back-door lab?" Andrei nodded. Vicktor's eyes darkened. "Who do you work for?"

Andrei ducked his head. "The KGB."

Silence rocked the car.

Gracie's breath lodged in her throat.

Vicktor's face washed white.

Andrei closed his eyes. "I'm not an agent. I merely obey orders and report what I see."

"You're a stoolie," accused Vicktor.

Andrei looked away, out the front window.

"How long?" Gracie stuttered.

He didn't look at her. "Ten years."

Something hard slammed into her chest and she gasped for air. Vicktor reached over the seat, and she was vaguely aware of him touching her hand.

"Start at the beginning," Vicktor said quietly.

Vicktor fought the anger roiling through him. The last thing he wanted to do was to come apart in front of Gracie. Andrei had been an informant, a plant assigned to Gracie. What had he told the secret police about his victim? Vicktor didn't know what emotion to give in to—anger or compassion. He held Gracie's limp, cold hand. The other hand gripped the handle of the gun, aimed at Andrei's ear.

Andrei continued to stare out the front window, eyes closed in private anguish.

"It started ten years ago. My brother was arrested for holding an evangelistic meeting. The KGB stormed the place and hauled him and three other brothers away."

Vicktor nodded, thankful he'd never been on a raid. Without *glasnost,* Roman could just as easily be sitting in *gulag* instead of being captain of his COBRA team.

"Like a fool I raced down to KGB headquarters, hoping to bail him out." Andrei opened his eyes. "They thought I was one of the conspirators against the state and locked me up." His voice constricted. "They questioned me."

Vicktor kept his face expressionless, but Andrei's words turned him inside out. Torture. The KGB, Vicktor's coworkers, had put Andrei to the vices. He lowered the gun an inch.

Andrei drew in a breath. "In exchange for my life, I agreed to work for the KGB."

"Your life?" Vicktor frowned.

"My life. They sent my brother to *gulag* as an example." His voice shook. "He died there two years later."

Gracie made a whimpering sound. Vicktor's gaze snapped to her crumpled face, the tears that edged her eyes.

Andrei jumped him. He grabbed on to the gun and angled it into the seat.

Vicktor slammed his fist into Andrei's jaw. "Let go!"

Andrei jerked back, blood in his eyes. "You're going to get us all killed."

"You're the one who's stalking Gracie."

"I'm trying to keep her alive!"

Vicktor wrenched the gun from Andrei's grasp. "Sit back, hands on the steering wheel."

Glowering, Andrei obeyed. "Listen, Shubnikov, you gotta believe me. I've been blocking for Gracie since they tried to gun her down. I would never let anyone hurt her."

Vicktor squinted at him. "What do you call betraying her, spying on her for two years?"

Andrei tightened his jaw. "Protection. I censored the information I sent back. I saw to it that they knew she was harmless." He stared hard at Gracie. "I took care of her."

Andrei's story rang true. *Perestroika* and *glasnost* didn't erase seventy years of suspicion. Americans all over Russia were stalked, spied on, followed. Whoever had assigned Andrei to follow Gracie lived by the old rules. "Who's your handler?"

Vicktor saw fear flicker in Andrei's eyes. The chauffeur shook his head.

"Please. I'll be dead by morning."

Vicktor glanced at Gracie. Her face was white with agony.

"How did you deliver your information?"

"At first, I called a special number. Now I just get sporadic phone calls and I have to leave my reports at the dead drop."

"A special number?" A chill crept up Vicktor's spine. "A KGB number?"

"I don't know. I called and had to ask for an extension."

Vicktor fought his racing pulse. "When did you stop calling?"

Andrei blinked slowly, looked down and away. "Years ago."

"You're lying. You called that number recently."

Andrei's gaze turned icy.

Vicktor forced the words through his dry mouth. "*It. Was. You.* You're the one calling Ishkov's old line. You're the informant. You called about Evgeny's murder, about the Youngs, and warned us about Gracie getting shot at at my father's flat. But...I don't get it."

Andrei sat in silence. Then, wretchedly, he said, "I want this to be over. I want Gracie safe, and I want to be done with this disgusting business."

Vicktor heard indictment in his words. *Disgusting business.* Vicktor's business.

Andrei wasn't the only one who was tired. "Do you know the Wolf?" Vicktor asked.

Andrei's confused frown seemed genuine.

Vicktor hid his disappointment. "Do you know who killed Evgeny Lakarstin?"

Andrei looked away. "Leonid Krasnov."

"L-Leonid the Red?" Gracie stammered.

Andrei nodded. "Maybe the vet was his connection to his medicine. Leonid called me the day before Lakarstin's murder and told me if anything happened to Leonid, to call the number. He was scared. And he asked me if Gracie knew anything about the medical notes Dr. Willie had."

A muscle tensed in Vicktor's neck. "Leonid worked for the KGB, too."

Andrei's silence answered his question.

"Leonid was a spy?" Gracie blurted in a squeaky tone, as if trying to wrap her brain around the words.

Vicktor sensed the pain in her voice and winced.

"We figure the KGB has spies assigned to all the missionaries."

Vicktor shook his head. "Can't be true. We're past that."

Andrei shrugged. "I'm still getting phone calls."

Vicktor chewed the inside of his mouth. "So Leonid the Red killed Evgeny. Why? Who killed Leonid?"

"I'm not sure."

Vicktor glared at him, feeling sick. "And the Youngs?"

Andrei's face twisted. He gazed out the window, beyond Vicktor. "I was trying to protect them. I didn't realize the medicine meant that much. I still wonder if he knew..."

Gracie gasped.

Vicktor clenched his teeth, wanting to hit something, like a chauffeur, until this pain in his chest dulled. "You killed them," he said quietly.

"No. But I saw them die. Leonid killed them."

The pain in Gracie's moan was so palpable, Vicktor felt it in his gut.

"Did you warn us of the attack on my father?" Vicktor asked, trying not to look at Gracie.

"I had no choice." Andrei's eyes glistened. "I don't want Gracie to die. Nothing she has is worth that."

He bowed his head, and Vicktor could see Andrei battle his emotions.

Andrei shook his head. "I want out." His eyes shimmered. "They are killing my friends. They want their information, and unless Gracie gives it to them, she's going to die."

"I don't have anything! I don't know what they want."

Gracie's wretched-sounding tone made Vicktor flinch.

Andrei looked at her, his expression pleading. "Gracie, they know you have it. I came to get you—"

"To turn her in?"

"No! To warn her…to warn you." Andrei's face sagged, aging quickly. Exhaustion hung in bags under his eyes.

"I thought if we could find it, we could use it to bargain for her life. I thought I could protect her. But, when they came after me at my mother's house, I knew. They don't care if they kill me, or her." His voice dropped to an agonized rasp. "I should have let you protect her from the first moment. I just didn't know who to trust."

Vicktor's mind went back to the moment in Gracie's flat, when he'd wondered whom Andrei had been working for.

The man had put himself between Gracie and the rest of the world because he loved this American woman. Vicktor lowered his gun slightly.

"We need to find what they want. I'll bargain with them, give you enough time to get Gracie out of the country." He looked away, out the window. "After that, I'll tell you everything. I don't care what happens to me, as long as Gracie is safe."

The hollow look on Andrei's face eroded Vicktor's resolve.

"Listen," Andrei said, his tone earnest. "They're after information that links Gracie to Dr. Willie and Leonid. Maybe it's the medical notes Leonid mentioned. Some sort of formula?"

"He has medical notes on his computer," said Vicktor. "But I don't think that's what they're after. There weren't any formulas, just records."

He lowered the gun and rested it on his lap. Andrei's eyes tracked to it.

"The computer was on at the crime scene," Vicktor continued. "If the information was there, the chase would be over." Medical notes. His memory ranged back to Evgeny's crime scene, the charred notebook in the trash can. "Maybe there aren't any notes."

"Yes, there are," Gracie said starkly.

Vicktor tightened his grip on the weapon and looked at her.

"Evelyn gave me a bunch of letters and a package to send in the States. There was a package addressed to a cancer hospital in Minnesota. I packed it to take home."

Vicktor shook his head. "Your place was searched, remember? It wasn't there."

Gracie leaned forward, her hands white on the seat. "Because my suitcases weren't there. I took them to Aeroflot to be weighed. We brought them home with us."

Vicktor's mouth opened in mute realization.

"They're still at the flat," Andrei said grimly.

Vicktor swallowed, glanced at Gracie. "Go," he said to Andrei.

Andrei turned and popped the car into drive. Momentum pressed them back into the seat.

"Where are we going?" Gracie asked in a whisper-thin voice.

"Home."

# Chapter Twenty-Five

She had to be shattered. Glancing at Gracie's hunched figure in the back seat, Vicktor noted that she looked wrung-out and defeated as she rubbed her upper arms and stared wanly out the window. He reached for her hand and snagged only air. She didn't even glance in his direction. He ached for her. He would be eviscerated if Roman, Yanna or David ever betrayed him the way Andrei had her.

The first hint of dawn pushed over the horizon beyond the river. The car idled, waiting for the morning ferry. Andrei lay slumped in the driver's seat, his arms banded across his chest, his face hidden.

A spring chill seeped into the car and up Vicktor's spine. Sleep lay like sandbags over his eyes but he sat board-straight in the driver's seat, holding the gun loosely in his lap. His gaze went from Gracie to Andrei. Not a word had passed between them during the hour-long ride to the ferryboat platform across the river from Khabarovsk. Andrei had stared straight ahead, face void of expression, while

Gracie slumped in her seat, twirled her hair and avoided Vicktor's searching looks.

He wanted to throw Andrei in the trunk and hold Gracie until the world righted itself. She had to hate the man she had called best friend, even if the guy had spent the last few days trying to save her life.

He should have seen through Andrei's veneer of loyalty. Vicktor was a trained agent and had been duped like a first-year rookie. *Idiot!* Just wait until Roman, or Arkady…or his father found out. Vicktor's grip tightened on the gun as he forced a cleansing breath.

A flock of sparrows began an early morning song as the sky turned periwinkle. Vicktor looked at Gracie. Her head drooped. He smiled. *Sleep, Gracie. Today you'll be flying home to safety. To peace.* His throat went dry. His grand master plan centered on flagging down a plane, shoving her aboard, and getting her as far away from Russia as he could.

As far away from him as he could…

Because, although she had told him her awful, rip-his-heart-through-his-ribs truth, she didn't want him to be a part of her life.

At least, not the way he wanted to be.

He closed his eyes, painfully aware that she'd done something dangerous to him. Like, made him feel alive and not nearly as tired or hopeless as he had been a week ago.

Her head bobbed forward and her hair fell across her face. He resisted the urge to brush her silky strands back, rub the softness against his fingers.

No, after her history, he wouldn't touch her again without a written, signed-in-triplicate invitation.

*You need more than me and Yanna, Mae and David. You need a Savior. And you need the love of a good woman.*

Roman's words. Pointed. Painful.

Vicktor glanced at Gracie, remembering his own words. *In general, women can't be trusted.*

Oh, yeah. Gracie had about as much deceit in her as a nun. On the contrary, her honesty made him flinch.

Like her admitting she'd been raped. That revelation turned him inside out, and as he let that ugly image sweep through his brain, he felt himself shake.

Why, *why* did God let bad things happen to good people while the rest of the world didn't get what they deserve?

Like him, for example. By rights he should be the one hobbling around on a cane. He pushed the thought from his brain before it could consume him.

A snore emerged from Andrei's corner of the car. Vicktor bristled and shot a look at the double-crosser.

Who was Andrei's boss? The Wolf? Utuzh had agreed the corpses were the handiwork of the notorious serial killer. Still, the idea that Andrei was the Wolf's pawn seemed a stretch.

Only, what if Andrei's boss was not only the Wolf, but also KGB? Vicktor rubbed his eyes.

He could use a little help.

*You have the truth, Vicktor, it's right in front of you.*

Even more than truth, Vicktor suddenly wanted hope—hope that things would improve for himself, for his father. Hope that his life wasn't a waste. Hope that he'd see his mother again.

And that was what Gracie emanated. Hope.

The ferry's whistle split the air. Vicktor pried open his eyes and spied a slow-moving car ferry chugging toward shore.

It shouldn't be too hard to get into Gracie's flat. She had the keys and his men had kept it under surveillance since Tuesday. Hopefully there was still a sentry there.

They should be in and out in a matter of minutes.

*They?* As in he and *Andrei?* Fatigue had obviously numbed Vicktor's brain. How stupid could he be? Andrei hadn't come to warn them—but to ambush them. The chauffeur may have duped Gracie for two years, but it took only two days for Andrei to completely string along a trained agent with years of military experience.

Andrei probably already had men at her flat waiting to gun them down the minute Gracie retrieved the package. On the other hand, if Vicktor left Gracie in the car, with or without Andrei, one of Andrei's henchmen could kidnap her and ransom her life for the information.

Vicktor needed backup. He reached for his cell phone. His thumb hovered over the keypad.

What if Andrei was not working for the FSB, but for some *former* KGB agent?

The collapse of Communism had hung hundreds of undercover KGB agents out to dry, leaving the new guard to deal with the backlash. Burrowed in their undercover trenches, most had tentatively surrendered, only to be quietly retired and removed from service. Many, however, had simply vanished. Dug in deep, they'd refused to surface. Dead maybe. Or addicted to their assigned lifestyle. All of them, however, were spies abandoned by their network, given their walking papers without so much as a gold watch for their years of loyal, stealthy service.

He would hate to meet one of the agents behind a Dumpster on a dark night. An animal in a corner has nothing to lose by pouncing.

If Andrei was connected to an old KGB agent, a swarm of ambitious FSB agents descending on Gracie's flat would alert Andrei's contact and destroy Vicktor's opportunity to unearth him.

Vicktor's brain throbbed with unimaginable possibilities. He focused on one thought—whoever was behind the lies, the betrayal and the secrecy was a murderer. And in today's Russia, the former USSR, a murderer paid for his crimes.

Andrei's chest rose and fell, his breath steaming a patch of window. Sunlight glossed the car hood.

Vicktor stared at Andrei, remembering the agony in his eyes as he'd admitted the truth. It had strummed a chord of sympathy. Vicktor had no doubt that he, too, would have sacrificed his honor to save Gracie, the woman he loved—

Where had that come from? Vicktor had definitely jumped into the realm of fatigue-induced insanity.

He and Gracie had about as much chance together as his father had of becoming a cop again.

There he went again, wishing for the never-weres-nor-could-bes.

Another horn sounded as the barge edged near shore. Vicktor reached over and shook Andrei, not gently.

Gracie's building shadowed a sleepy courtyard. The bread kiosk window was latched tight, but a green truck had backed up to the side door. Vicktor opened his car door and the smell of fresh bread taunted his empty stomach. Vicktor ignored it and beckoned to Andrei.

The chauffeur's face was waxed white with fear, which, in Vicktor's estimation, was a good sign.

In the back seat, Gracie was also a shade lighter. Both hands gripped Vicktor's gun. Her tired green eyes blinked in shock. "I can't do this, Vicktor."

Vicktor opened her door, keeping one eye on Andrei, who shifted from one foot to the other. "I know you hate it, Gracie, but it's the only way. Lock the doors, and if anyone comes, just point the gun. I'll be right back." He crouched beside her, touched her arm. It shook.

"Do it for me," he said quietly, hoping she wouldn't see fear in his eyes.

"I'm not shooting anyone."

"I didn't ask you to."

"Hurry." She put her hand on his and squeezed.

Words caught in his chest and he nodded.

She flashed him a quivering smile. "Be careful."

Today, his middle name was Careful. At least until he got Gracie on the plane for America. After that, he wasn't making any promises.

Vicktor glanced at Andrei. "Give the keys to Gracie."

Andrei obliged. The men closed the doors and Gracie locked them.

Then, with Andrei a pace in front of him, Vicktor strode toward the entrance to Gracie's flat.

Gracie turned the black gun over in her hands and wondered when she had abandoned her common sense. There was no way she was going to kill someone. *Kneecaps.* If she was being threatened, she might be willing to shoot at someone's kneecaps. In all likelihood, she'd miss and end up shooting herself.

Her best weapon was, without a doubt, prayer.

Gracie watched Vicktor and Andrei disappear into the shadowed entrance of her building. Then she leaned her head back against the seat.

"Lord, I don't know what is going on in there. I don't know why Vicktor is so afraid. I don't even know what to believe about what Andrei said, but You know, and I ask for Your presence here with us, with me, with Vicktor and with Andrei. Please help them get this information so I can get safely home." She paused and listened to the sound of the bread truck doors squeal on their hinges. "Lord, whatever lies ahead, I thank You for sending me to Russia, for allowing me to meet Vicktor, and…Andrei." Gracie swallowed, hard. "Please, help me to forgive Andrei. Please protect him." The bread truck began to pull away, and in its wake, wrens chattered their goodbyes.

"Also, please protect Vicktor. I…I don't know how I feel about him, but You love him and I pray he would see his need for You and turn to You. And, well, help me to be wise and trust in You."

There were so many other things she wanted to say, things that swirled in her heart but that seemed too fresh, too tender to admit aloud. Things that maybe a smart girl shouldn't be feeling about a man who lived in another country, who personified danger, who didn't share a belief in eternity with her. But also a man who pushed her fears into the night and made her feel safe…and beautiful.

And who would have predicted that? Dressed in her leopard-skin shirt and second-skin pants, her hair falling in tangles around her face, well, she knew she looked…well, there probably weren't words. But when Vicktor looked at her, she saw respect, and just enough awe in his eyes to make her feel whole and clean.

"Lord, forgive me for getting into trouble here. I'm sorry. Just…help me not to do something really, really stupid."

A gunshot cracked the air. Gracie jumped, nearly dropped her weapon. Her heart hammered through her chest. She flattened her cheek against the car window and craned her neck to stare at her ninth-story window. Dark as night.

Another *crack,* and her pulse roared in her ears. She glued her gaze to the entrance of her building. The gun shook in her hand.

A thousand minutes thundered by as she waited, gulping her heart back into her throat.

The two men staggered out. *No, oh please, no!* Her gun fell to the floorboards. Gracie fumbled for the latch, opened the door and fell out of the car.

# Chapter Twenty-Six

❦

Gracie cradled Andrei in her arms, his hot blood saturating her shirt. Gritting her teeth, she pressed her hand into the wet tissue of his jagged stomach wound. "What happened, Vicktor?"

Vicktor's hands shook as he redialed the cell phone. He couldn't look at her.

Andrei started to moan.

"Zero-one at Leningradskaya Street, building fourteen," he barked in Russian at the dispatcher who answered. "I need an ambulance and backup." He snapped the phone shut. Retrieving his trench coat, which lay in a pile beside the car, he knelt beside Gracie. "Put this on the wound and press hard." She took it without meeting his eyes.

Guilt churned in his chest. Vicktor rested the butt of his gun against his forehead, the cold metal shocking his sweaty skin. He'd been careful, checking the shadows as he shoved Andrei off the elevator in front of him…

They swept the flat together, Vicktor's fist knotted in the collar of Andrei's coat.

The trashed flat seemed untouched—boxes upended, closet doors thrown open, their contents spilled like the insides of a gutted animal. The house reeked of rotting tomatoes.

Gracie's bedroom was so quiet he could hear birds singing in the trees and the low rumble of a bread truck as it shuddered over hardened ruts in the courtyard. Vicktor flung open the bathroom door, smacking on the light. The smell of mildew stung his nose, but there was no one hiding behind the flimsy shower curtain. Or in the living room, or hiding in the odorous fog of the kitchen.

Not a trace of the agent he'd sent to guard the flat.

The fine hairs on his neck stood up.

He should have paid attention.

Gracie's two bulging suitcases sat where Andrei had left them, against the wall in the corridor.

Vicktor forced Andrei to his knees. "Open them."

He watched Andrei for any subtle movements as the man unzipped the first suitcase. It popped opened like overripe fruit, spurting bulky socks and sweaters into the hallway. Andrei lowered it onto its side and began to paw through the contents.

"Hurry up."

Andrei pulled out books and prodded hidden places under the folds of sweatshirts. "It's not here."

"Open the other one."

Andrei moved toward the second bag. It, too, spurted open. Vicktor pictured Gracie sitting on it to zip it closed. "Hurry."

Andrei rummaged through the clothes and souvenirs. "Gracie was wrong. The information isn't here." Andrei tossed out a wad of socks. Something shattered on the wooden floor.

Vicktor picked it up and grimaced when he found the smashed remains of a *zhel* ring holder. "Take it easy."

Andrei lifted a pile of jeans. "Got it." He shot Vicktor a look of triumph and held up a large manila envelope. Andrei studied it for a moment before Vicktor yanked it from his hands.

"University of Minnesota Cancer Center." Vicktor breathed for what felt like the first time in hours. Beside him Andrei climbed to his feet.

Whoever the assailants were, they had the speed of panthers.

The weight of a man on his back slammed Vicktor to his knees. Vicktor jerked hard with his elbow and rolled. The attacker tumbled off and Vicktor leaped to his feet.

A black Baikal pistol stared him in the face.

"Give me the envelope." A pig of a man with a ruddy face and dilated pupils, he glared at Vicktor. He wore a shiny black leather jacket.

"Nice coat," Vicktor said, and dropped the envelope.

As the man followed the envelope with his eyes, Vicktor cracked him in the chin with his right fist, deflected the muzzle of his gun with his left. The gun went off as the pig's head whipped to the side. Vicktor spiked him in the chest with his elbow. Breath wheezed out of him.

The pistol fell to the floor. Vicktor jumped for the weapon. Another shot sounded as he swept it up.

The pig pounced just as Vicktor turned, weapon in hand. Vicktor cuffed him hard. The thug dropped like a stone.

"Vicktor!"

Vicktor looked at Andrei and turned cold. Andrei clutched his stomach, blood spurting through his fingers. The other hand indicated the back of the other attacker as he escaped.

*Gracie waited downstairs.*

Vicktor started after the intruder.

Andrei's breath was ragged. "Stop, Vicktor. I shot him. He won't go far."

Vicktor hesitated.

Footsteps thundered down the stairwell.

"Are you sure?" Vicktor scrambled back to Andrei, already punching in zero-one. The chauffeur was white. He slumped against the wall, eyes big and scared, but nodded. He kicked a silver Tanager, no bigger than a lighter, toward Vicktor.

Disbelief froze Vicktor, even after the dispatcher came on the line. She hung up before he could recover. Andrei had had a gun this entire time and hadn't used it on him?

Gracie had been right. Andrei was the truest friend she could have here, despite his not-so-righteous role as traitor. A sheep among the wolves.

"I'm sorry, Vicktor."

Vicktor cringed. Andrei's saturated shirt dripped blood where a knife had dug a hole under his rib cage.

"Get me downstairs. I have to talk to Gracie." Andrei's voice wobbled.

"Of course." Vicktor felt ill, seeing the chauffeur's life ebb out.

Tucking the manila envelope inside his belt, Vicktor threaded an arm around Andrei and towed him to his feet. Andrei howled in pain. Vicktor dragged Andrei to the hall and called the elevator.

"Sergei—what about Sergei?" Andrei's voice was a scant whisper.

"Who's Sergei?"

Andrei coughed. "The one who jumped you."

Sergei. Andrei's boss? "Out cold."

Andrei slouched against him as Vicktor dragged him out of the apartment and laid him in Gracie's embrace....

"Hang on, Andrei," Gracie whispered. Andrei moaned.

Vicktor paced the yard. Where was the ambulance? He released a pent-up breath. Why hadn't he called Roman, or Arkady? He winced, indictment sinking razor claws into his heart.

Andrei's breathing was labored. Gracie sobbed.

Vicktor wanted to drop to his knees and howl. Hadn't she been through enough? Now he had to go and kill her best friend?

She met Vicktor's eyes, desperation screaming from her tortured expression.

Vicktor looked away, into the sky, at the pigeons, the spying babushkas, the impatient people in the bread queue—anywhere but at Gracie.

"I called the ambulance," he said starkly.

Andrei's skin turned a smoky gray, his lips purple; his life was pooling on the ground.

"No, oh no, Andrei," Gracie moaned. She bent her head close to his face, her hair and tears dripping into his eyes.

"Gracie," Andrei rasped, "I'm sorry…please…forgive me."

Gracie choked her sobs. "I already have, Andrei. I already have."

A small smile crossed Andrei's ghostly face. In the distance a siren whined through the air.

She couldn't stop shaking. Disbelief cut a jagged swath through her heart as Gracie hugged herself and watched the EMTs load Andrei's body into the ambulance. They'd made a gallant effort to revive him, despite their meager resources, Andrei still died before her eyes.

The wind nipped her ears, blew tears from her cheeks. Never in her worst nightmares had she believed she'd see the lifeless bodies of three of her best friends in one week's time. Agony forced her eyes heavenward. "Why?"

The sunrise had bruised the sky a deep purple, and gray clouds prophesied a misty day. Gracie bit the inside of her cheek, feeling scraped out from within. "I need You more than ever today, God," she moaned. "Hold me up."

Ten feet away, Vicktor stared unmoving at his bloodied trench coat. His wan expression betrayed tortured thoughts. He looked up and met her eyes. The agony in his gaze wrenched her heart. She took two steps toward him. He blinked and his expression hardened.

"We need to go. Now."

Gracie halted and glanced at the ambulance. "I need to call his cousin."

Vicktor closed the gap between them. "You can do that from my house. I have to change." He studied her. "And so do you."

He strode toward the car. Rattled by the steel in his voice, she blinked after him, then examined her clothes.

She was covered in Andrei's blood. It had turned the black pants a russet brown and saturated her leopard-skin shirt. Red etched the grooves of her hands. Her stomach lurched, a small moan escaped her lips and her knees gave way.

"Oh, Andrei." She crumpled to the ground, fell forward and covered her head with her hands, moaning. Andrei was gone. Killed because he'd been protecting her. She felt parted down the middle.

"Gracie! Oh no, don't do this. Please hold together."

Vicktor's arms enclosed her and she felt him pull her to his chest. He lowered his face close.

"I'm going to get you home. Don't be afraid."

Gracie dug her fingers into his shirt. "It's all my fault, Vicktor."

His sharp intake of breath was followed by a groan. "No. This is not your fault."

"Yes, yes, it is. Andrei was supposed to be protecting me."

"*Nyet*. Listen to me." He leaned away from her, grabbed her shoulders.

Gracie saw a haunted look creep into his face.

"If anything, it's my fault," he said.

She started to shake her head. His grim expression silenced her.

"I'm taking you home."

Then he lifted her. And she, because she was boneless with grief, let him. Somehow it just seemed easier to bury her face in his chest, curl her arms around his neck and hold on.

Larissa rolled up a pair of jeans and tucked them into her carry-on. She wouldn't have to take much. Looking at herself in the mirror, she ran a hand over her face, noticing the dry skin. She needed a tan, and perhaps a massage. She wasn't used to this kind of stress.

It would be over in a few hours.

She'd feel a lot better if Andrei answered his telephone. Where was he?

In her heart, she hoped he had found Gracie and coaxed the information out of her. She really didn't want Gracie to die. She put her hand to her throat and grimaced at the empty place there. Boris was definitely stressed. The man was practically coming unglued, pacing her apartment half the night. His plan would never work. She'd have to do it herself. Sometimes she wondered how he'd ever thought up the scheme in the first place. Dumb luck, perhaps.

His dumb luck was running out. And if she didn't help him, he was going to get them both killed. She picked up the necklace, broken in the middle, pried open a tiny link and wrapped the ends together. It would hold just long enough to help her finish the job.

Gracie sat on Vicktor's bed, numb, her arms wrapped around her knees, staring out the window.

A pigeon sat on a balcony just across the alley, and Gracie focused on it, on the movements of its tiny head, on the dark eyes. Andrei's brown eyes, thick with emotion, bored into her memory. She saw his fierceness, swelling when he kidnapped her from Vicktor. His words returned like a haunting prophecy. *I am so sorry I got you into this. But I swear I won't let him hurt you.*

Was he referring to Vicktor? Or someone else, someone he feared more? Gracie clutched her forehead with her hands and took a cleansing breath. Andrei, her best friend, her protector, her translator in this harsh Russian world, had died in her arms. Her clothes were stained with his blood.

Betrayer's blood.

Protector's blood.

He'd stood between the KGB and her for two years, and paid for it with his life. *Oh, God, why?* A fresh sob shook Gracie. *Please, don't let his death be in vain.* She crunched the envelope to her chest and raised her eyes to heaven.

She heard the water running in Vicktor's bathroom. Poor man. He'd looked hunted. It made her ache to think he blamed

himself for Andrei's death. The ride to his flat had been ago-
nizingly silent—Vicktor battling some unspoken pain, she
gulping back horror. She didn't want to admit how much she
longed to be safely tucked back inside Vicktor's embrace. But
he had no room for her.

His guilt took up all the space in his heart. She could see it,
even if he couldn't. Vicktor needed forgiveness like a person
needed air.

What did he have planned next? Where would she run to
that she couldn't be found? Or was Vicktor planning on giving away the envelope? To whom? Who wanted this information, and why?

Money. If Leonid truly had been cured of cancer, then the
antidote would be priceless.

And worth dying for. She ran a finger over the address Evelyn had written. This information would *not* land in the hands
of Dr. Willie's killer—not without the battle of her life. She'd
leave Russia with the notes.

Or die trying.

# Chapter Twenty-Seven

"C'mon, Vicktor, sort this out." Vicktor sat on the edge of his bathtub, the door securely locked, muttering to himself. Steam hung near the ceiling and sent rivulets of perspiration down his face. His clothes clung to him, sweat coursed down his back. He shoved his hand through his hair, then pushed his palms against his temples.

*Think.*

"*Sergei,*" Andrei had said. Vicktor flashed the face through his memory. When his FSB backup had arrived at Grace's flat, they'd arrested a reviving Sergei and hauled him outside. Slouched in the back seat of the squad car, he'd glowered at Vicktor. The thug had seemed familiar. Vicktor scowled, willing the memory to come to him.

They'd found the rookie FSB agent assigned to watch the flat trussed up on the balcony.

Vicktor stared at his hands, crusty with dried blood. It wasn't the first time he'd held a dying man, wasn't the first time his hands had been covered in blood. He felt cold now, however, seeing how red filled every pore, even the grooves of his fingernails. Self-condemnation hit him low and hard in his gut.

After peeling off his clothes, he stepped into the shower. The heat nearly took off a layer of skin. He turned and put his face in it, wanting it to hurt. When he could stand it no longer, he cranked on the cold and grabbed the soap. Blood pooled brown at his feet as he scrubbed.

Moments later, he was toweling off. He let the water run for Gracie who had insisted he shower first. He tugged on a pair of sweatpants, pulled on a T-shirt and wrapped the towel around his neck.

Steam drifted from the bathroom when he opened the door. The cool air hit him. "Gracie? It's your turn."

Silence.

He walked down the hall and stopped at the doorway of his bedroom.

She stood with her back to him, staring out the window.

"Gracie, you okay?"

She shrugged. He saw grief in the curve of her shoulders, her wretched posture. His heart ached, knowing he had caused it. He winced and ran a hand through his hair, wishing he could take them back ten hours to that moment in the garden and never let go. Something wonderful, magical, so right it hurt, had passed between them. And he'd killed it this morning. He clenched his jaw, willing himself not to fall apart in front of this woman who had more guts than anyone he'd ever met.

"I'm going to die, aren't I."

*Oh no, Gracie, please don't think that.* He couldn't stop the groan as he walked toward her. "Don't give up hope, Gracie." If the light in her eyes died, it just might kill him. He put his hands on her shoulders. "No, you're not going to die."

He lowered his forehead to her hair. Her smell played havoc with his emotions. How was he supposed to say goodbye to the one person that made him feel hope? He tried to keep the agony from his voice. "Not if I can help it."

She turned, and he was shocked—no, terrified—by the fierceness in her eyes. She lifted her chin.

"I'm ready to die. I don't want to, but I'm ready. I don't want you to give Dr. Young's medical notes to this maniac. I want you to send them to America."

He went dry-mouthed, picturing the worst. Gracie, shot dead, or worst, knifed by the Wolf. His body reacted to the picture, his breathing almost painful. He stepped back. "No."

She moved toward him and touched his face. "It could save lives," she said.

He fought to keep emotion from his voice. "We don't know that."

"I think we do. Leonid was cured. Dr. Willie gave his life to protect this information—"

"Or to protect you. He knew you had it."

She winced.

"I can't risk your life." He didn't care that he had just cracked open his chest, letting her get a full view of his desperation. Or that he was now reaching out, clutching her arms and trembling.

Yes, she saw the panic in his eyes, for her expression softened. "It's my life. I can. I want to."

*Don't look at me that way, Gracie. Please.* He glanced away.

"Besides," she said, and he heard a smile in her voice, "it would kill you to let the Wolf get this information, wouldn't it?"

He frowned at her. "Yeah. How did you know that?"

"The way you describe him. The way your voice turns cold and your face darkens. You have some sort of past with him, don't you?"

He licked his lips, aware for the first time that she might know him better than she let on. "Yeah, I do. He's my greatest mistake. I do want to get him. But the truth is, Gracie, that it would kill me if you died and he got away." He might as well declare his feelings with a megaphone. "If anyone is going to give their life for that information, it'll be me."

/

Her eyebrows lifted. "Vicktor. I'm ready to die. You aren't."

He flinched.

A ray of sunshine broke through the wall of clouds and a shaft entered the room, lighting her hair gold. He pushed her hair away from her face and tucked it behind her ear. "Well, then I'm not ready to lose you." What she didn't know was that if she died, he would, too. A little bit every day for the rest of his life.

"Gracie, what am I going to do after you're gone?" Had he really let that leak out? He opened his mouth, maybe to take those words back, but she was staring at him with a startled expression that turned him mute. Wide eyes, beautiful and huge, a slight smile that packed a whammy.

What was he doing sending her home?

A thousand images raced through his mind, Gracie reaching across the table to take his hand, her eyes tearing at his words at the *dacha,* her laughter when Alfred slobbered on her. She was so beautiful and giving and full of this unconditional love that it made his knees weak. In fact, it ripped the breath right out of his chest.

He already felt like he might be dying.

"Gracie, I know this sounds crazy. But maybe… Don't go. We'll find the Wolf, and until then I can protect you. And then you can be here and maybe we can figure out—"

"Vicktor," she said, but he couldn't hear the no. *Please.*

He leaned down and did the only thing he could think of to silence her.

He kissed her. Cupped one hand behind her neck, closed his eyes and touched his mouth to hers. Sweetly. Softly. She held her breath and trembled just slightly, and he felt pretty sure that he was going to dissolve into a puddle right there.

Her lips softened against his, full of trust. She mouthed his name, and his emotions climbed up his throat. *Gracie.*

She had her hand on his chest. But she wasn't pushing him away.

In fact, she was kissing him back.

It felt like a written and stamped invitation.

His arm went around her waist, and he pulled her to his chest and felt his heart move out of his body to a place where there was no past, no future, just now. Blessed, glorious now.

"Gracie," he murmured, not wanting to stop, but needing to know, please, that he wasn't scaring her. He had the barest grip on his self-control, and knowing that made him slow down.

Could it be that Mr. Reckless cared more about behaving himself than wrapping his arms around her, deepening his kiss and making her forget everything but a list of reasons why she should stay, forever?

Maybe he'd begun to think with his heart instead of his pride.

He felt her hands on his chest.

*Yes, okay, slow down.* With a ragged breath, he tore himself away. She met his eyes, a strange, pained expression on her face.

He felt kicked in the gut.

"No," she whispered.

No? She might as well have plunged a knife into his chest. Closing his eyes, he hoped she didn't see the effect her words had on him. He blew out a breath and released her.

"Sorry," he said. He couldn't look at her.

"It's not your fault," she said, but it didn't feel that way.

He sighed.

"I'm going to take a shower," she mumbled, and moved toward the door, away from him. Away from them.

He clutched the back of his neck. A muscle screamed, pulling taut. Dredging up his voice, he called after her. "How about some clean clothes?"

She turned and nodded. A tear edged down her cheek. He suddenly wanted to throw something, anything, hear it shatter and drown the agonizing wail inside his head.

*No?*

He strode past her to the closet. Pulling out a pair of black jeans and a denim shirt, he handed them over without looking at her.

"Thank you." Her voice trembled.

He held himself together until he heard the bathroom door close. Then he sank onto the edge of the bed, covered his face with his hands and listened to his heart shatter.

Gracie slumped against the bathroom door, giving way to the pressure in her knees.

She'd kissed Vicktor. And she meant *kissed* him. A one-hundred-percent, lean-into-it with-her-heart-in-her-throat kind of kiss. And he'd been so gentle, so perfect. Tears glazed her eyes.

What had she just done? She curled her arms over her head and groaned, still feeling his hands in her hair, her lips burning. Some missionary she was. She couldn't even behave herself.

Was it possible to fall in love with someone in three days? To let him move in and take over your heart? But love wasn't based only on feelings. Love meant commitment, sharing like goals, values, futures.

She and Vicktor were night and day. Light and darkness.

*Please, get me out of here, Lord. Save my heart from being totally skinned.*

Too late.

She curled the pile of Vicktor's clothing to her chest and buried her face in it. His clothes smelled like him. She inhaled, then with panic, dumped them onto the floor. She didn't want to think about his smell, or his incredible blue eyes, or the feel of his strong hands, or the way he scooped her into his arms, or even the tremor of his voice when he said her name.

Obviously grief and fear had her clinging to an emotional precipice, and with a nudge she could happily tumble over into Vicktor's arms and be lost forever. His gentleness, his protectiveness burrowed right to her heart.

Okay, yes, she loved him. Loved the fact that she felt beautiful and perfect in his eyes, that he'd do anything to protect her. The thought of leaving him made her grasp the edge of the sink, and haul in deep, pained breaths.

*I'm sorry, Lord. I am. Help me to leave him....*

Climbing to her feet, she peeled off her bloodied attire and stepped into the shower.

She'd just stay here, forever, in the bathroom. With the shower blanketing her in warmth, and cleansing her of the grief of the past twenty-four hours, and hiding her from the emotions that could only lead her, and Vicktor, to a place they couldn't bear. She crumpled into the bathtub, closed her eyes and lifted her face to the water.

Vicktor answered the telephone on the second ring. *"Slyushaiyu."*

"Sounds like you had a rough morning." Roman's voice was a balm on Vicktor's fraying nerves.

"I've had better."

"For what it's worth, I'm praying for you, pal."

Vicktor nodded, wishing Roman could pray Vicktor's way into Gracie's heart. "Thanks."

"I chatted with Preach last night, and he got your info. I copied it and sent it to your home address."

"Appreciate that."

"The bottom line is that cancer vaccines are a fringe method of treating cancer. They've found one to eradicate melanoma, but it has little effect on other cancers."

"So Young's remedy could be a breakthrough."

"If it works. You want me to come over there?"

Vicktor rubbed a screaming muscle in his neck. "No, thanks. I'll call if I need something."

"What are you going to do?"

Vicktor blew out a breath. "I have to get her safely home."

The silence on the other end of the line said his friend knew what that meant.

"I guess this is one of those times I'll ask you to pray to that God of yours." He couldn't believe he'd said that. But maybe it was time to invest in a little help. He'd contend with the cost later.

"You got it, Stripes," Roman said, then clicked off.

Vicktor rummaged through his closet until he unearthed a brown knit shirt. Kicking out of his sweatpants, he pulled on a pair of black jeans. He could hear the shower still running and wished it could wash away the horror of the last few days. He doubted Gracie would ever return to his homeland. The memories alone would keep her away. Regret tightened his empty stomach. Why had he allowed himself to open his heart? Hope had led him places that he, a smart man with a history, knew better than to tread.

Throwing his clothes into the clothes hamper, he also picked up a suit coat he'd draped over a chair. He'd turned into a complete slob, he thought wryly. He emptied the pockets onto the bed, intending to hang the jacket in the closet.

A piece of paper snagged his attention. He picked it up and memory jolted through him. The picture he'd found at the Youngs' apartment. A Korean and a Russian, arm in arm with Dr. Young. He squinted at the Russian. The face seemed familiar.

Vicktor flicked the picture with his middle finger. Pastor Mikhailovich. Sure, the guy who'd practically dragged Gracie out of the lighthouse restaurant. He'd seemed rattled by Vicktor's sudden appearance, even sweating. And something about his voice had struck a chord. Vicktor squinted at the Korean. His eyes widened. Gracie's words hummed in his ears, *You have the truth right in front of you, you just need to open your eyes to see it.*

Vicktor picked up the phone and speed-dialed Arkady, who answered on the second ring.

"I need you to do me a favor…" Vicktor started.

Five minutes later he hung up and called Yanna. Her businesslike voice softened when she heard his request. "I'll see what I can drum up," she answered.

"Great. We'll be by HQ in about an hour."

"I'll see you then," Yanna promised, and hung up.

Sitting down at his desk in the family room, he heard the shower turn off. And felt dread. Now Gracie would walk out of the bathroom, looking heart-wrenchingly gorgeous in his clothes, her green eyes shining like jewels. And he was supposed to turn off his feelings and not somehow get his heart cremated. He swallowed a rising panic and opened his laptop.

His modem connected, then he downloaded the message from Roman in seconds and hung up.

Dear Stripes: I got this from my sister. She says it's the best she can do under the circumstances. She's working with an indigenous tribe in Siberia at the moment.

Vicktor felt a shard of pity for Roman. Reading the name of his true love had to twist the knife in his friend's wounded heart.

Forwarded message from sarai@mail.ru
Dear Dave. I don't know how much I can help you, but this is what I know about cancer vaccines.

A cancer vaccine works much the same way as a small-pox vaccination, or a polio vaccination. It involves the administration of medicine to an individual which will stimulate the immune system to produce antibodies to a particular disease. The idea is that if a person is then exposed to this particular disease, the antibodies will evoke a response to eliminate the disease.

Cancer vaccines have been in the works since 1890, but since there are varied types of cancer cells, not one has been approved for therapy by the FDA. Studies show a significant percentage of success with melanoma (skin cancer), but for all other cancers, they are still under trial.

Vicktor's letter mentioned a veterinarian. Early rabies and even polio vaccines were made from the cells of animals. They often used a bacteria as a host cell to create these cells. Today, they are using what is called recombinant DNA technology to extract and manipulate cells of animals to form various vaccines. It is possible to use this genetic engineering to transfer a gene from one species into cells of another and let this transformed cell create a corresponding gene product. For example, they do this in the production of insulin.

Dave, scientists have been trying to create a cancer vaccine therapy for nearly a hundred years. If somehow a veterinarian in Siberia stumbled onto a possible therapy, the odds might be slim, but the stakes would be gargantuan. Pharmaceuticals would knock each other off just to get a sniff at the process. Cancer, the leading cause of death in America, could be given a death sentence. Millions of lives saved.

Tell Vita to be very, very careful.

Hello to Mom and Dad.

XOXO Sarai

Vicktor drummed his fingers on his desk and read over the letter again. Gene therapy. Animal antibodies. Could Evgeny have found a vaccine for cancer? And if so, who wanted it? Who wouldn't want it? The possibilities webbed his brain. Sarai's last line, however, glared like neon.

He had to get Gracie out of Russia—with the medical notes.

The door to the bathroom creaked open. Vicktor turned.

The sight of her knocked him breathless. Just what he needed. With her hair slicked back, swimming in his black jeans, and blue jean shirt, her tentative smile lit his heart.

"No," she'd said.

Oh, his world would be black when she left. Somehow she'd brightened his life, and after she left, his soul would be that much darker for the contrast.

Now, he had Andrei's death to contend with.

Vicktor fled to the kitchen, unable to face the despair he felt. She padded in behind him.

He grabbed a bowl. "I'll make us some eggs."

"I don't want eggs right now."

He turned, and she startled him by stepping closer. "I want to know what haunts you."

A lump lodged in his throat. No, she did not want to know that he woke every night wishing he could rip the heart out of a monster. No, she didn't want to know he was so desperately lonely that at times he longed to climb inside his computer, or that his heart was crumbling right here, knowing he was sending out of his life the one person he'd always dreamed about.

Or that he loved her, and it was only going to destroy him.

His heart thudded against his rib cage when she stole closer and hung a hand on his arm.

"Please? I really do care."

Oh, she had truly magical, heart-stopping, persuasive green eyes. He clenched his jaw. "How about some toast?"

"No. I want the truth."

He turned away from her and put the bowl back. Bracing his hands on the counter, he hung his head. "No, you don't."

Her hand on his back coaxed him. "Trust me, please?"

Trust her. Like she'd trusted him? He closed his eyes. "You might not like me when I'm done."

Softly, without a pause, she said, "Not a chance, Vicktor."

He turned and against his will he reached out for her.

She didn't resist him. Which made him want to cry. She fit so well in his arms. She leaned her cheek against his chest—her fragrance, fresh soap and his shampoo, reaching up like a caress. He felt her damp hair through his cotton shirt and was oddly warmed by it. He closed his eyes.

They stood in a quiet embrace while Vicktor listened to his heartbeat counting down their last moments together.

Vicktor reached down and cupped her chin, raising her face to his. Her eyes were a translucent, sea-green, brimming with something indescribable…something he hoped could be called love. He was afraid to ask, to speculate and let hope drive him insane.

"I—I'm so sorry about Andrei," he stammered. "I didn't know…it all happened so quickly…I couldn't—"

She stopped his words with two soft fingers to his lips. "It's okay. I know. And…I forgive you. I know it wasn't your fault, but you think it was…so, I forgive you, in Andrei's stead."

He winced and put her away from him. "No, Gracie, you can't forgive me." He pushed past her.

"Vicktor…"

He stalked out of the room and stood at the door to his bedroom. She padded up behind him, and he stiffened.

She curled her grip around his arm, pulling gently. No, he wouldn't look into her eyes and see the tenderness, the forgiveness written there. The back of his throat tightened.

"Vicktor, look at me."

Her plaintive voice was more than he could take. Reluctantly, he turned to face her. He kept his jaw, his body rigid. She ran her finger along his chin.

"Sometimes it's easier for people to live with self-punishment than it is to accept forgiveness. But in this case, you don't get to tear yourself apart with Andrei's death. It was a horrible, terrible murder, but not at your hands." Her eyes glistened. "Andrei is in heaven now, and I don't want you to live in hell, here on earth."

Heaven? "How can you say that? Andrei betrayed you." He felt himself loosing his grip, sliding down the slope toward desperation. "He lied, he was even a part of the Youngs' murder…and you say he's in heaven?" Vicktor shook his head. "I don't understand you, or your religion."

"'For God so loved the world that He gave His one and only son that whosoever believes in Him shall not die but have eternal life.' It's not my religion—it's God's grace. And He gives it to whoever asks."

"No way." He stepped away from her, into his room. He resisted slamming the door in her face, but every nerve in his body wanted to shake free of her words.

Sadness crept into Gracie's voice. "I know Andrei was a Christian. I know it in the way he talked, and even in his actions. He may have betrayed me, sinned against me, but Jesus can forgive any sin."

Vicktor stood straight, his fists in his pockets, and stared out the window. On the street below, a group of birds picked at the garbage. The pewter sky began to spit on his window. *Any* sin? "A year ago, I was involved in a foot pursuit of the Wolf. Against policy and my better sense, I ran into an abandoned building after the suspect." He felt her hand on his arm and tensed. "I was overpowered and lost my weapon. The Wolf used it during his escape and shot my father."

"The Wolf?" she asked softly, and he knew she was connecting the dots.

He didn't repeat himself.

"So you do have history with him. Painful history."

He hung his head. "Yeah."

"This is personal."

He drew in a deep breath and dared to look at her. Tears hung on her eyelashes.

"Very."

She didn't respond. He turned away from the pain in her face. His voice hardened. "I destroyed my father's career because I was proud and reckless." He stared out the window, refusing to see the judgment written in her eyes. Shame trapped words in his chest.

"And destroyed any chance of earning his respect," Gracie said quietly. "I think I finally understand."

The compassion in her voice made him bury his face in his hands. "Yeah. And now you understand why I can't go crawling to God for help. I don't deserve it."

"No, you don't."

He felt gut-punched. "Thanks."

"Your dad showed me your boyhood pictures." She put her hand on his cheek, turned his face. Her beautiful eyes searched his. "And now I know what's haunted you your entire life."

He looked away, but she moved in front of him, offering him no retreat.

"Your father's respect. His acceptance. You're out to prove you're just as good as your old man, aren't you."

He stared at her, unable to find words.

"The sad thing is, you never had to earn your father's respect." She paused as emotion filled her voice. "It's always been there." She put her hand on his chest, over his pounding heart. "I saw it on his face. The tone he used to describe your boyhood. I can't speak Russian, but I do understand the language of the heart. Your father is incredibly proud of you."

"How can he be?" Vicktor said, his voice low.

"Because you're his son."

Her words rocked him. He tried to edge away but she grabbed his hand. Her eyes flashed.

"God is like your dad. He wants to love you. But you can't see it. The only thing holding you back from forgiveness is your own stubborn pride. It kept you from seeing your father's love. Don't let it sabotage your salvation."

She took a breath as if fighting to control her emotions. "You're right, you know. About deserving forgiveness. You don't deserve it."

He flinched, but she touched his cheek. "But that's the point. You can't make it better, but God can. Remember what I said about God loving us when we were sinners? We don't have to prove anything to Him. We just have to *need* Him."

She moved away from him, took his other hand. He stared at it.

"God wants to forgive you, Vicktor. He wants to free you from grief and guilt. He wants to show you how much He loves you. But you have to ask."

Vicktor winced. Heaven help him, Gracie was right. He was his own enemy. Only, he'd lived with guilt for so long, how could he cope with freedom?

He sank to the bed and buried his face in his hands. "I...have a hard time...trusting this."

"You have to choose to trust, to believe. The first step of faith is the hardest. It *does* get easier."

She crouched before him; he felt her hands on his knees.

"God is trustworthy. He loves you more than you know." Her voice broke on the last words.

He lowered his hands.

She was crying.

*Crying.* For *him.*

He traced the tear lines down her face. He ached to believe her words. Wanted to stake his life on it.

And what did he have left? "I want to believe you." That admission felt...cleansing. It almost overwhelmed him.

Her breath caught. "You do?"

Vicktor dredged up his courage. "Yeah, I guess." He looked past her. "The fact is, Mae and Roman and David have been preaching to me for years. But, well, I guess I never saw my need for forgiveness." *Until now. When I want, so badly, to start over. To not wake up each day with hate. To look at the reflection in your eyes and feel clean.*

To know, for the first time, hope.

Gracie closed her eyes, tears streaming down her face. "Pray with me," she whispered.

He closed his eyes. Gracie took his hands and held them tight. "Oh, God, Vicktor here wants to be Your man. Please hear his prayer."

Strength had to be flowing from her warm hands because suddenly he felt his defenses crack. Everything, the grief, the anger, the hatred, the failure, even the fear spilled out in a voice that seemed somehow not his own, broken as it was. And yet, it was also very much his voice, a voice he'd longed to find. "God, I never thought I would need You. But I guess I do." He forced the words through the wall of emotions threatening to strangle him. "I have a lot of garbage in my life and I need to be forgiven. I need help."

He drew a shaky breath. "So, here I am God. Please forgive me for my sins and my unbelief. Please change my life and help me to know You..."

The words lodged in his throat, and he wrenched them free. "And help me to trust You." He heard a gasp, then realized it was his own. His breath drew with it the shackles of a thousand mistakes, the mantle of grief, the burden of self-reliance.

His pulse quickened, and in a blink he knew he'd been forgiven.

It sent him to his knees on the floor in front of Gracie. He felt tears on his cheeks. His eyes opened, his chest swelled with joy, and he smiled crazily at the woman kneeling before him.

Gracie's eyes were wide, sparkling, her mouth agape. She reached out and touched his face. "You wouldn't believe this— you actually look different! Like a mask has fallen off your face."

"Oh, Gracie, you didn't tell me I'd actually feel clean." He breathed deeply. "This is what it means to be saved?" What a glorious God in heaven who could make a man feel brand-new!

Delight danced in her eyes. "Trust me, it's just the beginning."

He put a hand over hers on his cheek. He had so much to be thankful for and much of it was grinning at him.

"What's all this?"

Vicktor turned and saw Roman leaning against the door-jamb, a curious smile on his face.

# Chapter Twenty-Eight

The elation lighting Roman's face made Vicktor forgive his friend for breaking and entering.

"Well, your good news tops mine," Roman said with a twinkle in his eyes.

"Spit it out," Vicktor demanded impatiently.

"So you were right on your hunch about the thug in Gracie's flat. Sergei Lasherov. Petty thief, sat some time in the zone two years back for possession of a weapon."

"And he was Andrei's boss?" Gracie asked in disbelief.

Vicktor reached out and pulled her close. He could barely think when she looped her arm around his waist. Like she belonged there.

Roman shrugged. "I don't know that. But I did find something interesting in his file." His smile dimmed. "He was an official snitch for the KGB."

Vicktor blinked at him, then groaned. He stalked away from them, wanting to bang his head against the wall. "I knew I'd seen him before. I arrested him once, only to have him vanish under the wings of the KGB."

"Right," Roman acknowledged. "He was one of the left-overs, caught between two systems. He worked undercover on various projects."

Vicktor glanced at Gracie. "Did one of those projects happen to be the Russian Church?"

Gracie stepped out of the car at the airport into the rain, hoisted a newspaper over her head and made a dash for the front doors. The Youngs' computer bag slapped against her side. Vicktor splashed one step behind her, nearly running her over. He flung open the door and they scurried inside. Gracie shook out her damp hair.

"Not a great day for flying."

Vicktor tucked a hair behind her ear and let his hand linger on her cheek. She leaned into it.

"I'm not leaving your side until you're on the plane."

She closed her eyes and willed herself to keep it together. So what, she was leaving. Vicktor was saved. And, well, that meant she wasn't leaving him forever, right?

Except, it felt that way. "So, let's get this over with." She fingered the airplane ticket Vicktor had picked up from Yanna. Flipping open the spanking new passport, she grimaced at the picture. "How did you get this in such a hurry?"

Vicktor curled his arm around shoulders. "C'mon, honey, I'm with the FSB, remember?"

"Gracie!"

Gracie whirled and barely caught Larissa as her friend flung herself into her arms.

She squeezed Larissa tight, reality hitting her hard. Her only other friend left in Khabarovsk.

"I was worried about you when Andrei didn't call me. He said he was going out to the *dacha*." Larissa's voice fell and she looked warily at Vicktor. "Did you see him?"

Gracie's answer caught in her throat. She nodded. How was she going to tell Larissa her cousin had been murdered? Larissa frowned, and looked beyond her.

"Where is he?"

Gracie noticed Vicktor's dark, warning look and scrambled for an answer. No, now was not the time, but she ached to tell Larissa, gently, instead of letting Vicktor do so. "He's at home," she answered truthfully.

Larissa's eyes narrowed, briefly, then she shrugged. "Well, I hope he doesn't miss saying goodbye."

Gracie swallowed a lump in her throat and shook her head. "He already did." Vicktor was standing behind Larissa, giving her the most compassionate look she'd yet seen on him. Not a trace of anger over Andrei's betrayal. Truly, a new creation in Christ.

And she'd been there to witness it. Despite Andrei's death, she felt like breaking out in the "Hallelujah Chorus." She treasured Vicktor's prayer in her heart. Wasn't that what salvation was all about—joy in the midst of sorrow?

Larissa peered at her over her wire-rim glasses. "Are you okay?"

Gracie nodded. "It's just hard to say goodbye." She noticed Larissa had worn the cross she gave her. She prayed her friend would never take it off, that somehow the message behind the symbol would sink in with her, just as it had with Vicktor.

Larissa stepped close and wrapped her arm around Gracie. "I have to tell you something. Can you come to the ladies' room with me?"

Gracie nodded.

Vicktor touched her arm. "Not so fast."

Gracie raised one eyebrow. "Are you coming with me?"

His expression told her he might.

"I'll be right out," she assured him, touched by the worry on his face. She reached over and tugged at his suit coat lapel. "Thanks for caring."

He pinched his lips together. The haunted look may have evaporated, but the fierce set of his jaw sent a shiver through her.

Oh, he cared. More than he should.

"I'll wait by the door."

Gracie strolled away with Larissa, feeling his gaze on her.

"He's a little protective, don't you think?" Larissa whispered in her ear. "Who is he?"

Gracie ducked her head, feeling her face heat. "He's a friend."

Larissa harrumphed loud enough to make Gracie elaborate, almost.

The rain pattered against the floor-to-ceiling windows facing the parking lot. A steel-gray sky obscured the sun, painting the lobby a dismal hue. Gracie scanned the corridor, fighting the claw of anxiety. Surely the Wolf wouldn't know to look for her here? With Andrei silenced, there was no one to spy on her. A bittersweet relief filled her. She sighed and felt Larissa's arm tighten.

"Are you sure you're all right?"

Gracie squinted at her. Larissa's angular face showed concern. Gracie patted Larissa's hand at her waist and nodded. She peeked behind her and spied Vicktor prowling ten feet away.

She nearly tumbled over the yellow Yield sign in front of the bathroom.

Larissa caught her. "'Cleaning,'" she translated, sounding disgusted. She tugged on Gracie's arm. "Who cares? C'mon."

Gracie made a face and followed Larissa into the bathroom. The door whisked shut behind her.

"What took you so long?"

Gracie stared gape-mouthed at Pastor Yuri Mikhailovich. Dressed in a crisp black suit and holding a briefcase, he wore an annoyed expression that stalled her heart. "W-what are you doing here?" she stammered.

"Did you get it?" he asked Larissa.

Gracie frowned and looked at Larissa, who loosened her grip on Gracie's waist and stepped away. Her expression changed, slowly, like all the color draining from a Technicolor movie.

Gracie saw her in planes of black and white, heard her friend answer from another place, distant, as if through a tunnel.

"*Nyet.*" Larissa pushed her glasses up on the bridge of her nose.

Gracie blinked, moved her head in jerks between Larissa and Yuri. The dank smell and dirty shadows shifting through the bathroom made her head spin. "Larissa?"

Her friend edged away. "I'm sorry, Gracie."

"What?" The bottom dropped out of Gracie's stomach.

"Please, give him what he wants." Larissa's voice was hard. "If you don't, he'll kill Andrei." She added a note of pleading to her voice.

Gracie could hardly breathe for the weight that settled in her chest. Larissa? Was she in league with Andrei? Had Gracie not one genuine friend in all of Russia?

*Vicktor.*

A wail started near her toes but she clamped down on it. "*Yea, though I walk through the valley of the shadow of death…*"

Well, what Larissa didn't know was that the Wolf had already done Yuri's job. She pressed a hand to her stomach and turned to Yuri. "What do you want?"

"The notes. Dr. Young's medical notes on Leonid Krasnov." A line of sweat trickled down Yuri's face.

As he took a step toward her, realization washed over her. She stiffened and met Yuri's dark eyes. "*…I will fear no evil…*"

"Over my dead body."

He laughed. "You have more spunk than Evelyn," he hissed. "Too bad."

He dropped the briefcase, caught her wrist in an iron grip and yanked. Pain shot up her arm. She fell toward him, crying out. He released his hold and clamped his hand around her windpipe, forcing her to her feet. His breath streamed across her face. Spittle edged the corners of his mouth.

She felt a burn at the base of her throat and gasped.

Yuri peered over her shoulder and smiled. "Just in time, Captain."

* * *

Vicktor's heart completely left his chest as he stared at the man squeezing Gracie's throat, a bowie knife pressed to her jugular. "Let her go," he demanded in Russian. Vicktor held his pistol in two hands, but with the man using Gracie's body as a shield, Vicktor couldn't get a clean shot.

"You don't remember me? I'm hurt." The man tightened his grip and Gracie whimpered.

Vicktor's hands tightened on the gun.

"Gracie, introduce me to your boyfriend." Yuri turned Gracie to face Vicktor.

Gracie's white face, the red marks streaming from the man's grip on her throat and the stain of blood on her collar sent a white-hot fury through him. Then he met her eyes, and turned cold.

*No, Gracie, no, no.* She was ready to die for her beliefs. He shook his head, pleading with her.

"You shoot, and I take her head off."

Vicktor focused on the man. "I know you. We've met, haven't we?"

"A couple times." Sweat glistened on the man's forehead, and when he smiled, memory stabbed Vicktor.

"You're the pastor," he said starkly. "Yuri Mikhailovich."

The pastor tipped his head, his eyes never leaving Vicktor's. "I want Dr. Young's notes."

Vicktor squinted at him. "We've met a couple times…" he repeated, turning over Mikhailovich's words.

Mikhailovich looked at him and laughed. "And again, I have bested you."

Vicktor went weak. That laugh. The laugh that gave sound to his nightmares. The laugh that echoed through the abandoned building.

A predator's laugh. *The* predator.

"You'll never get away," Vicktor growled. "I know who you are."

The Wolf's face twisted. "I have spent nearly thirty years in well-cloaked cover. I will walk out of here and no one will stop me because I am Pastor Yuri Mikhailovich, head of the Russian Church." He tightened his grip on Gracie, who whimpered. "Besides, I'm on your team. You can't arrest a fellow KGB officer."

"The KGB doesn't have spies in the church anymore." Vicktor glanced at Gracie's balled fists, her hand on her satchel. "You were ordered to come in years ago." If she could just move two centimeters…

"You don't understand the type of commitment it takes to be an agent," the Wolf snarled. "A true KGB agent doesn't abandon his ideas just because the party changes hands in Moscow. I spent three decades listening to idiots babble. I was poor, laughed at… I even had to pay allegiance to the glory-hungry Americans." Bitterness laced his voice. "I deserve a little payback, don't you think?"

Vicktor shuffled a step closer. Maybe he could knock her aside…

Gracie gasped.

"Be careful, Captain."

Vicktor froze. "You worked for Ishkov, didn't you?"

Yuri shrugged.

"And you killed him and everyone who knew it." His mind listed the Wolf's victims, former agents, informants, prostitutes. They suddenly webbed together with stinging clarity.

"I had to keep my cover."

"Why?"

"Missionaries are worth their weight in gold. They bring in huge amounts of cash and humanitarian aid." He smiled caustically. "We can't let them wander freely around the city."

Vicktor took a calming breath. "You killed Evgeny and the Youngs."

"And Krasnov. Unfortunately, I didn't get Andrei, but I heard his death was especially poignant." He smiled, his head tilting in mock pity.

Gracie's friend Larissa made a sound like she'd been hit in the gut. Vicktor didn't spare her a look. Gracie's eyes filmed, and adrenaline surged through Vicktor's body. *Patience.*

"Let her go, Mikhailovich. She'll give you the information. Just let her go." His voice was cool, but inside he was shredding, fast. *No. Not again.* The plea started in his gut and rattled through him. *Please, not Gracie.* He locked her terrified gaze and felt pain sear through him.

"Drop your weapon, kid," the Wolf said icily.

Gracie's whimper sent Vicktor's pistol crashing to the floor.

"I want Young's notes."

Vicktor indicated Gracie's shoulder bag. "Let go of her and I'll hand them over."

"I am a fool?" He switched to English. "Drop your bag, Miss Benson."

Gracie shook her head. A wild look entered her eyes.

"Gracie, drop the bag," Vicktor said in a low tone.

"Never."

He wanted to strangle her himself. Eyes on the Wolf, he strapped down every emotion and spoke in a monotone. "If you meant what you said about trusting me, prove it. Drop your bag."

Her mouth opened, and he knew he'd hit deep and hurt her. Like she hadn't proven her trust in him over and over and over. Stiffly, Gracie slid the computer bag off her shoulder. It thumped to the floor.

The Wolf kicked it toward Vicktor. "The notes," he repeated.

With jerky movements, Vicktor grabbed the bag, wrenched open the zipper and yanked out the manila envelope. He held it out to the Wolf.

"Drop it on the floor."

Vicktor obeyed. At the slapping sound of Dr. Willie's life work offered as a sacrifice to the Wolf, Gracie flinched.

"Thank you. See that closet behind you?"

Vicktor shot a look over his shoulder. The janitor's closet. *Oh, God, I was serious about needing You. Now would be a good time to show up*. He turned back to the Wolf, fresh out of ideas. "Let her go. You got what you wanted."

"And have you track me across Russia?" The Wolf snorted.

"You could kill me," Vicktor taunted. "That would keep me out of your hair." Gracie's choked sob sent daggers through his heart. But he was serious. He'd go to his grave this second if it meant Gracie might live.

"And let you escape the shame of knowing you failed… again?" Yuri smirked. Sweat glistened on his fat cheeks. "Some punishments are worse than death."

Vicktor calculated the distance to his pistol. Ten centimeters from the Wolf's foot, but only a body length if he dove.

"Get in, now, or your girlfriend dies in a Russian bathroom." He made his point by pressing the knife against Gracie's flesh. She refused to cry out, but Vicktor wanted to when he saw blood trickle across the blade.

Vicktor swallowed, every muscle aching to spring. He forced himself to open the closet door.

"Larissa, tie him up," ordered the Wolf. Larissa avoided Vicktor's eyes as she dug through her backpack and unearthed packing tape. She wrapped his wrists tight behind his back, then wound it around his mouth. Vicktor couldn't bear to look at Gracie.

"Now, shoot him."

Larissa paled. "*Nyet*. I'm not killing a cop."

"Pick up his gun and shoot him now, Larissa. Or he'll find us, and destroy our plans."

Larissa glanced at Vicktor, then back to Gracie. Then she bent and picked up the gun.

Vicktor braced himself, and for a last painful moment, met Gracie's beautiful eyes. They went wide, and then she screamed.

"No!" She fought Yuri's hold as Larissa leveled the gun at Vicktor and pulled the trigger.

# Chapter Twenty-Nine

❦

*No, oh please, Lord, no!* Gracie's knees buckled as Larissa lowered the gun and slammed the closet door.

*Vicktor.* She moaned, and began to shake. "Vicktor!"

"Calm down," Yuri snapped. "Or you're next."

Gracie felt warm blood trickle down her chest. The prick of the knife burned at the base of her throat. She couldn't look at Yuri, but his foul breath washed over her face, turning her stomach.

"Go ahead. I don't care."

"Get up." He grabbed her by the hair, wrenched her to her feet.

She stared at the closet door, her heart screaming for the man who'd given his life for hers.

"Larissa, give me the gun."

Yuri held out his hand, but instead of taking the gun, he yanked Larissa toward him. Before Gracie could jump, Yuri had stabbed her.

Larissa fell, eyes open, onto the floor. She clutched her

stomach, blood pouring from between her fingers. "Boris...I trusted you."

"*Da, Tovarish.*" He laughed, and it sounded more animal than human.

Gracie stood frozen, unable to breathe.

Yuri grabbed her by the back of her neck. "I'm going to put my knife away, but let's hold hands, since we're such good friends." His fingers dug into her and she bit back a cry. A moment later, he released her and grabbed her hand. "Let's go, dear. We have a plane to catch."

Gracie tried to yank her hand away, but he jerked hard, nearly tearing the limb from its socket. She bit her lip, refusing to acknowledge the pain, amazed that she could feel anything.

Shock had her lungs, her heart filled her throat.

Yuri picked up Vicktor's gun and pocketed it. Then, he lifted the envelope. "Open it."

She glared at him, grabbed the package and pulled out Dr. Willie's notes. "Satisfied?"

"Yeah. Perfect." He snatched the pages away from her. "Thanks."

She looked away.

"Now, if you'll come quickly, and quietly, I'll call zero-one when we get to our destination. Maybe they'll arrive in time to save your friend Larissa's life."

Larissa? What about Vicktor? If there remained a remote chance he had only been wounded, and could be rescued...

Yuri pulled her out of the bathroom, walking as if there was nothing unusual about Gracie holding hands with the head pastor of the Russian Church, who had exited the women's bathroom. Gracie scanned the lobby. It teemed with activity. Three long lines snaked from departure counters. A sea of people and not one of them familiar. Her chest constricted, her feet felt leaden. *Please, God, get me out of this safely. Again.*

Yuri pushed through a line of people and stalked toward the departure gate. A lone woman in a navy blazer with tired eyes stood sentry. She stopped him and Yuri pulled out a black passport. Flipping it in front of her face, he snorted at her. She paled and shooed them through.

Gracie's brain could hardly keep up with her feet. Yuri had been after the medical notes the entire time? From his heated discourse with Vicktor, she knew there was more to the tale than just Dr. Willie's medical notes. He'd betrayed her, his Church, her friends. He'd probably killed Dr. Willie and Evelyn, maybe even Leonid and Andrei. She glanced at him, noticing the sweat dripping off his sideburns, the folds of skin pushing into his dress shirt at the base of his neck. He'd tricked them all. Like a wolf in sheep's clothing, he'd moved among his flock, devouring. Disgust twisted her stomach.

He pulled her through the departure lobby, then out the glass doors onto the tarmac. The rain had slackened to a drizzle. It pelted the back of her neck and slicked her hair to her face. She stumbled blindly, wincing under his grip.

Thunder droned in the distance. In bewilderment Gracie searched for the source and her knees weakened at the sight of a small airplane, gunning its jets in preflight.

"I'm not getting on a plane with you!" Gracie tore at his fingers, fighting his grip. She kicked at him and landed a glancing blow on his shin. He jerked her hard, snapping her head back.

"I don't want to hurt you," he growled, "but I will."

His words jolted her and she stumbled. He yanked her along with him, jogging toward the plane.

The sound of the plane engine took possession of her senses. "No!" she screamed again, digging her heels into the tarmac. "Don't think for a second I don't know you plan to kill me! You've killed everyone I care about." Her voice shook. "You'll probably dump me out over the ocean!"

"Not until I'm out of Russian airspace."

"No." If he was going to kill her, he had to do it here, now. Then Vicktor's little army could shoot him out of the sky.

He cuffed her and she tasted blood. Clamping a hand around the back of her neck, he squeezed until she doubled over in pain.

"I'm running out of patience," he hissed.

She staggered toward the plane. He pushed her up the steps and she fell onto the thinly carpeted floor. Yuri stepped up behind her and grabbed her by the collar.

"Get up."

Gracie clenched her teeth and got to her knees. Yuri stabbed her hard in the back with his fingers and she swayed down the aisle.

"Over there," he said, pointing to a row of seats. "Sit down and buckle up."

Her heart lodged in her throat, Gracie fell into the seat. Yuri hollered to the front and returned to close the side door. The plane started to move. Gracie bit her lip and clutched the armrests as the ground seemed to travel by, gaining speed. *Oh, God, now what?*

Vicktor didn't know where he was hit, but his entire body burned. Mostly his head, but he had to think that was from falling. He had a bump, but there was no sting of a gash.

But his shoulder screamed, and that, along with the stink of cleanser and bleach told him that this wasn't heaven.

He was still alive.

And, hopefully, so was Gracie. Vicktor didn't know how long he'd sat there, counting his heartbeats. He twisted his hands and the tape cut into his skin. Still, it gave slowly and he wiggled his hands, now slick with blood, free. Releasing his feet, he then worked off the tape over his mouth.

The first kick at the door made him double over in pain. Okay, so maybe he *was* shot. He touched his arm and winced, feeling moisture between his fingers. Probably adrenaline had muted the pain.

But no kind of adrenaline would dull the pain of losing Gracie. He kicked the door again, adding a growl to his efforts. The door shuddered and held.

Figures that Russia would build a fortress to protect their cleaning supplies while they let killers waltz in and out over a paper-thin border.

Probably, by now, the Wolf was halfway to some anonymous island.

Vicktor couldn't believe he'd done it again. Failed someone he cared about more that life.

Closing his eyes, he could hear only the drip of the faucet and the sound of his own harsh breathing.

Gracie was a dead woman. The Wolf was a cold-blooded killer, and Vicktor had let the animal walk away with the woman he loved. *Loved?* Vicktor leaned his head against the cement wall and gulped searing breaths. Yes, loved. Everything inside him ached to be around her, to hear her laugh, to see the sun in her eyes. She was hope and faith and life—so much life that the world dimmed in comparison. And it wasn't until forgiveness unlocked his shackles that he realized this was the woman with whom he wanted to marry, have children and grow old.

She believed in him.

And the Wolf had her.

If ever he needed help from above, it was now. Fighting the cloying smell of cleanser, he tried to form coherent thought. He should have put together that Yuri and the Wolf were one and the same. Of course. If he'd been thinking with his cop brain instead of his heart, he would have connected the dots, seen the trail from Andrei, to the Church, to the KGB, to the KGB-connected crimes and finally to the Wolf. *Oh, God, what have I done?* Raising his eyes, he searched for a speck of light. "God, I have nowhere else to turn. Please, save Gracie."

Gray light streamed into the closet as the door eased open. Larissa's pinched face wedged into the crack. "Help me," she begged. "I'm sorry." Tears trailed down her cheeks.

Vicktor got to his feet and slammed the door open with the palm of his hand. He stared at the pitiful girl, who had collapsed onto the floor. He pulled off his jacket and pressed it against her wound. She moaned.

"I'll get help."

He scrambled out to the lobby and nearly crashed into Yanna. She grabbed his forearms, her dark eyes fixing on his.

"Slow down, Stripes." Her eyes widened. "You're bleeding."

"What are you doing here?"

Yanna indicated a group of COBRAs hauling a snarling, handcuffed man to his feet. Blood trickled from a freshly opened wound on his head. "Just trust your friends for once, will you?"

Yuri stood in the aisle, one hand on each row of seats, eyes narrowed as he watched the pavement roll by. Gracie licked parched lips and hung her head, wondering what it would be like to die. If only she could have saved Dr. Willie's notes.

She heard Yuri's grunt of pain before she saw him stagger forward, then crash to the floor with a grunt.

What?

Roman! Gracie unhooked her belt and scrambled to her feet. Roman straddled Yuri's waist, his hand around Yuri's throat.

"You okay, Gracie?" Roman asked, not looking at her. Yuri cuffed him. Roman's grip turned white on Yuri's neck.

Gracie covered her mouth as Yuri's contorted face colored a dark red, his lips purple.

"Roman, look out!"

Yuri had flushed out Vicktor's little black gun from somewhere beneath him. He shoved it into Roman's temple.

Gracie screamed. "No! Yuri!"

Roman released his grip and backed off. Gracie's eyes were glued to Yuri as Roman pulled her behind him. "Please, Yuri, don't shoot," she begged as Roman's body became her shield.

Yuri inched back and climbed to his feet. He trained the weapon on Roman as Yuri felt for the cockpit handle, opened the door and slipped inside.

Roman spun toward her, and the grim look on his face made her flinch. "Open that door and jump out right now."

Gracie reeled, blinking at him. "The plane's moving."

Roman's blue eyes turned to steel. "I know."

The cockpit door opened. A woman in army fatigues scuttled out and slammed the door. Her eyes were wide, her face slightly flushed. A shock of curly red hair fell from the bun at the nape of her neck. "He doesn't want me to drive," she said in English.

Gracie fought Roman, gripping the seat. "You're an American?"

The woman nodded. "Let's get off this plane, *now*."

Roman pushed Gracie toward the door. Her feet dug into the carpet. "You're trying to kill me!"

"The clock is running, people. Move!" the woman barked.

Gracie didn't want to decipher the meaning of those words. Roman reached past her and unlocked the door. It swung open, nearly sucking Gracie out. Icy rain stung her face.

"No!" she shrieked, bracing herself in the doorway. The plane was moving so fast.

"I'm sorry!" Roman yelled above the din. His hand clutched her upper arm. "You have to jump!"

"Thou art with me; thy rod and thy staff they comfort me…"

Gracie screamed and flung herself into open space.

# Chapter Thirty

⌭

Vicktor jumped aboard the luggage car and gunned it. Beside him, Yanna clung to the seat. The rain streaked in cold torrents down his back. He squinted and drove like a madman toward the taxiing AN-2. Heaven help the Wolf if he harmed one hair on Gracie's head.

His heart nearly stopped when he saw someone jump from the plane. Two more bodies followed. Vicktor gripped the steering wheel harder.

As the plane accelerated down the runway, Vicktor made out Roman, rolling to his feet and limping over to one of the others. Shock ripped through him when he recognized Mae, her hair unfurled and glistening amber in the drizzle. That meant the figure sprawled flat and unmoving was Gracie. *Please, no.* He slammed the pedal to the floorboards.

The plane screamed as its front wheels lifted.

Vicktor's eyes were glued to Gracie. She wasn't moving. He felt his heart leap out ahead of him as he slammed on the brakes and jumped from the vehicle. "Gracie!"

She raised her head just before he skidded to his knees at her side.

"Vicktor?"

He took her in his arms. It was quite possible he was going to turn into a sniveling, oh-no-don't-look mess right here, with Mae and Roman and Yanna watching.

"Vicktor! I thought Larissa had…" She pulled away from him, stared at his wounds. "You're shot."

She'd just jumped from an airplane and she was worried about *him?* His voice cracked, letting out his emotions. "I'm fine. Larissa just clipped my arm."

She looked like she might cry. "Is Larissa dead?"

He ran his hand down her check. "I don't know. She freed me and all I could think of was getting to you. I think Yanna called for help."

"Oh." Her expression began to crumble and she balled his jacket in her fists. "Oh."

"Gracie." He pulled her into his arms and held tight, trying not to cry himself. Except, his were tears of relief. "You scared me," he choked out.

"I scared myself," she said into his wet shirt. But she didn't let go.

He held her away from him again and scanned her for injuries. Her pants had ripped open at the knees and an angry abrasion on her leg was quickly turning purple. He rubbed his hands over her arms, down to her wrists, and cringed at the scrapes on her palms. "Nothing broken?"

"Not yet." She cupped his cheek and brought his gaze to hers.

In her eyes welled an emotion he could only hope was love. *Please, let it be love.*

Because he knew he loved her.

But he couldn't say that. Not here, not on the tarmac, with the rain pummeling them. He buried his face in her soggy hair, let relief shudder through him. "I thought the worst." Not just thought it, but believed it, mourned it, had felt his heart crushed beneath it.

She drew away, searching his face. "But you prayed, didn't you?"

He nodded. Was it possible she could see right to his very soul?

Yes, it was. And, what was more amazing…it didn't terrify him.

She smiled. "Kiss me, Vicktor."

Kiss her? Okay. That he could do, even right here in front of Yanna, and Roman, and even Mae. He took Gracie in his arms and showed her how much he loved her. Gently, not letting his hunger overwhelm her, his restraint speaking louder than anything else might. But enough.

And she surrendered. It felt so sweet he hoped it would never end. She kissed him back, knotting her hands in his shirt, holding on tight until he had to pull away and whisper the words that pulsed in his heart. "I love you, Gracie."

He hoped she could see it in his eyes. He willed her to see it, to know that she had helped set him free and taught him everything, including how to trust.

She traced his mouth with her finger. "I can hardly believe it, but I love you, too." Then she blushed, washing away the gray pallor of her rain-drenched skin, leaving her breathtakingly gorgeous with her golden mop plastered to her head, her eyes bright and alive.

*She loved him, too.* He curled her to his chest, closed his eyes and grinned like a silly man.

"What took you so long, Stripes?" Roman clamped him on the shoulder, his eyes mischievous.

Vicktor shrugged. Beyond him, he saw the Wolf's AN-2 arch in the sky, then nose-dive.

Vicktor yanked Gracie into his embrace and ducked his head just as the plane slammed into the ground. The explosion rolled over the tarmac.

Roman crouched beside them, shielding himself with his arm.

"What was that?" Gracie exclaimed, turning, searching for the source.

"Oh, just some fallout from damage I did to the steering," Mae said. "Sadly, it was only supposed to incapacitate him, buy the COBRAs some time. But when the Wolf's pilot caught us…well, Roman and I had to stick around and see if we could save your skins."

"The Wolf?" Gracie stared at the flames. "Was he on the plane, too?

Vicktor nodded, swallowed. "Yeah." As Vicktor drew her in tight, Gracie buried her hand in his shirt and pulled him even closer.

And that's when he realized he'd not only been forgiven, a thousand times over, but been blessed more than he'd ever deserve.

Grace drew back and blinked at Mae. "Who are you?"

A smile inched up Vicktor's face. "Gracie Benson, I'd like you to meet Captain Mae Lund, United States Air National Guard."

Gracie struggled to her feet, Vicktor assisting. "Mae?"

Vicktor nestled Gracie against his side as she shook Mae's hand. "I've heard about you."

Mae laughed. "Glad to meet you, too, Gracie. You're an extraordinary woman to win Vicktor's heart."

Vicktor ducked his head, and heard Gracie laugh at his blush. "He's got an extraordinary heart."

The whine of emergency vehicles soured the air. "Let's get you inside and warmed up before your plane takes off," he said quietly.

Gracie frowned, her eyes glistening. "No, I can't leave yet."

The desperation in her voice tugged at his heart.

Vicktor pressed a kiss to her forehead. "Trust me."

Gracie sat in the airport cafe, fingering her coffee cup and shooting daggers at the vile clock that ticked down her last moments with Vicktor. Her fingers were threaded through his under the table. His thumb stroked her hand in long sweeps, sending waves of yearning through her. *Why, God? Why did You drop someone wonderful into my life, only to yank me away?*

Then again, maybe it was enough that God *had* dropped Vicktor into her life…and saved them both. And now that Vicktor had his shoulder bandaged—pending stitches—she might be able to breathe freely.

Her flight hadn't been called to board yet, but the announcement was imminent. She tried to focus on the conversation around her, thankful it was all in English.

"So how did you know Yuri was after Gracie?" Yanna asked, leaning toward Vicktor. She kept smirking at Gracie, obviously gleeful that Roman's and her matchmaking had been a success. Gracie fought embarrassment. It had been ages since she'd been the willing recipient of a man's affection. It took some getting used to.

"I found a photo of Yuri, Dr. Young and a Korean named Pastor Yee at the Youngs' flat. When I found out Leonid had killed the Youngs, and they'd been framed, I called Arkady and asked him to ask Pastor Yee—formerly from North Korea—if his visa had ever been stolen," Vicktor explained.

"Pastor Yee said he lost his passport about a year ago," Roman continued. "He didn't know if it was stolen, but we figure the Wolf/Yuri used it to create the fake documents framing the Youngs. Arkady called me when he couldn't reach Vicktor. He told me you were at the airport, and Yanna and I figured that Yuri might try to ambush you there. We also checked the outgoing flights and discovered that his pilot, a comrade from the KGB era, had filed a flight plan. We couldn't ignore the coincidence."

"It's a good thing you have well-placed friends, Stripes," Yanna said.

"And she's not only talking about Comrade Major Malenkov." Roman's eyes gleamed. "He authorized the call to Mae, who was thankfully already here, filing her preflight plan." He thumped Vicktor on his non-bandaged shoulder. "You need to check your cell-phone batteries, pal."

Vicktor winced and dug into his pocket. The phone hadn't a spark of life. "Even if you'd called, I doubt I would have thought of Yuri hiding in the bathroom. And it was only when I saw him, and strung together his KGB history and the M.O. of the crimes, that I realized his true identity. I only wish I'd connected the dots sooner."

"Pastor Yuri was your serial killer?" Gracie winced.

"Gracie, don't you understand *any* Russian?" Vicktor asked, shaking his head.

She made a wry face and shrugged.

"Yes, he was the Wolf. He was also KGB and a plant in the Church for over a quarter of a century."

Shock sent her chin downward. "A plant in the Church?"

Roman folded his hands on the table. "It was common practice for the KGB to assign someone to the Church to watch them. Christianity was a crime in the former USSR. Most non-churched kids grew up believing it was a cult and members were closely watched."

"Yuri sent people to *gulag?*" Horror turned Gracie's voice whisper thin.

Roman bowed his head. "My guess is yes."

Silence around the table made his statement resonate. Vicktor squeezed her hand. Roman shifted in his seat. Pity stabbed her heart. Russians had so many reasons not to trust one another.

Gracie shot a furtive glance at the clock. "Who cooked up the plan to get Yuri?"

"The COBRAs had eyes on you all the way from the building to the plane, but no one could get a clean shot with you kicking your way across the tarmac."

"She does pack quite a wallop," Vicktor teased. He leaned over and kissed her cheek.

Gracie wrinkled her nose. "Sorry."

"Mae and I were at the plane and she was cutting the aileron cable to a thread. Under pressure on takeoff it would snap. Sadly, the pilot caught us. We had to subdue him, and she took over controls while I waited in the luggage bay for you to board." Roman folded his hands on the table. "I'm just glad we were able to get you off that plane before he took off."

Gracie rubbed the scrape on her chin. "I'm walking away with a few bruises, Roman. Please, don't ever push me off a moving plane again."

Roman laughed. "I'll try to keep that at a minimum."

"Well, I'm glad I got to meet the woman who snared Vicktor's heart," Mae said. She combed her hair with her fingers, then fastened the red mane into a bun. "I can leave knowing he's in good hands."

"I'm in very good hands," Vicktor echoed. "Thanks to Gracie, and Roman, and you, Mae."

"And Yanna," added Mae. "She was the one who dug up the file on Yuri, and confirmed his status as inactive/active KGB plant."

Vicktor tipped his head to Yanna. "Thanks, Yanna. But I was referring more to your faithful prayers, Mae."

Surprise limned Mae's face. Gracie had the sudden urge to let out a Russian "ooh-rah!"

"I became a Christian this morning."

Mae's gape turned into a joyous smile. "Will miracles never cease?"

Vicktor shrugged, and Gracie noticed a hint of blush on her stalwart cop. It tickled her heart. Oh, underneath that hard-as-granite exterior, Vicktor was a big softie.

"Flight 248 to Anchorage, now boarding."

Gracie went cold. She raised her gaze to Vicktor. His tortured expression made her want to weep.

"C'mon," he said in a low voice. His face chiseled out a smile.

She dredged up one to match.

He held her tight until the last person had passed through Customs. Then, in front of all his friends, Vicktor cupped Gracie's face in his hands and kissed her. Thoroughly, with enough love for her to carry with her, and hopefully believe, deep inside, that he meant his words. "Hope dies last in Russia, Gracie. I will see you again."

She nodded. Then she turned and ran through Customs, taking his heart with her. He waited until she was through, then shuffled back to his friends.

"I can't believe you're letting her go," Yanna said, her eyes sparking. "Just like that." She snapped her fingers.

"No, it's not 'just like that.'" He imitated Yanna's actions. "She's the one. She's the woman I've been waiting for."

Roman rested his hand on Vicktor's shoulder. "Do you trust her?"

"Absolutely."

All three friends stared at him. Vicktor pressed the floor with his shoe.

"There's always the Internet," Roman said.

"We can put her on our chat list," Yanna added.

Vicktor swallowed with difficulty. How was he going to live beyond this moment? He felt a chill creep over him.

"Well, gang, the fun's over." Mae fitted on her cap. "I need to run. I have a fistful of soldiers and one very crabby major to fly home." She one-finger saluted them. "I'll see you on the Net." Whirling, she speed-walked away.

Vicktor followed her with jealous eyes.

Abruptly, she turned, cupped her hands and yelled, "You know, when you fly Aeroflot, you're considered on Russian territory until you get off the plane in America."

The seat belt light dinged off as the plane leveled. Gracie stared out the window for a last glimpse of Russia before they ascended into the clouds. "Goodbye, Vicktor." Her heart constricted and she blinked back tears. The plane jetted into the cloud cover, obscuring Russia in a fog.

Disbelief twisted her empty stomach. Yuri Mikhailovich, head of the Russian Church was a spy, a traitor.

All the good friends she'd had in Russia had either betrayed her, or given their lives to protect her. She knew she had barely skimmed the grief that would come. For the moment, her rawest emotions had to do with missing the man she had thought, five days ago, that she could least trust. But she'd learned trust was a choice, and not only that but God had seen her fears and given her life into the hands of a man who'd proved himself worthy.

Imagine that. She thought of Vicktor's arms around her, and how he'd trembled with relief when he'd found her alive on the runway. She closed her eyes, aching as if a chunk of her heart had been ripped out of her chest.

She loved him. She'd started loving him when he'd tracked her down and scared the life out of her on the train, and when he had bought her a new dress and her reflection had sparkled in his eyes. Most of all when she'd unlocked her secrets and seen his compassion. She wanted to love him more, know him more. He'd abandoned his plans for revenge, and instead had prayed. Vicktor had so much potential to be a man of God. She ached to watch the Almighty take over Vicktor's life and change it.

That would be loads of fun across the ocean.

She leaned her forehead on the Plexiglas window. The sun glinted brilliantly across an endless landscape of fluff. Below the mantel, these same clouds wept upon her Russia.

Gracie reached down, slid the laptop computer from under her seat and plopped it on the seat beside her. Overwhelmed with regret, she rubbed the case with her palm. "I'm sorry, Dr. Willie." His life work lay in cinders in Khabarovsk Airport. Her eyes burned at the injustice. So many lives sacrificed for nothing.

She wondered if her office really had been trying to contact her, or if Yuri had been simply trying to oust her from Vicktor's protection that day at the lighthouse restaurant. Lowering her tray, she hoisted the computer onto it and grabbed the air link hookup.

She unzipped the leather case and opened it.

A thick sheaf of papers had been wadded inside. Clipped to them was a small note.

Gracie, I hope these turn out to be worth it. I know they brought me to you—and you to me. Remember me when you are drinking coffee in Duluth. I love you. Vicktor.

Gracie unclipped the note and clutched it to her chest. Then she peered at the title page of the stack of A-4 paper: "Scientific Explorations and Experiment Results of Trichinosis Virus Vaccination by William Young, M.D."

*Trust me, Gracie.* Vicktor's voice, with the slight accent that curled her toes and sent ripples down her spine, reverberated through her mind.

Gracie closed her eyes. *Hope dies last.* She pressed her fingers to her lips, remembering the sweet taste of Vicktor's kiss, promising, loving. She would pray and wait, just as she had for Vicktor's salvation. *Oh, God, thank You. Thank You for adopting Vicktor into the family.*

Her eyes fluttered open. She had finally led someone to Christ. God had used her for the work of Vicktor's salvation.

The thought made her tingle. So maybe she wasn't a joke. Maybe, in fact, it was more about her needing God and God doing His thing in amazing ways. Using the darkest moments to bring light, and joy, and salvation.

Simply because they'd needed Him.

"The poor will eat and be satisfied. They who seek the Lord will praise Him—may your hearts live forever."

So, maybe this wasn't goodbye. Maybe, in fact, God was just getting started.

She leaned back, closed her eyes and let herself rest.

"Okay, Captain, you're free to unbuckle." The flight attendant freed herself from the jump seat, leaving Vicktor to wrestle himself out of the restraining harness. He got to his feet and peeked through the blue curtain separating the seats near the cockpit from first class and coach. "I don't see her."

Humor played on the flight attendant's face. "Seven-A, sir."

Standing tall, Vicktor smoothed his still-damp suit coat and entered the compartment.

Gracie sat slumped in her seat, her eyes closed, clutching Dr. Young's notes. He smiled. So she'd found them. While Gracie had waited in his office at FSB HQ, he'd emptied the envelope, made a copy of the first page, then tucked the real notes in with the computer, just in case.

Leaning over, he tapped her on the shoulder. "Miss?"

"Yes?" She didn't open her eyes.

"Can I sit with you?"

Slowly, she looked at him. Now, *that* was the smile he'd been hoping to find.

"You see, I'm with the KGB and I've been searching all over for you."

This time, she didn't kick him.

\* \* \* \* \*

# A NOTE FROM THE AUTHOR

King David is one of my favorite biblical heroes. Throughout the Psalms and through his mistakes and victories, he displays emotions I can embrace. And, whether he is dancing (half-naked!) or moaning that his heart has turned to wax, he displays a faith in God that surprises me. David made no bones about it—he needed God. God was his entire life, and he had no problem saying, "God, I'm your guy…so please come and help me!"

I have to admit, David's brazen faith astounds me. It wasn't that he was without sin (murder and adultery come immediately to mind). So where did this confidence come from?

His confidence comes from God's unfailing love—which He proves to David, and to His chosen people. Psalm 22, verse 24, gives me hope that this confidence can be mine, also. "For He has not despised or disdained His afflicted one; He has not hidden His face from him but has listened to his cry for help."

David didn't deserve God's love. He didn't earn it. He simply needed it…and received it.

I wrote *In Sheep's Clothing* in Russia, back in 1998 when we were missionaries there. At the time, I had four children under the age of seven, was homeschooling and lived on the ninth floor of a high-rise apartment that had water pressure only from midnight to 4:00 a.m. (Which meant I did my laundry and dishes in the middle of the night.) I had no telephone (no e-mail!), no car, and my husband worked over an hour away in a tiny village. I felt a little… um…overwhelmed.

I'll never forget the day my husband came home, weariness and distress in his eyes. He told me a horrific tale of espionage and a KGB plant in the church where he'd been working. Right then, the seeds for *In Sheep's Clothing* were sown, along with a deep grief over what the members of that church had suffered at the hands of their so-called pastor.

Also living in Russia at the time were two other missionaries. Not long after we moved there, they were murdered. This rocked my world. Here I was, "suffering" for the Gospel, and everything I'd counted on (namely, the safety of my family in this foreign land) seemed to crumble.

I was tired and afraid. And, like Gracie, or Vicktor, I had my own gaggle of "demons" whispering lies into my ears. Like "You were foolish to bring your children so far overseas." Or "What do you hope to accomplish?"

Truly, I was in a place of need. What could I do to make my family safe and leave a lasting impression on my world, when it seemed that darkness stalked me on all sides?

Nothing—except trust the Lord. Writing this book became a catharsis for me. I learned, as Gracie and Vicktor do, that God's favor (or His forgiveness) can't be earned. It's a gift. And in order to receive it, all I have to do is need Him. I learned that God was my strength when life felt too big, or too dark. And I learned that with God there is always hope.

That's the secret David had. The belief that when he got on his knees and asked, God would provide.

God provided in so many ways as I wrote. I am deeply grateful for the support and encouragement of the following people:

Karen Solem—for finding a home for *In Sheep's Clothing!* Thank you for your part in making this dream possible.

Krista Stroever and Joan Marlow Golan—for your enthusiasm and for believing in me. Krista, your letter (even without the stickers!) is one of my all-time favorites!

Constantine Utuzh—Now in Heaven. A man of conviction and passion, he made me realize how important small acts of kindness can be.

The Far East Russia CoMission teams from 1994-1998. (Especially the ladies!)—The friendships forged during these times made living in Russia a billion times easier.

Alexi and Cindy Kalinin—I can't help but think of you when I read Gracie and Vicktor's story. Your friendship is among my most cherished.

Ellen Tarver (and Daniel and Tom!)—Thank you for reading *In Sheep's Clothing,* and later for saving me from being locked in my room all day. Your friendship is such a blessing.

David Lund—Thank you for reading *In Sheep's Clothing,* and for believing in me even when I had my doubts. You're such a blessing to me.

Andrew and my sweet children—For all those moments when I read aloud over dinner, or shooed you away with a death-glare, or talked plot endlessly…thank you for listening politely, for understanding and most of all for believing in my dreams. I'm so grateful for you.

# DISCUSSION QUESTIONS

1. *In Sheep's Clothing* opens with Gracie confronting the end of a season of her life. What seasons of life have you experienced? Gracie also feels as if she hasn't accomplished anything with the opportunities God has given her. Have you ever felt like a failure on the inside when others consider you a success on the outside?

2. Vicktor is a man who has regrets in his past that compel him to go on the hunt for his friend's killer. Do you think regrets are a good motivation for actions or behaviors? Have you ever had a regret that has motivated you to do something out of your comfort zone?

3. Vicktor has a group of friends that he considers his closest—yet his best friend, David, is only available online. With the advent of the online world, more and more good friendships are located online, with many of these friends never meeting. Do you have a good friend online that you have never met face-to-face? How has e-mail changed your relationships, either local ones or long-distance?

4. After seeing her friends' murder, Gracie tries to flee for the American consulate, via the train. In the same situation, what would you have done? Would you have trusted an FSB agent if he came after you on the train?

5. Gracie has a spiritual revelation while hiding at Andrei's mother's house. What is it? Discuss how it changed her outlook. Does it have any application to your own life?

6. When Vicktor changes Gracie's appearance, how does it change the way she feels about herself? Why? Have you made any appearance changes that have changed the way you feel about your life, or your circumstances?

7. Vicktor is deeply affected by the revelation of Leonid the Red's cure. Why? Discuss how his mother's death affected him spiritually. Have you ever felt that God betrayed you? Why did Gracie's spiritual answer to him on the way to the dacha make him angry? What might you have said to Vicktor's questions?

8. Gracie comes to believe that she's been using her fear of men to not fully trust God. Why? How does she make a leap of faith?

9. Gracie believes Andrei is in heaven. Why? Not that we can judge a man's heart, but do you agree with Gracie's thinking? Why or why not? Why does her faith in grace upset Vicktor?

10. Gracie is finally able to make an analogy about grace that affects Vicktor. Discuss that analogy and why it made a difference, finally, in Vicktor's relationship with God. Does that analogy have an impact on you, and why?

11. How did God use Gracie to heal Vicktor's emotional and spiritual wounds, and vice versa?

12. What do you think will happen with Gracie and Vicktor's relationship?

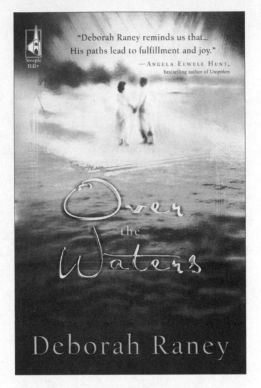

# From *USA TODAY* bestselling author Deborah Bedford comes BLESSING

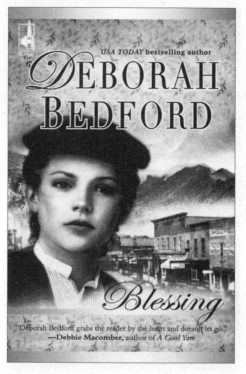

The secret beneath Uley Kirkland's cap and mining
togs is unsuspected in 1880s Tin Cup, Colorado.
She longs to hide the clothing of deception and
be honest about her feelings for handsome stranger
Aaron Brown. But while Uley dreams of being
fitted for a wedding gown, the man she loves is
being fitted for a hangman's noose, and she is
the inadvertent cause of his troubles.

The truth will set them free, and
Uley will do whatever it takes to
save Aaron's life—even risk her own.

**Steeple Hill®**